Praise for *The Naked Viscount*

Starred review "A laugh a minute.... Brimming with sex, schemes, and sass, MacKenzie's books ... are so addictive they should come with a warning label." —Shelley Mosley, *Booklist*

"Ah, another naughty, *Naked* hero to brighten MacKenzie's irresistible romance. There's plenty of sizzle, delicious repartee (filled with double entendres), excitement and mystery to satisfy anyone who needs a bit of love and laughter to brighten their day."—Kathe Robin, *Romantic Times BOOKreviews*

"Charming, yet darkly dangerous.... If you want to smile, sigh, feel a tug of the heart, and be drawn into a bit of danger, read a Sally MacKenzie romance." —Connie Payne, OnceUponARomance.net

"Naked, naughty nobles with a dash of intrigue and a side of romance all blend together for one delicious dessert in the form of a romance novel."—Joyce Greenfield, ReaderToReader.com

Praise for *The Naked Baron*

"Sweet and sexy Regency tale."—Maria Hatton, *Booklist*

Top pick! "Naked and naughty—that's the kind of hero MacKenzie stakes her reputation on, and it's also the kind that readers adore. With their humor and heated love scenes, her books sparkle and light up readers' hearts. Her feel-good stories are just what we need."—Kathe Robin, *Romantic Times BOOKreviews*

"Caution: Reading *The Naked Baron* may cause spontaneous smiles and feelings of happiness!"—Connie Payne, OnceUponARomance.net

"Sally MacKenzie may have penned her best *Naked* book yet, raising the bar for the entire series. With unforgettable characters and blazing passion, *The Naked Baron* is a book to be savored over and over again." —Lettetia, SingleTitles.com

Praise for *The Naked Marquis*

"*The Naked Marquis* is an endearing confection of sweetness and sensuality, the romance equivalent of chocolate cake . . . every page is an irresistible delight!"—Lisa Kleypas, *New York Times* bestselling author

"With a delightfully quirky cast of characters and heated bedroom encounters, MacKenzie's latest *Naked* novel delivers a humorous, sprightly romance." —Kathe Robin, *Romantic Times BOOKreviews*

"Charming . . . funny . . . full of delightful characters . . . *The Naked Marquis* merits a place on the keeper shelves of readers of the traditional Regency and the spicier Regency-set historical romances alike."—Jane Bowers, RomanceReviewsToday.com

"*The Naked Marquis* is a delicious indulgence. Treat yourself!"—Connie Payne, OnceUponARomance.net

Praise for *The Naked Duke*

"MacKenzie sets a merry dance in motion in this enjoyable Regency romp."—Maria Hatton, *Booklist*

"This is a funny, delightful debut by a talented writer who knows how to blend passion, humor and the essence of the Regency period into a satisfying tale."—Kathe Robin, *Romantic Times BOOKreviews*

"Debut author Sally MacKenzie has penned a marvelously witty novel. . . . Readers who enjoy a large dose of humor will love *The Naked Duke*. The characters are charming, and the pace is quick. It is the perfect book for a cozy winter retreat."—ARomanceReview.com

The
Naked King

Books by Sally MacKenzie

THE NAKED DUKE

THE NAKED MARQUIS

THE NAKED EARL

THE NAKED GENTLEMAN

"The Naked Laird" in LORDS OF DESIRE

THE NAKED BARON

THE NAKED VISCOUNT

"The Naked Prince" in AN INVITATION TO SIN

THE NAKED KING

Published by Zebra Books

The
Naked King

SALLY MACKENZIE

ZEBRA BOOKS
KENSINGTON PUBLISHING CORP.
http://www.kensingtonbooks.com

ZEBRA BOOKS are published by

Kensington Publishing Corp.
119 West 40th Street
New York, NY 10018

All Kensington titles, imprints, and distributed lines are available at special quantity discounts for bulk purchases for sales promotion, premiums, fund-raising, educational, or institutional use.

Special book excerpts or customized printings can also be created to fit specific needs. For details, write or phone the office of the Kensington Special Sales Manager: Attn.: Special Sales Department. Kensington Publishing Corp., 119 West 40th Street, New York, NY 10018. Phone: 1-800-221-2647.

Zebra and the Z logo Reg. U.S. Pat. & TM Off.

ISBN-13: 978-1-4201-0255-0
ISBN-10: 1-4201-0255-9

First Printing: June 2011
10 9 8 7 6 5 4 3 2 1

Printed in the United States of America

Chapter 1

Stephen Parker-Roth landed in a large puddle. Mud and water splashed into the air, soaking his breeches, spattering his coat, and decorating his face with flecks of dirt. He wiped a blob off his right cheek with a clean corner of his cravat and frowned at the perpetrator of this sartorial disaster. "You have deplorable manners, sir."

The miscreant blinked at him, tongue lolling. He looked not the slightest bit abashed, damn it.

"This wouldn't have happened if I weren't very, very drunk, you know."

The fellow tilted his head to one side.

"You doubt me?" Stephen leaned forward and poked his finger at the large beast to emphasize his point. "I warn you, I'm an exceedingly dangerous man. I've won brawls from Borneo to Buenos Aires to Boston. More than one blackguard has rued the day his path crossed mine."

The dog barked, a rather surprisingly deep, ringing sound, and put his head down on his front paws. His hindquarters remained in the air, tail waving like a flag in a stiff gale.

Stephen unbent enough to scratch the creature's ears. "Ah, well, I won't hold your ignorance against you. You're just a . . ." He frowned. "No, you can't be a homeless cur—you're far too clean. How is it you're roaming Hyde Park by yourself?" His fingers found a collar in the dog's deep fur—and then he noticed the leash dragging in the grass. "Oh ho, you're not alone. What have you done with your master, sir?"

The dog's ears pricked up. A woman's voice, rich and incredibly alluring, called out, "Harry!"

"Or mistress . . ." Stephen found himself addressing empty air. Harry was already bounding across the grass to a figure about a hundred yards distant. Stephen squinted in the sun. The female wore an enormous bonnet and a dress that looked like an oversized flour sack.

Pity. A voice that evoked twisted sheets and tangled limbs should not belong to an antidote.

The woman stooped to reclaim the leash, and Harry promptly began towing her back toward him. He'd best stand, then, like a gentleman should.

He struggled to his feet. The mud didn't want to let him go. MacInnes was going to have an apoplexy when he saw him. Why his valet, who didn't blink at tending his gear in the Amazon or the wilds of Africa, got as priggish as a damned dandy when they reached England's shores was beyond him.

Eh. The change in altitude was not felicitous. He bent over, resting his hands on his knees, and swallowed several times until the landscape stopped whirling and his last meal agreed to remain in his stomach. It would be shockingly bad form to greet the lady by casting up his accounts all over her slippers.

"Harry! Slow down!"

Even sharp and breathless, her voice sent a jolt of pleasure through him. He leaned forward a bit more to shield any obvious evidence of his interest.

Rein up, you cawker. She might have buck teeth and garlic breath; she might be toothless and eighty years old.

He glanced up. Well, not eighty. She was moving too quickly to be that ancient.

The dreadful bonnet slid back off her head as he watched. Ah! Now he saw the purpose of that hideous headgear—it hid her riot of bright red curls. They glinted in the sunlight like dew-kissed roses.

She had spectacles, too, that looked to be in danger of falling off her rather prominent nose, and delightfully full lips, currently twisted into a grimace. She wasn't beautiful, but she was definitely attractive.

Who was she? A maid assigned to walk the family dog? No sane butler or housekeeper would give this girl that task—the dog was walking her, not she the dog. A lady of the night? Unlikely. It was now an awful hour in the morning, and he'd never heard of a dasher with a large obstreperous dog, the voice of a siren, red curls, and spectacles. A fallen female with those striking attributes would be the talk of the male *ton*. Perhaps she was a widow.

Or married. Damn, he hoped she wasn't married. He didn't dally with married ladies.

He shook his head. Was he insane? How the hell had dalliance crept into his thoughts?

He was drunk. That was it. Very, very drunk.

And she was very flushed and very annoyed. She was glaring at him.

He *was* covered in mud—his shoes squelched with the stuff—but that wasn't his fault. Her dog was to blame.

Harry dragged her the last few yards and plopped down at his feet. The girl's brows were the same shade as her hair. She looked more like a flame than a rose, actually. Was she as fiery in bed?

He closed his eyes briefly. If he could remember how many glasses of brandy he'd had, he'd vow never to have so many again.

He regarded her glowering countenance. "Er, good

morning." He sounded perfectly sober, if he said so himself. "It's, ah, a lovely morning, isn't it?"

"No, it's not." She blew out a short, sharp breath and pushed her hair back out of her face. Her green eyes were as stormy as a wind-tossed ocean, full of passion . . .

Perhaps he should swear off brandy entirely, though drink had never made him so lustful before.

"I mean . . ." She swallowed, obviously trying to get her spleen under control. "That is, yes, it is a lovely morning. How nice of you to say so after Harry caused you to fall into the mud. I apologize for his behavior."

Mmm, that voice. He'd so like to hear it threaded with need and desire, panting his name—

Definitely no more brandy.

"He's a sheep dog," the woman said. "I imagine he was trying to herd you away from the puddle, not into it." She reached back to reclaim her bonnet.

Oh, no. He couldn't let her cover her beautiful curls again with that monstrosity. He plucked the millinery mistake from her fingers and dropped it into the mud, mashing it down with his foot for good measure.

"My bonnet!" Lady Anne Marston gaped down at her poor bonnet, flattened under this rude person's shoe. What sort of gentleman attacked a woman's hat?

No sort of gentleman. The man might be handsome as sin with his startlingly clear blue eyes and shaggy, sun-streaked hair, but handsome is as handsome does—she had learned *that* lesson beyond hope of forgetting—and destroying a woman's bonnet was not handsomely done.

She drew in a breath to tell him exactly what she thought of such behavior—and stopped. Was that brandy she smelled? Certainly the man wasn't foxed at ten o'clock in the morning!

"Your bonnet is an abomination," he said.

"It is not!" And now he was insulting her as well. That was her favorite bonnet under his foot. It might not be stylish—*she* wasn't stylish—but she liked it. She'd had it for years.

"You didn't buy it in London, did you?"

"Of course not. London bonnets are frilly, silly dabs of straw and feathers and gewgaws. I need something serviceable."

She should leave. Yes, the man had landed in the mud, but it was probably more his fault than Harry's. Drunkards were notoriously unsteady. She tugged on Harry's leash, but the idiotic animal stayed where he was, at this human animal's feet.

"Serviceable?" He ground her poor hat deeper into the muck. "How could this atrocity be the least bit serviceable?"

"It protected me from the sun"—*and kept critical eyes off my disreputable hair.*

She would admit that last only to herself, certainly not to him. What did this fellow know of the matter anyway? He didn't have red hair—though, being a man, he probably wouldn't care if he did.

He snorted. "It protected you from the sun and every male who saw you in it, I'll wager."

Oh, she'd like to kick the cod's head exactly where it would hurt him most. He didn't think she was some silly miss on the catch for a husband, did he? "I'd hoped it would protect me from annoying men"—she sniffed, giving him her best pretention-depressing look—"such as yourself."

He chuckled. "Now that's put me in my place, hasn't it? And here I just rescued you from the ugliest bonnet in Britain." He leaned forward slightly, sending another whiff of brandy her way. "When you go looking for a replacement, try Madam le Fleur's in Bond Street. Fleur's hats are far more attractive."

Of course this fribble would be an expert in female fashion. She jerked on Harry's leash again; Harry merely yawned. "You are drunk, sir."

He nodded, looking not the least bit repentant. "I'm very much afraid I am."

"Did you rise early, then, to begin your debauchery?" It was a shame—in an academic, aesthetic sense only, of course—that such a handsome man was so dissipated.

"No. I haven't yet been to bed."

"You haven't?" She looked at his clothes more closely. Under all the mud they were indeed evening wear.

And under the clothes were exceptionally broad shoulders, a flat stomach, narrow hips . . . She flushed. Damn her coloring. She squeezed her eyes shut and drew in a deep breath—still tainted with the scent of brandy. What was the matter with her? Yes, even drunk this fellow was terribly attractive, but he was a man, and men were only trouble. She'd sworn off the breed years ago.

"But while I haven't engaged in any debauchery yet this morning . . ."

He paused suggestively, and, damn it, she couldn't keep her eyes shut. She looked at him.

". . . I'd be willing to attempt some now, if you'd like." He waggled his eyebrows.

Much to her surprise, she had to swallow a laugh instead of a gasp.

His eyes gleamed and his lips slid slowly into a smile—with dimples, blast it all. "Care to tuck me into bed?"

"No!" He was the very worst sort of London coxcomb, just the kind of male she'd worried about encountering on this unfortunate trip. So why was she finding him so amusing? The horrifying truth was part of her did wish to tuck the handsome rascal in. "Behave yourself."

She would not let herself be taken in again. This man might not seem at all like Lord Brentwood on the surface, but his heart was likely as black. His heart and another, specifically male organ.

"Oh, well." He shrugged. "I'll be off to bed straightaway then once I've seen you home." He raised his brows, looking ridiculously hopeful. "If you're certain you'd not like to read me a bedtime story at least?"

She turned another laugh into a cough. He was indeed an accomplished seducer if he could charm her well armored heart. She must be sure to keep her half sister away from him. At eighteen, Evie was too young to have learned to be suspicious of handsome scoundrels. "Quite certain. And there is no need for you to escort me."

"Oh, but there is. You know I wouldn't be a gentleman if I didn't see you safely home."

She turned her nose up at him. "You are not a gentleman—and I am quite all right by myself."

"No, you're not. A gently bred woman needs a male to protect her."

She glared. "I have Harry—he is both male and protective."

"And you have no control over him."

"Oh, and I have more control over you?"

The moment the last word left her lips, she froze, as if she'd shocked herself, and then flushed. Her eyes dropped in apparent embarrassment—and focused on his crotch.

Damn. He wasn't about to hide behind his hands like a bashful virgin, but if she stared at him much longer, she would get quite an education in male anatomy.

"I assure you, I can find my way home by myself." Her eyes moved on to her dog, thank God. "Forgive me for not apologizing earlier for the state of your clothing. I intended to immediately"—her eyes came back up to scowl at him—"and would have if you hadn't accosted my bonnet."

"I wouldn't have accosted your bonnet," he said, stepping on it once more and twisting his foot to grind it farther into the grime, "if it hadn't so vilely accosted my eyes and my male sensibilities."

She pressed her lips into a tight line, obviously wishing to brangle with him, but equally obviously restraining herself. Too bad. He found sparring with her surprisingly stimulating.

She took a deep breath, causing her formless bodice to swell in a rather interesting fashion. "In any event," she said, "Harry was at fault." She dropped her eyes to his muddied cravat. "Your clothing is likely irreparably damaged; my father will wish to make it right. Please have your bills sent to Lord Crane."

"Ah." That was why he didn't know her. Crane spent even less time in London than he did. "So you're Crazy Crane's daughter."

He was sober enough to notice her flinch, but she must be used to hearing that nickname. Everyone called Crane crazy. His passion for finding antiquities was even greater than Stephen's for discovering new plant species. The word at White's was the earl had come to Town—briefly, as it turned out—to fire off his daughter on the Marriage Mart. Stephen frowned. He was drunk, but he wasn't completely disguised. Wasn't this girl too old to be a debutante?

"So you're here to find a husband?" he asked.

Her brows snapped down as her eyes snapped back to his face. "Of course not." She curled her delightful upper lip slightly. "Were you quaking in your boots?"

"Don't have boots." He lifted his foot to show her and almost left his shoe in the quagmire. "And you don't scare me. I've been dodging debutantes for years—though you do seem a little long in the tooth to be just making your bows."

"I am twenty-seven"—it sounded as if she were gritting her teeth—"not that it is any of your business. It is my half sister who is being introduced to the *ton.*"

"Ah!" He nodded. Now he remembered. "You're Crane's older daughter, the one by his first wife. The bluestocking as opposed to the—"

A sliver of sobriety wormed its way into his sodden brain. He coughed.

"As opposed to the beauty." She sounded indifferent, but he saw the hurt in her eyes before she turned abruptly and started walking briskly toward Grosvenor Gate. Even Harry gave him a reproachful look as he left.

Damn. That hadn't been well done of him. He should let her go. She would not want to spend another moment in his presence.

He couldn't let her go. He did *not* break hearts, nor offend anyone, at least unintentionally. He had to apologize. He took off after her.

Crane's daughter—what was her name? Damned if he could remember. No one at White's had talked much about the bluestocking. She had a long stride, but was hampered by her skirts, and Stephen was used to walking long distances. He caught up to her quickly.

As he feared, she was crying.

"Go away." She wouldn't look at him.

"Look, I'm sorry. I didn't mean that quite the way it sounded."

She snorted—and then had to sniff repeatedly. He offered her his handkerchief.

"Thank you." She glared at him briefly, her eyes quite red behind her spectacles.

He took Harry's leash so she could blow her nose, which she did rather defiantly. She stared straight ahead, refusing to meet his gaze.

"And I was not affected in the slightest by your words. Of course not. I merely had a speck in my eye. It is true my sister is a beauty; I have hopes she will have a wonderful Season." She sent him a pointed look then. "She is much too young for you, however."

She looked like an angry kitten, trying to be fierce with its tiny claws and teeth. And he *had* hurt her feelings; he had sisters; he knew when girls felt wounded.

He felt an odd warmth in his chest. A bout of indigestion, most likely. He'd certainly had too much to drink. Once he saw Lady . . . Lady . . .

"You never did tell me your name."

She shrugged. "And you never told me yours."

"So I didn't." He inclined his head. "Stephen Parker-Roth, at your service."

"What?" She stumbled on a crack in the pavement. He reached to grab her, but she avoided his hand. *"The King of Hearts?"*

"Well, yes, some people call me that." He cleared his throat. "I'm rather good—or lucky—with cards."

Cards? Anne sniffed. "It's not *cards* you're good with."

"It is."

Damn it, the rogue looked like a blasted choir boy, as sinless as a cherub, but she knew through long association with her half brothers not to trust that mask of innocence. "Oh?" She allowed her skepticism to show in her voice.

He had the grace to laugh. "I grant you my skill with cards is not the only reason I got that dam—er, unfortunate nickname." He raised his brows. "How do you know it, Lady—" He frowned. "Devil a bit, I *still* don't know your name."

She might as well tell him. He would learn it soon enough once the Season got underway. "My name is Lady Anne Marston."

"Lady Anne," he said.

Her name sounded like someone else's when he said it—someone beautiful, or at least someone interesting. Someone he was interested in.

Idiot! Only a complete noddy would think the King of Hearts could have the slightest interest in a red-headed, bespectacled bluestocking. She wasn't the beauty of the family; she was very ordinary looking, except for her lamentable hair.

She was *glad* he wasn't interested in her. She wasn't interested in him.

She was a terrible liar.

"So how is it, Lady Anne, that you know my nickname when you have so recently arrived in Town? If gossip is correct, the earl dumped you—" He coughed. "I mean *deposited* you at Crane House just yesterday."

Dumped was the correct description. Papa could barely stand to pause the coach long enough to let her, Evie, and the boys out. He certainly hadn't waited for their baggage to arrive; he and Georgiana were far too anxious to get to the docks and board their ship for Greece. Fortunately Cousin Clorinda, being in London already, had moved in the day before, but things were still very much at sixes and sevens.

"The London papers come even to the country, you know."

He raised one eyebrow and looked annoyingly superior. "So you can peruse the gossip columns?"

She raised her eyebrow back at him. "So I can read the entire paper."

And, yes, perhaps she had paid particular attention to gossip concerning the K— of H—. She'd taken an interest—a *scholarly* interest—in him. She'd come across an article in Papa's *The Gentleman's Magazine* a year or two ago, an account Mr. Parker-Roth had written describing one of his plant hunting expeditions. He'd sounded exceptionally intelligent and rather intrepid—

obviously he'd learned how to be as cozening in print as in person.

She flushed. She'd dreamt about him once or twice, too. She was lonely on occasion—well, most of the time. She may have sworn off men, but somehow he'd caught her fancy. What harm was there in a little romantic woolgathering? She was never going to meet him.

Except she just had.

One would think a twenty-seven-year-old spinster would have more sense, especially a woman with her experience.

Traffic was beginning to pick up. The streets and walks had been deserted when she'd left Crane House earlier—a very good thing as she'd had to run to keep up with Harry. Of course now the stupid dog was walking sedately at Mr. Parker-Roth's side.

"The *ton* is always making up nicknames for people," he was saying. "They'll probably christen you and your sister as soon as you attend your first social event."

"I sincerely hope not." Blast it, how was she going to navigate these treacherous social waters with only Cousin Clorinda to help her? She bit her lip. It was just like Papa and Georgiana to go off to dig in the dirt, leaving her in charge of the children. Not that Evie was a child any longer. Of course not. They wouldn't be in this mess if she were.

She swallowed a sigh. Thankfully, Evie was a sensible girl—but Anne had considered herself sensible once, too. All it had taken was one experienced, London rake paying her a little attention—

Dear God, what if Brentwood was here in Town?

No, she couldn't be that unlucky. She'd been reading the gossip columns very carefully for weeks and had not seen his name.

But if he *were* in London—

"A penny for your thoughts, Lady Anne."

Her heart thudded into her throat. "I wasn't thinking about anything."

"No? You looked—"

"Oh, yes, look, here we are at Crane House." *Thank God!* "What a surprise. I don't know how we got here so quickly." She was blathering, but if she kept talking, he couldn't ask her questions she didn't want to answer. "Thank you for escorting me and for taking charge of Harry. If you will just give me his leash, you can get"—she hadn't been about to say he could get to bed, had she?—"that is, you can be about your business." She smiled, or at least tried to, and held out her hand. If she was lucky, she would never see him again.

Ha! She might hope she wouldn't see him, but she was here for the whole cursed Season. She couldn't hide in her room and send Evie to the parties and balls with only odd, elderly Cousin Clorinda as chaperone.

Perhaps Mr. Parker-Roth would leave London tomorrow to hunt for greenery in some exotic—and very distant—location. She would add that thought to her prayers tonight.

"Lady Anne," he said, looking far too serious all of a sudden.

"Mr. Parker-Roth, I should go. Cousin Clorinda and my sister must be wondering where I am."

She glanced up. What if someone looked out a window and saw her conversing with Mr. Parker-Roth? She and he would be quite recognizable—neither was wearing a hat. Their faces were evident for any curious spectator to see.

Whom was she kidding? It wasn't only her face she had to hide—her unfortunate hair was a blazing beacon, proclaiming her identity to anyone not color-blind.

Perhaps no one would look. It was early for most of the *ton* . . . but Lady Dunlee lived next door and she had a nose for even the faintest whiff of scandal. Cousin Clorinda had warned Anne about the woman the moment Anne had crossed Crane House's threshold— and Lady Dunlee herself had already stopped Anne to let her know the boys had been teasing her nasty gray cat.

"But I never properly apologized," Mr. Parker-Roth said. Harry sat calmly at his feet. Why wouldn't that dog behave for her?

"No apology is necessary. Now, please—"

He touched her lips with his gloveless fingers. She froze.

Oh.

His skin was slightly rough—he clearly used his hands for more than raising a quizzing glass or shuffling cards—and warm.

All of a sudden, she didn't care about the windows overlooking the square.

"I don't want you to think you aren't beautiful." His fingers slipped sideways to cradle her jaw; his thumb moved back and forth over her bottom lip. "You are."

He was an enchanter, that was it, weaving a spell around her. Faintly, very faintly, she heard the voice of reason warning her about gossip and Lady Dunlee, about boorish and unprincipled villains, about the complete idiocy of believing her fantasies lived in the real world, but for the first time in a decade, she ignored it. Her hands crept up to rest on the King of Hearts's broad, solid chest.

In her dreams, he had not only been handsome, he'd been kind and honorable.

She wanted a taste of what this man could give her. Just this once. Just for academic purposes. To impress upon herself that dreams were not real and men were indeed best avoided.

She smelled the brandy on his breath again. "You're

drunk." She spoke to him, but she was reminding herself.

"Yes." His words whispered past her cheek. "But I'm not blind."

His mouth brushed hers. Her lips tingled, feeling suddenly swollen. This kiss—if you could call it a kiss—was nothing like the hot, wet, slobbery affairs she'd endured from Brentwood. Being kissed by Brentwood had been an attack—this was something else entirely.

Comfort, not lust. An invitation, not a command.

Beguiling, seductive, making sin seem like a divine gift . . .

"Anne."

She loved the sound of her name in his voice. A little shiver slithered through her and she sighed, tilting her head more, like a sunflower seeking the sun.

He made a small, satisfied noise and nibbled on her bottom lip while his free hand, the one not grasping Harry's leash, slid to the back of her head.

An odd warmth gathered in her belly. Something hard and frozen began to melt. She leaned into Mr. Parker-Roth's strong body, wanting—needing—more of his heat.

And then she heard the hiss of an angry cat and Harry's answering bark. Mr. Parker-Roth jerked backward. She felt herself wobble and grabbed his coat.

"Hold tight," he muttered. His arm locked around her waist as they lost their battle with gravity and tumbled toward the pavement.

"*Oof!*" He flinched as he took the brunt of the impact.

She was not a featherweight. "Are you all right?"

"I'll live." His voice had an edge of pain.

"I'm so sorry!" She relaxed against him for a moment. His body was so hard under hers. Pleasantly hard. And something else of his was getting hard as well . . .

Her face burned. What had she been thinking? Here she was, sprawled across a man in a public square and from the feel of the sun on the back of her legs her skirt was up around her knees. And from the feel of the man below her, he was having the expected reaction. How mortifying. And if anyone saw them . . .

She started to scramble off him. He held her still.

"Let me go." She tried to twist free. "Think of the scandal if we are observed."

He flinched again and tightened his hold on her back . . . well, a bit lower than her back.

"Mind your knee, love."

"Oh." Her leg was now between his. Her knee was indeed very close to—"I'm so sorry."

"That's all right. No permanent harm done." He smiled a little tightly. "I hope. Now, we'll just have—"

That's when she heard the sharp intake of breath.

"Trouble," Mr. Parker-Roth muttered.

Anne looked up. Lady Dunlee stood not ten feet from them, a look of delighted horror on her face.

"Lady Anne—and Mr. Parker-Roth! What in the world are you doing?"

Chapter 2

Stephen rubbed his temples and tried surreptitiously to lean against a sturdy wingback chair in Lord Crane's bookroom. Tiny devils with sledgehammers were banging away on the inside of his forehead and the high-pitched yammering around him only added to his misery. He'd give his damn fortune to be back in his bedchamber, curtains drawn, icepack on his head. But he was, for all his faults, a gentleman. He couldn't leave Lady Anne to face the music—or screeching—alone.

He glanced over at her. She looked more than capable of defending herself. At the moment she was glaring at her elderly cousin Miss Clorinda Strange and Lady Dunlee, her mouth set in a tight line, her brows almost meeting over her nose. He'd swear her nostrils flared. If he were closer to her, he'd probably see green sparks shooting from her eyes.

"Cousin Clorinda, Lady Dunlee, you are making far too much of this incident."

"Far too much?" Lady Dunlee sniffed and raised her eyebrows. "I don't see how one can make 'far too much' of a lady disporting herself with abandon in a public square—and with the King of Hearts, no less." She shot him a pointed look. He smiled back as blandly as possible.

"Anne." Miss Strange was scowling. She'd not looked pleased when they'd interrupted her—she'd been perusing some large, musty tome when Lady Dunlee had burst in, dragging them along in her wake. "Is this true?"

Lady Anne turned a lovely shade of red. "Of course not. I was not disporting myself with"—Zeus, she turned even redder—"I wasn't disporting myself at all."

Damn, he'd like to disport himself with the lady in a private room, on a large, soft bed. Odd. He'd never been drawn to bespectacled spinsters dressed in sacks before, but there was something about this spinster . . . She'd been delightful in the square. Shy, hesitant, yet curious, too—quite the contrast from her prickly behavior up to that point.

"Oh, no?" Lady Dunlee said. "I saw you in Mr. Parker-Roth's arms. You were running your hands over his chest before you kissed him and threw him down on the ground to have your wicked way with him."

Lust shot directly to his, er, brain, so he momentarily lost track of the conversation. Fortunately instinct prompted him to step quickly behind a chair, shielding his telltale bit from Lady Dunlee's sharp eyes.

Lady Dunlee had misconstrued the scene, of course, but he wished she'd had the right of it. He was more than willing to let Lady Anne have her wicked way with his poor self.

How wicked would her way be? Mmm, that was an interesting question to contemplate. If her imagination faltered, his was more than adequate for the task. Much more. It was currently producing a number of delicious images, completely inappropriate for his present location. But if he and Anne were in his bedchamber—

"Mr. Parker-Roth, did I just hear you groan?" Damned

if Lady Dunlee's eyes didn't drop to his nether regions, still well hidden behind the wing chair.

"I don't believe so, madam, but I do have a touch of the headache."

The blasted woman kept her eyes focused on where his unruly cock was misbehaving and arched a brow. "I bet you do."

She couldn't see through the chair, could she? He felt a hot flush sweep up his neck, but he did his best to ignore it. At least this corner of the room was too shadowy for his heightened color to be easily discerned . . . he hoped. He glanced at Anne.

She appeared to be too mortified or too furious to form a coherent sentence. Her mouth was open, but only strangled sounds emerged.

Unfortunately, Miss Strange's voice was working perfectly. "Anne, were you actually on the ground with a *man?*" She might as well have said "soul eating devil."

Her voice drilled right between his eyes. He rubbed the spot with his index and middle finger and leaned a little more against the chair. At a guess, Miss Strange was not a huge admirer of the male of the species. Not surprising. He couldn't imagine any of his sex admiring her. She looked like an elderly heron, all stiff and angular, with a long neck and beak-like nose. She wore her gray hair in a bun so tight her watery blue eyes bulged.

"Oh, yes." Lady Dunlee wasn't even trying to hide her glee. She glanced at him again before dropping her voice to a stage whisper. "Lady Anne's skirts were up around her knees, and Mr. Parker-Roth's hands were on her"—she dropped her voice even lower—"derriere."

Lady Anne moaned—and not with suppressed desire. No matter. The sound, throaty and deep, caused his eager cock to grow another inch.

Blast it, this was most definitely not the time or place to entertain salacious thoughts concerning Lady Anne.

They were in a very sticky situation. Lady Dunlee was by far the biggest gossip in London if not in all of England.

Miss Strange's jaw had dropped almost to her slippers, and her throat worked exactly as if she were indeed a heron trying to swallow a large fish whole. "Ah, ah."

"I fell." Lady Anne had found her lovely voice again. "I wasn't . . . there was nothing . . ." She took a deep breath and scowled at Lady Dunlee. "It was all your cat's fault."

Good God, didn't Anne realize she was teetering on the edge of social annihilation by accusing the woman's pet of misbehavior? It was akin to jumping in front of a speeding carriage. Lady Dunlee could— and likely would—take instant umbrage and flatten Anne's reputation with just a well chosen word or two.

He cleared his throat. "Perhaps we should sit down and discuss the matter over a nice, calming cup of tea." He'd prefer a large glass of brandy, but even his sodden brain knew he dare not ask for that. At least his dimensions had subsided sufficiently so he could risk Lady Dunlee's scrutiny long enough to take a seat. In fact, other pains were overtaking the ache in his crotch. His shoulder and hip throbbed from where he'd landed on the pavement and his head threatened to explode. His knees felt a touch wobbly and his stomach was considering revolt.

The ladies ignored him.

Lady Dunlee had swelled up like an angry feline. "How can you possibly say Miss Whiskers is to blame for your sins?"

"Because she *is* to blame." Lady Anne clasped her hands as though to keep from strangling Lady Dunlee. "And they aren't sins."

Lady Dunlee's eyebrows disappeared into her hair. "Rolling around on the ground in passionate—"

Anne cut her off. "The entire incident was an

accident. If your cat hadn't darted past just then, Harry would not have taken off after her and pulled Mr. Parker-Roth backward, causing us both to fall."

"Ah." Lady Dunlee's lips pulled into a rather dangerous smile. "And I suppose Miss Whisker's presence somehow compelled you to kiss and caress Mr. Parker-Roth *before* your dog pulled you over?"

"No. I mean I didn't." Lady Anne's complexion got even redder. "That is, *he* kissed *me*."

The silence that followed this announcement was deafening.

"So the beast forced himself on you?" Miss Strange choked on the words. Two pairs of feminine eyes—Lady Anne had the grace to examine the floor at her feet—swiveled toward him.

"Er . . ." If he remembered correctly Lady Anne had been a very willing participant in that kiss. Surely he remembered correctly? He wasn't that drunk—he'd never been so drunk as to take liberties with an unwilling woman.

"No, of course he didn't force himself on me, Cousin," Lady Anne said, her cheeks still bright red. "Don't be ridiculous."

Miss Strange patted Anne on the shoulder. "There, there. No need to be embarrassed. It's not your fault." She glared at him. "Everyone knows men are all too often driven by their baser instincts."

Anne stepped away from her cousin's touch. "You sound like the worst horrid novel, Clorinda. Mr. Parker-Roth did not attack me." She shrugged one shoulder, looking most uncomfortable, but compelled by honor to tell the truth. "He may have initiated the encounter, but I didn't exactly struggle."

Not exactly. He bit back a smile. Not at all.

He cleared his throat, bringing the ladies' attention back to him. He couldn't let Anne dig herself deeper into a hole. A hole? Ha. He felt parson's mousetrap yawning before him like a bottomless abyss, but there was no way to avoid it now; they might as well step in with as much grace as they could.

"Of course you weren't struggling, dear heart." Three jaws dropped at the endearment. "Why would you?" He moved to take her hand in both of his before turning to the other women. "My apologies, ladies, for letting passion rule my better judgment, but I'm afraid it's been so long since I've seen my betrothed, I couldn't contain my happiness."

"Betrothed?" All three women spoke together in the same tone of incredulity. They were like a damn Greek chorus. Three pairs of eyes goggled at him now.

"I'm sure you didn't tell me you were betrothed, Anne." Miss Strange's tone was an odd mix of confusion and horror. "I would have remembered if you had. And your father didn't mention it in his letter." She paused, her brow wrinkling. "At least, I don't think he did. I grant you he ran on so about his silly antiquities I did skim a lot of his missive."

Anne tried to tug her fingers out of his grasp, but he wasn't about to let her go. "I didn't tell you, Cousin, because Mr. Parker-Roth and I aren't—ouch!"

She glared at him accusatorily; he smiled. He was sorry to have squeezed her so hard, but he couldn't let her ruin his attempt to save her reputation. Couldn't she comprehend? All they had to do was fabricate something remotely plausible. Lady Dunlee might doubt their story—most likely would doubt it—but she couldn't know for certain what the truth was. He and Anne would have all Season to convince her and the *ton* of their devotion.

He lifted Anne's fingers to brush his lips over them— and smiled a little more as she blushed and tried again to snatch them out of his grasp. This charade might even be pleasant. And should it—as it likely would—end in matrimony . . . Well, he'd been thinking just this evening—or was it this morning?—that he needed to give in and look about for a bride. He'd just turned thirty, he'd narrowly escaped a marriage trap two months ago, and his older brother and younger sister were both wed and busily procreating. Hell, after his second bottle of brandy, he'd admitted to himself he didn't much care to live out his life as old Uncle Stephen.

Not that he'd be given that opportunity, of course. When he'd been home for his nephew's christening, Mama had been hinting—rather more than hinting—that he should embrace the joys of matrimony sooner rather than later, and with John and Jane both taken care of, she would turn the complete focus of her marital machinations on him—Nick was still too young, the lucky dog.

He'd laughed when he'd watched her drag John up for the Season year after year and push eligible young ladies into his path—he would not be laughing so heartily if he were Mama's victim. Frankly, he'd been a little surprised she hadn't followed him to London when he'd left the Priory after the christening. Thank God for baby Jack. But he had little doubt the joys of grandmotherhood would not supplant the duties of motherhood—as Mama saw them—forever.

Truthfully, marriage shouldn't be that onerous. This farce had saved him the annoyance of shopping for a bride—or having Mama shop. Once he was wed, he'd be off looking for plants on foreign shores most of the time anyway. It might even be convenient to have a woman on his estate to warm his bed and tend his children when they arrived. It wasn't the marriage his parents had—it wasn't the marriage he'd thought he'd have—but it was the exact sort of arrangement much of the *ton* enjoyed.

He studied Lady Anne's expressive face. She was so full of emotion, she looked ready to explode. How would she look full of passion, naked in the center of his bed?

Delightful.

She should keep his nuptial bed very warm indeed.

"I know we aren't ready to make a formal announcement, my love,"—she scowled at him—"but now that Lady Dunlee and your cousin have found us out . . ." He turned to the queen of London gossip. "We can ask you to keep our little secret, can't we, Lady Dunlee?" He managed to keep a straight face at the absurdity of his request. He might as well ask the sun to change places with the moon.

"Of course." Lady Dunlee's eyes gleamed with excitement. "You can rely on me. I won't tell a soul."

Stephen believed her. She wouldn't tell a soul—for however long it took her to toddle across the square to the house of her bosom friend and equally accomplished gossip, Melinda Fallwell.

"I still think the earl would have made it a point to say something to me if he'd known about this betrothal." Miss Strange's nostrils twitched as if she smelled something rotten.

What was the matter with the woman? His and Anne's betrothal might be a complete sham but why would she wish to discuss that in front of Lady Dunlee? She must see the woman was dying for the smallest crumb of gossip, and here she was offering the gabble-grinder a veritable feast.

Stephen forced himself to smile. "I gather Lord Crane was in a hurry to catch his ship."

"In a hurry?" Anne said. "That hardly describes it. Papa almost shoved us out of the carriage while it was still moving. He certainly didn't pause to have a word with you, Clorinda."

"No, he didn't." Clorinda nodded. "The man's obsessed with bits of pottery and broken statues. Queer as Dick's hatband about it, if you ask me—always has been. We were surprised he got his head out of the dirt long enough to marry your mother, Anne. And the current countess . . . she's as daft about debris as he is."

"Georgiana does share Papa's passion," Anne said, trying not to sound disgruntled. Papa and Georgiana never thought twice about taking off at a moment's notice, leaving her to manage everything at home. She'd got used to it, but to expect her to handle Evie's come-out as well . . . What in God's name had they been thinking? She knew nothing about the London Season, never having had one herself, and it was clear to her Clorinda would be no help. And now with this nonsensical betrothal to complicate matters . . .

All she needed was for Brentwood to put in an appearance, and this disaster would be complete.

"And I really don't see how you are one to talk, Clorinda," Anne said. "You have your nose forever buried in some ornithological tome."

"That's an entirely different matter. I'm studying living, breathing creatures." Clorinda sniffed. "Your father and the countess are pawing through history's middens"—she wrinkled her nose in distaste—"picking through someone's garbage."

Mr. Parker-Roth cleared his throat.

"Oh, what is it?" Anne looked at the man in exasperation, but her damn heart stuttered the moment her eyes focused on him. He was so incredibly handsome. Women must stare at him wherever he went.

Idiot! Of course they stared at him—he was the King of Hearts. All the *ton*'s females vied for his attention.

"I don't believe we need to take any more of Lady Dunlee's time, do you?" Mr. Parker-Roth was saying.

He tilted his head slightly toward the woman and raised his eyebrows significantly. "I'm sure she must have other commitments."

"Oh." Anne glanced at the annoying busybody. Lady Dunlee's beady little eyes fairly glowed. Clearly she was gathering bits of gossip like a squirrel gathering nuts for the winter. At any moment her cheeks would start to bulge. "Yes, indeed. Please don't let us detain you, Lady Dunlee."

"Tut, tut. Don't be silly." She smiled as if she were some completely harmless matron. "As it happens, I have nothing pressing to attend to. Please, carry on. Just pretend I'm a potted palm."

A potted palm with a tongue that runs on wheels. "I wouldn't think of it," Anne said. "I know you are a very busy woman." *Busy about other people's affairs.* She walked briskly to the bookroom door and opened it. Mr. Parker-Roth gestured for Lady Dunlee to precede him. The woman hesitated, but finally must have concluded—correctly—she had no choice in the matter. She dragged her feet, but she went.

Anne looked at her cousin. Clorinda had already returned to the book she'd been reading when Lady Dunlee, full of moral outrage, had barged in with them. "Coming, Clorinda?"

"Hmm?" Clorinda turned a page.

"Are you coming to see our guests out?"

Clorinda waved her hand vaguely, her nose still buried in her book. "You can do that without my help."

"Very well. I'll—"

"Just do be careful." Clorinda marked her place with her finger to glance up at Anne. "Mr. Parker-Roth is very pleasant to look at, I grant you, but he's also a bit of a rake. They call him the King of Hearts for a reason, you know."

"Yes, I know." And didn't Clorinda know the man

was standing in the corridor right behind her? Anne heard him choke back a laugh. Lady Dunlee snickered.

"Just thought I should put the word in your ear, Anne," Clorinda said, returning to her reading. "Having spent your whole life in the country, you're hardly up to snuff."

"Thank you, Clorinda." One didn't need to come to London to learn about libertines, but Anne didn't wish to discuss that topic whilst the current libertine and the queen of London gossip listened. She pulled the door closed behind her and avoided her guests' eyes. "This way," she said.

She started briskly toward the front of the house. She'd be extremely happy to see the back of Lady Dunlee—and Mr. Parker-Roth, too, of course. Once they were out the door, she could finally get on with her day. She'd planned to take her paints out early to explore the back garden, but first Harry had needed a walk and then the . . . incident with Mr. Parker-Roth and Lady Dunlee had occurred, and now she'd completely missed the morning light. Blast! As soon as her unwelcome guests had departed, she'd hurry upstairs and . . .

No, the way this day was going, she'd never be so lucky. The boys were sure to be into some kind of mischief—she almost hoped they were teasing Miss Whiskers again—and she was supposed to take Evie shopping. A proper come-out required an annoying amount of clothing.

She glanced over her shoulder. Lady Dunlee was peering around as if trying to memorize every detail her greedy little eyes beheld. Papa must not have invited her in on his rare visits to London. She snorted. Why would he? He might be more focused on Greek and Roman artifacts than English society, but he could recognize trouble when it lived next door.

Lady Dunlee must have heard her snort and was now looking at her inquiringly.

"Er . . ." What to say? Lady Dunlee obviously expected something. "I do apologize for Harry's behavior." She was saying that a lot today, not that she meant it this time either—Lady Dunlee should have kept her cat inside.

"That's quite all right." Lady Dunlee turned to examine a naked statue of Apollo through her lorgnette. "No permanent harm done. Miss Whiskers has likely found her way home by now."

"Then you'll want to hurry off to let her in," Anne said hopefully. She reached for the door, but Mr. Parker-Roth's large hand grabbed the knob first.

Lady Dunlee tore her eyes away from Apollo's fig leaf. "Oh, I'm sure my butler has already done so, unless Miss Whiskers chose to stay on the front step. She likes to lie on stone that's been warmed by the sun. I image it's quite cozy, don't you?"

Anne blinked. She hadn't ever considered the matter. "I . . . I suppose you are right."

Lady Dunlee nodded. "Of course I'm right." She stepped past Anne, but paused on the threshold to give her a stern look. "Before I leave, I must insist you keep your dog under better control in the future, Lady Anne. Miss Whiskers and I will not be pleased if we are constantly disturbed by the brute."

Miss Whiskers had been the one doing the disturbing this morning, but Anne managed to keep from saying so. "Yes, indeed. I will try to keep Harry away from your cat."

Lady Dunlee nodded toward Mr. Parker-Roth. "I'm sure your betrothed can help. Oftentimes large dogs need a man's touch."

"Exactly." Mr. Parker-Roth wrapped an arm around Anne's waist. "I'll be happy to take Harry in hand."

Anne stiffened at his touch. Lady Dunlee's lorgnette had snapped up and her enlarged orb was now staring at his hand on her waist. She tried—halfheartedly, but she did try—to shrug out of his embrace, but he wouldn't let her go. Instead his hand slipped a little lower so it lay on her hip just below her stays.

Oh! She felt each finger as if it were burning a hole through her dress and chemise. The hard strength of his arm and the warmth of his body all along her side made it very difficult to think clearly.

Well, perhaps thinking wasn't the issue. Her head insisted she should move away, but her body . . . She drew in a deep shuddery breath, filling her lungs with his scent, a heady mix of brandy, damp broadcloth, eau de cologne, and . . . man.

A heavy liquid warmth settled low in her belly.

Oh, God. She'd never felt this way before, even when she'd thought herself in love with Brentwood. It could not be good.

"I will see if I can train Harry to behave in a more gentlemanly fashion," Mr. Parker-Roth was saying. "As I've been in London and Lady Anne's been in the country, I haven't had the opportunity until now to do so—and of course manners in the country are more relaxed."

"Indeed they are, sir," Lady Dunlee said, scowling at him, "but I hope manners are not so relaxed as to approve the behavior I just witnessed in the square. You know, if Lady Anne does not, that London society will not tolerate such conduct."

"I—"

Mr. Parker-Roth didn't let Anne squeeze a word in. "I beg your pardon for my lack of decorum, Lady Dunlee. I can only plead temporary insanity. I'd not seen Anne in far too long." Mr. Parker-Roth managed to look suitably contrite—he'd probably perfected that charmingly apologetic expression as a boy.

Good Lord, Lady Dunlee dimpled up at him. "Of course you have my pardon, sir, as long as I have your vow to control your emotions in the future. I quite understand the fervor of young love."

Anne had to choke back a laugh, turning it into a cough. Lady Dunlee had at least forty, if not fifty, years in her dish. Young love must be a very faint memory.

"But I would be terribly remiss," Lady Dunlee continued, "if I didn't point out many people will wonder at this sudden betrothal. You can't wish to make things more difficult for Lady Anne and her family."

"Of course I don't."

Anne barely heard Mr. Parker-Roth's words. *Many* people would wonder? What a horrifying thought.

She must have made a sound, because Lady Dunlee raised her brows, giving her an alarmingly arch look. "You are very lucky, Lady Anne. Countless society maidens will take to their beds in a fit of the dismals when they hear Mr. Stephen Parker-Roth is no longer available."

Her stomach sank to the bottom of her slippers. This *must* be a nightmare. She would wake up in a moment safely tucked into her bed at Crane House.

"Oh, yes, society will be abuzz with the news of your betrothal." Lady Dunlee gave what looked suspiciously like a skip as she cleared the threshold.

"But you promised not to say a word," Anne called after her.

The woman just smiled over her shoulder and waved her hand. Instead of turning to mount the stairs to her house, she headed off across the square. A large, gray cat darted out from under a bush to rub itself against her ankles.

"At least Miss Whiskers is safe," Mr. Parker-Roth said, closing the door.

Anne glared at him. "I don't care about that stupid cat—where is Lady Dunlee going?"

"To Melinda Fallwell's. She lives at number forty-nine."

"Who's Melinda Fallwell?" Anne pointed to the door. "And aren't you leaving, too?"

Mr. Parker-Roth took her arm. "Melinda Fallwell is London's second greatest gossip—second to Lady Dunlee, of course—and, no, I am not leaving. We need to discuss our betrothal. Where can we be private?" He started back down the corridor, opening doors and peering in. "Ah, this will do nicely."

He pulled her into what Hobbes had called "the, ahem, Oriental room" when he'd given Anne a quick tour of the house the day before. She called it the harem room. It was furnished with low couches and oversized pillows. Gauzy striped curtains festooned the ceiling and hung down the walls giving one the feeling of being inside a large tent.

Mr. Parker-Roth picked a brass statue off the mantel. His eyes widened and he chuckled. "Interesting decorations you have, Lady Anne."

She had a bad feeling about this. "Everything was here when we arrived." She snatched the statue out of his hands and looked at it. There was a man and three women and they were—

"Dear God!" She stuffed it behind one of the couches. As soon as she got rid of Mr. Parker-Roth, she would examine all the knickknacks and pack away the inappropriate ones before the twins found them. This looked like just the sort of room ten-year-old boys would love. "Apparently collecting erotic—I mean *exotic*—items runs in my father's family."

"Apparently." The annoying man had found another inappropriate sculpture on the mantel.

"*Will* you put that down?"

"I don't know. It's rather . . . stimulating, don't you think?" Mr. Parker-Roth sent her a heated look. His thumb was rubbing slowly over the brass woman's extremely prominent breasts.

"No, of course not." If he wanted prominent breasts, he would have to look elsewhere.

And why was she thinking of breasts at all? How shocking.

Her body wasn't shocked. Her little breasts felt oddly sensitive, almost achy, as if they'd like Mr. Parker-Roth to touch them as he was touching the statue. "Didn't you drag me in here to discuss our b-betrothal?"

He put the statue back on the mantel and smiled. "Yes, I did." His voice sounded like sin as he came toward her. He *looked* like sin.

He's the King of Hearts, you ninnyhammer. Seduction is his middle name.

She looked for a sturdy settee to dodge behind, but the damn room had nothing so conventional. She grabbed a fat pillow instead and held it in front of her like a shield.

He stopped a good two feet from her and frowned. "You aren't afraid of me, are you, Anne?"

"Of course not." God help her! His look of concern made him even more alluring.

She wasn't afraid of him; she was afraid of herself.

What was the matter with her? Had she forgotten the last time she'd let her body rule her head? Ten years ago, she'd gone with Lord Brentwood into Baron Gedding's garden and come back without her virginity. She would not be so stupid as to make that mistake again.

Well, she couldn't, could she? Virginity once lost was gone forever.

"I won't hurt you." Mr. Parker-Roth actually looked worried. "I thought you knew that."

"You're drunk."

He shook his head and winced. "Not any longer—or at least not enough to mask my other aches and pains." He looked at her intently. "But even drunk I'd never force myself on a woman."

He wouldn't have to. Women would force themselves on him.

She dropped the pillow back on the couch, feeling a little ridiculous. "About this sham betrothal?"

He studied her for another minute and then shrugged, running his hand through his hair. "I do think it's the only way to save your reputation and salvage your sister's Season."

She had a very uncomfortable feeling he might be correct. She didn't care about her reputation—she didn't have one to salvage—but she'd fight tooth and nail to protect Evie's chance to enjoy a London Season and perhaps find a suitable husband. "If Lady Dunlee would keep the story to herself, we might be able to get by."

He rolled his eyes. "Yes, and if I had wings, I might be able to fly across the Thames."

"But—"

"But I am sure Lady Dunlee and Melinda Fallwell are setting out this very moment to share the tale—in strictest confidence of course—with ten or twenty of their closest friends. It will be all over London by nightfall."

"No."

"Yes. You don't have to be familiar with London to know how gossips operate. There are plenty of those in the country."

"Oh, yes, I know." Though somehow the story of her downfall had never spread, probably because only she and Brentwood knew about it. She was not about to say anything, and Brentwood likely had forgotten it the moment he'd pulled her dress back down. From what she'd heard later, she was only one of his many conquests.

Damn. They had only arrived in London yesterday. How could she have made micefeet of everything so quickly?

"Hey." He touched her shoulder. "Don't look so glum. We'll muddle through."

She tried to smile.

He cupped her cheek. "It would be easier to pass the story off if we seem to like each other, you know. Given the rather passionate display Lady Dunlee witnessed, we might even wish to appear somewhat ardent. Restrained, of course, but just barely—giving the impression that the moment society looks the other way, we'll be in each other's arms."

"How are we to do that?"

He grinned. "Well, to begin with, I don't think you should glare at me all the time. Do you suppose you might be able to manage that?"

"I might." Her eyes focused on his lips. Her brain told her that was a stupid thing to do, but her eyes refused to listen.

His lips had felt so good.

"That's it. You are doing an excellent job of not glaring at me now." His voice had dropped. His arms came around her. They felt good, too.

"Hmm." His lips were now so close and coming closer. He brushed them over her mouth, but it was not enough. She must have whimpered slightly, because he came back.

He didn't mash her lips against her teeth. He didn't try to force his tongue down her throat. He didn't haul her body up against his so tightly she couldn't breathe. He didn't do any of the things Brentwood had done.

He held her firmly, yet gently, and slowly, leisurely, explored her mouth, filling her with a dark, liquid heat that pooled between her legs.

She knew what happened between a man and a

woman. It was embarrassing and painful . . . but that was not what many of the married women said. No, they smiled and giggled and blushed when they talked about their marital duties.

Perhaps the act was different with different men like kissing appeared to be.

Her body insisted everything would be different, better, with Mr. Parker-Roth.

"Anne," he said, his voice slightly breathless, "there's no one here to fool. You're supposed to be pushing me away and giving me that evil look of yours." He kissed the corner of her mouth. "You're supposed to be lashing at me with your sharp tongue, telling me to stop."

He kissed her again, his hands bringing her closer, up against the hard ridge of his erection.

Nerves fluttered through her. Brentwood had done a similar thing . . .

But his hands had been rough. She'd felt trapped.

She didn't feel trapped now. She felt welcomed.

The King of Hearts had earned his title; there was no question about that.

He urged her toward one of the couches, but it was too low. She lost her balance and tumbled against him, ending in a tangle of skirts and legs as the carefully closed, but unfortunately unlocked, door flew open and Harry bounded in.

Chapter 3

Of course the dog hadn't opened the door himself. Stephen looked over to see who else was in the room. A boy about ten years old stood in the doorway frowning at them.

"Anne, what are you doing with that gentleman?" he asked.

Anne was making embarrassed panicky noises, struggling to right herself with Harry's dubious help. Her knee was again in danger of putting paid to any hope Stephen might harbor of fathering children. He grasped her elbows and lifted her off him, then stood and helped her up.

"Philip," she said sharply, straightening her spectacles. Her hair was dangling down her back and her bodice was in some disarray. "You should knock before you enter a room with a closed door." She frowned at Harry who was still barking. "Oh, hush, you silly dog. I can't hear myself think." She tugged at her bodice and looked waspishly at Stephen. "Do you see any of my hairpins?"

Philip was apparently far too polite to point out Anne was not currently in the best position to lecture him on proper behavior, but he wasn't too polite to make a simple observation. "I don't believe Papa would approve, Anne."

Anne turned a darker shade of red. "Uh, that is . . . well . . ." She cleared her throat. "You aren't old enough to understand, Philip," she said in what sounded like her best older sister voice.

Stephen smiled as he looked for hairpins on the couch. He'd heard his sister Jane try that tone with Nick, but since there was only four years between them, it hadn't been very effective.

Ah! He dug his fingers between the cushions and found two hairpins. How had they got down there? No matter. They should do. He wasn't an expert in women's coiffures, but he had helped his sisters—not Jane so much, but the younger two—with their hair often enough he could make Anne somewhat more presentable.

He straightened. Philip was watching him, a very serious expression on his face. Good. The lad *should* keep an eye on any man paying his sister attention.

"Here, let me—Hey, sir!" He frowned down at Harry who, in his enthusiasm, had so far forgotten himself as to jump up and put his paws on Stephen's breeches. "I do not care to be mauled by you. Sit." Harry complied, his tongue hanging out, his tail beating a tattoo on the floor. He stared up at Stephen with clear canine devotion.

Anne's brother relaxed, obviously feeling his dog was a good judge of character.

Anne reached for her hairpins. "Thank you. I'll take those."

"Oh, no, you won't," Stephen said, holding them away from her. "I'll attend to your hair."

She scowled at him. "You will not."

"You won't be able to manage without a maid and a mirror, I imagine."

She sniffed and looked down her nose at him. "You

are mistaken. I'm not one of your London ladies who need such help."

He laughed. "Stop fussing. I won't stab you with the pins, if that's your worry." He gathered a handful of hair. Mmm. The silky curls wrapped around his fingers like soft vines.

Anne huffed. "Are you going to pin the hair up or hold it all day?"

He grinned. "Well . . ."

"Anne!" Two more people burst into the room—a young woman and a boy identical to Philip except for the sticking plaster on his forehead. Harry leapt up, barking enthusiastically.

The woman, a petite vision with golden curls and flashing blue eyes, screamed. "What are you doing to my sister, sirrah? Unhand her at once!" She lunged for the brass statue standing on the table just inside the door. "George, get Hobbes. Philip, help me." She wrestled with the sculpture.

"Evie," Anne began, but no one paid her any attention.

Philip frowned. "What are you going to do with that, Evie?"

"Knock the villain's brains out, of course." She grunted. "*Will* you help me? It's heavy."

Meanwhile George, ignoring his instructions, advanced on Stephen with clenched fists. "Move away from Anne, sir, or you will be very sorry."

"Take a damper, bantling." Stephen tried hard not to laugh as he quickly finished pinning Anne's hair back into some semblance of order. Anne was apparently too embarrassed to speak at the moment, and Evie was still jerking on the statue without budging it an inch.

"I don't see why we should brain a guest," Philip said. He stooped to scratch Harry's ears.

"Oh, for goodness sake"—Anne had finally found her voice. She sounded completely exasperated—"will you show some sense, Evie?"

George chose that moment to attack, but Stephen, being the second oldest of six children, caught the boy easily and held him firmly, but gently, as he kicked and squirmed.

"George! Where are your manners?"

"I won't let him hurt you, Anne."

"Does it look like he's hurting me?"

George stopped struggling to peer at Anne. "No."

"Of course I'm not hurting your sister," Stephen said, cautiously letting George go. "That would be a daft thing to do to my betrothed."

Stunned silence greeted this announcement, and then, just as in the study earlier, three shocked voices spoke at the exact same time. *"Betrothed?"*

Anne made a noise that sounded suspiciously like a moan and dropped her head into her hands.

"You're going to marry *Anne*?" George blinked. He flopped down on the couch that Stephen and Anne had so recently vacated. "Don't you mean Evie? She's the beautiful one."

"Of course he doesn't mean me, you cabbage head." Evie had stopped struggling with the statue and now clasped her hands under her bosom. "That's wonderful, Anne. I'm so happy for you. I'd quite given up hope you'd ever marry."

Anne's head snapped up and she glared at her sister. "I'm not a complete antidote, Evie."

Evie shrugged. "Of course not, but you've never shown the slightest interest in any man." She flushed. "Mama thought you might be . . . different."

"What do you mean, 'different'?" Philip asked. He and Harry had gone over to join George.

"Nothing. She means nothing," Anne said. She was

going to die of mortification. What must Mr. Parker-Roth think? She couldn't bear to look at him.

George rolled his eyes. "Oh, yes, she does mean something otherwise she wouldn't have said 'different' in just that way."

"It's something Papa will explain when you are older," Evie said, her cheeks rather pink.

At least Evie's brain had finally caught up with her mouth. Anne would have to have a word with her about that. They weren't in the country any longer. Letting one's tongue run on unchecked could be disastrous in London. The gossips—

Oh, why did she even worry about Evie saying the wrong thing? Anne had already done the wrong thing in a spectacular manner. To be discovered embracing—rather more than embracing really—the King of Hearts by the Queen of Gossip . . . Anything Evie did could only pale in comparison.

And then if her scandalous mistake with Lord Brentwood should come to light . . .

Anne rubbed the space over her nose, right between her eyebrows. Her head was beginning to throb.

"Does Papa know Anne's betrothed?" Philip asked. "He didn't say anything before he left."

"He must know, Philip," Evie said. "There are settlements and other things of a legal nature to be arranged. Depend upon it, he just forgot to tell us."

Philip nodded. "Like the time he bought all Baron Redlawn's library. We were so surprised when the first cartload pulled up at the house."

"And of course Papa and Mama were away," Evie said. "You had to sort it all out, remember, Anne?"

"Botheration!" George said. "You aren't going to go on and on about those dratted books again, are you?"

He looked up at Stephen. "Are you infernally bookish as well?"

Stephen smiled somewhat cautiously. "No, not *infernally*."

"George, what a question to ask Mr. . . ." Evie's mouth hung open a moment, a startled, blank expression decorating her beautiful features. She turned to Anne. "Did you tell us your betrothed's name?"

"You didn't give me much chance, did you?" Lady Anne said, a touch waspishly. She turned to Stephen. "Sir, as I'm sure you've surmised, this is my sister, Lady Evangeline, and my brothers, Philip—Viscount Rutledge—and George." She looked at her siblings. "And this is Mr. Parker-Roth."

Evie extended her hand. "Very nice to meet you, Mr.—oh!" She snatched her hand back before Stephen could touch her fingers. "But—" She bit her lip. "I must have misunderstood. I thought you were married, sir."

"That's his *brother*, Evie," Anne said.

"Indeed, my older brother, John." Stephen smiled. "I'm the second son, Stephen Parker-Roth."

Evie's eyes widened. "The King of Hearts?" She shot Anne an odd look.

"Er, yes," he said. He'd never been much pleased with that sobriquet, but he was heartily sick of it now. "I'm rather good at cards, you see."

"*Cards*? But—"

Anne cut her sister off. "Cards," she said with a note of finality and a significant look at the boys.

Philip's eyes lit up. "We shall have to play some day, sir."

"Watch out," George said. "Phil fleeces us all, even Papa."

"Stubble it, you lobcock!" Philip glared at his brother

and then turned back to Stephen. "We only play for pins, sir, not that I could get the better of you, of course. But it's true none of the others has much of a head for cards. They can't remember what's been played."

"A common failing." Stephen smiled. "I'll be happy to play with you when I'm not squiring your sisters to the Season's entertainments."

"Oh, will you, sir?" Evie sounded thrilled. "Escort us to all the balls and parties, that is."

Anne looked alarmed. "Don't be silly. Of course he won't. Mr. Parker-Roth is far too busy for that."

"Of course I will," Stephen said, reaching over to take Anne's hand. He thought at first she was going to protest, but at the last minute she must have realized how odd that would look—the boys might not remark on it, but her sister would—and let him wrap his fingers around hers. "What could be more important than attending the *ton*'s gatherings with my betrothed?"

"Indeed!" Evie almost bounced with delight. "I confess I was quite worried about my come-out. My particular friend, Constance Donbarton, warned me I would have a hard time of it, even when we thought Mama would be here to chaperone me. Mama is a rector's daughter, you see, and Papa, though an earl, only goes to London when he must. Constance says the *ton* considers him peculiar, which isn't surprising since he is rather."

"Papa's not peculiar," Anne said, tugging to free her hand from Stephen's grasp. He didn't let her go.

"You know he is, Anne. He thinks of nothing but antiquities."

Anne grumbled. She could not deny that fact.

Evie looked earnestly at Stephen. "Papa's mama is sadly departed and his only sister has also gone aloft, so I have no one to help ease my way into society. It might be different if Anne had had a Season and was married to someone of importance, but she didn't and isn't, if you see what I mean."

"It's very clear, Evie." Anne sounded as if she'd prefer to shout her words.

"And you must agree Cousin Clorinda will be no help at all, Anne. Rather the opposite—she's even more of a bluestocking than you are."

"She is not." Anne's scowl became even more pronounced. "I mean, she's much more of a bluestocking than I."

Evie ignored her, looking hopefully again at Stephen. "You have a sister, do you not, sir? I believe your consequence, especially as Anne's betrothed, might be enough to do the trick, but female assistance must always be preferred."

"I have three, but I expect you mean Jane since Juliana and Lucy aren't out yet," Stephen said. "If you read the gossip columns as your sister does"—he shot Anne a speaking look, which she ignored—"you might have seen Jane mentioned rather prominently the year before last."

Evie's face fell. "Oh, yes, now I remember . . . the scandal with Viscount Motton. But they wed, didn't they?"

"Indeed they did and with no lasting damage to their social prominence, I believe. However, Jane has never been a great fan of the Season, and she firmly believes country air is far superior to London's soot for her son, so she's not planning to come to Town anytime soon." He also suspected she might be in the family way again, but she and Motton hadn't said so yet. "The only Parker-Roth you might encounter this Season besides me is my younger brother, Nicholas, who's just finished his studies at Oxford."

"Oh, well, I'm sure you must know everyone." Evie looked both hopeful and nervous. "With you to guide us, I'll fare much better than if I had only Cousin Clorinda and Anne to rely on."

"Thank you for the vote of confidence," Anne said dryly. She did have to admit to some relief, though. Evie was completely correct—Anne knew next to nothing about London society. She'd woken up in a cold sweat early this morning—one reason she'd been out walking Harry—terrified of putting a wrong foot forward and blighting Evie's chances. And she'd already done that . . . but Mr. Parker-Roth's presence at their side would definitely help.

She couldn't risk ruining Evie's Season; who knew if Papa would think to give her another. Evie was too beautiful and vivacious to be condemned to spinsterhood or forced in desperation to marry one of the fat, old men hanging out for a young wife at home.

"I do have a friend or two who's stepped into parson's mousetrap," Mr. Parker-Roth was saying. "I'll wager their ladies will be more than happy to help steer you past society's treacherous shoals."

Evie clasped her hands together again. "That would be splendid."

"And you said your younger brother had just finished Oxford, didn't you, sir?" George asked.

Mr. Parker-Roth smiled. "Yes. Do you plan to go to Oxford yourself, George?"

"No. Or, that is, I don't know. Philip's the scholar, not me." George shrugged and looked at Philip. "I was just wondering . . ."

". . . if your brother—or, if not he, then a friend of his—might be interested in being our, well, tutor?" Philip finished.

"Except he wouldn't have to do lessons," George hastened to add.

"He'd just have to take us around London to the museums," Philip said, "and . . . balloon ascensions."

"And Astley's Amphitheatre."

"And the Royal Menagerie."

"And all the things a boy should see in London," George finished, "but which we won't see if it's left up to Anne or Evie or Cousin Clorinda."

"Papa said he'd find us an amiable fellow to keep us out from under the women's feet," Philip said, "but then he got wind of the new antiquities discovery and forgot."

"Papa forgets everything when anyone mentions antiquities," George said.

Two identical faces stared up at Mr. Parker-Roth, hearts in their eyes. The man smiled as though he really understood how the boys felt.

Anne felt an odd sensation in her chest, as if her own heart had turned over. "I'm afraid Philip and George are right," she said. "Papa did neglect to make any arrangements for them—or if he did, he didn't tell us what they were. And I expect Evie and I will be too busy to do much with the boys. Nor can I see relying on Cousin Clorinda—"

"Cousin Clorinda? You couldn't be so shabby as to stick us with her!" George said. "She'd probably lock us in the library. Phil might survive, but you know I ain't bookish. I'd cock up my toes from boredom in a trice."

Anne frowned. "A little reading would do you good, George."

"You saw her try to get me to read that damned—"

"George!"

"—deuced book on some stupid bird last night."

"And I saw how you gave her palpitations when you told her the only good bird was one turning on a spit," Evie said, laughing.

"Yes, well, I did say I couldn't see relying on Clorinda," Anne said. "I suppose I could send you and Philip about with a footman, but I can't like that, either. I wouldn't put it past you to bamboozle the poor man into letting you do any hare-brained thing that occurred to you."

"Let me talk to Nicholas," Mr. Parker-Roth said. "He's not in Town yet, but I expect him any day. If he can't ride herd on these fellows, I'm sure he'll know someone who can."

"That would be very kind of you." Anne glanced at the clock on the mantel and blushed. Oh dear, it would have to go, too. The male and female figures entwined around the timepiece were misbehaving in a shocking manner. *Who* had been in charge of decorating this room? "Look at the time—or well, don't look. But I'm afraid Evie and I need to get ready to go shopping."

Mr. Parker-Roth's eyebrows went up. "You sound as if you're contemplating a trip to Newgate Prison rather than a pleasant excursion to Bond Street."

"There's nothing pleasant about shopping." Anne could feel her stomach clenching already. She hated going to the mantua-maker. She was too tall and too thin and had red hair—Mrs. Waddingly's face always fell when Anne came through her door. She'd taken to urging Evie to precede her; the anticipation of dressing her beautiful sister helped keep the poor woman from complete despair.

"Mama mentioned Miss Lamont as a dressmaker, Mr. Parker-Roth," Evie was saying, "but Mama is not much for fashion either. Nor is Cousin Clorinda—she just shrugged and said one place was as good as another when I asked her."

Mr. Parker-Roth's eyes widened and he deftly turned a laugh into a cough. The man was the King of Hearts. He must be very familiar—*intimately* familiar—with ladies' clothing makers.

"I'm afraid I can't agree with your cousin," he said.

"Nor can I advise visiting Miss Lamont. Do you know where her shop is? I've not heard of it."

"No-o." Evie looked at Anne. "Do you know, Anne?"

"Of course not. I assumed Clorinda would."

"Then I think Miss Lamont," Mr. Parker-Roth said, "as estimable as she may be, must be eliminated."

"I suppose you are right." Evie bit her lip. "But then what are we to do?"

Anne knew what she would like to do—forget the whole thing, but even she realized she and Evie couldn't attend the Season's entertainments dressed in their country clothes.

"I will be happy to help. I happen to know a few of the more fashionable shops." Mr. Parker-Roth didn't even have the grace to blush. "I'd be delighted to accompany you and act as your guide."

"You don't need to—" Anne started to say.

"That would be wonderful—" Evie said at the same time.

They stopped and stared at each other, and then Anne looked at Mr. Parker-Roth. "People will remark on it if you escort us to the dressmaker's."

He grinned and his damnably attractive dimples appeared. "No, they won't. I'm sure it is unexceptional for a man to help his betrothed and her sister find their way when they are so newly arrived in Town. It would be more remarked upon if I deserted you in your hour of need."

"Well . . ."

"Mr. Parker-Roth must be correct, Anne," Evie said. "He certainly wouldn't do anything to put you in a bad light." She laughed, shaking her head. "I still find it difficult to comprehend you're betrothed." She gave the fellow a sly look. "Not that I didn't notice how you paid particular attention to any mention of Mr. Parker-Roth in the gossip columns, Anne."

Mr. Parker-Roth's eyebrows shot up.

She was going to strangle Evie, if she didn't die of mortification before she could wrap her hands around her sister's neck.

"But where did you meet Anne, sir?" Philip asked, looking up from rubbing Harry's belly. "She's not been to London—she's not been anywhere."

"And you haven't been to Crane House," George said.

Anne's stomach dropped. Dear God! Trust the boys to ask the obvious question. She and Mr. Parker-Roth had not yet concocted a plausible story—they hadn't had time.

She flushed. And the time they'd had, they'd not spent wisely.

"I'll let Anne tell you our story," she heard Mr. Parker-Roth say.

What?

Everyone looked expectantly at her. Her brain—the part that wasn't cursing a certain society gentleman—froze. "I, ah, met Mr. Parker-Roth at, er, Baron Gedding's house party."

She closed her eyes briefly. Why the hell had she said that? She never wanted to consider that horrible gathering again.

"At Baron Gedding's?" Philip naturally sounded confused. "When were you at Baron Gedding's, Anne?"

"A long time ago." Now she would really sound like an idiot. "Right around the time you were born."

"I remember," Evie said. "I haven't thought about it in years—I was only seven when you went. You did come back different." She frowned. "But I'd have said you were rather sad and quiet. You should have been happy if you'd fallen in love."

What could she say? She hadn't fallen in love of course; she'd been unceremoniously flung out of it—or at least her youthful dream of it.

The days after the house party had been terrible. Her view of the world and her place in it had undergone a sea-change; there was no going back to the innocent, trusting girl she'd been.

At least her courses had come right after she'd got home, so she hadn't had to worry there'd be a child as the result of her wrong headed encounter with Brentwood.

"And, you know," Evie was saying, "I think you've been sad ever since."

Sad? She might not have been merry as a grig, but she hadn't been constantly Friday faced either.

Mr. Parker-Roth finally came to the rescue, in a manner of speaking. "Ah, but you see, we were far too young to consider marriage then—or, at least I was— I was only nineteen."

And probably well on your way to being crowned King of Hearts, Anne thought—*and not for your card-playing prowess.*

"So we had to part." He took Anne's hand again. "And, being only nineteen, I'm afraid I was somewhat cavalier in my leave-taking. I believe I may have wounded Anne."

Anne cringed at the romantic nonsense. George, gagging dramatically, hands around his throat, flopped backward on the couch.

Evie, however, swallowed the story as if it had been published by the Minerva Press. She sighed as she looked at Anne. "So that's why you never showed particular interest in any of the gentlemen at home. You've been pining for your true love."

Philip looked doubtful. "But for ten years, Evie? That's a long time."

"Not for true love," Evie said.

Anne thought she might join George, who was now

rolling his eyes and making quite amazing faces of disgust.

"Did you never see each other again till now?" Evie asked, clearly hoping they had.

"Well, I was out of the country a lot, you know," Mr. Parker-Roth said, "hunting plants for my brother. But I believe we did meet again, didn't we, dear heart?"

Think. Had she ever been away from home another time?

Yes—when Grandpapa had died.

She'd gone to Cambridge in Papa's carriage with only a maid as a companion. Papa had left for some antiquity-rich patch of ground in Yorkshire before they'd got word. The twins had been sick, so for once Georgiana had stayed with her children.

"We did manage to see each other two years ago in Cambridge when my mother's father passed away."

She shouldn't try to maintain this fiction, but she didn't have much choice. Evie and the boys could never keep a secret, and while the twins probably wouldn't have occasion to let the cat out of the bag in a socially damaging situation, Evie would. She only hoped no one from that damn house party was in Town. Who had been there besides Baron Gedding and Lord Brentwood? She didn't remember.

"Ah, yes," Mr. Parker-Roth said. "We had those few sweet, stolen moments before I had to leave for the jungles of South America."

Must he mouth so *much* romantic twaddle? She frowned at him.

He grinned and pulled his watch from his waistcoat pocket. "If I'm going to escort you shopping, ladies, we'd best bestir ourselves."

"You might wish to go home first, sir," Philip said. "You're rather muddy."

Mr. Parker-Roth looked down at his spattered breeches and ruined shoes. "So I am—very good point,

Philip. I'll go back to my rooms to change, and then return for you ladies in"—he consulted his watch again—"an hour's time, shall we say?" He looked at Philip and George. "And I'll see you both once my duties to your sisters are completed."

"Yes, sir," Philip said.

"Huzza!" George cheered while Harry barked in support. "We'll finally get out of this house."

"You've only been here since yesterday, George," Anne said. "You've hardly been imprisoned."

Mr. Parker-Roth laughed. "Even a few hours can feel like a hundred to a ten-year-old boy, eh, George?"

"Yes, sir!"

Mr. Parker-Roth smiled and kissed Anne's hand. "Till later then."

Damn it all, Anne thought as she watched him go, she should not feel bereft at the King of Hearts's departure.

Chapter 4

Stephen almost had to push Lady Anne through the door to Madam Celeste's shop. He'd wager if he hadn't been standing behind her like a wall, she would have fled. He'd never seen a female so skittish about dressmakers.

Evie wandered farther into the shop, looking around with wide eyes at all the bolts of fabric and pattern books, but Anne stopped stiffly right inside the door.

Celeste was at the counter with an older, very stylish white-haired woman—Lady Brentwood. Fortunately Lady Brentwood's unpleasant son, the marquis, was not with her—not that the reprobate made a practice of hanging about his mother's skirts. God, no. But Lady Brentwood's were about the only skirts the blackguard didn't frequent.

People might call Stephen the King of Hearts, but men called Brentwood the king of another female body part. More and more of society's doors were closed to him. He was a *very* dirty dish—and a constant source of heartache for his mother.

Lady Brentwood was just completing her business.

She turned and smiled at him, though her smile looked rather tired and sad. "Mr. Parker-Roth, how pleasant to see you."

"Lady Brentwood." Had he felt Anne stiffen even more? He glanced at her. Her face was ashen. He put his hand on her elbow in case she needed support. "May I present my companions Lady Anne Marston and her sister, Lady Evangeline?"

Evie smiled easily, but Anne stood like a broken puppet. What was the matter with her?

"Lord Crane's daughters," Lady Brentwood was saying. "So nice to meet you. Your cousin Clorinda is a particular friend of mine, so I knew you were expected in Town."

"Ah," Anne said. Her lovely voice sounded strangled, but Lady Brentwood seemed not to notice.

"I'm giving a card party this evening—just a small gathering. Perhaps you can attend?" Her smile flickered. "I will confess I'm not completely without ulterior motives. I'm hoping my son will be there. As you may discover some day, mothers never give up on their children's happiness. I keep praying he will find a woman to marry."

"Oh," Evie said, obviously delighted at her first London invitation. "May we go, Anne?"

"I do not know our plans," Anne said. "We have just arrived in London." Her voice was tight now; clearly she'd gleaned Brentwood's reputation from the gossip columns.

Lady Brentwood's expression drooped. She'd noted Anne's reserve—unfortunately, Stephen would wager she was all too familiar with that reaction. "I had hoped . . . Clorinda said . . . well, she happened to mention you were still unwed, Lady Anne."

Something about Anne's stillness made him fear

she was going to explode at any moment. Poor Lady Brentwood did not merit that.

"Ah, but Miss Strange was missing a few facts, Lady Brentwood," he said quickly. "Lady Anne isn't wed, but she *is* betrothed . . . to me."

He heard Celeste and her assistant, patiently waiting nearby for them to finish their conversation, suck in their breath. Lady Brentwood merely smiled, this time with genuine happiness.

"How wonderful. My sincere congratulations to you both. Your parents must be delighted."

Mama certainly would be delighted . . . if she knew.

Evie was opening her mouth, probably to enlighten Lady Brentwood concerning the somewhat sudden nature of the betrothal announcement. He felt very sure they could leave that detail to the gossips.

"Indeed," he said before Evie could speak. "And that is why—as you can see—I'm selfishly depriving Miss Strange of the pleasure of shopping with the ladies"—Anne snorted, but he felt it wisest to ignore that—"and have brought them to Celeste so she might work her magic on their wardrobes."

"Very good." Lady Brentwood's eyes actually twinkled. "And I know Clorinda was delighted to cede this duty to you, sir, though I suspect she never intended to accompany the ladies in the first place." She turned to Anne and Evie. "Don't worry; I believe you can put your faith in Celeste. She is an excellent dressmaker"—she laughed—"and Mr. Parker-Roth will give you splendid advice. I do hope, once you consult your appointments, that I might see you tonight, even if my original hope will be unrealized."

Evie made a credible curtsey and Anne managed to produce a polite murmur as Lady Brentwood departed.

What was the matter with Anne? He would have

thought she'd have been a bit more gracious. Well, there was no time to consider the issue; Celeste was upon them.

"Ooo, Monsieur Parker-Roth!" Celeste said, hands outstretched. "Eet is tres magnifique to see you—and with two belles jeunes femmes aussi!"

She was almost leaping with joy; he felt like the Prodigal Son. It had been only two months since he'd parted ways with his last mistress, but Celeste had clearly been missing his blunt.

Her sharp eyes studied Anne; she raised her eyebrows slightly—not surprising as Anne had chosen to don a dress almost as hideous as the abomination she'd been wearing this morning in Hyde Park.

"As I'm sure you've surmised"—by what Celeste saw as much as by what he'd said—"Lady Anne and Lady Evangeline will need all new clothes for the Season."

Celeste knew that however crazy Crane was, his pockets were deep. Her smile widened, if that were physically possible. "Bon!"

Anne squared her shoulders, taking a deep breath as if readying for battle. "My sister is the one making her come-out, madam. She will need . . ."—she paused, glanced at him, and then frowned at Celeste—"whatever one needs for such an undertaking."

Celeste clapped her hands. "Mais oui. Ball gowns and walking dresses and . . . oh, so many things." She surveyed Evie. "You are tres jolie, mademoiselle, but my dresses—they will make you even more beautiful. The London bucks will be dazzled; they will throw themselves at your feet. Your papa will have many, many offers for your hand."

Evie smiled and blushed. "Thank you, Madam Celeste, though I can't imagine . . . well, I hope there's some truth to what you say."

"Of course there is! Ask monsieur." Celeste turned

to him. "Is it not the case that my dresses are sought after by all the London ladies?"

"Yes, indeed. I wouldn't have brought you here, Evie, if I didn't know Celeste to be extremely skilled at what she does."

He thought he heard Anne mutter something about the King of Hearts and legions of women, but he ignored her.

"Just so." Celeste turned to Anne. "And for you, my lady? You must also need many things?" She carefully avoided looking directly at Anne's dress.

Anne made an annoyed little sound, almost a growl. "I suppose I'll have to get a few dresses, but I'll not need as many as Evie."

"Not true, my love," Stephen said, tweaking one of her curls, and then removing his hand before she could swat his fingers. He noted Celeste's delighted gaze. If his ears didn't mislead him, her assistant sighed behind them.

"Lady Anne will have to play the chaperone, but I'm hoping her sister won't need too much supervision." He leaned closer to Celeste, dropping his voice conspiratorially. "I'm planning to lure my betrothed into as many darkened gardens as I can manage."

Celeste giggled. "Oh, the other ladies, they will be tres desole that le Roi de Coeurs has finalement lost his heart."

He'd swear Anne was vibrating with anger beside him—she wouldn't darken his daylights here in Madam Celeste's shop, would she? He looked down at his bride-to-be in what he hoped was a besotted fashion. She was not holding up her end of things—her eyes were narrowed, her nostrils flaring, and her lips were pressed into a tight, thin line.

"When is the wedding to be, monsieur?" Celeste

asked, obviously hoping to have the making of Anne's dress.

"We haven't set a date. I'm, of course, anxious to wed as soon as possible, but my sweet termagant is threatening to make me wait till the end of the Season."

He kissed Anne's fingers—she tried to snatch them from his grasp, but he was stronger than she—and then smiled at Celeste. "We haven't yet put a formal announcement in the papers. The earl had to go out of town rather unexpectedly, and Lady Anne naturally wants to wait until her father is back to make our engagement common knowledge. I'm sure we can rely on your discretion?"

"Mais oui. Certainement. I am most discreet. Do not worry, monsieur."

He didn't worry. He knew Celeste would spread the news far and wide as soon as they left her shop, but as Lady Dunlee and Mrs. Fallwell had already been busy about that errand, her efforts would amount to only a very small swell in the tidal wave of gossip.

"Mr. Parker-Roth." Anne sounded as if she were speaking through clenched teeth.

Celeste took one look at her and took Evie's arm. "Come, mademoiselle," Celeste said, "permit me to show you some of my sketches whilst monsieur speaks with your sister."

Celeste took Evie over to a table covered with pattern books to begin choosing dress styles, colors, and fabrics. If Evie were like most women he knew, she'd be occupied for quite a while.

They were barely out of earshot before Anne exploded. "Are you *insane?*" she hissed. "The news will be all over London by nightfall."

This female was definitely not like most women of his acquaintance. She almost reminded him of his sister Jane, though he had far from brotherly feelings for Anne, of course. "It already is all over London. Remember Lady Dunlee?"

Anne groaned. "Oh, blast. What are we going to do?"

He glanced at Celeste. She met his gaze over Evie's bowed head and smiled saucily, winking as if she thought Anne was suffering from frustrated desire. If only.

"We are going to be betrothed, at least for this Season," he murmured by Anne's ear. Hopefully Celeste would assume he was whispering love words. "Your reputation—and your sister's Season—will be ruined if we aren't. Remember the scene that necessitated this charade?" And what happened later in the odd harem room, but he chose not to mention that. He certainly remembered. He'd been reliving every exquisite detail from the moment he'd left Crane House—the sweet, heady scent of Anne's skin; the damp heat of her mouth; the pressure of her body against his.

He'd had his share of women over the years—all right, maybe more than his share—but he hadn't been this intrigued by a female in a long, long time, if ever.

"Of course I remember. How could I forget? I've never been so embarrassed in my life."

He wasn't usually attracted to viragos. Some men thought fiery women burned up the sheets once on their backs, but in his experience women who argued and nagged in the drawing room did exactly the same in the bedroom. Anne was different though. He'd wager his annual income her prickliness sprung not from bad temper but from something else . . . at a guess, something to do with the Marquis of Brentwood.

"I can't believe I participated in such a scene," she was saying, shaking her head. She frowned at him. "If you hadn't been drunk—"

He put his finger on her lips and felt her breath suck in. Her eyes widened.

"If you'd slapped me soundly, Anne, I would have stopped. Even drunk, I would have stopped. As I told you before, you don't have to fear me."

She jerked her head back. "I'm not afraid of you, you big coxcomb."

She was lying. She *was* afraid, if not of him, then of something. What?

He would find out eventually—but not now. He grinned instead and tilted her face up with the edge of his hand. "You seem rather . . . jumpy around me. Was your sister correct? Have you been pining for me?"

She flushed and her eyes slid away from his. "Of course not. I just met you."

"True. But I've observed sisters usually know the worst truths."

Her gaze flashed up to meet his and then dropped again. He released her, and she stepped away, turning her back on him and walking toward Evie and Celeste. "Have you found the perfect dress yet, Evie?" Her gay tone sounded more than a little forced.

Lady Anne Marston was an interesting puzzle. Spirited and shy; bold yet timid. Maddening.

It was a good thing he liked puzzles.

"Many dresses, Anne." Evie was breathless with excitement. "Carriage dresses and evening dresses and ball dresses and walking dresses. Oh, look at this darling habit." She sighed. "I do wish we'd brought horses to Town."

"Well, we didn't, and a good thing it is. Think of the expense. Horses eat their heads off." Anne sounded so waspish Celeste and Evie stared at her.

It was going to be a *very* interesting Season if Anne was determined to pick fights with everyone she encountered.

"I don't have horses in Town since I'm not here much," he said, "but I have friends who keep a full stable. I'm sure I can find you a mount, Evie."

"Mais oui, mademoiselle." Celeste nodded vehemently. "You must go riding in the Hyde Park. Eet is de rigueur."

Celeste was, of course, trying to coax a few more pence into her purse, but she was correct. "In any event you'll need a habit for all the house parties you'll attend."

Evie's face lit up—and Anne stiffened like a poker.

Hmm. His betrothed obviously did not approve of house parties, and since it sounded as if the only house party she'd ever attended had been Baron Gedding's ten years ago . . .

He must find out what had happened at that ill-fated gathering. Gedding was in Town—and Stephen prided himself on his ability to extract information from people so discreetly they weren't aware of what they were revealing. The man was such a jaw-me-dead getting him to talk would not be a problem; steering him in an informative direction, however . . . that would be the challenge.

"And you, Lady Anne," Celeste was saying, "you must also have dresses. Pardon-moi, but this"—she gestured at the rag Anne was wearing—"eet will not do at all." She chose a few sketches and offered them to Anne. "Regardez these, s'il vous plaît."

"No, I . . . that is, I won't . . ." Anne looked at the papers in Celeste's hand as if they were poisonous snakes.

"Let me see." Stephen took the sketches and flipped through them. He stopped at one of a ball gown with an especially low bodice. "Here you go. This would look splendid on you, Anne, in moss green to match your eyes."

Anne glanced at the drawing. "No, I don't think so."

He frowned at her. "Why not?" He held it up for Evie and Celeste to see. "Don't you think this gown would suit Anne?"

"It would *not* suit me." Anne almost strangled on the words. For a man with a supposedly discerning eye, Mr. Parker-Roth had failed to discern an obvious problem—her poor little breasts were far too small to be displayed in such a way, even with the heroic efforts of an exceptional corset.

"It's very pretty, Anne." Evie studied the picture. "It hadn't occurred to me—I mean it's nothing like what you usually wear—but I think Mr. Parker-Roth is right. It would look very good on you. What don't you like about it?"

"Oui, Lady Anne, what is the problem?" Madam Celeste smiled, but Anne could hear a touch of exasperation in her voice. "The dress is tres jolie—you will be beautiful in it. All the men will envy monsieur."

They were all mad—or blind. "The dress is very pretty; it just will not look good on me." She felt herself flush, damn it.

Mr. Parker-Roth—and Evie and Madam Celeste—all stared at her as if she were a bedlamite. "Let's see what else there is." She grabbed for the sketches, but Mr. Parker-Roth held them out of her reach.

"Enlighten us, Lady Anne," he said. "Why won't the dress look good on you?"

She turned to Madam Celeste. The woman was a dressmaker; she must understand. Mrs. Waddingly, the dressmaker back home, certainly had. She was always adding another row of lace, a bow, or a knot of ribbons to Anne's bodices in a vain attempt to hide her deficiencies. "You must have something of a more modest nature."

"Modest?" Madam Celeste looked from Anne to Mr.

Parker-Roth. "I do not comprehend. What is not modest?"

Surely the woman wasn't going to force her to spell it out? "Something with a higher neck, perhaps?" She smiled somewhat desperately she feared. "I'm only a chaperone, you see. I don't wish to bring attention to myself."

Madam Celeste's jaw dropped. "Only a chaperone?"

"Yes, of course. It's my sister's come-out after all, not mine. I will be sitting along the wall with the other mature women." That had certainly been her plan as soon as she'd realized Georgiana was leaving her in charge of Evie's Season. And especially now that she knew Lord Brentwood was here; she would rather not encounter the man.

"But you are monsieur's betrothed! All the eyes of London will be upon you!"

"Surely not." Anne felt ill.

"I'm afraid Celeste is probably correct, Anne," Mr. Parker-Roth said. "People do take an inordinate amount of interest in my life—you saw how often I was mentioned in those infernal gossip columns. It's extremely annoying, but inevitable whenever I'm in London."

"Oh." This just got worse and worse. How was she ever going to survive this Season? "But can't they look at me in a dress with a high neck and long sleeves? I get chilly so easily."

Madam Celeste looked horrified, probably wondering how much she could pay Anne not to tell anyone who had had the making of her dresses.

Mr. Parker-Roth laughed. "You won't get chilly in a London ballroom. Trust me, they are stifling." He shook his head, but his eyes were uncomfortably penetrating. "You don't want everyone whispering I'm marrying a quiz, do you? Not that I care what the society cats say, but the gossip and sniggering will cause you and probably Evie some discomfort, and I confess it will make me angry on your behalf."

"And there is no need for it," Madam Celeste said. "Pardonnez-moi, my lady, but you are being tres silly. Everyone will envy you; you are the betrothed of le Roi de Coeurs. You have succeeded where so many others have failed. Why would you not wish to wear a gown that matches your beauty?"

"Oh, dear heavens." Anne sat down abruptly. This was shaping up to be a complete nightmare.

Mr. Parker-Roth sat down next to her. "It won't be so bad, Anne. I'm sure Madam Celeste is overstating the case. Yes, people will be curious, but many will be happy for me—for us."

"Um." She stared at the table, though she didn't see it. It would be bad enough if she were really Mr. Parker-Roth's betrothed, but she wasn't. She would be forced to act that part with all the *ton*—all the nasty, gabble-grinding *ton*—watching her every move.

She *was* going to be ill.

She covered her face with one hand and waved the other in Madam Celeste and Mr. Parker-Roth's direction. "Why don't you just pick out a few things for me?"

Madam Celeste did not need to be told twice. She spread her sketches out on the table at once and began talking in a very animated way to Mr. Parker-Roth.

"Anne," Evie said quietly, "are you certain you don't want to look at Madam Celeste's drawings? Her dresses are wonderful—nothing like the plain old things Mrs. Waddingly makes up."

"No. I'm sure madam and Mr. Parker-Roth know what is fashionable." Since she was such a stick, it wouldn't matter what they hung on her frame. She would still look like a boy in his older sister's dress.

Evie cleared her throat hesitantly. "I never liked to

say it, but I do believe the clothing you wore at home . . . that is, I think Mrs. Waddingly does not know how to make dresses that compliment your figure."

"That's because I don't have a figure, Evie." Anne did not begrudge her sister her curves, but she would admit to a small pang of jealousy in the present circumstances. Any dress would look lovely on Evie.

"That's not true at all. You are just thinner than many women."

"Mmm." She hadn't been quite so thin ten years ago—she'd still had a bit of baby fat—but she'd never been voluptuous. Why had Brentwood singled her out—a skinny, red-headed, bespectacled, awkward miss?

He must have been bored or there must have been a wager involved. That was all she could surmise from the many times she'd pondered the matter.

"Here, Anne, let's see how this color looks on you." Mr. Parker-Roth had concluded his discussions with Madam Celeste and now had a swatch of reddish cloth dangling from his fingers. That jolted her out of her reverie. She gaped at him.

"Are you blind?" How could he overlook the mass of red curls on her head? "I can't wear red."

"Let's see if you can or not." He held out his other hand to help her up. "Come stand before Celeste's mirror and we'll see what colors become you."

"Brown." Though she couldn't really say brown became her; it just didn't call attention to her. Her dreadful hair did that well enough. "Mrs. Waddingly always made my dresses in brown."

Madam Celeste smacked her hand hard against the tabletop and Anne jumped.

"Mon dieu! This Madam Waddingly is an imbecile of the first order—and blind aussi. She should not be permitted to make the dresses—or even to own a thimble."

Madam Celeste pointed an accusing finger at Anne's frock. "That . . . thing—bah!" She wrinkled her nose in disgust. "It is the color of mud—non, of horse dung. I would not let a *dog* wear it."

Mr. Parker-Roth raised an eyebrow. "It's not a pleasant shade, I'll grant you that. As soon as your new dresses arrive, Anne, you must burn it and all the other things this misguided Mrs. Waddingly made for you." He grinned. "I'll help, and I daresay Evie and the boys will as well. What do you say, Evie?"

"Oh, yes—I'll be delighted to set fire to Anne's old wardrobe. And I will gather all the things for the bonfire if Anne is hesitant to do so."

"I am not going to burn the clothes Mrs. Waddingly made," Anne said, frowning at Mr. Parker-Roth as she stepped in front of the mirror. "What a shocking waste of money that would be."

Madam Celeste grunted and muttered something under her breath. The only words Anne could discern were "monsieur" and "naked."

"Of course not," Mr. Parker-Roth said, a bit more loudly than necessary. He stood behind Anne and smiled reassuringly at her in the mirror—only she didn't feel precisely reassured. She stepped back—and bumped into his hard body.

He glanced over his shoulder at Madam Celeste. "Why don't you take Lady Evangeline back to get her measurements?"

Madam Celeste's answering smile was not reassuring at all. "An excellent idea, monsieur. You will help Lady Anne choose colors while we are gone."

"Just so. I'm sure it will take us a while, so don't hurry back."

Madam Celeste's smile broadened. "Oui, mademoiselle and I, we shall have much to do with the measuring and the pinning." And she winked at him.

What exactly was Mr. Parker-Roth planning? "I'm sure I should go with Evie. I—"

Madam Celeste shook her head so briskly her gray hair floated about her head. "Mais non, Lady Anne. Mademoiselle and I do not need you, do we, mademoiselle?"

Evie's eyes were far too full of mischief. "Of course not. We've already selected some styles and colors, Anne. How can you help with the measurements?"

"Nevertheless, I should be with you." Mr. Parker-Roth's hand was now on her elbow. His fingers held her gently; his thumb stroked little circles on the inside of her arm. She could smell his cologne.

"Do not be silly," Madam Celeste said, standing and gesturing for Evie to precede her to the dressing room in the back. "You will be most in the way." She looked over at her assistant, who'd been straightening ribbons and other trimmings. "Betty, come with us, s'il vous plait."

"Yes, madam." Betty flashed Anne a knowing smile as she ducked through the door behind Evie and Madam Celeste.

Anne bit her bottom lip. Damn it, she and Mr. Parker-Roth were completely alone now and likely to be that way for the next little while unless a new customer entered.

Her stomach fluttered in an uncomfortable manner. Is this how a mouse felt when cornered by a cat? She certainly was trembling like a frightened mouse.

No, that wasn't true—she wasn't frightened. She was . . . excited. If she were a mouse, she most ardently wished to be caught.

Stupid! All Mr. Parker-Roth need do was stand close to her, and her resolution and common sense fled. "I really should go back with Evie."

His lips turned up slightly. They were very nice lips, narrow and firm, not wet and thick like Brentwood's.

"You really shouldn't." His voice stirred the tendrils of hair that had got loose over her ear. "You will disappoint everyone—Evie, Madam Celeste, Betty"—he slid his hand up her arm—"me."

"Oh." She closed her eyes for a moment. Was he seducing her? One would think she would know seduction, but this was a completely different experience than her unpleasant encounter with Lord Brentwood.

Mr. Parker-Roth did not utter a word to persuade her into sin—he didn't have to. He just stood there behind her, his thumb rubbing slow, lazy circles on her arm, as if he had all day, as if there was nothing more he wished to do with her than stand close and touch her.

She drew in a deep, shuddery breath. His scent and his heat were everywhere. Her small breasts felt swollen, and she ached low in her belly—lower even. Her knees threatened to give out. She wobbled slightly and Mr. Parker-Roth's—Stephen's—arm came around her waist to steady her.

He drew her back against him. She felt his hard form from her shoulders to her bottom.

"Look in the mirror, Anne," he whispered, his lips brushing against her earlobe.

She saw their reflection. Dear heavens! She appeared completely wanton, sprawled back against him, her mouth open, her cheeks flushed. She shut her eyes immediately. "Oh, I—"

"Mmm, you smell good." He kissed a spot just under her ear, sending a shiver cascading through her, and, hussy that she was, she tilted her head to bare a little more of her neck.

She felt him smile against her skin; then his lips

wandered slowly down her jaw. Would he kiss her mouth if she turned her head?

No. He stopped at her cheek. "Temptress," he said.

That was a bucket of cold water. Brentwood had said the same thing, right before he . . .

She straightened and glared at him. "I'm not. Don't be ridiculous."

His eyebrows shot up. He was so close she could trace them with her finger—but of course she would never do such a shocking thing. "I'm not being ridiculous. This is the third time you've tempted me into improper behavior."

The third time? "No, I—" There had been the first disastrous event that Lady Dunlee witnessed and then the incident in the harem room and now . . . "You were drunk before." She sniffed his breath. "Are you drunk still?"

"Of course not. And I'll let you know I do not make a practice of kissing well-bred young women even when I'm in my cups."

"I'm *not* young."

"You're younger than I am."

They stared at each other for what felt like a full minute; then Mr. Parker-Roth grinned and kissed her on the nose. "We can argue about this later—I look forward to it—but we do need to attend to selecting colors, Anne. Evie and the others will not stay in the fitting room forever."

"Well, of course not. And there's no need to bother with that red—oh."

Mr. Parker-Roth draped the fabric across her bodice, covering the brown. She blinked. Something about the color made her skin glow. The change was remarkable.

"And what of this?" He substituted a deep green swatch that almost matched her eyes.

"It *is* rather nice." And it would be lovely, if she could wear it in a room by herself. "But won't I stand out in colors so . . . dramatic?"

He grinned and tweaked one of her curls again. "Anne, you will stand out no matter what you wear." His eyes grew serious. "You must stop trying to hide your light under a bushel."

"What light?" She made a face at herself in the mirror. "You forget—Evie is the beauty; I'm the blue-stocking."

"Hey." He turned her and tilted her chin up so she couldn't avoid his eyes. "None of that." His lips pulled slowly into a smile. "I'm not aware of any law that states bluestockings can't be beautiful, but if there is one, I'm afraid you've broken it."

"Don't be—"

Stephen's mouth covered hers, taking her words and her breath away.

She found she didn't care. She was much more interested in how his lips moved over hers, how they urged her to open for him, how his tongue slid into her mouth, filling her yet making her hungry for more.

He broke the kiss off too soon; she moaned a little in protest.

"Shh, love," he whispered, his forehead resting against hers, "we are about to have company."

"What?" Her eyes flew open, and she scrambled away from him. She looked around; Madam Celeste was standing in the doorway to the dressing room area, laughing.

"Oh, monsieur, you must save your lovemaking for a place more private. What will mademoiselle think of such carryings on by her sister?"

Stephen took Anne's hand and tugged her to stand next to him. "She will think the truth, won't you, Evie?

That I am head over heels for Lady Anne." He pressed a kiss to Anne's palm. "And now I believe Lady Anne is ready for you to take her measurements, madam. Come sit with me, Lady Evangeline, while we wait."

"But . . ." There would be no hiding her meager proportions in Madam Celeste's fitting room.

"Come." Madam Celeste stepped aside and gestured for Anne to go first, probably so she couldn't turn tail and flee. "We will free you from that drab cocoon and turn you into the butterfly, oui?"

If only that were possible. Anne looked at Mr. Parker-Roth and Evie. They both made shooing motions, urging her to go off with Madam Celeste.

Ah well, it was clear she had no choice in the matter. She'd have to submit to Madam Celeste's transformative abilities, even if she emerged only a rather ungainly moth.

She took a sustaining breath and led the way back to the dressing room.

Chapter 5

"Will Madam Celeste really be able to get a ball gown made by tonight?" Evie flushed and looked at Anne. "I mean two ball gowns, of course."

"I told her to do yours first, Evie," Anne said as they climbed the steps to Crane House. "I can wear one of my old dresses."

"No, you can't." Evie looked at Stephen. "You won't let her do that, will you?"

"Of course not. There is no need to worry, however. Celeste will have gowns done with time to spare. She is extremely gifted and has exceptionally talented assistants."

He reached for the doorknob, but before his fingers could close around it, the portal was flung open and a very untidy looking butler was revealed on the threshold. His cravat was askew and his hair was disarranged as if he'd been running his hands through it.

"Hobbes," Anne said, alarm clear in her voice, "whatever is the matter?"

"Oh, my lady, I—" Hobbes tried to assume a stoic, butler-ish demeanor, but failed miserably. He wrung his hands. "The young gentlemen have gone missing."

"Gone missing?! What do you mean, 'gone missing'?" Anne asked sharply, pushing her way past the luckless butler and looking around the entry as if the boys might be hiding under a table or behind a chair. "Where could they have gone?"

"I don't know, my lady." Hobbes looked at Stephen like a drowning man going down for the third time.

"You don't *know*?" It was a wonder Anne didn't grab Hobbes by the neck. The man clearly feared such action; he stepped back out of reach.

"Anne, if Hobbes knew where the boys were, they wouldn't be missing." Giving the man an apoplexy wasn't going to help matters.

Anne looked as if she wished to tear Stephen's head from her shoulders. "I know that, damn it." Tears filled her eyes.

"Anne, this is London," Evie began, "I can't think—"

Anne cut her sister off. "Exactly. This is London where all manner of villains live. It is not the country. The boys know their way around the country, and everyone knows them. But here—they may be trapped in a narrow alley by a gang of thieves at this very moment."

It looked as if everyone, including Hobbes, was going to cry.

"Anne, we are in Mayfair, not Seven Dials. I don't believe we need fear for the boys' safety." Stephen turned to Hobbes. "When did you discover them missing?"

"About ten minutes ago, sir. And I should say the dog is missing as well."

"Ah, there's your answer," Stephen said, looking at Anne. "The boys took Harry for a walk."

"But wasn't one of the footmen supposed to do that?" Anne asked Hobbes. It didn't bode well for whichever hapless footman had failed in his duty.

"Yes, my lady. However, Miss Strange wished some

furniture rearranged. Charles, a very responsible lad I must say, let the dog out into the back garden, but the animal was not content there. Lord Rutledge and his brother said they would take it to the park in the square, and Miss Strange agreed."

"Where *is* Cousin Clorinda?" Evie asked.

"She went to visit Lady Brentwood, my lady, shortly before the young men went missing."

All the color drained from Anne's face. Now what was amiss? She looked as if she were on the verge of collapse again. Stephen took her arm. "Have you sent anyone to look for the boys, Hobbes?"

"Aye. Charles and the other lads searched the square thoroughly, sir. They have just returned. We were going to send for Miss Strange when you arrived."

"Clorinda will be of no help," Anne said, jerking her arm out of Stephen's hold. She appeared to have shaken off whatever fit had befallen her. "We need to expand the search at once, spreading out in all directions. I will go—"

"You will let Hobbes and the footmen attend to it," Stephen said firmly. He turned to the butler. "Send men out as far as Park Lane and Oxford, Mount, and Bond streets. If they still don't find the boys, have them regroup and try farther afield, but I strongly suspect young Philip and George will come home on their own in a little while."

Hobbes looked very relieved to be given orders. "Very good, sir."

Anne was not relieved; she was incensed. "You are far too highhanded, sir. My father put me in charge of my brothers' welfare; of course I will help in the search."

"The footmen will do very much better without you."

"They will not."

He was not going to waste time arguing with her as

she clearly was not of a mind to be persuaded. If she'd bother to give the subject even a moment's thought, she'd realize if she went out, the men would be distracted by their need to keep her safe. "You will not go with them."

"I won't stay home," she said, looking a bit desperate. "I can't."

Evie put her hand on Anne's shoulder. She looked worried, too, but not as frantic as Anne. "I'm sure the boys are all right. They are together and they have Harry."

"But this is *London*, Evie. Anything could happen."

If he didn't get Anne out of here soon, she'd work herself and Evie into a full-fledged case of hysteria. "Now that I think of it, it's most likely Harry remembered his fine romp through Hyde Park this morning and insisted on taking your brothers there."

"Oh." Anne frowned for a moment and then nodded, the dark cloud lifting from her features. "Yes, of course. You must be right. I think I can retrace our route. It is certainly worth a try." She was out the door as she finished her sentence.

Wasn't she going to wait for him? "Hobbes, you'll organize the operations?"

"Yes, sir. Right away."

"And you'll be all right here, Evie?"

Evie smiled. "I'll be fine. You'd better go after Anne, though. She might be halfway to Park Lane already."

"I don't doubt it—and don't worry. We'll find the boys."

Evie frowned. "But Hyde Park is quite large, isn't it?"

"Yes, but Harry struck me as a very intelligent dog. If we don't find him, he'll find us."

He heard Evie laugh as he dashed out the door. As she'd predicted, Anne was not waiting politely for him at the bottom of the steps. He caught a glimpse of her hideous brown dress turning the corner toward Park Lane before she was completely hidden from view. He strode after her. The woman would keep him on his toes once they wed.

He stumbled, but quickly caught his balance. Was he actually going to marry her?

It looked very much as though he was. His honor demanded it.

His honor and other things. He grinned. He was quite looking forward to their marriage bed.

If anyone had told him yesterday he'd be betrothed today to a woman he'd just met, he'd have called the fellow a fool. On the other hand, some of his best decisions had been made on the spur of the moment. After years of navigating unknown terrain and negotiating with natives and other plant collectors, he'd become very good at making split second decisions. He trusted his gut.

And his gut liked Anne.

He had to admire her dedication to her family. So many society women concerned themselves only with themselves and their amusements. Not Anne. She'd take as passionate care of their children as she did her brothers and sister. And she was already used to managing an estate with little or no guidance—Crazy Crane must be gone as much as Stephen.

Now why did the thought of leaving Anne on his estate sit like a rock in his belly? It was the perfect situation. He couldn't have found a better bride for his purposes if he'd conducted a thorough search of the *ton*'s ballrooms. He must still be feeling the residual effects of too much brandy.

He turned the corner and saw her about ten yards ahead, striding purposefully along in that frightful frock. At least she didn't have this morning's dreadful bonnet to complete the fashion disaster, though this selection wasn't much better. He lengthened his own stride.

"You should slow down, you know," he said when he caught up to her. He didn't try to get her to take his arm. It was clear she'd have no part of that.

She spared him a glance. "Why? Am I moving too quickly for you?"

"No, but we are creating a bit of a spectacle." He nodded at a group of bucks sauntering down the other side of the street. One of them had stopped to put his quizzing glass to his eye. "And don't, I pray you, stick your tongue out at that fellow."

Anne slowed a little. "I would never do something so ill-bred, but I can't imagine why those men feel the need to take note of me."

Poor Anne. London society was going to be a very rude shock for her. Why hadn't she ever had a Season? Was it because of the boys? She would have been around seventeen when they were born, and he'd wager twins could throw the most ordered household into disarray. But then why hadn't she come up to Town the next year? Lady Farrington, Crane's older sister, had still been alive then and in fine fettle—she could have sponsored Anne.

"Well, besides the fact you are a strikingly beautiful unknown"—in a dreadful dress, but he didn't say that, of course—"I was chasing you down Upper Brook Street."

That stopped her cold. "You weren't chasing me."

"Well, actually, I was." He took the opportunity to put her hand on his arm.

She scowled, but left her hand where it was as they started walking again. "That's horrible." She darted another glance at the group.

"That's London. The *ton* is always watching and

gossiping. I'll wager any number of busybodies is peering out their windows right now as we pass."

"No!" Her head swiveled toward the houses in time to see the curtains on the two closest twitch back into place. "How can you stand it?"

He shrugged. "I'm used to it. I've learned not to care too much what people think—though I grant you, it's far easier for a man to disregard society's opinion than for a woman. Women have to be much more careful of their reputations."

"Yes."

Now why the hell was she flushing and looking so miserable? "Is something the matter?"

"N-no." She cleared her throat. "Of course not."

She clearly wasn't going to confide in him now. No matter. He would find out eventually what was troubling her. "And I confess it helps that I'm rarely in Town."

She glanced at him. "Why are you here now? I thought you'd be off exploring some foreign jungle."

It was a good question; he'd been asking it himself recently. Usually he couldn't wait to set off on another expedition, but of late he'd had little enthusiasm for travel.

"My good friend the Earl of Kenderly married in February so I wanted to be in England to celebrate with him. And my older brother's first son was born last month." He laughed. "Poor Jack is mostly a red-faced, screaming little lump of humanity, but John and Meg are both besotted with him."

"Give him a month or two." Anne smiled. "I remember how tiny the twins were when they were born. We weren't at all sure they would live, yet look at them now." Her smile abruptly turned to a scowl. "I would like to look at them now. What were they thinking, going off like that?"

"I imagine they weren't thinking at all. In my experience, ten-year-old boys don't look much beyond the present moment."

"That may be true of George," Anne said, worry twisting her features. "He has a sad tendency to leap before he looks, but Philip is almost preternaturally careful."

They reached Park Lane, and Stephen had to grab Anne's arm to keep her from dashing out in front of a carriage. "Here now, I'd say George is not the only impetuous one in your family."

She flushed. "There was much less traffic when I was here this morning."

"Of course. Everyone else was still in bed, sound asleep." He took her arm firmly and guided her across the street and through the gate into the park. The path west to Kensington Gardens ran straight ahead; the path south to the Serpentine and Rotten Row was on their left.

Anne stopped abruptly. "Hyde Park is so large." Dismay clouded her eyes. "How will we ever find them?"

"Don't worry. We'll find them." He started down the path toward the Serpentine, but Anne dug in her heels.

"Wait! How do you know they went that way?"

"I don't—"

"Exactly. You don't. They could just as easily have taken this other path. We shall have to divide up. I'll go—"

"You will go with me, my girl. You are not venturing off on your own, so disabuse yourself of that notion immediately."

"Don't be ridiculous. There are two paths and two of us, ergo—"

"When did you know young boys and dogs to stick to paths?"

That stopped her in mid-word. "Oh."

"Precisely. Furthermore it is completely beyond the pale for a young woman—"

"I am not a young woman."

Mr. Parker-Roth turned his eyes heavenward as if looking for Divine support. "Right, you are ancient. People will still talk if you amble around the park unescorted."

"I don't care what people say. I care about Philip and George and their safety."

"And I care about *your* safety. Hyde Park is no longer infested with highwaymen, but that's not to say it's safe for a woman alone." Mr. Parker-Roth grinned suddenly. "If nothing else some drunken buck might accost you."

She had to laugh in spite of her worry; the man was impossible. "But you assured me you weren't drunk any longer."

"And I'm not, so you are quite safe as long as you stay by my side."

"But . . ." She looked at the other path. They would waste so much time if they chose the wrong direction.

"Come, Anne." Mr. Parker-Roth took her arm firmly. "If you'd let me finish my sentence earlier, you would have heard me say I don't know, but I suspect the boys—or at least Harry—were headed to the Serpentine. That was your goal this morning, wasn't it?"

"No, at least not intentionally. I was just following Harry."

"There you go. I imagine Harry smelled water and was making his way there when I distracted him."

"I suppose you might be correct." She fervently hoped he was as she fell into step beside him.

"Of course I'm correct." He shook her arm a little.

"And do stop worrying. The boys are likely having a wonderful time and won't thank us for interrupting their fun."

The knot of worry in her gut tightened into anger. "Oh, I intend to do more than interrupt them." She'd wring their necks.

"Watch your step there." Mr. Parker-Roth guided her around a pile of dog droppings. He grinned and raised an eyebrow. "Look familiar?"

"No, you dreadful man. Harry's . . . that is when Harry . . ." She laughed. "This is a completely inappropriate topic, but no, I don't think that's evidence Harry has been this way."

He nodded. "Just thought I should check."

They walked along the path in companionable silence. What was it about this man that gave her such a feeling of comfort? She should be frantic about the boys, but she wasn't. She trusted Mr. Parker-Roth had the matter in hand.

That was a dangerous thing. Look at what had happened when she'd trusted Lord Brentwood.

No, the situations were not comparable. She was far older and wiser now—and Brentwood would never have taken an interest in her family.

She glanced up at Mr. Parker-Roth's profile. What if she'd really met him at Baron Gedding's house party? She'd certainly never have gone into the garden with Brentwood.

Mr. Parker-Roth was sinfully handsome with his shaggy sun-streaked hair, blue eyes, and long lashes, but more importantly he looked happy, as though he found life amusing. Lord Brentwood had always looked vaguely angry and a bit tortured.

If only she could do it all over—

Bah, it was a silly waste of time to consider such things. The past was the past. She had gone to the party, and she'd done what she'd done. No amount of wishing or regret would change that.

And there was no reason to think the King of Hearts would have noticed her at Baron Gedding's party had he been there—or today if he weren't forced to do so by his misplaced sense of chivalry.

"Have I a smut on my cheek?" Mr. Parker-Roth looked down at her, one brow lifted.

"What? No, of course not."

"That's a relief. You were studying my face so intently I thought I must have dirt on it." Both eyebrows rose in mock horror. "Never tell me I have some deformity that's escaped my notice all these years?"

She flushed. "I apologize for staring."

His firm lips slid into a slow smile bringing his dimples out of hiding. "Anne, you can stare at me anytime you like."

Now she must be even redder. She tore her eyes away from his face. She should be thinking about Philip and George, not Mr. Parker-Roth's lips and dimples.

"You're worrying again, aren't you?"

"No." She shrugged. "Well, perhaps a little. Are we almost there?"

"Almost." He touched her cheek. "Don't be too hard on the boys."

"Too hard? They are frightening us all to death."

"I know, but they likely have no idea the fuss they've caused. They know where they are. They know they're safe. I'll wager they will be astounded when they learn you've been worried. And that's what they must be taken to task about. A gentleman never causes a lady undue worry."

She almost laughed at that. How could the King of Hearts say such a thing with a straight face? Brentwood certainly didn't subscribe to that philosophy. Even her father thought of himself—and his antiquities—before anyone else. He'd headed for the dock yesterday without the least concern for how she would manage Evie's come-out.

"I can't believe—" Wait! Was that . . . ? "I think I hear . . ."

"Yes, I'd say that's Harry's bark," Mr. Parker-Roth said. "Those trees are blocking our view at the moment, but—"

Anne didn't wait. She picked up her skirts and ran. It was farther than she'd thought. She stopped, a little winded, and leaned against the last tree before the broad expanse of lawn down to the Serpentine. There, a hundred yards or so down the river were two boys and a dog herding a bevy of swans.

"Have we found them?" Mr. Parker-Roth asked, coming up beside her.

"Yes! Oh, dear God, there they are." The tight knot of worry in her stomach released with a flood of tears.

Mr. Parker-Roth gathered her up against his broad chest and held her as she soaked his shirt front.

"I'm sorry," she muttered into his cravat. "I'm not usually such a watering pot."

He hugged her a little tighter, and she rested her cheek against his chest. "You've just gone through a bit of an upheaval, coming to London and being saddled with the responsibility of your sister and the boys," he murmured against the top of her head. His voice was calm and reasonable as if it were perfectly normal to have a woman sobbing in his arms in the middle of Hyde Park. "And then to have the boys wander off . . . It would be odd if your nerves weren't a trifle overset."

"Perhaps." She inhaled deeply. He smelled so good. She'd stay here in his comforting embrace just a moment longer . . .

"Parker-Roth." A man with a distinctively deep, gravelly voice spoke behind her. "How odd to see you here and in such an"—the man coughed suggestively—"interesting position."

No! She stiffened and then pressed herself more tightly against Mr. Parker-Roth, wishing she could miraculously vanish. That voice . . . She hadn't heard it in ten years. Maybe she was mistaken. Maybe it wasn't—

"Brentwood," Mr. Parker-Roth said, his tone cold.

Chapter 6

What had the bastard done to Anne? When she'd heard his voice, she'd clutched Stephen so tightly he'd thought Satan himself had appeared.

Brentwood *was* a blackguard. Stephen had conceived his disgust of the marquis at Eton when he'd come upon the cur trying to drop a new student head first into the jakes. All the other boys had stood around watching, afraid to intervene. Brentwood used his rank and greater size—he'd got his growth early—to bully anyone he chose.

Stephen had been too furious to care. He'd tackled Brentwood and, with the help of the erstwhile victim—now his good friend Damian, Earl of Kenderly—given him a taste, quite literally, of his own medicine. It had taken days and endless scrubbing for Brentwood to free himself from the stench.

It was one of Stephen's favorite memories of his Eton career.

Brentwood usually gave him a wide berth. What—ah. A breeze brought him the scent of brandy. Hyde Park seemed to be a favorite location for inebriated gentlemen today.

"I'd always thought you such a d-discreet fellow,"

Brentwood was saying, "and here I find you making love in the middle of the park to a female in the drabbest dress I've ever had the horror to see." Brentwood waggled his eyebrows. "I suppose the awful garment must hide a body so d-delicious even the King of Hearts can't restrain himself."

He turned to the woman on his arm. "You should see if she wants to join your establishment, Mags. It would be better than working the park"—he chuckled— "though I suppose she don't care if she gets grass stains on that d-dress."

Mags—Madam Marguerite, the proprietress of Le Temple d'Amour, one of the rougher brothels in Town—laughed. "I could use a new bird, 'specially if the King of Hearts has taught her some tricks. Hey, girl, turn around so we can see you."

Anne tried to burrow farther into him.

"I suggest you and your companion continue with your stroll, Brentwood," Stephen said, rubbing Anne's back. He'd like to toss them both in the Serpentine, but that would involve letting go of Anne—or, more to the point, persuading her to let go of him. She was now gripping him so firmly he might bear a bruise or two.

"If you're taking a mistress, man, let me give you a hint—buy her some new clothes." Brentwood laughed, sending a cloud of brandy-laden air Stephen's way. "The female members of the *ton*—especially Lady Noughton—will be d-devastated to hear the King of Hearts has lost—or is at least lending—his heart to some fair Cyprian." The marquis grinned. "Introduce us. I want to be the first to know her name."

Anne tightened her grip even more. He *would* have bruises.

"No." He spoke forcefully enough to cause Mags to step back, but Brentwood was too drunk to hear the warning. "Perhaps I was not clear earlier—move on."

"Oh, now, don't keep the girl to yourself, Parker-Roth."

Brentwood reached for Anne, but before he could get within half a foot of her, Stephen knocked the miscreant's hand aside.

"Ow!" Brentwood cradled his injured fingers. "No need to be nasty."

Stephen caught Brentwood's gaze and held it. "Try to touch the lady again, and I'll break your hand."

There was an awkward silence.

"Better let him be," Mags said, tugging on Brentwood's arm. "I's seen that look often enuff when gents are fighting over a whore. He's like a mad dog, protecting his bone."

Brentwood straightened his cuffs, favoring his injured fingers. "Mad, indeed. I—"

The rest of Brentwood's words were drowned out by furious barking. Harry was tearing up from the water, teeth bared, aiming for Brentwood. Smart dog.

Mags screamed, and Brentwood turned a pasty shade of white.

"I believe the animal doesn't care for the color of your waistcoat, Brentwood," Stephen said.

Brentwood glared at him. Mags had already decided flight was her best recourse and had taken off, skirts hiked up above her knees. The marquis stood firm—until Harry was about a yard from him. Then he, too, took to his heels.

Harry gave chase, barking and snarling for a short distance before trotting back to them, tongue lolling from his mouth, apparently of the opinion he'd vanquished the villains.

"Well done, Harry," Stephen said.

Anne finally loosened her grasp on him and went down on her knees, wrapping her arms around Harry's neck. "Good dog, Harry, good dog." She buried her face in Harry's fur.

Stephen looked for Brentwood and Mags, but they were long gone. Unfortunately, they were sure to discover Anne's identity shortly. How many other oddly dressed women had been seen with him today? Hell, there must be so many rumors flying through society about Crazy Crane's eldest daughter, no other gossip could be discussed.

Philip and George finally reached them. Both boys were remarkably dirty.

"Hullo, sir," Philip said, somewhat breathlessly. "I'm sorry Harry chased away your friends."

"Don't be," Stephen said. "They weren't my friends. I was delighted to see Harry run them off."

"Oh." Philip clearly didn't understand, but he didn't let his incomprehension trouble him long. "You must come see the swans. Harry was herding them, Anne; it was so funny." He looked at his sister who was still kneeling on the grass next to Harry and his mouth dropped open. "Have you been crying?" Since Anne's poor eyes were red and her face blotchy, the observation was not beyond even a ten-year-old boy's powers of discernment.

"No." She sniffed. "I haven't."

This amazing lie kept them all silent for a moment.

George, clearly more accustomed to tumbling into bumble-broths than his brother, asked cautiously, "What's the matter, Anne?"

"Nothing." She burst into tears again, hiding her face back in Harry's fur.

Philip and George looked up at Stephen with identical expressions of bewilderment.

"Your sister is merely a trifle upset."

They blinked at him.

"Anne doesn't usually cry," Philip assured him.

"She's usually pluck to the backbone," George agreed. "You mustn't think you're getting a watering pot for a wife."

Philip nodded vigorously. "Anne's the best of sisters, sir. She might not be as pretty as Evie, but she's much more practical. She's the one our housekeeper, butler, and estate manager come to, not Mama or even Papa."

"You'll be glad to have her, really you will." George shrugged. "And you're too old to want a pretty wife anyway, aren't you?"

Stephen kept his jaw from dropping, though only just. He couldn't decide whether to give the boys a severe dressing down or to laugh. They reminded him of a trader on the outskirts of Rio who'd tried to sell him a broken down pony. It wasn't *belo*—beautiful— he'd said, but it was very *inteligente*.

No wonder Anne didn't value her beauty properly. And the twins thought he was too old to care about his wife's appearance? His lips twitched. Thirty must seem ancient to ten.

"You are laboring under some misapprehensions, boys. First, I find your sister Anne quite beautiful."

Anne's head snapped up and she joined the boys in gaping at him.

"And second, not that physical appearance alone should govern one's actions, but I daresay no man is too old to value a beautiful wife. And third, thirty—my age—is *not* old."

"Oh." Philip's forehead wrinkled. "But Reverend Braxton's wife is ugly. She has a squint and crooked teeth."

"And Mrs. Trent, the butcher's wife, looks like a sow," George added. "She even grunts like a pig."

"Boys!" Anne sniffed and got to her feet, wiping her eyes on her sleeve. "You shouldn't say such things. Mrs. Braxton and Mrs. Trent are both very kind and upstanding women." She sniffed again, more desperately. Stephen handed her his handkerchief.

"Thank you." She blew her nose vigorously. "I do apologize. I seem to have left my own handkerchief at home again."

"You're quite welcome," he said. "I'm always happy to help a maiden in distress."

"But if I continue on this way, I'll soon have your entire supply in my possession."

George shrugged. "Mrs. Braxton makes jolly good apple pies and Mrs. Trent lets us play with her cats, but that don't change the fact they're both ugly."

"But why were you crying, Anne?" Philip asked.

Anne frowned at him. "Because I was worried about you and George. We came back from the dressmaker's and found you gone. No one knew where you were. Hobbes was frantic—the house was in a complete uproar. In fact, the servants are all out now searching for you."

The boys looked astounded. "But we aren't lost," Philip said.

"You know where you are, yes, but no one else does." Stephen looked sternly from one identical face to the other. "I thought we'd agreed I would take you out once I returned with the ladies."

"Well, yes," Philip said, "but Harry needed to go for a walk, sir."

"And this is where he wanted to go," George said. "He dragged us along after him, really he did. And it's very safe here. We weren't in any danger."

Anne's brows snapped down and she opened her mouth as if to read the boys a thundering scold.

"I suggest we return to Crane House," Stephen said, taking her arm. "You'll want to let Hobbes know as quickly as you can that we've found the boys."

"But—"

"You can lecture them much more comfortably at home and be subject to far fewer curious stares."

Anne looked around. The two couples taking in the park air were indeed looking their way and whispering together.

"Yes, of course." Anne fixed the twins with a glare that promised serious retribution. "We will discuss this further when we get home."

They started back up the path, the boys trudging along beside them, looking very gloomy.

"If Papa had engaged a tutor," Philip said, "this wouldn't have happened."

George kicked a pebble off the path. "We can't just stay at Crane House all the time. It's a dead bore. There's nothing to do."

"It's true, Anne," Philip said. "Cousin Clorinda won't even let me read the books in the library anymore."

"Philip," Anne said, "what happened?"

George laughed. "She found him looking through a book with drawings of naked people in it while you were gone."

Philip flushed and glared at his twin. "You were looking at it, too. That's why she came over. If you hadn't made that noise, she wouldn't have known about it, and I could have put it back on the shelf."

"What?" Anne spoke so sharply, Harry barked. "What book?"

Philip shrugged, turning even redder. "Just some book. I couldn't read the title. It was in a foreign language. That's why I pulled it off the shelf, so I could see what it was about."

Given the artwork in the harem room, Stephen thought he knew exactly what the book was about.

"And all Evie talks about is clothes and parties," George said. "She was never so much of a feather head at home. And you're always worrying about something, Anne."

Anne frowned. "Of course I'm always worrying; there's a lot to worry about. Papa and your mama didn't warn me they were going off and leaving me in charge of Evie's come-out. I know nothing about London society."

"Isn't Cousin Clorinda taking charge of Evie?" Philip asked.

"Do you see Clorinda taking charge?" Anne's beautiful voice was rising. "No, she's in the library or off visiting friends." She took a deep breath, obviously trying to get herself under control. "And anyway, George, we've hardly been in London twenty-four hours."

"Well, it *seems* like forever," George muttered.

"Can't you show a little patience?!"

Both boys startled at Anne's sharp, loud tone. Clearly it was time to separate her from her brothers. "Why don't you two run along with Harry?" Stephen said. "We'll catch up to you when you reach Park Lane."

He didn't need to make the suggestion twice. The boys, recognizing an opportunity to escape when they heard one, took off without a moment's hesitation.

Anne scowled after them. "They got off far too easily."

"Because you didn't get to ring a peal over them?"

"Yes."

"I thought you were going to treat them to a bear garden jaw once you all reached Crane House?"

"Yes, but it won't be the same. I can never stay angry at them." She looked up at him, worry shadowing her lovely features. "But they need to know they can't go off like that."

"I think they realized that when they saw how upset you were."

They walked on a few paces in silence. Stephen

watched Anne frown down at the path, obviously chewing over the exchange with her brothers in her mind. She clearly loved them very much.

"I'm certain Nicholas or I can solve your tutor problem by the end of the week," he said.

She sighed. "That would be wonderful—thank you." She looked up, a half smile on her lips but anxiety still clouding her eyes. "I do worry too much, I know. But the boys—George particularly—are so high-spirited. They know their way around the country, but London is a very different matter."

"I agree they shouldn't be let roam unsupervised here in Town." He paused and looked at her thoughtfully. "One never knows when one might encounter someone one wishes to avoid."

Anne paled and looked away.

"Are you going to tell me why you are afraid of Lord Brentwood?"

"I'm not afraid of him!"

"No? Then why did you plaster yourself to me back there?" He smiled. "Not that I'm complaining, you understand."

She closed her eyes as if in pain. "I . . . perhaps I am a little afraid of the marquis."

He put his hand under her chin, tilting her face toward his. "Look at me, Anne."

She shook her head slightly and tried to pull away, but he wouldn't let her.

"Anne."

She sighed and opened her eyes. Tears shimmered over the green like rainwater on Amazon leaves. One tear spilled over and slid down her cheek. He caught it with his thumb.

"You don't have to be afraid of Brentwood. He's a damnable bully, I know. He has been for as long as I've known him. But you are betrothed to me now. I will protect you."

More tears spilled over and she jerked her face away, turning so he couldn't see her expression. "I'm not really your betrothed, and you can't protect me."

She hurried after the boys, and he let her go.

"There's Charles," George said as Stephen caught up to them. He waved at the footman, who was on the other side of the street.

"Thank you for your escort, Mr. Parker-Roth." Anne addressed his cravat. "We won't take any more of your time. Charles can see us safely home."

"But I'm happy to—"

She met his eyes briefly. *"Please."* One word only, but the desperation was clear. She dabbed at her face with his crumpled handkerchief.

"My sister is right, sir," Philip said, somewhat stiffly. "We have taken too much of your time."

The boy wasn't going to regret his moment of irresponsibility too much, was he? "Then I'll leave Lady Anne in your capable hands, Lord Rutledge, and I will see you and Master George tomorrow. Will the afternoon be convenient?"

Philip nodded. "Oh, yes, sir."

"But you must promise me you won't give the ladies any more cause to worry."

"We won't, sir. You have my word."

"George?"

"We'll be little angels."

Stephen laughed. "Oh, I'm not asking for miracles. Just endeavor to stay out of trouble. Can you manage that?"

George gave him a cocky grin. "Do I have to promise not to worry people or to stay out of trouble? Because they're not quite the same thing, you know."

"Just don't wander out of the square and try not to

do any damage, all right? And do leave Lady Dunlee's cat alone."

"All right."

Anne had regained her composure. She offered him her hand. "Thank you again for all your help today, Mr. Parker-Roth. I sincerely appreciate it."

He took her hand and kissed it. "My name is Stephen, Anne. I am your servant as always—and I will see you this evening at the Earl of Kenderly's."

"What? You are mistaken, sir."

"No, my love, I am not."

"Come *on*, Anne," George said. Charles had crossed the street to meet them and was shifting from foot to foot.

"We have no invitations," Anne said.

"You will."

"And I have nothing to wear." She lifted her chin.

He grinned. Good, she'd got back some of her fire. "Ah, ye of little faith. Celeste can work magic—you'll see."

He bowed and left, smiling a little at the sound of her sputtering.

"Boys," Anne said, "will you take Harry out of here? His tail almost sent that purple vase flying off the table." They were taking tea in the green sitting room, which was much too small for three women, two boys, and a large dog.

"It's an ugly vase." Philip grabbed Harry and hugged him. "It would be better broken."

George flung himself onto the floor, too, wrestling Harry away from Philip and almost knocking over a Chinese pig with his foot. "If we broke all the ugly things in this house, there'd be nothing left."

"I don't think Papa would like that, George," Evie said, saving a shepherdess from Philip's elbow.

George paused, letting Philip pull Harry out of his grip, and his eyes lit up. "A shilling says he would."

"Good heavens!" Clorinda put her hand to her breast, wrinkling her nose in distaste. "Are they always so . . . active?"

"Yes." Anne fixed the boys with the look she'd perfected over ten years of managing them. "We are not wagering on that or anything else, George. Now please take Harry away."

"Shall we take him outside?" Philip asked.

"Take him anywhere as long as it's not here—*and* as long as you stay in the square or in the back garden. Don't go wandering off again."

"We won't. We gave our word to Mr. Parker-Roth, right, George?"

George shrugged.

"*George.*" Anne had perfected a no nonsense tone as well.

"All right. Yes. We won't wander off." George looked a trifle sulky. "Mr. Parker-Roth did say he was coming to-morrow, didn't he?"

"Yes, he did, so you have less than twenty-four hours to wait."

"That's a long time."

"George, it's—"

Fortunately Mr. Hobbes brought in a tray of cakes at that moment.

"Hooray!" the boys shouted in unison. In a burst of noise and action, they left, taking Harry and at least half the cakes with them.

Clorinda sighed and looked sadly at the tray. "I do hope Mr. Parker-Roth produces a young man to take charge of those devil—I mean darlings soon." She reached for the largest slice of seed cake the boys had left.

"I'm sure he'll do his best," Anne said.

Clorinda nodded and then continued with the topic

the boys' commotion had interrupted, speaking around a mouthful of cake.

"I still don't understand why you are resisting Lady Brentwood's gracious invitation to her card party tonight, Anne." She washed the cake down with a sip of tea. "We are very fortunate she happened to be having it this evening. It will be an excellent way for you and Evie to meet a few people before you're thrown into society." She took another bite. "And if we're very lucky, Evie will meet an eligible parti immediately, and I can return to the library. Your papa may have his faults, but he has an excellent library."

Anne almost wished she could call Philip, George, and Harry back into the sitting room. "After today's excitement, I think a quiet evening at home would be more in order."

In the normal course of things, Clorinda might be correct; if the hostess was anyone other than Lady Brentwood, Anne would agree to attend. The woman seemed very pleasant, but Anne had no desire to attend an event with Lord Brentwood present. And to expose Evie to him—no, it didn't bear thinking of.

She repressed a shudder. She wanted absolutely nothing to do with that family. "It is not as if Evie has never been about in polite society, Clorinda. She's attended any number of events at home."

Clorinda snorted, sending some cake crumbs tumbling down her bodice. "Bah, the country! Bears no resemblance at all to London society—as different as chalk from cheese. Far too many girls come to Town thinking they can go on as they did in the country and fall flat on their faces—figuratively speaking for the most part—at their first ball."

Evie leaned forward in her chair. "I'm not tired, Anne," she said, "and Cousin Clorinda may be right. Perhaps it would be good for me to get my feet wet in this small pond"—she smiled—"or puddle, really. Lady Brentwood was very nice when we met her at the dressmaker's shop. I think I'd like to go."

"But what would you wear?" Anne saw a possible winning argument. Evie wasn't vain, but she appreciated beautiful clothes. "Our dresses haven't arrived yet."

"Oh." Her sister looked crestfallen. Anne steeled her heart. She knew beyond a doubt it was best they both avoid this gathering.

Clorinda helped herself to another slice of cake. "I'm sure you have something you can wear. It *is* only a small party after all. Marion understands you've just arrived in Town."

Anne took advantage of Clorinda's full mouth. "Lady Brentwood may understand, but what about her guests? London is bristling with gossips."

Unfortunately, Clorinda was a fast and efficient chewer. "As you learned this morning to your detriment, my girl."

Anne flushed. She'd momentarily forgotten about Lady Dunlee.

"It will be good for you to face the smaller dose of gossip you'll encounter this evening, Anne," Clorinda said, looking almost sympathetic. "You can see which way the wind is blowing and prepare yourself. Better to face a few old cats now so you're ready for the ballroom full you'll encounter in a day or two. You don't wish to be taken unawares—that would be fatal."

Anne had a vivid mental picture of a roomful of hissing, snarling felines, from barn cats to she-lions, fur on end, tails twitching, massed and waiting to shred her to pieces with their claws.

She must have moaned aloud, because Evie leaned forward and put a comforting hand on her knee. "Don't worry, Anne. Surely Mr. Parker-Roth will be there to support you."

He wouldn't be. He'd be at Lord Kenderly's. She hadn't mentioned that invitation to Clorinda since it had not arrived—just as the dresses he'd assured her would come from Madam Celeste's had not. Mr. Parker-Roth with his false promises was proving no better than Brentwood. She only hoped he came through for the boys. He couldn't be so cruel as to raise their hopes if he had no intention of fulfilling them, could he?

"Hmph." Clorinda inspected the sweets tray again. She had finished all the seed cake, so she selected a piece of gingerbread. "I wouldn't bet on Mr. Parker-Roth's attendance, though Marion did invite him, of course."

Anne sat up straighter. "I wasn't counting on seeing him. I'm sure he must have many other engagements."

Clorinda raised an eyebrow. "Only one engagement I'm aware of."

"That's not what I meant, and you know it."

"Temper, temper," Clorinda said, wagging her finger. "You have to smile and look bored no matter what anyone says to you."

"But surely you're mistaken about Mr. Parker-Roth, Cousin." Evie sounded shocked. "And you too, Anne. Why wouldn't he come?"

Clorinda shrugged, popping the gingerbread in her mouth. "He's the King of Hearts. He's adept at slipping out of uncomfortable situations."

"But he's quite taken with Anne."

"No, he's not, Evie." Anne reached for her teacup, but pulled her hand back when she realized how badly it was shaking.

Everyone—everyone but Evie, that is—must know her betrothal wasn't going to last. The King of Hearts promising to wed a red-haired, gawky female like herself when he had all of London, if not all of England, at his feet? Not likely.

Clorinda nodded. "You are too naïve, Evie, that's why you need some Town polish. The man got caught stealing a kiss. What else was he going to say?" She treated Anne to a pointed look. "Once the Season's over, people will forget, as long as Anne doesn't do anything else to disgrace herself."

Anne's stomach sank even more, but Clorinda wasn't being cruel; she was being candid. It just wasn't pleasant to hear it.

"But Clorinda, Mr. Parker-Roth is truly quite taken with Anne." Evie giggled. "You should have seen them at Madam Celeste's."

Anne closed her eyes briefly. If she died of embarrassment now, she'd save herself weeks of suffering. "Appearances can be deceiving."

"Appearances can be damning, missy," Clorinda said sternly. "If you behave circumspectly during the Season, I think you can survive this peculiar betrothal. But act like a hoyden and your reputation will be in tatters. The *ton* have long memories, you know."

"I know."

Clorinda's voice gentled. "Don't be too hard on yourself, Anne. The King of Hearts is a genius at making women feel emotions they should not be feeling. Don't fall prey to his blandishments, my dear. He is very charming, and he will be paying you marked attention, but you must not forget it means nothing. Keep your wits about you. You want people to forget you, not pity you, when there's no wedding."

Anne nodded. She knew Evie was looking at her with big, shocked eyes, but she couldn't meet her glance—she'd cry if she did. Stupid. Clorinda was just saying what she already knew.

Thankfully, Clorinda turned her attention back to Evie. "Marion said her son, the marquis, might stop by." She sniffed. "Well, truthfully, she planned the event partly in the hopes he might see some woman he'd consent to marry."

"Lady Brentwood mentioned that." Anne clenched her hands in her skirts. It was a wonder she hadn't hit the woman at Madam Celeste's though, of course, Lady Brentwood had meant no harm. Anne hadn't considered it before, but it must be hell to be the mother of such a dirty dish. "I got the impression you encouraged her to think I might be a matrimonial candidate."

"Well, you are still unwed—and as far as I knew, not spoken for. A twenty-seven-year-old spinster can't be too choosy."

"But the Marquis of Brentwood?" Anne's stomach twisted.

Clorinda had the grace to blush. "I can't say I care much for the man—truthfully, he's broken Marion's heart too many times to count—but he *is* a marquis." She looked back at Evie. "He's a peer you can practice on."

"Clorinda!" Anne couldn't believe what she was hearing.

"I meant practice her social graces on, of course."

"Lord Brentwood is not the sort of person Evie should know."

"Of course he's the sort of person Evie should know, though I grant you he is no longer accepted in the best houses," Clorinda said, a touch of exasperation in her voice. "He's a marquis."

"But he's not a nice marquis." Anne knew she sounded like a goose-cap, but she was desperate. She—and Evie—could *not* go to this party.

"Anne, most of the *ton* isn't particularly nice. Frankly, they are, for the most part, spineless idiots. I didn't say Evie should encourage the fellow."

"I don't see how it can hurt to go, Anne," Evie said. "I'm not a complete ninnyhammer. I won't be bowled over by a title. Surely you know that."

"Yes, but . . ." Damn it, now she was insulting Evie.

She did know her sister wouldn't be taken in by Brentwood—Evie was much smarter than Anne had been and, in any event, Anne would be there to see Brentwood didn't lead Evie astray. The truth was Anne couldn't bear to see Brentwood again so soon and at such a small event where there would be no hope of avoiding him. "It's just that—"

"My lady." Hobbes entered the room carrying a white square of vellum on a tray. "A note from Lord Kenderly. His servant awaits your reply."

Anne sucked in her breath. Could this be the promised invitation? Her heart began to pound.

"The Earl of Kenderly? What can this be about?" Clorinda snatched the note off the tray and opened it. "My word! Lord Kenderly begs the pleasure of our company at a light repast prior to his ball this evening."

Anne was almost dizzy with some odd emotion— a mix of relief and happiness with a touch of . . . something else. It looked as if Mr. Parker-Roth *was* a man of his word—at least in regard to obtaining invitations. Sadly, the dresses weren't here, but he didn't have complete control over that. He'd most likely fallen prey to an overambitious estimation of Madam Celeste's abilities.

Clorinda was holding the note to her thin bosom. "This is an amazing stroke of luck. How do you suppose we got on Lord Kenderly's guest list?"

"I believe Mr. Parker-Roth may have mentioned the

possibility when we were with the boys in Hyde Park this afternoon," Anne said, addressing her hands. She could feel Clorinda's eyes on her, but she wasn't about to meet her quite possibly probing look.

"See, I wasn't mistaken," Evie said. "Mr. Parker-Roth *is* taken with Anne."

"Hmm," Clorinda said. "It is certainly very kind of him to arrange this—the ball will be the event of the Season, and if Lord and Lady Kenderly take you up, Evie . . . Well, they are the best *ton*, you know."

"Then shall I tell Lord Kenderly's footman you will attend, my lady?"

"Yes, indeed, Hobbes. We cannot turn this opportunity down. Oh, and do send my regrets to Lady Brentwood."

Anne was torn between relief and panic. At least now she wouldn't have to face Brentwood, but she would be pitchforked in amongst another group of the *ton*—and she still had no suitable ball gown. She'd never cared much about her clothes—serviceable was all that mattered—but the thought of wearing the drab gown she'd had for at least five years was unaccountably depressing . . . especially as Mr. Parker-Roth would see her in it.

Hobbes paused on the threshold. "I'm afraid with all the excitement today I forgot to mention packages from Madam Celeste's establishment arrived while we were out searching for the boys. One of the housemaids put them aside. Shall I have them sent up to your rooms now, Lady Anne?"

Evie clapped her hands; Anne almost did. "Yes, please, Hobbes."

"And should I also tell Lord Kenderly's footman that you accept Mr. Parker-Roth's escort this evening? I was given to understand Mr. Parker-Roth was at Lord Kenderly's home when the invitation was sent."

"Yes, Hobbes," Clorinda said, "that would be fine."

"What did I tell you," Evie said once Hobbes was out of earshot. "Anne's betrothal is *not* a sham."

Clorinda looked at Anne thoughtfully. "I admit Mr. Parker-Roth is making some effort to give that appearance."

If only it were more than appearance, Anne thought, as she and Evie went upstairs to examine Madam Celeste's packages.

Chapter 7

"So tell me why I had to invite Crane's daughters to this evening's blasted festivities?" Damian Weston, Earl of Kenderly, poured two glasses of brandy and handed one to Stephen, sprawled in a comfortable leather wing chair by the fire in Damian's study. Damian lowered himself into the matching chair and stretched out his long legs, crossing his ankles. "I didn't know you were an intimate of Crane's."

"I'm not."

"A friend of Lady Crane, then?"

"No." Stephen took a sip of his brandy. If Damian had been to White's or Tatt's or anywhere the men of the beau monde congregated instead of holed up here working on some obscure Latin translation, he'd already know the story.

Why couldn't Stephen just tell him the whole now? He'd have to do so before Anne arrived this evening.

The words stuck in his throat. The thing seemed reasonable when he was with Anne—and after Lady Dunlee had caught them in the square, he hadn't felt he'd had any options—but now . . . Damian would

either call him a fool or fall on the floor laughing—
or both.

It didn't help that just a few weeks ago he'd teased
Damian about *his* precipitous marriage here in this
very room.

"They're new to Town—just arrived yesterday—and
don't know anyone. Their cousin Miss Clorinda
Strange is nominally their chaperone, though the
older sister, Lady Anne, looks to be saddled with the
real work of bringing Lady Evangeline out."

"I see." Damian looked at him over the rim of his
brandy glass before taking a swallow. "And when did
you establish the Benevolent Society for the Welfare of
Young, Marriageable Misses? I confess I missed the announcement."

Stephen shifted in his chair. "I just thought these
girls could use a hand."

"Oh?"

Silence was one of Damian's tricks. He'd make a non-
committal, questioning sort of sound and wait for his
victim to fill the void with noise—usually incriminating
words.

Stephen kept his mouth tightly closed and stared
back.

Damian's lips twitched. "Don't want to tell me,
hmm? I'll find out, you know."

"Oh, I know. I'm sure I'll tell you shortly. It's all over
Town anyway—which you'd know if you ever went out."

Damian laughed and blessedly turned his penetrating gaze to the fire. "I have heard the younger daughter is quite beautiful."

"She is—and she's barely out of the schoolroom."

"Yet old enough to wed. That's why she's here, isn't
it? To find herself a husband."

"Perhaps. Certainly to get some Town polish."

Damian's voice was suspiciously bland. "And you're going to help with the polishing."

His tone rankled. "I am *not* interested in Lady Evangeline."

"Oh, ho." Damian regarded Stephen, eyebrow raised. "The gentleman doth protest too much, methinks."

Stephen had an irrational urge to plant his fist between Damian's eyes. "Good God, you are by far the most annoying of my friends, Kenderly."

Laughter came from the study doorway, and Damian's face assumed the besotted expression Stephen had come to expect whenever the earl heard or saw his wife. They stood to greet Lady Kenderly.

"Of course Mr. Parker-Roth isn't interested in Lady Evangeline, Damian," she said, stepping in and closing the door behind her. "How could he be? He's betrothed to her older sister."

Damian let out a long, low whistle and his damn eyebrows just about disappeared into his hairline.

"I was going to get around to telling you," Stephen said.

"Then please excuse me for stealing your news, sir," Lady Kenderly said, coming over to them, "and for intruding into your private meeting as well." She glanced at Damian. "I did knock, but I suppose you were too immersed in your conversation to hear me."

Damian took his wife's hand and brought it to his lips. "You are always welcome wherever I am, Jo."

Stephen averted his eyes; watching his friend act the devoted husband was not the most edifying of sights. Hard to imagine, but Damian used to be a very rational fellow.

Fortunately *he* would never be such a love struck noddy. No, selecting a bride by accident—when the

bride was a sensible, capable female like Lady Anne—
was a very good thing.

He glanced again at Lady Kenderly. He hadn't spent
a lot of time with her, but she seemed somehow different this evening. She was tall and slender . . .

Hmm . . . perhaps not so slender?

"What brings you here, my love?" Damian asked as
he helped his wife into the chair he'd just vacated.

She laughed again. "Disaster in the kitchens!"

Damian scowled. "This infernal ball! You know I
told you you shouldn't undertake such an exhausting
project, not in your condition."

Ah, ha, so old Damian *had* been his usual efficient
self, getting his lovely wife with child without wasting
a moment.

Lady Kenderly smiled and patted her chair arm.
"Do sit down and stop glowering at me, dear. I am not
exhausted. Your inestimable housekeeper is handling
all, smoothing Cook's ruffled feathers as she's done for
years, long before I came on the scene."

"You're certain?"

"Completely." She grinned. "Though just in case I
am wrong, I have come here to hide until the storm
blows over."

Damian wasn't totally mollified. "You know we could
easily cancel the whole business, disinvite everyone,
and spend a quiet evening together."

"I know no such thing! We would upset countless
people—even disappoint a few, I imagine—as well as
set our own house in an uproar. If you think Cook is
displeased now, I shudder to consider what she will say
if you tell her all her work was for naught." Lady
Kenderly looked at Stephen. "And of course Cook
wouldn't say a word to Damian; she would never consider speaking directly to the Master! But depend on
it, we would all suffer."

Stephen smiled. "Surely your cook would not complain if you are in a delicate condition?"

Lady Kenderly blushed.

"Ah, so you noticed my slip, did you?" Damian said. "We have not made the news public—it's still early days yet, you know."

"And you think I would blab the story all over Town? I am not one to bruit your business about as I would hope you'd know."

Damian caught Stephen's gaze and held it. "As neither am I one to do so about your affairs. What *is* your interest in Crane's older daughter, Stephen? You know you can trust Jo and me. Indeed, you've asked our help by including the ladies on our guest list tonight."

"Yes, Mr. Parker-Roth. I may be new to your circle of acquaintances, but please rest assured you can rely on my discretion," Lady Kenderly said. "Frankly, I found the rumors of your betrothal hard to credit, even though I heard basically the same story from multiple sources. Now that you've confirmed the tale is true, the question remains—why?"

Stephen let out a long breath. "If you've heard the rumors, you know why."

"I've not heard the rumors," Damian said. "Enlighten me, if you please."

"Lady Dunlee caught me kissing Lady Anne on the walk outside Crane House."

Lady Kenderly cleared her throat delicately. "It was rather more than that," she pointed out. She turned to Damian. "Lady Dunlee found him flat on his back in front of Crane House with Lady Anne sprawled all over him."

A hot flush crept up Stephen's neck. "I was distracted when Lady Dunlee's demented cat showed up. Lady Anne's dog took off after the cat and, since I was still holding the lead, I fell down. As I was, ah, also holding Anne, she fell, too. On top of me."

He cleared his throat. Two pairs of eyes—one brown, one blue—blinked at him. The silence stretched out, but there was no way in hell Stephen was breaking it.

Damian frowned. "This is rather sudden. Have you known Lady Anne for a long time? I don't believe I've seen her in London before."

He should have told Damian from the beginning; if he had, he could have shaped the story to his liking. This piecemeal approach made it all sound so . . . odd. "I met her this morning."

Damian sat stunned for a moment—Stephen took a little pleasure from that; he'd never dumbfounded the man before.

"Ah. So, do I have this right? You met Lady Anne this morning for the first time, took her into a passionate embrace, and kissed her so thoroughly you so lost awareness of your surroundings as to be pulled over by a dog." Damian rolled his eyes. "Well, you'd already lost awareness of your surroundings if you were kissing a woman on a public street, especially one frequented by society's premier gossip, Lady Dunlee."

Stephen studied his clasped hands. "We talked for a while first."

"Ah, wonderful. So at least you had some conversation before you accosted the woman."

"I didn't accost her."

"She accosted you?" Damian sounded bemused.

"No, of course not." Stephen shrugged. "It just . . . happened." He coughed. "I was rather drunk at the time."

"I see." Damian sat back and stared at him. "I've never known you to be an amorous drunk."

Lady Kenderly laid a hand on Damian's knee. "It doesn't matter what happened; what matters now is what happens next." She frowned at Stephen. "How do you feel about Lady Anne? Do you *wish* to marry her?"

What kind of question was that? "What I wish or don't wish is immaterial. I've compromised a lady and I must make amends. My only option is marriage."

Lady Kenderly sighed and looked heavenward. "You are just like a man, seeing everything in black and white."

"Stephen isn't just like a man," Damian said, chuckling. "He *is* a man."

Lady Kenderly rolled her eyes this time. "I *know* that. I haven't been so blinded by my love for you, my lord, that I can't see beyond the end of my nose."

Damian bristled, suddenly frowning. "Here, now, Jo, you'd best not be wanting any other men!" He sounded only half joking.

"Don't be silly. Looking and wanting are not the same thing at all, at least for women." She laughed. "Or, not wishing to speak for all my sisters, at least not for *this* woman." She looked up at Damian, a teasing note in her voice. "You keep me far too busy for my affections to wander."

"I do, don't I?" Damian had a very self-satisfied grin on his face.

Stephen shifted in his seat. He was glad Damian was happily married, but he did not care to observe the heated look the man was exchanging with his lady. Surely they hadn't forgotten his presence?

Lady Kenderly patted Damian on his thigh—rather too close to a certain organ for Stephen's comfort—and laughed again. "Here we are, putting poor Mr. Parker-Roth to the blush. What are we thinking?"

Stephen was all too aware what Damian must be thinking. The earl opened his mouth as if he were going to answer the question, but then, fortunately, thought better of it. He grinned while Lady Kenderly turned to Stephen.

"Getting back to your problem, Mr. Parker-Roth," she began.

"Oh, no, don't feel as if you need to get back to my problem, Lady Kenderly." Stephen would be delighted to let that topic drop. "As I say, I don't have any problems. No problems at all." He took out his pocket watch. "I see I should be—"

Lady Kenderly put her hand on his wrist. "Sir, I cannot believe you really wish to wed Lady Anne."

Was Damian's wife a lack-wit? "As I've said, my wishes have nothing to say to the matter."

"They have everything to say to the matter!" Lady Kenderly tightened her grip on him, shaking him a little, and then released him and sat back. "I realize you've compromised the girl—"

"She's hardly a girl. She's almost my age."

"Ah," Damian said. "Then she should have known what she was about. Perhaps she's a conniving minx out to trap herself a wealthy husband."

Anger surged in Stephen's gut. "She's no such thing."

"She is a little long in the tooth to be unwed," Lady Kenderly said. "She might be more than a little desperate."

"She is *not* desperate." Stephen drew in a deep breath. He didn't usually have any trouble controlling his anger. "Her stepmother, the earl's current wife, gave birth to twins when Anne should have made her come-out, so Anne never came to Town."

"Not for all these years?" Damian sounded skeptical.

"I take it she's had so many responsibilities, marriage never seriously crossed her mind. You know how Crane will take off at a moment's notice when he gets wind of any new antiquity. Apparently Lady Crane is also keen on the subject and travels with him. Anne is put in charge of the family when they leave, including now." He looked back at Lady Kenderly. "Crane and his wife dropped everyone at Crane House and immediately departed for foreign shores, leaving Anne to manage her sister's come-out alone."

"Heavens!" Lady Kenderly looked properly horrified. "Has she no one to assist her?"

"Only her elderly cousin, Miss Clorinda Strange."

"That odd woman who's obsessed with birds?" Lady Kenderly asked.

Stephen nodded. "The same."

"Isn't she the harridan who attacked Lady Wappingly last Season because she had plumes from some exotic bird on her bonnet?" Damian asked. "Snatched the thing right off Lady Wappingly's head, calling her any number of unpleasant names." He laughed. "The caricaturists had a grand time with that. The drawings were in the windows of all the print shops for a week or more."

"Quite possibly. I didn't come up to London last Season." He'd stopped down at the Priory to deliver the plants he'd brought back from the Amazon for John, and then he'd gone off again.

"Ah, that's right." Damian grinned. "Now that I think on it, I guess it's time for the annual Parker-Roth scandal. Your sister entertained the gabble-grinders the Season before last with her hurried marriage to Viscount Motton and staid old John shocked the *ton* last year. Now it's your turn."

"Very funny." Damian was right, though. He hoped Mama and Da had become inured to tittle-tattle regarding their children.

"Gentlemen," Lady Kenderly said, "you have strayed far from the point. Let us return to the crux of the issue." She looked at Stephen. "Do you love Lady Anne, Mr. Parker-Roth?"

"Do I love her?" Stephen gaped at Damian's wife. "I've only just met her."

"Jo, let me put it in terms my *male* friend might understand." Damian grinned. "Do you lust after her?"

Bloody hell. Stephen felt a hot flush climb his neck. Did he lust after Anne? He pictured her in her hideously drab, shapeless brown dress.

No, he didn't.

He sighed, running his hand through his hair. "It's more complicated than that."

"How can it be more complicated?" Damian reached for the brandy he'd abandoned on a side table when his wife had arrived. "You either want her or you don't. I'd say you don't." He took a sip. "You can't marry her if you don't desire her. That would be hell."

"Hell for her, too," Lady Kenderly said.

Blast and damn. His insides were all twisted up. He didn't know how he felt, which was a completely foreign state of affairs for him. He *always* knew his own mind.

He might not know his mind, but he knew his duty. "I compromised her; I have to marry her." He shrugged. "I've just turned thirty—it's time I wed." He tried to grin. "My mother certainly thinks so."

"Thirty is not ancient," Damian said. "You have plenty of time. It's not like you have a title to secure."

Lady Kenderly sucked in her breath and said in mock anger, "So that's why you wed me!"

"Don't be ridiculous, Jo. I wed you because I was mad for you." Damian shook his head. "You can't marry the woman if you don't like her, Stephen. I'll tie you up and ship you off to the Continent before I'll let you do that."

"You're welcome to try." Truth was Damian was almost as good a fighter as he. He didn't think the earl could get the better of him, but he wasn't one hundred percent certain. "And I do like Anne."

"Well, that's something," Damian said. "So at least it won't be a completely cold marriage of convenience." Damian pulled a face. "Be sensible. You don't want a polite, lukewarm arrangement. It would be one thing if you came from chilly stock, but I've heard the stories about your parents and your sister Jane—hell, everyone thought John was the Parker-Roth with ice in his veins and look what happened with him. You're the King of Hearts—you can't marry without love."

Stephen felt trapped and angry. "I detest that nickname, Damian, as well you know."

Lady Kenderly touched his knee. "But you've just met Lady Anne. I can see having an immediate physical reaction, but you said you don't lust after her. You can't know her well enough to know if you like her or not."

"Lady Kenderly, I pride myself in being a good judge of character; I've had to be. Out in the wild, in the jungle or on the savannah, often among natives who may not speak English, all you've got to go on is your gut."

Damian nodded. "That's true. And I would agree you've got excellent instincts where people are concerned. You had the wisdom to befriend me, after all."

"I just didn't care to see you go head first into the privy courtesy of Brentwood."

"Details, details."

"Oh, do be serious, Damian," Lady Kenderly said. She nodded at Stephen. "I understand what you mean, Mr. Parker-Roth. I've observed that myself. Some people have an unerring sense of whom to trust; others are always falling into disastrous 'friendships.'"

"Exactly. Anne is trustworthy and responsible, and she sincerely loves her half sister and half brothers when she could easily be surly and resentful. She guides them with an excellent mix of firmness and sympathy."

"She sounds like a damn paragon," Damian said.

"I won't have you disparaging her, Damian."

Lady Kenderly held up her hand. "Gentlemen, please. Then let me ask you this, Mr. Parker-Roth."

"Lady Kenderly, if your hard-headed husband here does not object, I'd be happy to have you call me Stephen." He smiled wryly. "I would say our conversation has strayed beyond the formal."

Lady Kenderly smiled. "I would like that. Damian speaks so highly of you."

"Jo, you can't tell him that," Damian said in mock alarm. "It will go straight to his head; there'll be no tolerating him."

Lady Kenderly snorted, but otherwise ignored her husband's comment. "And you must call me Jo, Stephen, though you may wish to call me 'damn Jo' as Damian sometimes does when I ask you this last question."

"Take care, old friend," Damian said. "You are in trouble now. Jo's questions can be like rapier thrusts to the heart."

Jo spared a glance at her husband. "Really, dear, I'm not certain you're helping matters." She turned back to Stephen. "You said you'd kissed Lady Anne, Stephen. Would you do it again?"

Stephen flushed. A rapier thrust indeed.

"Of course he would do it again, Jo," Damian said. "He's a man—we've established that."

"Yes, and Lady Anne is a lady. One kiss might be a mistake, but two—well, I think that must show some attraction or affection—"

"Or lust!" Damian laughed. "And if there's some spark, it may grow into a raging fire, eh, love?"

"Exactly." Jo lifted her brows and considered Stephen.

"So, Stephen, would you kiss Lady Anne a second time?"

Talk about raging fires—Stephen was certain his face resembled a conflagration. He cleared his throat. "I already have."

Jo clapped her hands. "Excellent. Then I have great hopes for you. And I shall be happy to help your Lady Anne find her way—not that I am an expert in the social scene, of course, being so new to it myself, but Damian is a man of great consequence as he periodically likes to remind me."

"Now, Jo—"

"Oh, hush, Damian. I am teasing you." She grinned at Stephen. "I suggest you stay betrothed for the Season and see how your feelings grow. If you find you cannot love Lady Anne—or if she cannot love you—then you can end your betrothal quietly when the Season is over."

Stephen was not sure how it happened that Damian's wife had taken charge of his marital situation, but he feared somehow she had. "But I will not be ending the betrothal."

She stood and shook out her skirts. "You know, Stephen, I do think you might not." She kissed Damian on the cheek. "Now if you will excuse me, I will go see if Cook has been calmed and our food tonight will not be a complete disaster."

Anne stared at the dress on the bed. She had hoped Madam Celeste would have chosen the green fabric first, but no.

"It's very . . . red, isn't it?" Evie said, doubt clear in her voice. "Do you think it will go with your hair?"

Anne sighed. "I suppose we will find out, won't we?

And if it doesn't, I can always wear my best ball gown from home."

They both looked at that poor, drab dress, draped over a nearby chair. Anne had got it out of the wardrobe once she'd unwrapped the package from Madam Celeste. It was brown and sadly out of date, but at least she would blend into the background if she wore it.

She certainly wouldn't blend into the background in the red dress. She'd look like a, a . . . well, she wasn't certain what she would look like. She ran her hands over the silky fabric.

Her first reaction when she'd seen the dress was to bundle it back up. She might have done so if Evie hadn't come in.

She shouldn't waste time trying it on, but it felt so soft. Her fingers lingered over the cloth. And the little swatch of fabric Mr. Parker-Roth had held up against her skin in Madam Celeste's shop had made her look . . . different. Almost pretty.

She looked at Evie again and smiled. "At least you will make a spectacular debut, and that is all that matters." She shook her head in wonderment. "You always look beautiful, but tonight . . ." She sighed happily. "Tonight you are exquisite."

Evie preened in front of the mirror, unable to contain her excitement. "The dress is lovely, isn't it?"

The dress *was* lovely—delicate white muslin with small puffed sleeves and a wide blue ribbon around the waist that exactly matched Evie's eyes. "Yes, but the girl in the dress is even lovelier."

Evie took one last look at herself and then turned back to Anne. "I'm sure Madam Celeste wouldn't make a dress for you that wasn't flattering, Anne, and Mr. Parker-Roth surely must have excellent taste. He helped you choose the color, didn't he?"

"Yes, but the small bit of fabric we looked at in Madam Celeste's shop didn't seem so overwhelmingly red. I'm sure to look like a ripe tomato."

Evie giggled. "Don't be silly. You are far too thin to look like a tomato of any sort." She picked up the dress and shook it out, the bright satin whispering over itself. "It's not red, really, but coquelicot. There are definitely tones of orange."

"Hmm." The dress was simply cut with few embellishments. Clean, uncluttered, and so very bright. It looked almost alive in Evie's hands.

"Come, Anne, try it on. Mary went to help Tredlick get Cousin Clorinda ready, so I'll act as your maid."

Anne had the oddest feeling that if she put that dress on, she'd turn into someone else. Ridiculous, of course. But still . . . it would be very hard to avoid attention in that gown.

Evie shook the dress again. "You don't have all night, you know. Mr. Parker-Roth will be here shortly."

On odd thrill shot through her, and her stomach shivered. Mr. Parker-Roth would see her in this dress . . . was that a good thing or not?

More to the point, why did she care?

"Very well." She let Evie help her into Madam Celeste's shocking creation. The cloth smelled sweet and new; the satin slid sensually over her skin, caressing her body, hugging its contours in a way Mrs. Waddingly's dresses never had, and falling to swirl around her feet. Something, some new energy, thrummed through her. She felt more alive than she had in a long, long time— since before Baron Gedding's house party.

She kept her eyes closed, afraid to see how garish she must appear. She wanted to look beautiful for once. She didn't want to take off this new gown and put on her boring, old dress that she'd worn to countless assemblies and balls for the last five years. She was suddenly heartily sick of it.

"Oh, my." Evie's voice had a very peculiar tone to it, almost one of awe.

Anne forced one eye open to peek at her reflection. "Oh!" She opened the other eye and gaped at the woman in the mirror. Was it truly she? She raised her hand to touch her face, and the woman in the mirror did the same.

Through some miracle, Madam Celeste had crafted the dress so Anne actually appeared to have a figure. The neck was cut rather low over her small bosom and the skirts flared out from a high, but defined waist. The color, rather than making her look like a clown or, far worse, a cheap whore, made her skin glow and her eyes appear greener. "I look almost pretty."

"Pretty? You look"—Evie paused, apparently searching for the proper word—"ravishing. Mr. Parker-Roth won't be able to take his eyes off you. I suspect all the men we meet tonight will be unable to look at any other woman present. I am quite put in the shade."

"Don't be silly." Anne managed to tear her eyes away from the vision in the mirror, though she couldn't resist darting glances at herself. "I am an elderly spinster, very much on the shelf. No one will give me a second glance."

"You are not on the shelf—or won't be much longer. You are betrothed to Mr. Parker-Roth." Evie grinned. "I am counting on him to discourage all the other men from flocking around you."

"Flocking around me like a gaggle of geese? Now you are being completely absurd." She wished she could share the story of her betrothal with Evie. It would be a relief to have someone know the truth. Perhaps if she swore her to secrecy—

"Here I am, miladies. Did ye think I'd forgotten ye? I had to—lordie!" Mary stopped just inside the door to Anne's room, her mouth hanging open. "Lady Anne, is that really ye?"

Anne felt herself flush. "Of course it is, Mary." She gestured to Evie. "Isn't Evie beautiful?"

Mary took in Evie's dress and then returned to consider Anne. "Aye. Lady Evie is always a treat, and that dress is very special, but ye, milady . . ." She shook her head and then grinned slyly. "I'm guessing ye'll be having a very short betrothal."

"Mary!" Anne was certain her cheeks were now bright red. Evie was blushing, too, but laughing as well.

"Mark my words," Mary said. "Once that man sees ye in this dress, he'll be running for a special license." She winked. "He'll want ye out of the dress and in his bed as quick as may be."

"I'm sure you should not be saying such things." Anne could barely get any words out, she was so embarrassed— embarrassed and something else. Nervous, yes. And excited. It would be nice to have a man—to have Mr. Parker-Roth—look at her with some admiration in his eyes.

Mary shrugged. "Yer both old enough to be thinking of marriage—and marriage beds." She pulled out the dressing table chair. "Now come, I need to get ye ready and be quick about it. Hobbes just sent word up that Mr. Parker-Roth has arrived. Miss Clorinda has already gone down." She pushed Anne into the chair. "We don't want to keep the poor man waiting, especially waiting with Miss Clorinda. She's sure to set his teeth on edge in no time." She pulled a brush through Anne's unruly hair.

"I can't wait to see Mr. Parker-Roth's face when he catches sight of you, Anne," Evie said. "I think Mary's right. He'll be completely entranced."

Anne smiled weakly. Her odd excitement had just

exploded into a flock of butterflies, fluttering in her stomach, her bosom, her throat—everywhere. She watched Mary tame her hair, weaving a few flowers artfully through it.

"There ye go, milady. Ye do look a picture."

Anne got up so Evie could take her place. Her knees were not quite steady. It would be a wonder if she didn't tumble down the stairs to land in a heap at Mr. Parker-Roth's feet. That would make a lovely impression—and send him running away from her as far and as fast as he could go.

Chapter 8

"The girls should be down in a moment," Clorinda said. "Their maid is just finishing their hair."

Stephen nodded. He hoped Anne and Evie would be down very soon. He wasn't certain how much more he could take of Miss Strange. The last five minutes had felt like fifteen. Worse, he could tell she was working up to some topic he was certain to find unpleasant.

He was right.

"The wags call you the King of Hearts," she said, "and I hear the title is well deserved." She waggled her graying brows and slapped him on the arm.

He stepped out of reach. "Gossip always distorts its subject far beyond the bounds of truth."

"Oh, come now, sir. You are a great favorite with the ladies—admit it!"

He was not going to admit anything. "Miss Strange, I fail to see the point of this conversation." Not that it was actually a conversation, of course. Conversation required at least two willing participants—there was only one here, and it was not he.

Clorinda frowned at him. "The point, sir, is that you are an experienced man of the world, a man who knows his way around the boudoir. Poor Anne is a mouse to your cat. You will gobble her up in one mouthful."

Damn. He should not be entertaining salacious thoughts while standing in the Earl of Crane's entry hall with elderly, odd Miss Clorinda Strange, but his rational, proper brain seemed to have lost control of his irrational, lusty nether regions. The thought of gobbling up Anne was wildly appealing.

He was going mad. He'd told Damian and his wife he didn't lust after Anne, and he'd told the truth. He liked her, yes, but she wasn't really the sort of woman to stir his animal instincts . . . so why were those instincts stirring? Stirring to the point of an embarrassing display—thank God the flickering candlelight hid as much as it illuminated.

And if Clorinda thought Anne a meek little mouse she did not know her cousin very well. "I am betrothed to Lady Anne, madam. I will not be gobbling"—he coughed, feeling his misguided manhood leaping at the thought of anything dealing with his mouth and Lady Anne's person—"I am not a threat to your cousin. On the contrary, my duty is to protect her."

She hit him again, this time with her fan. He stepped back another pace.

"Very nicely said, sir, but you and I both know this betrothal is all a humbug. Astounding that such a skilled flirt as the King of Hearts would be caught stealing a kiss from a dusty old spinster, a woman so firmly on the shelf she's become part of the woodwork, but I suppose stranger things have happened. It's very kind of you to try to guard Anne's reputation."

"It is not kindness, madam." His voice rose. How dare the woman call Anne an old spinster? "It is my duty and my pleasure."

Clorinda snorted. "Pleasure? Come, come, sir. You'll

find your pleasure elsewhere, I don't doubt." This time she hit her own hand with her fan, slapping it against her palm, as she appeared to mull the problem over.

Blast it, did she think he was just like so many of the other society men?

Of course she did. She knew him only by his bloody nickname. She didn't know *him* at all.

"I would be remiss in my duties if I did not point out what should be obvious, Mr. Parker-Roth. While Anne has far more years in her dish than a normal debutante, this is, in a way, her come-out as much as Evie's. Not that she's looking for a handsome, titled husband, of course. That would be ridiculous. But the truth is she has never experienced a London Season, and I worry she'll be so caught up in the excitement and, well, magic of the balls and whatnot that she'll lose her good sense. In short, I fear she may be susceptible to your charms." She snorted. "Well, truly, what woman isn't?"

Zeus, was he blushing? Surely not.

"However, in the normal course of events, she'd be in no danger of having her heart bruised. She could admire you from afar with the rest of the silly geese and none would be the wiser. But because of this bizarre betrothal, her name will be linked with yours, and she'll likely spend some time in your company—tonight's invitation to Lord Kenderly's is a prime example."

Clorinda shook her head sadly and sighed. "I am very much afraid dear Anne might be in danger of losing her heart to you, sir. When you call off the betrothal after the Season, it will be a severe blow to her, even though she should know better."

The anger that had been growing in his gut with each of Clorinda's words turned to cold rage. He'd admit he was confused. He didn't know or understand how he felt. But he knew this without question—Anne was not the pitiful figure Clorinda described.

Too many words struggled to be said. He swallowed. He was not going to show his heart, whatever it contained, to this woman, but at least he could state the obvious. "Madam, an honorable man does not break a betrothal."

"Oh, yes, I know that. Of course, I will prevail upon Anne to end it. Or if she won't listen to me, she'll listen to her father. You don't have to worry you'll be trapped. I'm only asking you to take care not to injure poor Anne too deeply."

Stephen pressed his lips together. He'd swear he couldn't remember ever being so angry. He wanted to shake Clorinda so hard her ugly purple turban tumbled off her head. He wanted—

"Heavens!" Clorinda's eyes grew wide and her jaw dropped. She was staring up the stairs.

He followed her gaze. There on the landing stood Lady Evie. Celeste had done an excellent job with her gown. It was appropriately virginal, not too plain, but not too fussy, and it highlighted Evie's ethereal beauty perfectly. He'd wager many a male head would turn when Evie walked into Damian's ballroom.

He noted all that without thought, taking in the details in one glance. Then his eyes moved on to the cause of Clorinda's shock.

Heavens indeed—or would that be Heaven? Anne was . . . hell, she was out and out spectacular. The red gown hugged instead of hid her curves—her lovely hips, her narrow waist, her small but tempting breasts. Her hair had been dressed so it appeared to be on the verge of tumbling over her creamy neck and shoulders. She looked like a flame come to life.

He'd been mistaken—he did feel lust for Anne. Pure, hot lust hit him in the gut—well, perhaps not exactly the gut.

He finally turned his attention to Anne's face. Hmm.

Her sweet full lips were drawn into a tight, narrow line; her cheeks glowed with something more than the effects of the gown's splendid color; and her lovely eyes were full of green fire.

They met his, almost shooting sparks the length of the staircase. His wonderful Anne was furious. He was in for a fight.

He repressed a smile. How fortunate that he loved this kind of battle.

Anne was so angry she could spit. No, she wanted to fly down these stairs and kick the bloody King of Hearts in exactly the place it would hurt him most.

So an honorable man didn't break a betrothal he didn't want? So Clorinda or her father would prevail upon her to end it?

So silly, naïve Anne, poor old spinster, might lose her heart to London's darling?

"I'm sure Mr. Parker-Roth doesn't want to get out of the betrothal," Evie whispered. "Cousin Clorinda has no idea what she's talking about."

Anne didn't yet trust herself to speak.

"I think the man looks quite smitten," Evie said. "You must not regard Clorinda's remarks."

"Oh, I don't." Anne had finally found her voice. It was tighter than she would have liked, but at least she wasn't crying. "You go first, Evie. We shouldn't keep everyone waiting."

"Yes. All right." Evie gave her a searching look before she began to descend the stairs.

Poor silly spinster Anne took a sustaining breath, straightened her spine, and lifted her chin. She would not be an object of pity, especially in the damn King of Hearts's eyes.

She felt rather exposed in this blasted gown, but she

would brazen it out. She would force herself not to cringe when people looked at her. She'd managed it ten years ago.

When she'd got home from Baron Gedding's house party, she'd been certain everyone could immediately discern her fallen state. She'd hidden herself away, laughingly easy to do with Georgiana's painfully pregnant condition and then with the birth of the twins. No one questioned that she was needed at home; no one expected her to attend assemblies or other social gatherings. She had Evie and the boys to care for.

By the time the household was back on an even keel, she'd managed to construct a public mask she could hide behind. She hadn't forgotten how to don it. She settled her features into a pleasant, neutral expression and followed Evie down the stairs.

Unfortunately, her old mask hadn't had to contend with the King of Hearts. The annoying man kept his eyes glued to her, his lips curved into a small, almost feral smile. She felt his look in a most embarrassing section of her body.

She also felt her damn skirts caressing her legs with each step. She held them up slightly, but she couldn't hold them completely away from her body. She had a shift on, for God's sake, but Lady Celeste had made it so it might as well be nonexistent for all the help it was providing her at the moment.

By the time she reached the bottom of the stairs, her emotions were a roiling mass of anger, shame, and . . . something she couldn't identify. Mr. Parker-Roth was still watching her in a very hot, intent way. He clearly wanted her. Not for marriage—he hadn't denied he'd be happy for Clorinda or Papa to make her cry off— but for something.

And what did she want him for?

Her nipples tightened at the thought. Dear God, they

weren't making little tents in her dress, were they? She'd thought this new corset was cut scandalously low. She kept herself from looking down to check only through the strictest willpower while she ordered her wayward thoughts to behave as a proper spinster's should.

They refused. Perhaps it had something to do with this sinful gown—and Mr. Parker-Roth's very sinful eyes, so full of temptation—but part of her anger seemed to have been transmuted into some other very odd, very strong, very *hot* emotion. Something she'd never felt before.

Was this lust?

"Don't you think that dress is a bit, a bit . . ." Clorinda frowned. "It is definitely not in your usual style."

Anne flushed, but whether it was from Clorinda's comment or Mr. Parker-Roth's eyes or her own growing heat, she couldn't say. "Thank you, Clorinda. Since my usual style is brown and shapeless, I will take that as a compliment."

"Anne's dress is beautiful, Cousin Clorinda." Evie sounded most indignant on her behalf. "And it looks beautiful on her."

"It certainly will attract a lot of attention. Are you sure you want that, Anne?" Clorinda's tone left no doubt that Anne should definitely not want it.

Anne shrugged—and felt the satin slip over her nipples. "I can't control what the silly *ton* chooses to look at. I like the dress." The only attention she wanted was Mr. Parker-Roth's, and she was getting a lot of it at the moment. He'd taken her hand and was raising it to his lips.

Damn the fashion for wearing gloves. His mouth touched the soft kid on the back of her hand—no kissing the air above for him—but kidskin was not as expert at transferring sensation as bare skin. Still, the pressure of his lips on her hand quite took her breath—and any coherent thought that had managed to form in the puddle that was her brain—away.

She studied his bowed head. What *did* she want him for? He was hers, in a manner of speaking, until the end of the Season.

Her blush must now be as bright as her dress.

"Anne's gown is exquisite," Mr. Parker-Roth said, "though nowhere near as lovely as the lady who wears it."

Hobbes presented their coats, and Mr. Parker-Roth left her to assist Clorinda, who looked a bit like she'd bitten into a lemon, and Evie.

When he returned to help her, he somehow made the simple task of putting on her cape tantalizing. He stood a little closer to her than quite proper and extended his hands farther, bringing the cloth all the way to her throat instead of merely settling it over her. Then his fingers smoothed the fabric over her shoulders, causing her heart—and another part of her anatomy— to throb.

Her head told her to ignore these hot feelings; her body told her to enjoy them—and look for more.

He put her hand on his arm and covered her fingers with his. His touch felt both protective and possessive.

"Shall we go?" he said, turning to look at Clorinda and Evie. Anne had to swallow a giggle. The other ladies were gaping at him. Evie appeared delighted; Clorinda, incredulous.

"Mr. Parker-Roth," Clorinda said, "I thought we understood each other."

Mr. Parker-Roth inclined his head. "I believe I understand you, Miss Strange, but I sincerely doubt you understand me."

"Well!" Clorinda looked at Anne. "I warn you, miss. Be careful of wolves in sheep's clothing."

"Of course, Clorinda," Anne said, though the way

she was feeling at the moment, perhaps Mr. Parker-Roth was the one who should take care.

The man laughed. "No one has ever accused me of resembling a sheep, Miss Strange."

Clorinda drew in a sharp breath, her nostrils quivering with offended sensibility. "You are impertinent, sir." She straightened her turban and sniffed. "Come, we should be going. We don't want to keep Lord and Lady Kenderly waiting." She turned on her heel and sailed out the door Hobbes was holding open.

Evie gave Anne a significant look—not that Anne could decipher its significance—and followed Clorinda, leaving her alone in the entryway with Hobbes and Mr. Parker-Roth.

She came back to earth with a proverbial thud. What was she thinking? She was furious with Clorinda, but she had to admit her cousin had a point. Much as she might try to play at being a seductress, she was at heart a country mouse—currently with her fingers on a wolf's arm. If she didn't take care, she'd be an appetizer for his next meal.

She jerked her hand back. No luck. His grasp was gentle, but unbreakable.

"Will you let me go?" she hissed, trying to free herself again while throwing a furtive glance at Hobbes. The butler was doing an excellent impression of a deaf and dumb doorpost.

The annoying Mr. Parker-Roth smiled. "No," he said. His smile widened to a grin. "Never."

She rolled her eyes. "Don't be ridiculous. I . . . You . . ." She wanted to expound on his duplicity in pretending to care for her when they both knew this betrothal was a hoax, but she restrained herself.

"I'm not being ridiculous, Anne. I would be delighted to explain to you in detail"—he treated her to an especially heated look—"here and now how I feel about you, but I don't believe Clorinda's patience or Hobbes's very proper stoicism can survive that conversation."

She glanced back at Hobbes. The tips of his ears were bright red.

"We will just have to have that discussion later, in a more private setting. Don't you agree, Hobbes?"

Hobbes's cheeks bloomed to match his ears, but he smiled and nodded nonetheless. "Indeed, sir. An excellent notion."

"Hobbes!"

"Now, Lady Anne, don't be silly," Hobbes said. "And don't listen to Miss Strange."

"See? Hobbes is a very wise man."

Anne knew her jaw had dropped again. If she kept up this way, she could hire herself out as a fly trap. "But—"

Clorinda's voice came wafting in from the carriage, "Will you two hurry up? We don't have all night."

"Very true." Mr. Parker-Roth urged her forward. "I'll bring the ladies home safely, Hobbes."

"Very good, sir."

Mr. Parker-Roth waved off the footman as they approached the carriage and offered Anne his own hand to mount the steps. She took it, but stopped when she looked inside the coach. Damn. Now she realized the significance of Evie's look. The traitor had taken the seat next to Clorinda, leaving the opposite bench—the very narrow bench—free for Anne and Mr. Parker-Roth.

"Have you grown roots, my love?" she heard Mr. Parker-Roth say from behind and then she felt his large male hand on her derriere. His palm, four fingers, and thumb burned straight through to her skin.

"In you go." He gave her a little push. "Clorinda wishes to be on her way."

She scrambled over to the far corner, squeezing herself into it to leave Mr. Parker-Roth the lion's—or, in this case, wolf's—share of the bench.

It was a wasted effort. Mr. Parker-Roth sat as close as possible to her. Any closer and he'd be sitting in her lap.

"Are you making room for someone else?" she muttered as the carriage lurched into motion.

He leaned even closer. "Pardon?"

She gave him a little nudge with her elbow. "You are crowding me, sir."

He gave her a lazy smile and placed her fingers on his thigh! She would have snatched them right back, but they were, once again, trapped under the warm weight of his hand.

She'd never touched a man's thigh before, even Brentwood's.

There had been very little touching with Brentwood. A brush of hands, a stolen kiss—and then that disastrous morning, when, with barely a greeting and no kiss at all, he'd tossed her skirts up and done *that* to her. Thank God no one had come upon them.

She wouldn't think of it. She *couldn't* think of it. All her attention was focused on the muscular male thigh under her fingers. It was so hard and warm.

Evie grinned, arching her brows as if to say *I told you so.*

Cousin Clorinda glared, first at their hands and then at Mr. Parker-Roth's face. The gentleman gazed blandly back.

"Sir, I am not accustomed to such scandalous behavior."

"There is nothing scandalous about our behavior, Miss Strange. Anne is my betrothed, and we are in the privacy of my carriage. I am merely holding her hand, not making wild, passionate love to her."

Anne could not be the only one to blush furiously at that statement, though to give Cousin Clorinda her due, the woman seemed more annoyed than embarrassed.

Mr. Parker-Roth shrugged; he was so close, she felt his shoulders move. "And who is to spread the unremarkable tale? You?"

"Of course not." Clorinda favored them with another glare and then sniffed, turning her attention to the window.

Anne stared out the window, too, and tried to ignore the man next to her.

She failed miserably. He was now drawing lazy circles with his thumb on her palm. She closed her eyes to better concentrate on the sensation. Mmm. She shivered.

He leaned closer again, his weight pressing her against the carriage wall. "Cold, sweetheart?" His whisper teased her ear.

"N-no." She cleared her throat. "No." She was not cold; she was hot—very, very hot. And embarrassingly damp.

The carriage hit a bump, and the seductive devil braced himself—totally unnecessarily, she was sure—against the wall on her side of the carriage. She had a very close look at his waistcoat and cravat. His scent—shaving soap and linen and man—filled the air around her. She shivered again.

"Are you sure you aren't cold?" He righted himself, a task that for some odd reason required him to slide his hand over her lap. "I could put my arm around you, if you like." His eyes—his very blue eyes that were only inches away—laughed at her.

"Will you sit back? You are smothering me."

"My apologies."

He did sit back then, but his thigh was still touching hers. It rubbed and pressed against her with every bump—and there were countless bumps. She'd not noted before how uneven the London streets were.

The odd, hot feeling was growing in her again. Her nipples were hard; her breasts, sensitive; and the place between her thighs was damp and achy. She needed his—

No! She drew in a sharp breath. She never wanted anyone to touch her *there* again. Once had been more than enough. It had been painful and messy and embarrassing.

"Are we almost there?" She suspected Mr. Seducer Parker-Roth had instructed his coachman to take the long way to Kenderly House—most likely by way of Yorkshire.

He smiled at her, a private, sly smile that only increased the annoying need in her. She'd wager all her pin money the fellow knew exactly how she felt.

"Yes. In fact, I believe the coach is slowing now."

Thank God! Anne tried to keep her relief from showing on her face.

"Well, it's about time." Clorinda didn't bother to hide *her* relief. "I thought we would never arrive." She fixed Mr. Parker-Roth with a penetrating gaze as the footman opened the carriage door and let down the steps. "I hope you know what you are about, sir."

"Oh, I do." Mr. Parker-Roth's voice was cool and firm. He stepped out to help the ladies.

Anne took her first deep breath since she'd entered the coach. She hadn't been this agitated since the damn house party. When she'd come home from that devastating visit, she'd felt so stupid and so . . . dirty. She'd felt as if everyone had been laughing at her, Brentwood included. All the other girls had seen what Brentwood was; they'd avoided him. But she hadn't. She'd been the only silly idiot—

No, she wouldn't berate herself. That was one of the terms of the peace she'd made. There could be no looking back. She'd accepted her . . . mistake and its consequences. She'd stopped dreaming of a husband and children.

Except, apparently, she hadn't.

"Anne, love," Mr. Parker-Roth said from the carriage door, "are you going to sit in my coach all night?" He grinned—she could see the whiteness of his teeth in the darkness. "I could climb back in and show you all the lovely things we could do there, if you like. It would surely scandalize your sister and cousin and it would most likely be outside even a liberal interpretation of acceptable conduct between betrothed, but I'm game if you are."

She repressed the tiny voice that suggested she call his bluff and propelled herself toward the door. "Oh, no. We don't want to keep Lord and Lady Kenderly waiting."

He took her hand and held it, looking directly into her eyes, his face surprisingly serious. "Anne, I don't give a damn about Lord and Lady Kenderly's convenience, and their party can go on without us with my blessing."

"Oh." Her heart thudded in her chest. He really wouldn't take her back inside the carriage and show her all those . . . things, would he?

He looked like he definitely would.

Chapter 9

Anne's hand trembled in his grasp. She looked both horrified . . . and tempted. He was a beast to tease her, but he couldn't help himself. He was too damn happy.

He'd been attracted to her even in her ugly dress and bonnet, and he'd certainly admired her mind and personality, but it was a great pleasure—and relief—to feel consuming lust for the woman he was compelled to wed.

He turned her hand over and pressed a kiss to her palm, grinning when he heard her quick intake of breath. She was so unspoiled and responsive—such a change from the experienced widows he was used to. "That is just the first of many kisses I plan to give you tonight," he whispered.

Her eyes widened.

"Will you two hurry up?" Clorinda's voice came from Kenderly's doorstep. "We can't be announced until you join us."

"But unfortunately," he murmured, "it appears I shall not be allowed to give them to you in my oh-so-comfortable carriage."

"Of course not!" Anne was sputtering again, full of delightful outrage.

He'd best not tell her now about Damian's garden. It had a number of splendidly leafy, dark bowers, perfect for private . . . conversations. He'd taken several widows out to explore the secluded spots over the years, but this time would be different. This time he'd be taking his betrothed. He would kiss her thoroughly, and then give her the ring that was currently burning a hole in his pocket.

"Mr. Parker-Roth, please," Clorinda said. "We are waiting."

"And not very patiently, eh?" he said to Anne. She choked on what might have been a giggle as he helped her down the steps and placed her hand firmly on his arm. "Here we are. You may knock, Fredrick," he told his footman.

Fredrick, the impudent fellow, grinned before plying the brass knocker.

Huntington, Damian's butler, opened the door almost immediately—he'd likely been waiting on the other side, wondering what was taking them so long—and bowed. "Mr. Parker-Roth, ladies, please come in."

Huntington handed their things to a footman and preceded them to Damian's drawing room. Lady Kenderly—Jo—came over the moment they were announced, towing along a mustachioed, bespectacled, white-haired man.

"How lovely to see you again, Stephen," she said. "I'm so glad you could come."

He bowed, grinning at her. "Thank you for including us at the last minute."

"I am delighted to add your friends to our group." She nodded to the man at her side. "May I introduce Lord Ramsey? Miss Strange, I believe you are already acquainted with the baron."

"Yes, indeed," Clorinda said. "Dickie and I have known—and argued with—each other for years." She sniffed. "I would say we disagree on every ornithological issue."

"Not every one, surely," Lord Ramsey said.

Clorinda raised an eyebrow. "We cannot even agree on what we disagree about."

Ramsey laughed. "Surely you can agree you'd rather discuss birds than the bird-brained goings on of the *ton*?"

"Well . . ." Clorinda was obviously struggling with her desire to disagree and her dedication to the truth. "Perhaps."

"No doubt about it. Party's an insufferable bore—if you'll pardon my saying so, Lady Kenderly. I wouldn't be here if the invitation were from anyone but your husband, the earl. If you'll excuse me and Miss Strange?"

"Of course."

"I don't know that I agreed to go converse with you, Dickie. You're being a bit highhanded—as usual."

Lord Ramsey took Clorinda's arm. "You always were one to bite off your nose to spite your face, Clorinda. Do put aside your fussing and let me tell you about my great tits. I have quite a flock of them on my property."

"I don't know why I should be interested in your tits," Clorinda said, but she allowed herself to be led away to a quiet corner.

"It would be nice if those two made a match of it," Jo said, watching them go.

"Do you think so?" Evie wrinkled her brow. "Wouldn't they just fight all the time?"

"Ah, but sometimes the making up is worth it." Jo glanced across the room at her husband.

"I wouldn't think Cousin Clorinda would give any male without wings and feathers a second glance."

"Anne!" Evie stared at her sister in surprise.

Anne flushed. "Oh, please excuse me. My wretched tongue. I should not have said that."

"But it's true." Stephen laughed. "Or at least, I would have wagered on it until this moment."

"No, I think you are right," Jo said, shaking her head. "Lord Ramsey's been a widower for three years now; if he'd had any interest in acquiring another wife, I imagine he would have already done so." She shrugged slightly and smiled at them. "I just like to see people paired up, now that I'm happily wed. And speaking of that, how remiss of me." She turned to Anne. "I should have wished you happy the moment we met."

Anne looked like a startled deer. She glanced up at Stephen. Surely she wasn't going to tell Jo they weren't really betrothed?

"Oh, I know you haven't announced it yet—Stephen told us when he asked us to include you tonight. I've already congratulated him." Jo met his eyes. "I'd say he was quite taken with you."

"And you'd be completely correct, Jo."

Jo's smile widened. "Splendid. I confess Damian and I had our concerns—only because it seemed so sudden and the particulars sounded a bit odd—but now I see everything is as it should be. Amazing how one can attain clarity of vision in what seems like only a moment, isn't it, Stephen?"

"Indeed it is." He smiled down at Anne. Now he only had to persuade his prickly beloved to see things his way.

Anne took a sip of wine and surveyed the dinner table. There were eighteen people gathered there—the Marquis of Knightsdale and his wife had been delayed—

and all were good friends of the earl and his countess. Everyone was smiling and in animated conversation. Clorinda and Lord Ramsey sat together down the table, arguing about something avian no doubt, and Evie was chatting with a pleasant looking young man whose name Anne couldn't for the life of her remember.

Sadly she couldn't remember much of the pre-prandial conversation either. Oh, everyone had been very polite and no one had asked her about the rumored betrothal, but they must all have supposed it to be true since she was there. She should have felt at ease, but she hadn't. She'd felt like an imposter.

She *was* an imposter—and if these people discovered her real secret, they would give her the cut direct. Unmarried women who'd misplaced their virginity were not good *ton*.

And if Stephen found out . . . She closed her eyes.

With Brentwood in London, the question wasn't "if" but "when."

The butler appeared at the dining room door. "Lord and Lady Knightsdale have arrived, my lord."

"Splendid." Lord Kenderly and all the men stood as the couple entered. "So glad you could make it."

"My apologies, Kenderly. One of the children wasn't feeling well, and Emma wished to be certain everything was in order before we left."

"I hope it's nothing serious," Lady Kenderly said.

"Oh, no." Lady Knightsdale smiled as she took her seat. "Just a slight fever. Our older son had it first and now it is moving through the family. Nurse has everything well in hand, but of course I still worry."

"Of course." Lord Kenderly gestured around the table. "I believe everyone is known to you, except perhaps for Lady Anne Marston and her sister, Lady Evangeline, Lord Crane's daughters. They just arrived in London yesterday; we were delighted they could join us."

"My pleasure," Lord Knightsdale said, bowing, but his lady did not look so pleased. She frowned at Anne before turning to speak to Lord Westbrooke.

"I don't believe Lady Knightsdale cares much for me," Anne whispered to Mr. Parker-Roth who was sitting on her right.

"Oh, don't mind Emma," he said, taking a swallow of wine. "She can be somewhat fierce if she thinks her family is endangered, but she has a heart of gold."

"Emma?" Anne darted another glance at the woman and then darted her eyes back to Mr. Parker-Roth when she saw the marchioness was looking at her again. "How is it you are on such close terms with Lady Knightsdale?"

The annoying man grinned. "Never say you're jealous!"

She felt herself flush. "Of course not. I'm just surprised, though I suppose I shouldn't be. You obviously move in the first circles."

Mr. Parker-Roth laughed. "Oh, I don't know Emma from Town. Her sister is married to my brother."

"Oh." That was right. She remembered the account of the scandal in last year's papers.

"Unfortunately, that connection is enough for her to take an interest in me. I'm certain she'll approach us at the ball to ask pointed questions about the betrothal rumors—and she won't be quite as polite as everyone else. But Knightsdale will rein her in."

"Ah." Lovely. Perhaps Anne could manage to hide in the retiring room all evening—but then who would keep an eye on Evie? The way Clorinda had her head next to Lord Ramsey's, it didn't look as if she would be taking on that responsibility.

"I don't believe I've seen you in London before,

Lady Anne." The Duke of Alvord, on her left, claimed her attention. "Surely this can't be your first trip to Town?"

"But it is, your grace." The Duke of Alvord was one of the most powerful men in England, yet Anne had liked him and his American-born wife the moment they were introduced. His amber gaze held intelligence and humor.

"You didn't have a come-out?"

"No. My stepmother was increasing with my twin brothers when I should have come to London." It was a good excuse, and one she'd given so many times it slipped from her tongue with ease. It was true—to a point. If she'd insisted, Papa would have had some female relative bring her out. His sister, Lady Farrington, had offered. But Anne hadn't wanted to go to Town, and Papa hadn't pressed the matter. "And once the babies were born, I was needed to help with them and Evie."

"I see." The duke's gaze was thoughtful. "Are you looking forward to taking your bows now?"

"Oh, I plan to stay very much in the background, your grace. This is my sister's come-out, not mine."

The duke grinned at her. "Pardon me for bringing it to your attention, Lady Anne, but you will never be successful at fading into the background. Your beauty and your betrothal to the King of Hearts here will make you the center of much interest."

"Oh." Her cheeks flamed yet again. She felt Mr. Parker-Roth's hand cover hers under the table and give her fingers a comforting squeeze.

The duke looked puzzled. "Have I spoken out of turn? I do apologize, but the news of your betrothal was all over White's this afternoon. I didn't think it a secret." He shrugged, smiling. "The truth is, if it was supposed to be a secret, it's not any longer."

"Exactly." Mr. Parker-Roth looked down at her, giving her hand another surreptitious squeeze. "We'd planned to wait until Anne's father came home to make a formal announcement, but that was before Lady Dunlee spotted us. There's no point now in waiting as everyone *does* know. I'll send a notice to the papers when I get home tonight."

The papers! Anne's heart clenched, and black specks danced before her eyes. To have this pretend engagement appear in black and white in every breakfast room in Mayfair, by every cup of chocolate or coffee or tea . . . The scandal would be tremendous when they called it off, even if they waited until the Season was over.

No. A heavy chill settled in her stomach. Not the end of the Season. She was forgetting Brentwood. Once he read the announcement, he'd reveal her secret.

Oh, dear God, she'd become a joke. Her name would be bandied about in all the gentlemen's clubs. Lewd prints would appear in the shop windows. Everyone would turn from her in disgust. Everyone— especially Mr. Parker-Roth.

She tried to swallow her panic. It would be a relief not to hide her . . . situation any longer. She'd go home and live quietly. Papa wouldn't throw her out—would he? No, of course he wouldn't. He needed her to run the estate.

She just wished there was some way to save Evie's Season.

Mr. Parker-Roth was knocking his knife against his glass to get everyone's attention. He stood, pulling her up beside him. Her knees barely supported her weight.

"Friends, I have an announcement to make." He grinned. "Perhaps it's not much of an announcement as the duke just told us the rumor has already reached

White's, but nevertheless I wish to tell you myself that Lady Anne has agreed to make me the happiest of men."

"A toast," the Marquis of Knightsdale said, getting to his feet. All the other men rose as well. The marquis held up his glass. "To Parker-Roth and Lady Anne— may they find the happiness together we all have found"—he gestured to the married couples at the table—"and, to Lady Anne especially, welcome to my extended—very extended—family."

"Here, here!" Lord Kenderly raised his glass as well, and they all drank.

"A kiss, a kiss," Lord Westbrooke said as soon as he'd swallowed his mouthful of wine. "Give your lady a kiss, Parker-Roth."

"Robbie!" Lady Westbrooke yanked on her husband's coat. "Behave yourself."

"Now, Lizzie, I'm only giving the man an excuse to do exactly what he wants to do." The earl grinned.

"But think of poor Lady Anne's blushes."

Lord Westbrooke shrugged. "She can't get any redder than she is, can she?"

"Robbie!"

"I think your husband has an excellent notion, Lady Westbrooke," Mr. Parker-Roth said.

Everyone laughed, but Anne looked at Mr. Parker-Roth in horror. He wouldn't—would he?

He would. He bent his head and kissed her very gently on the mouth. It was a soft, incredibly sweet touch, and it took her breath away.

Someone—some laughing male—shouted, "Huzza!" and everyone clapped enthusiastically. Mr. Parker-Roth smiled at her, and then she was allowed to collapse, gratefully, back into her seat.

She looked down at her plate so she wouldn't have to meet anyone's eyes. If only she were really betrothed to this man—

But she wasn't.

Lord Kenderly stood. "To save poor Lady Anne further blushes, I will make an announcement of my own, one I know I can trust you all to keep in confidence."

"Aha!" Lord Westbrooke was grinning again. "So you wasted no time, did you?"

"Nor did you, Robbie, if I recall correctly," Lord Knightsdale said.

The duke leaned forward and looked first at Lord Westbrooke and then at Lord Knightsdale. "Could we allow Kenderly to actually make his announcement? Perhaps he merely wishes to tell us he is anticipating a bumper crop of corn this harvest."

"Right," Lord Westbrooke said. "And I'm the Queen of Sheba."

Lord Kenderly held up his hands, laughing. "Gentlemen, peace. Westbrooke is correct in his assumption; Lady Kenderly is indeed in the family way."

Everyone clapped again, and the parents at the table—which seemed to be most everyone—proceeded to offer a quantity of good-natured advice.

Anne forced herself to smile. All the women—except Clorinda and Evie—were about her age, and they all had, or were expecting, children. If she were really betrothed to Mr. Parker-Roth—well, it sounded alarmingly like she *was* betrothed to him, but more to the point, if she were really going to *marry* the man—she could be a mother this time next year.

Oh, God. Pain lanced through her, leaving behind an empty ache. She wanted a baby. She wanted a husband and a family and a home that was her own, not her father's or her stepmother's, but she'd thrown all that away when she'd let Brentwood under her skirts.

Damn it, she'd been only seventeen. She'd made one mistake—a large one, yes, but only one. She shouldn't have to pay for it the rest of her life.

She pretended to laugh at something Lord West-brooke said.

But life wasn't fair; she knew that. She'd thought she'd come to terms with that truth long ago. People made mistakes, and sometimes those mistakes did change their lives. A mother looked the other way and her child ran out to be crushed under a cart's wheels. A man on a horse rushed a gate and came home on a hurdle, dead of a broken neck.

A foolish girl fancied herself in love and broke society's cardinal rule.

It could have been worse. They could have been seen. She could have been forced to marry Brentwood. Living with him, sharing his bed, day after day, year after year, would be a far worse life than the one she had now.

She heard Mr. Parker-Roth laugh, felt his touch under the table, and wished . . .

No. She would not wish for what couldn't be.

"It's very crowded, isn't it?" There was a note of trepidation in Evie's voice.

Stephen was standing in Kenderly's ballroom with Anne and Evie at his side. Clorinda, ceding her chaperone duties completely to Anne, had secluded herself with Lord Ramsey behind a bank of potted palms to continue their discussion of great tits, black-tailed godwits, and other feathered subjects.

"All the better," Anne said. "You'll meet so many eligible men tonight, Evie. I'm sure you won't sit out a single set." Anne sounded confident, but the look she gave him was worried.

"Your sister is quite right, Evie." He had little doubt the girl would take. She was beautiful and an earl's daughter, even though the earl was Crazy Crane. Perhaps most importantly tonight, however, she was a favored guest of Lord and Lady Kenderly. "You'll be a great success."

Evie's wide smile made her even more beautiful. "You really think so?"

"I do indeed. We just have to find you your first partner, and then the men will be lining up behind him. Your feet will ache from dancing by the end of the night." He looked around the room. It should be easy enough to find a suitable man. There were plenty here to choose from, and more were still pouring into Damian's ballroom. Jo should be very pleased. Her first society gathering was going to be a shocking squeeze.

Davenport had chatted with Evie during dinner— he'd be an adequate choice. Where had the fellow got to? Ah, there he was, poor man. Lydia Fitzwilliam had already sunk her claws into him. Well, no matter. There were others—

Damn. Emma was coming their way, Knightsdale in tow. It had been a great piece of luck one of her children had taken sick—not that he wished the youngster ill, of course, but not having to face Emma before dinner had been a blessing. He'd known it was too much to hope she'd leave them alone all evening— she'd thrown Anne so many pointed looks across the dining room table, she likely upset the poor girl's digestion. Anne *had* looked a bit peaked by the end of the meal.

"Hallo, Emma; Knightsdale," he said.

Emma barely glanced at him, though Knightsdale gave him a commiserating look.

"Lady Evangeline, Lady Anne," Emma said, "I'm so sorry we didn't have an opportunity to chat before dinner." Emma addressed both Crane's daughters, but her attention was solely on Anne.

"And I was so sorry to hear one of your children is ill," Anne said. "I do hope it's nothing serious."

Ah, Anne had made a wise move in mentioning Emma's boys. Surely that must cause her to rise in Emma's estimation.

"Oh, no. A mother is always concerned, of course, but Henry—that's our second son—is a hardy little fellow and usually weathers these things better than Charlie, his older brother."

"That's a blessing," Anne said, nodding. "I've noticed the same thing with my twin brothers—illnesses always affect one more than the other."

"Really?" Emma's eyes brightened. Perhaps she would refrain from discussing anything more alarming than the croup. Stephen began to relax. "You've had charge of your siblings' care?"

"Oh, yes," Evie said, managing to squeeze in a few words. "Mama and Papa are often gone, so Anne has looked after us. She's the best of sisters."

Emma beamed at Anne. "I'm happy to hear it. I raised my sister as well, you know, and I've found the experience helped when I had my own sons, though of course each baby is different, which I'm sure you'll discover, Lady Anne, once you marry Stephen and start a family. And speaking of Stephen"—Stephen snapped back to attention. *Oh, damn, here it comes.*—"I must say your betrothal came as a complete surprise."

Emma turned her gaze to him. "Why didn't you tell us you were considering marriage when we saw you at Jack's christening?"

Stephen looked to Knightsdale for help, but the marquis merely raised an eyebrow. Clearly, Knightsdale smelled a rat. "It wasn't a settled thing then."

"It wasn't?" Emma looked at Anne, who just shook her head. "But you must have had some inkling. That was only a few weeks ago."

"Well, I might have had an inkling, but I wasn't about to share an *inkling* of marriage with my mother."

Of course, he hadn't known Anne existed a few weeks—a few *days*—ago, but he wasn't about to tell Emma that.

"Well, no, I suppose not. But surely you wrote to inform them once it became more than an inkling? We just got a letter from Meg and there wasn't even a whisper of your betrothal in it."

Right. He should post a letter to Mama immediately. "Even if I had, there wouldn't be room for that with all the baby news." He chuckled. "I'd never have believed it if I hadn't witnessed it myself, but I do think my brother has finally discovered something that's of more interest to him than his beloved plants."

Emma was not buying his theory. "Oh, I know Meg would have squeezed in a mention of something this extraordinary. Even a new baby can't completely distract from the betrothal of one's brother-in-law, especially a brother-in-law known far and wide as the King of Hearts." She smiled at Evie. "But I imagine you knew all about the engagement, Lady Evangeline. Women are so much more forthcoming than men."

Evie shook her head. "Oh, no, Anne hadn't breathed a word about it to me, though I suppose it's possible she'd mentioned it to Papa and Mama. I only found out about it when we reached London. It was quite a shock." She paused and seemed to think perhaps her last comment hadn't struck the proper note. "A *pleasant* shock, of course. I am very happy for Anne. She'd never shown any interest in the gentlemen at home, but now I expect that was because of her attachment to Mr. Parker-Roth. They have been in love for years, you know."

Emma's eyebrows disappeared into her coiffure, and Anne's face rivaled her hair and dress for brightest hue. Stephen hoped no one was taking note of them, but he knew better than to bank on that. It was time to bring this uncomfortable conversation to a close.

"And now we are finally betrothed," he said, lifting Anne's hand and kissing it. "I couldn't be happier. I hope you will both wish us well."

"Of course," Knightsdale said. Emma looked as if she'd like to argue, but thank God she kept her tongue between her teeth. The marquis had taken her arm, so perhaps he was exerting a little pressure. "Have you set a date for the nuptials?"

"We thought we'd wait until the Season was over and Lord and Lady Crane have returned," Stephen said. "Isn't that right, my love?"

It took Anne a moment to realize "my love" referred to her. She nodded somewhat weakly.

"Hmm." Knightsdale studied her. She managed to lift her chin and meet his eyes, making his forbidding expression soften somewhat.

"Lady Dunlee has been spreading a rather alarming tale, you know." Emma's eyes shifted between Stephen and Anne as if she couldn't decide which to blame. "She said"—her eyes slid over to take in Evie, and she pressed her lips together. "She said she witnessed an inappropriate degree of warmth between you and Lady Anne, Stephen, on a public square."

Knightsdale covered his wife's hand. "I don't believe Parker-Roth's behavior is really our concern, Emma." The gaze he directed at Stephen, however, clearly delivered the message that if any of Stephen's actions cut up Emma's peace, Stephen would pay the price.

Stephen looked back at him, but it took some effort. He was used to standing up to strong men—plant hunters had to deal with difficult and dangerous fellows routinely—but the marquis was especially intimidating. This particular expression was one he must have cultivated as a captain in the army, before his brother's death catapulted him into the marquisate.

"It *is* our concern. He's Meg's brother-in-law."

"Yes, but I hazard to guess Meg would not thank you for meddling, my dear." Knightsdale let his eyes linger another moment on Stephen. "Parker-Roth is fully aware of his responsibilities, I'm sure."

"Of course," Stephen said. "You can rest easy, Emma." He smiled somewhat bitterly. "I really am not a care-for-nobody, you know."

Emma flushed. "No, of course you aren't. I didn't mean to suggest . . . well, I suppose I may have suggested, but I didn't . . . that is, I apologize if I gave offense." Emma smiled at Anne. "You are quite fortunate in your choice, Lady Anne. I do not wish to give you a false impression."

"No, ah, you didn't." Anne glanced up at Stephen and smiled. "Er, thank you."

"And to make our family gathering complete," Knightsdale said, "I do believe I see Nicholas approaching."

"Nicholas?" Stephen turned and grinned as he saw his brother wending his way through the crowd. Splendid. He could foist Evie off on Nick once the music started. "My valet must have directed him here." He stepped forward to intercept him.

"Hallo, Stephen," Nick said. "Have you heard the wild tales circulating about you? Lady Dunlee apparently saw you kiss—ow! You trod on my foot, you oaf!"

"Exactly," Stephen hissed. "And I'll stomp on it again if you don't show some sense. Open your eyes, you nodcock."

"What? I don't—oh." Nick finally looked over Stephen's shoulder.

"Yes, oh." Stephen turned and drew his brother into

the circle. "Lady Anne, Lady Evangeline, may I present my scapegrace younger brother, Nicholas?"

Nick nodded at Lady Anne, and then stared at Evie. At least his eyes didn't start from his head. He even managed a credible bow. "My pleasure, ladies. Knightsdale, Emma, good to see you again."

"Lady Anne is my betrothed, Nick; her sister, Lady Evangeline—Evie—is making her come-out."

Nick managed to tear his eyes from Evie to goggle at Stephen. "I'm sorry." Nick laughed and shook his head. "I thought you said Lady Anne was your betrothed."

"I did."

Nick's jaw dropped, damn it. Stephen heard Knightsdale muffle his laughter.

"So it's a surprise to you, too, Nicholas?" Emma asked.

Nick transferred his gaze to Emma. "Rather." He moved his foot as if he feared Stephen would stomp on it again and swiveled his eyes to Anne. "But I'm delighted to welcome you as a new sister, Lady Anne"— his eyes went back to Evie—"and to become better acquainted with your family."

The orchestra was finally tuning its instruments. The dancing would start in a moment.

"Nick," Stephen said, "I believe Lady Evangeline is in need of a partner."

"What a coincidence," Nick said. "So am I." He bowed to Evie. "Would you care to stand up with me for the opening set, Lady Evangeline?"

Evie laughed shyly. "I would be honored to, sir."

"And I would ask you to join me, Lady Anne," Knightsdale said, "but I suspect Stephen here would take issue with that."

"Precisely, Knightsdale. Very astute of you." He laid Anne's hand on his arm. He was eager to partner her—and very uneager to partner Emma, which would be his fate if Knightsdale made off with Anne. He did not wish to spend the set dancing around Emma's questions as well as the ballroom.

He led Anne onto the floor, trying to ignore the stares and whispers. He hoped the musicians would play a waltz. He would very much like to waltz with Anne, but he wished it could be somewhere more secluded.

He smiled down at her as they waited for the set to begin. He'd have his secluded time with her. Once this set was over, he'd take her out into the garden, into one of Damian's leafy bowers. He'd kiss her and then he'd slip his ring on her finger, making this betrothal official.

He could hardly wait.

Chapter 10

The orchestra began the opening strains of a waltz and Anne's stomach sank—before it leapt into her throat as she felt Mr. Parker-Roth's arm slip around her back.

She looked up at him as she placed her hand on his shoulder. She could see the very faint shadow of his beard and the sweeping curve of his lashes over his clear blue eyes; she breathed in his scent, a mix of wine and soap, linen and man; she felt the strength of his arm and the broad solidity of his shoulder.

She'd been closer to him the times he'd kissed her, but in some odd way this seemed almost more intimate, perhaps because they were in public, with everyone watching them. As they moved through the opening steps, the music wove its magic around her, heightening her feeling that she'd stepped into a fairy tale with a happily-ever-after ending.

She had to say something, anything, to break this hot, drugging spell. Her voice wavered slightly.

"I should warn you I've never waltzed in company." Damn. She shouldn't have said that, but it was true. Worse, she'd never waltzed with a man before. The only time she'd performed the dance was at home, helping Evie learn the steps. Waltzing with Mr. Parker-Roth was a very different experience. He was so much taller and larger and harder than she. "I will probably tread all over your feet."

Mr. Parker-Roth chuckled. "I'm willing to risk it. You're doing fine."

It was a wonder she was, she was so on edge. "I suspect your toes haven't been flattened only because you are an excellent dancer."

The right corner of his mouth turned up in a half smile. "Oh, no, I assure you I've had my feet trampled by any number of society misses." He turned her so his hand slid over her back to her waist and she sucked in her breath. "Why haven't you waltzed before, Anne?" One of his brows rose skeptically. "Don't tell me the waltz wasn't danced in your neighborhood, because I won't believe you. Most of the *ton* haven't considered it scandalous for years. Even the patronesses at Almack's approved it long ago."

She flushed. The waltz *had* been considered too shocking ten years ago, the last time she'd danced in public. "The waltz is danced at home, just not by me."

"Why not?"

Why wouldn't he let the subject be? He must be able to discern she didn't wish to discuss it. She glanced at the other dancers and saw Evie smiling up at Nicholas. Her heart swelled with pride, distracting her for a moment from her own problems. Evie was so beautiful tonight, she was sure to be a success. It was almost worth all the worry and discomfort to see her shining in a London ballroom.

"Why not?" Mr. Parker-Roth asked again. "You aren't lame or disabled; quite the contrary. You have natural grace. You're a beautiful woman. You must be very popular at home."

The man was incredibly persistent. "I was very

popular with the hostesses. They counted on me to keep the older guests company."

"So you were nursemaid to the ancients? Did you enjoy hob-nobbing with the deaf and toothless?"

"No. I mean yes." She laughed. "You are being intentionally difficult. No, I wasn't a nursemaid at all. I was happy to be helpful—and, yes, I did enjoy the rational conversation of the more mature members of our society."

"Hmm." His eyes captured hers—she had never before appreciated how much eye contact was involved in the waltz. "That still doesn't answer the question of why you weren't waltzing. Surely no hostess would expect you to stay the whole time amongst the elderly, or, even if she did, the men of the neighborhood wouldn't let you languish there."

"But everyone at home knows I don't dance."

"You do dance. You're dancing now."

She wrinkled her nose. "Only to avoid an awkward, likely quite unpleasant, conversation with Lord and Lady Knightsdale."

He inclined his head in acknowledgment of her point. "I grant you, it did seem an excellent time to retreat. Emma can be a dashed terrier if she scents a bit of mystery."

Ha! He could give Lady Knightsdale a few lessons on doggedness himself. "Then I will try to avoid her in the future."

He snorted. "Good luck with that. There's no dodging Emma if she's determined to get to the bottom of something."

Nerves twisted in Anne's gut. The Season was going to be torture with everyone pulling at her. She looked longingly at the chaperone's corner—and noticed all the chaperones were looking back at her and whispering. Was her hem torn? She glanced down to be sure all was in order.

"Emma can be annoying," Mr. Parker-Roth was saying, "but her heart's in the right place, so I generally forgive her." He grinned. "Or leave the country. That's one of the splendid things about my expeditions—I can get away from an overzealous family. If you think Emma is bad, wait until you meet my mother."

Mother? Her nerves exploded into full-blown alarm, crashing up from her stomach to her head and producing a sudden throbbing ache. She hadn't considered his mother.

"Your mother isn't planning to come to Town for the Season, is she?" If she were, Anne swore she'd find some way to flee back to the country. Clorinda would just have to step up and fulfill her duties, or Georgiana and Papa would have to drag themselves back from their blasted antiquities.

"I doubt it, not with a new grandson to dote on. I suspect even her artist friends won't be enough of an attraction to lure her to London this Season. She likely commissioned Nick to purchase all her brushes and paints. He's a bit of an artist, too, so she can trust him to get exactly what she wants."

"Really? I will have to ask him which shops he favors." Dear Lord, it wasn't just the chaperones staring at her, it was everyone. She'd assumed—obviously naïvely—that once the dancing started, people would lose interest in her.

"Do you paint?" Mr. Parker-Roth asked.

"Yes." She would just try to ignore them. "I've no great skill, but I find it relaxing. I particularly enjoy painting flowers and plants."

"Ah. So you have an interest in botany?"

"I do, though I can't say I'm a scholar of the subject." It was hard to ignore the number of females glaring at her as if they'd like to do her an injury. "I've even read some of your travel accounts in *The Gentleman's Magazine*. I think it's a shame—more than a shame—women can't organize their own expeditions."

He laughed. "My mother's friend Agatha Witherspoon and her companion Prudence Doddington-Prinz do—they often go off on foreign jaunts, not that I would recommend it. When we're married, you can come with me, at least until our first child is born." His blue eyes held an oddly possessive, protective look. Her stomach shivered with . . . what?

Not with anticipation of traveling to foreign climes and painting exotic vegetation. Oh, no. It was something else entirely she looked forward to—

Children. His children and hers . . .

But he would be gone, searching for plants all over the world, leaving her in England to raise those children herself. She knew first hand the pain of having parents who were always somewhere else.

The orchestra played the last note. They were near the windows to the gardens. A cool breeze slid over her arms.

"Would you care to stroll outside for a little while, Anne? You look a bit flushed."

She was flushed both from the exertion of the dance and the turmoil of her thoughts. "I shouldn't."

"But will you?" He leaned closer. "We are betrothed."

"No, we're not."

He took her hand and lifted it to his lips. "We are. The announcement will be in all the papers tomorrow."

Damn. How had her life got so out of control so suddenly? "I should look for Evie." She glanced around for her sister and encountered a particularly acid glare coming from a beautiful, raven-haired woman in a dress even redder than her own. The lady looked as if she were deciding how best to separate Anne's head from her shoulders. Heavens! Who was she?

"Evie is fine. There, see? She's talking to Nick; it looks like he's introduced her to one of his Oxford friends." Mr. Parker-Roth put her hand on his arm. "Come, Anne. A stroll in the foliage won't hurt you. It's stuffy in here."

"I already have a heaping serving of scandal on my plate."

"It's not scandalous to go for a stroll outside during a ball. It wouldn't be even if we weren't betrothed."

True, if a stroll was all Mr. Parker-Roth intended, but something about the look—the heat—in his eyes made her think he had other activities planned.

"No, I—" She glanced over at the nasty, dark-haired beauty again. Good. The woman had found another male to interest her. She was talking to—

Brentwood. Oh, dear God.

She grabbed Mr. Parker-Roth's arm and dragged him into the darkness.

Stephen didn't know why Anne had changed her mind about the garden, but he wasn't arguing. He stepped onto the terrace, and relief slid over him with the night breeze. Damn, he'd swear he had a target painted on his back tonight. He'd half expected to feel a knife slice between his shoulder blades during that waltz. He stretched his neck and rolled his shoulders slightly. Even women he hardly knew had been looking daggers at him.

"How refreshing," Anne said. She glanced at the two other couples who'd sought the evening air and almost ran toward the farthest, darkest part of the terrace. Interesting. He followed along in her wake. When she reached the steps to the garden, she hurried down them. Even better.

"Take my arm, Anne. The path can be a bit uneven."

"Oh, yes. Thank you." She looked over her shoulder. Did she fear a stab in the back, too? He'd hoped she hadn't noticed, but she'd been getting any number of killing looks as well.

He covered her hand with his as they strolled down the gravel path. It was quiet here in the garden. Damian had ordered lanterns hung from the trees so his guests wouldn't stumble, but fortunately no one else had yet decided to go exploring. They would be the first—and he knew exactly where he was headed.

The music faded and the garden grew darker the farther they walked from the house.

Anne looked back again and stumbled. He caught her. "Careful."

"Yes, of course. I'm not usually so clumsy. I"—she started to look again, but stopped herself—"I should pay more attention to where I'm putting my feet."

"I won't let any harm come to you, my love." He wouldn't let her fall—and he wouldn't let the harpies hurt her either.

Maria had been the worst. Damn it, she couldn't have expected him to dance attendance on her; he'd ended their connection two months ago, when she'd tried to trap him into marrying her at Baron Greyham's house party.

He still couldn't believe she'd had the effrontery to try such a trick. She'd been a widow for five years. She knew very well how the game was played. She was a complete lunatic if she'd actually thought he'd marry her. Even if he'd had an interest—which he most certainly hadn't—he'd have wagered his yearly income she'd have rejected him. He'd always thought she meant to move up the peerage ladder—poor dead

Noughton had been a mere baron. And her newest flame bore that theory out. Why else would she have taken up with the Marquis of Brentwood?

Now *there* was a match made in hell. Maria was beautiful, but spoiled and demanding; Brentwood was a nasty bully, balding, portly, and sneaky. Maria must have brought him—Damian would never have invited the blackguard. In fact, Damian would not have invited Maria—it was thanks to him and Jo Stephen had escaped her clutches in February. She and Brentwood must have sneaked in.

Damian had let the vegetation grow a little wilder here at the far reaches of his garden. The trees crowded the path so Stephen and Anne had to walk very close together. He grinned as he slipped his arm around her to guide her. He might be the King of Hearts, but Damian was the Prince. The earl knew to a nicety how to create an atmosphere conducive to seduction.

"It was very generous of Lord and Lady Kenderly to include us at the last minute," Anne said. She looked over her shoulder once more.

"They were happy to do so." He directed her down a side path to a delightfully concealing willow tree. "Why do you keep looking behind us?"

"What?" Anne started to look again, but stopped herself. "Oh, er, I was admiring the earl's house. It's so beautiful all lit up with candles, it's almost magical."

He laughed. "You're a terrible liar."

If there'd been enough light, he was certain he'd see a bright flush spread over Anne's face. "I'm not . . . that is, I'm . . . well, it's . . . it *is* very pretty." She turned around to show him and finally realized the view of the house was completely obscured by vegetation. "Oh."

He drew her under the willow. No one could see them now, but enough moonlight filtered through the branches that he could make out her expression. "Are you anxious, dear heart?" He brushed a strand of hair off her forehead. "Don't be. I said I wouldn't let anyone harm you."

She made a noise, something between a gasp and a giggle, and shook her head. She took a quick step back.

"Eep!" She wobbled and started to fall, grabbing for him at the same time he caught her around the waist, hauling her up against his chest.

"Are you all right?"

She clung to him. "Yes," she whispered. "I stepped on my hem." She looked up at him.

Her lips were so close. Her body was plastered up against his, and her light, lemon scent clouded his thoughts. His hands slipped over her satin dress, over her back, her waist, her rounded hips, urging her even closer, settling her against his most insistent ache.

Celeste was a witch. She'd meant to drive him mad with lust when she'd made this garment. She was probably laughing right now, imagining him battling his male urges.

Let Celeste laugh. He had better things to think about.

"Anne," he murmured, brushing her cheek with his lips.

"Ah." He heard her breath catch as he traveled on to her jaw. Her hands slid up his chest to his neck; her body, all soft and feminine, collapsed bonelessly into him. "Oh."

He smiled against her skin, a surge of lust and protectiveness flooding him. She had given up fighting and had put herself in his hands, literally. His heart—and another organ—swelled. He would not betray her trust. He would love her and care for her; wed her and keep her safe; give her children . . .

He buried his face in her hair and inhaled. Mmm. She smelled so good.

He'd always given more thought to *not* having children than having them. He'd taken scrupulous care that none of his pleasant liaisons led to progeny. But when he joined with Anne . . .

The obvious part of him throbbed at that thought, eager to get to the joining immediately.

He nuzzled the warm place where her jaw ended right below her ear, reveling in the drugging scent of her skin and hair, listening to her small, breathy gasps. She moved against him, pressing her hips more tightly against his erection. He was going to explode.

He couldn't lay her down here in Damian's garden, but, Zeus, he wanted to. If they were already married, he'd slip out the back gate and hurry home to bed with her. But they weren't married, not yet. He needed to show some patience—he needed to find some control.

He moved down her throat to where her neck met her shoulder. She tilted her head to give him room and moaned.

Blast! His store of patience was severely depleted and his control was almost nonexistent; waiting until the Season's end to marry was likely going to be physically impossible. He'd die of priapism long before then.

He outlined the neck of her gown slowly with his finger and watched her bite her lower lip. She arched a little, as if to encourage his explorations. He smiled.

He'd persuade Anne to wed by special license. People might talk, but they would talk anyway. Both Jane and John had married under scandalous circumstances; he'd just be carrying on the Parker-Roth tradition.

He dipped his finger a little lower so now he was

tracing the line of Anne's delightfully low cut stays. She sucked in her breath and arched a little more.

Celeste was a master seamstress. Of all the dresses he'd encountered over the years, her designs best combined an elegant appearance with a multitude of seductive details. He slid his finger just a little lower and grazed Anne's delightfully pointed nipple.

He kissed her mouth to muffle her moan.

And really there was nothing wrong with anticipating their vows a little . . . just not on the ground in Damian's garden. There would be other opportunities. He *was* the King of Hearts, though in the past he'd had little need to find private corners at public places for his rendezvous; his widows usually just invited him into their beds. But once in a while they wanted a little variety to flirt with danger, perhaps, or just to feel the sun on their naked skin.

Mmm. He would love to see Anne naked.

He slipped his hand fully into her bodice and lifted free one breast. He couldn't rearrange her clothing too much—they did have to reenter the ballroom shortly—and he couldn't leave wet stains on the satin, but he could, if he were careful . . .

He bent his head and ran his tongue slowly over one tight, hard nipple.

Anne squeaked and her hands flew up to grab his head. Her fingers twisted in his hair, but they couldn't seem to decide whether to push him away or pull him closer.

"Oh, oh, oh." Her hips rolled against his front in a delightfully stimulating manner. "Oh, sir. Oh, Mr. Parker-Roth, you must . . . oh!"

He'd love to torment her further, but her hips were tormenting him a bit too much. He couldn't have any obvious stains on his clothing, either.

He laughed and lifted his head, keeping her breast

cupped in his hand. "Anne, love, my name is Stephen. You can't keep sirring and Parker-Rothing me." He kissed the top of her breast. "We are betrothed, and I'd say our relationship is now rather intimate, wouldn't you?"

"No." She looked down at her breast in his hand. Her fingers were still in his hair. "Y-you shouldn't do that." She was panting slightly.

"I know, but you are too tempting." He took out his handkerchief and slowly, carefully dried off her breast and nipple. "We don't want to spot the satin, do we?"

She shook her head, watching his hand move over her. Her fingers had released his hair, but were now gripping his shoulders. He tucked her back into her stays and adjusted the neck of her dress, taking some time to smooth the satin over both breasts and down her sides, hips, and stomach.

"Stop that, sir." She still hadn't let go of him. Perhaps she couldn't. He rather fancied he was helping her keep upright.

"Knees a little wobbly, Anne?"

She glared at him, but she still didn't let go. "Sir, we should not be out in the garden alone."

He clasped her waist and kissed her. "Stephen, Anne. My name is Stephen."

She pulled her head back, but she didn't struggle in his hold nor did she let go of him. "Sir."

"Stephen." He kissed her again, soft kisses, just pressing his lips to hers. They couldn't afford deeper kisses now. They did need to go inside shortly. They might already have been out here too long. They were betrothed, true, but he didn't care to have their absence become a topic of gossip in the ballroom.

"We should go," Anne said. "I need to see how Evie is doing."

"We will go once you call me 'Stephen.'"

She finally took her hands off his shoulders to push on his chest. He let her go, and she glared at him. "Very well, *Stephen*."

He grinned. "Have I told you yet what a beautiful voice you have? My name sounds splendid coming from your lips, even in that annoyed, martyred tone." He leaned closer. "It will sound even better when it's said with passion."

She sucked in her breath and her glare sharpened. "Don't be ridiculous." She took a step back. "Now, I've said your name. Can we go?"

"In just a moment." He reached into his pocket.

She put her hands on her hips. "Not another requirement. You said we would go in once I said your Christian name. I did so. You are not very honorable if you add—oh." She whipped her hands behind her back. "What's that?"

"What does it look like?" He held the ring up, but the moonlight didn't do it justice. "It's your betrothal ring. I owe you one, and I think this is perfect—a ruby to match your hair"—he captured her left arm and pulled it gently so her hand appeared from behind her back—"and your temper."

"I don't have a temper." She fisted her hand so he couldn't take off her glove.

"No? Then it is red to match your passion—yours and mine." He peeled her fingers back one by one and slowly tugged off her glove.

She was shaking her head back and forth as she watched him slip the ring onto her finger.

"I will just have to give it back to you." She cleared her throat, still staring at the ring.

"It looks better in the light."

Her eyes snapped up to meet his. "Oh, no, I didn't mean . . . I'm sure it's beautiful." She looked back at the ring, and her voice dropped to a whisper. "I'm sure it's perfect." She started to tug it off. "I just can't keep it."

He put his hand over hers, stopping her. He wanted her to keep the ring, even if she did end the betrothal. He'd chosen it for her; it would never look right on another woman's hand. But he knew better than to say that. He didn't wish to have the blasted ring thrown at his head and be forced to search for it in the dark and the leaves and dirt. "Then give it back to me at the end of the Season. For now, you must wear it or people will talk."

He put her hand—the hand with his ring—on his arm and started back to the main path. This had not turned out as he'd imagined it. He'd expected—no, obviously he could never expect anything with Anne. She was far too unpredictable.

He lengthened his steps. They did need to get back to the ballroom. If they were lucky, they'd arrive before the next set started.

"I'm sorry you've been put to all this trouble," Anne said, "and expense." She looked earnestly up at him. "I will take very good care of your ring. I promise I shan't lose it."

Irritation twisted in his gut. "It's your ring, Anne. You can throw it in the Thames if you wish."

"No." She frowned at him. "I am just borrowing it. I told you that."

"And I told you it was yours. I have no need of it. I'm certainly not going to give it to the next woman I become betrothed to." He rarely got angry, but he was feeling uncommonly out of sorts at the moment.

"But it must have been very costly."

"So? Do you think me a pauper, Anne? I might not have a title, but I'm quite plump in the pocket. I have my own estate in Devon. You needn't worry you'd starve if we wed."

She snatched her hand from his arm and hissed at him. "You are being purposefully obtuse. Since we are not really betrothed, I cannot accept such an expensive gift from you. You must assure me you'll take it back when our charade is over or I will not agree to wear it another moment."

"And you are being purposefully difficult." He clenched his teeth. His voice would carry more than Anne's lighter tones, and they were too close to the ballroom now to brangle. Someone would be sure to hear and spread the tasty gossip that the newly betrothed pair was already squabbling.

She put her hands on her hips again. Wonderful. If anyone was watching, he or she could easily guess what was transpiring.

"Will you be more discreet?" It was his turn to hiss.

Anne looked exceedingly mulish, even in this dim light. "Will you agree to take back the ring when we end this betrothal?"

"Very well." He could agree to that, since he wasn't going to end their engagement, and he was determined to persuade this prickly woman she didn't wish to end it either. "Now let's change the subject, shall we? Tell me what—or who—in the ballroom sent you dragging me off into the bushes."

Chapter 11

Anne's stomach performed a pirouette. Thank God it was empty or she'd have decorated Mr. Parker-Roth's handsome eveningwear with a mortifying display.

She'd forgotten for a moment—she couldn't go back inside. Brentwood was in there. She pressed her hand to her lips and swallowed determinedly.

"Anne, what's amiss?" Mr. Parker-Roth gripped her shoulders. He sounded most concerned.

When was the last time anyone had shown concern for her?

"Shall I call for the carriage? It will take but a moment. I'll have you home in a trice."

Yes, that was it. She would say she was ill. She *was* ill—very, very ill. She could go back to Crane House—

No, she couldn't. People would notice and speculate; the gossip would only get worse. And this was Evie's come-out. If she left, Evie would insist on leaving, too. She couldn't allow that. There were so many extremely eligible men in the ballroom.

"No." She took a deep breath. She was a mature woman. She could do this. "I'm f-fine."

"You don't look fine." One of his hands moved to

her chin, but she stepped back, careful this time to raise her hem so she didn't trip.

She knew he was frowning at her, but she wouldn't look him in the face. She stared at his waistcoat instead as she tugged on her glove, covering up his betrothal ring.

"Something is the matter, Anne. What is it? Why did you drag me into the garden?"

She couldn't tell him about Brentwood. She'd never told anyone that story. "It's nothing. I apologize. I was overcome by the crowds and the heat."

She could feel his eyes boring into the top of her head.

"Anne, I'm not a fool. Tell me what is bothering you."

He was not going to let her escape without an answer, but what could she say? Not the truth. Her thoughts darted like dragonflies, unable to light on a plausible reason for her dash into the darkness. If only he would leave her be. It was rude of him to press her so, but then she was rapidly coming to realize he was not one to let something as inconsequential as polite manners stand in his way when he wanted something.

"Anne."

He was losing patience, though what could he do if she refused to answer? He couldn't choke the truth out of her.

She didn't care to find out to exactly what lengths he'd go to satisfy his curiosity. There had to be . . . ah, of course. "If you must know, I found it extremely unsettling to be glared at by so many women."

There was a telling pause. Excellent. She'd got under his guard and scored a flush hit. She found the courage to look up. He was frowning.

"Glared at?" He cleared his throat. "Don't you mean

stared at? Our betrothal was a bit of a bolt from the blue, after all. People are naturally curious."

"Perhaps the men are curious; the women are angry. They believe the King of Hearts has been stolen from under their noses by Crazy Crane's bluestocking daughter."

His frown deepened. "Damn—I mean, dash it. I don't understand why women—some women," he amended, raising his brows and giving her a significant look, "fancy themselves in love with me. I assure you I've never encouraged them to think so."

Oh, she understood completely, as she was one of that silly sisterhood, though fortunately he hadn't puzzled that out yet. "The angriest of them all was that black-haired woman."

"What black-haired woman?" Did she detect a slight thread of discomfort in his voice?

"The beautiful one, of course."

He grinned at her. "I've been looking at only one beautiful woman tonight, and she has distinctly red hair."

She rolled her eyes. "Well, this woman was definitely looking at you. She was standing with Lord"— she swallowed—"with Lord B-Brentwood."

He clasped his hands behind his back, and his expression—and his voice—grew guarded. "Oh, you mean Baron Noughton's widow. You think her beautiful? I do not." There was a tinge of bitterness in his words. Had the woman broken the King of Hearts's heart? She looked like the sort who would do so if she could—elegant and cold as ice.

"Since you mention Brentwood," Mr. Parker-Roth was saying, "let's talk about him. Was it his unpleasant presence that sent you fleeing into the vegetation?"

She couldn't lie, but she might evade the truth a

little. "Why would you think that? I've had nothing to do with the marquis"—*for the last ten years.*

He just looked at her and let the silence stretch out. Damn it. She bit her lip hard to keep from blabbing all the embarrassing details of her supremely ill-considered connection with Brentwood.

Mr. Parker-Roth was obviously a master at getting to the truth of things, a skill that must have stood him in good stead when negotiating for rare plants. She should try silence the next time she wished to discover what mischief the twins had been up to.

"I will find out, you know. You could save us both some trouble by telling me now."

"What, and deny you the fun of ferreting out the story?" She was becoming hysterical. She drew in a deep breath. "Not that there is a story to tell—there isn't." She forced a smile. "Surely we've been out here too long? We should go back into the ballroom."

"Very well." He offered her his arm. When she took it, he laid his hand over hers, holding her still. Alarmed, she looked up.

"As I told you in Hyde Park—don't be afraid of Brentwood. He's a bully, but like most bullies, he's a coward at heart. He can't hurt you."

"Ah." Mr. Parker-Roth was wrong, of course. Brentwood *could* hurt her and with her, Evie. All he need do was let the word out she was no better than she should be.

"If he bothers you at all, tell me. I'll handle him."

"Hmm, yes. Thank you." By then it would be too late. Once Brentwood told Lady Dunlee or any of the gossipy *ton* the story of Baron Gedding's house party, Evie's Season would be at an end. She, Evie, and even Cousin Clorinda would all be treated to the cut direct. Papa would come back to find them in deep disgrace, if not already returned to the country.

It would serve Papa right for abandoning them in Town.

No, it wouldn't be Papa's fault this time. This time the blame could—should—all be laid at her door.

She walked with Mr. Parker-Roth back toward Lord Kenderly's ballroom, feeling much like she imagined one might feel walking to the French guillotine.

Stephen leaned against a pillar and watched Anne waltz with Damian. The red satin skirt of her ball gown outlined her long, slim legs as she moved gracefully around the room. She was so beautiful. She'd only needed the proper clothing—the proper dressmaker— to reveal what her sack-like dresses had hidden.

He shifted position slightly so his breeches didn't outline an especially long, thick part of his body.

She smiled at something Damian said, and an unpleasant sensation twisted his gut. Zeus! Was this jealousy? Ridiculous. Damian was one of his best friends—and very happily married at that—yet at the moment Stephen had an almost overwhelming urge to forcibly remove him from Anne's vicinity.

It was going to be a very trying Season if he was doomed to suffer jealous pangs every time another man paid Anne the slightest attention. He could better spend his energy figuring out what was upsetting her.

For example, why hadn't she waltzed before? It made no sense. She wasn't some young girl from impoverished circumstances; she was an earl's daughter. Her father might be eccentric, but he wasn't so eccentric men would avoid her. They certainly weren't avoiding Evie—she'd not sat out a dance all night. So why had they avoided Anne at those country assemblies?

True, the hideous dresses she'd favored could not

have helped, but they hid only her physical charms. Any man who spoke with her for more than a few minutes would realize she was passionate, strong-willed, and courageous.

Either all the males in Crane House's environs were idiots or Anne had wanted to be avoided. Why?

He'd wager it all came down to Brentwood. He needed to have a word or two with the blasted marquis. Where the hell was he?

Ah, there. He was lurking by some potted palms and watching Anne, the blackguard. This would be an excellent time to—

"You've been ignoring me, darling."

Oh, damn. "Hullo, Maria." He straightened and tried to appear not too displeased to see Lady Noughton. "Were you looking for the marquis? He's hiding in the palms over there."

"I'm looking for you, Stephen." She ran her hand up his arm. "I've missed you."

He stepped back out of her reach. "Oh, I sincerely doubt that, Maria."

"But it's been months since I've seen you." She pushed her lower lip out in what he'd once thought was an adorable pout. Now it just looked excessively silly. The woman was almost thirty, far too old to try to play little girl games.

"Two months, and I was painfully clear at the time that our liaison was over."

"No, I—"

"Maria, there were at least two other men besides me who were enjoying your favors when we parted." He didn't mind sharing, but there was a point where it became ridiculous and, frankly, somewhat repulsive. "I can't imagine Fortingly and Haltington have abandoned you."

"Well, no, but—"

"And obviously Brentwood has now joined their number."

"Yes . . ."

"And you are even wearing the diamonds I know you bought with my parting gift." They were draped around her neck. He thought them rather garish, but Maria had always liked large, flashy jewelry.

"They *are* lovely." She ran her fingers over them. "But that still doesn't mean I haven't missed you. Haven't you missed me?"

"No."

She looked rather startled at his bluntness and then laughed. "Perhaps you don't realize it. I imagine it was frustration that drove you into this sudden betrothal. I mean, kissing a woman on the street?" She shook her head. "If you had those needs, you could have come to me."

It was difficult to know how to respond to that. "You've been listening to rumors, Maria. You can't believe everything you hear."

"Ah, so you aren't betrothed! I told Wally—"

"Wally?"

"Lord Brentwood. I told him it was all a hum."

"Actually, you *can* believe that part. Lady Anne and I are indeed betrothed. You may wish me happy."

Maria looked as if she'd choke to death if she tried. Why the devil did she care? Yes, she'd convinced herself she wished to marry him in February, but now she must have her eye on Brentwood—and *he* had a title.

"Of course I hope you will be happy." Her tone clearly indicated this was a hope she'd be glad not to have fulfilled.

"Thank you. Now, if you'll excuse me?"

Her hand shot out to capture his wrist. "A new set is forming. Let's dance to celebrate your good news."

"Maria—"

"Oh, Stephen, don't be so stiff. I'm not asking you to come to my bed, just the ballroom floor."

At this point, it would look odd if he didn't dance with her. People were throwing them curious glances; it had never been a secret that he and she had a "connection." "Very well."

He glanced over at Anne as he led Maria out. Damn it. She was with Brentwood, and she did not look at all happy about it.

"Don't worry," Maria said, tugging him away from the couple. "Your precious betrothed will be fine with Wally. What could happen to her in Lord Kenderly's ballroom?"

True. Anne should be safe here, and, whatever her history with Brentwood, the marquis was a member of society. He might not be welcome in the homes of the highest sticklers, but he was at many gatherings—invited, or as Stephen suspected tonight, not. In any event, Anne would have to become accustomed to seeing him in public.

"Oh, lovely," Maria said as the orchestra played the opening notes. "Another waltz."

"You must have improved with age, my dear, to have captured the King of Hearts's fancy," Brentwood said as the music began—another waltz.

Anne tried not to cringe when he touched her. Damn. He obviously remembered every detail of that disastrous time at Baron Gedding's estate.

She stared down at his cravat. There were snuff stains on the linen, and he smelled of oil and dirt. If he'd looked like this ten years ago, she'd never have given him a second glance let alone gone off into the leafage with him.

"That dress is certainly an improvement over the frocks you wore at the house party."

"London dressmakers are more au courant than those in the country, I suppose. This woman seemed particularly skilled with her needle."

He laughed, sending a fetid cloud of garlic and onions into her face. "Yes, Celeste is very talented. I recognize her work—but then, it doesn't take much discernment to identify the dressmaker. Parker-Roth takes all his women there."

How dare he insinuate she was one of Mr. Parker-Roth's "women"? She might not be truly betrothed to the man, but she most certainly wasn't his mistress. She glared at him. "If you plan to be offensive, it would be best if we end this dance now." She should have refused to stand up with him, but that would have added to the gossip. She'd already waltzed with Mr. Parker-Roth, so she couldn't insist she didn't dance at all.

She could tell by the look in his eyes he was disappointed she hadn't turned into a shaking blancmange.

"My, my. The kitten has claws."

"I am hardly a kitten, as you well know." She shifted her feet to avoid getting trodden on. Dancing with Lord Brentwood was a bit like dancing with a bull—not that she'd ever danced with a bull, of course. But he was large and lumbering.

"No, you're an old cat, aren't you? You must be so relieved to have finally caught a husband—and the King of Hearts! How did you manage it? One would think Parker-Roth would be more nimble at escaping parson's mousetrap."

Mr. Parker-Roth was certainly more nimble than Brentwood on the dance floor.

She ignored Lord Brentwood's insulting question and looked around the ballroom. "Lord and Lady Kenderly must be delighted. Their ball is a shocking squeeze." Blast. Mr. Parker-Roth was dancing with Lady Noughton.

Brentwood had followed her gaze. "You don't mind your intended waltzing with Maria?"

"Why should I?"

"That's right, you're new to Town. Let me enlighten you. Maria—Lady Noughton—is Parker-Roth's mistress. Some amongst society thought they might wed." He smiled. How had she never noticed his teeth were crooked and rather stained? "There's no reason why they shouldn't. Maria is perfectly good *ton*—her father and her husband were barons—and Parker-Roth is only a commoner, after all. This sudden betrothal was quite a shock for the poor woman."

Anne didn't care a farthing about Lady Noughton's heart—she doubted the woman had one—but she did care about Mr. Parker-Roth's. She could tell when she'd mentioned the widow earlier there'd been something between them. Was that why he'd been drunk in Hyde Park? Had they had a falling out and he'd been drowning his sorrows? That must have been why he'd kissed her; she certainly wouldn't normally inspire passion in such a man.

Surely he'd find a way to let Lady Noughton know his betrothal was temporary—

She was letting Brentwood confuse her. If the woman was Mr. Parker-Roth's mistress, he could tell her whatever he wished in bed.

Damn it, Brentwood's hand was wandering. It came to rest on her derriere; she stepped on his toes as hard as she could.

"Ow!" He scowled at her, but he removed his roving fingers.

"Oh, I'm so sorry. I was distracted by something brushing the back of my dress. I do hope it won't happen again." She smiled.

He grunted. "As I said, everyone thought Parker-Roth would wed Maria—Maria certainly thought so."

"But as I'm sure you know, the world is full of disappointments." She let her elbow swing wide as he started to crowd her side. He dodged.

"Ah, but will Parker-Roth be disappointed?"

What did he mean by that? She wasn't about to ask. "Mr. Parker-Roth and I understand each other. I assure you, you need not busy yourself in our affairs."

Brentwood looked thoughtful—or as thoughtful as the idiot could look. "So he knows you're not a virgin?"

This was plain speaking indeed. Pray God no one could overhear their conversation or wonder why she'd suddenly assumed a hue a shade darker than her dress—damn her coloring. "You are offensive, Lord Brentwood."

"But does he know? Perhaps you've already been in his bed? That's what some of the gossips say." He leered at her. "Did you scream his name when you came like you screamed mine in Gedding's garden?"

She was not embarrassed now, she was furious. She should not continue this conversation, but the anger and hurt and, yes, hatred, that had been festering in her for ten years—and perhaps even the weight of this false betrothal ring—made her reckless. "Your memory is faulty. I don't know—or care to know—your Christian name, Lord Brentwood. If I screamed on that cursed day, it was from pain and shock."

She stopped and tried to jerk her hands out of his hold. He wouldn't release her. Another couple collided with them.

"Our apologies," Brentwood said, starting to waltz again. She was forced to move with him.

"My, my, such venom." His nasty little eyes studied her; she forced herself not to look away. "You *are* much more . . . interesting than you were in your youth. You know, from the rumors flying through the *ton*, I was certain you'd already warmed Parker-Roth's bed, but now . . . I think not."

He nodded, his smile turning even more unpleasant. "He does think you're a virgin, doesn't he? I wonder if he would withdraw his offer if he learned he's getting damaged goods."

She was certain silence was the best response. She hoped so, since she couldn't manage to speak.

"Men can be odd about the women they choose to wed, my dear. Parker-Roth may not have a title and he may be only a second son, but I'll wager he still has the silly notion he should marry a virgin. He'll be sadly disappointed on his wedding night, won't he, when there's no blood on the sheets?"

Oh, God. Dread spiraled in her stomach.

But, no, she needn't worry. They weren't actually going to marry—there would be no wedding night.

The thought didn't make her happy.

Brentwood leaned closer, choking her with another blast of garlic and onions. "Lady Anne, I believe it's my duty as a fellow male to alert poor Parker-Roth." He nodded, his little, rat-like eyes never leaving her face. "Indeed, I should drop a word of warning in any man's ear who might be so led astray."

He smiled in a very nasty manner. "But then Parker-Roth would be caught on the horns of a dilemma, wouldn't he? Call off the wedding and risk society's condemnation or go through with the ceremony and wed you." He gave a gusty, false sigh. "No, I think it best if I just spread the word of your infamy, don't you? It could so easily be accomplished. You've already set the stage with that scandalous public kiss. Just a word here and there, and you wouldn't find a single door in Mayfair open to you—or your lovely sister. Too bad her Season would be ended before it truly has begun."

"You wouldn't—"

"Oh, but I would, Lady Anne. I most certainly would."
He smiled again and her stomach knotted. "I might
even be tempted to whisper the truth in your little
sister's ear. I could take her on a garden stroll and . . .
enlighten her. She's far more beautiful than you were
when you were her age."

"You wouldn't dare." Anne tried to swallow her
horror. She knew he *would* dare.

Brentwood laughed. "Oh, my dear, of course I
would, and I'd enjoy every moment of it. However, I
might be persuaded to hold my tongue—and other
organ—if we came to an agreement, you and I."

"An agreement?" The words were forced out of her.
She couldn't let Evie be hurt if she could prevent it.

"An agreement, yes. A night in my bed for my silence. That's not so much to ask, is it? I'll even give you
a little time to accustom yourself to the thought—or to
grow wet and eager with anticipation, hmm?"

The only thing that was going to grow wet was Brentwood's waistcoat and breeches when she vomited all
over them here in Lord Kenderly's ballroom.

"A week from tonight, shall we say? Yes. A week from
tonight we'll be waltzing again, but in my bed." He
turned her hand over and pressed a kiss to her wrist.
"Trust me—you will enjoy it."

Thank God the music finally ended.

Chapter 12

"Take the carriage home, Albert," Stephen said as he followed the ladies up to Crane House's front door. "I'll be a while—I shall walk home."

"But, sir—"

"That will be all, Albert." Stephen was not in a mood to bandy words with his coachman.

Albert set the horses in motion.

Clorinda paused and frowned at him as Hobbes opened the door. "What do you mean you'll be a while, sir? It's late; you are not invited in."

"I'm inviting myself in, madam. Lady Anne and I have things to discuss." Evie was frowning at him, too. He glanced at Anne; she was studying her gloves.

It had been an extremely strained carriage ride from Damian's town house, so different from the trip there. The tension between him and Anne had killed even Evie's excited discussion of her first London ball. He was sorry for it, but he could not turn his thoughts from the spectacle of Anne waltzing with Brentwood.

And Anne had been on edge herself. It wasn't only his ill-temper that had poisoned the atmosphere.

"It can wait until the morning, sir," Clorinda said.

A small, reasonable voice whispered in his heated brain, agreeing it might be better to put off any discussions until his spleen had settled. He silenced the voice. "It cannot. I must speak with Anne tonight."

"You are very rude." Clorinda turned as if to block the doorway. Hobbes, standing behind her, wrung his hands.

"I am very determined."

"Anne," Evie said, "do you wish to speak to Mr. Parker-Roth? If you don't, I'm certain Mr. Hobbes will deny him entrance."

Hobbes's eyes widened and he looked around rather wildly, as if searching for a few strong footmen to assist him. Wise man. Stephen didn't want to hurt the fellow, but he was not going to be deterred.

"Oh, this is ridiculous," Anne finally said, throwing him a distinctly annoyed look before she stepped past Clorinda. "Of course the man can come in if he wishes." She nodded at Hobbes as she entered the foyer. Hobbes smiled in evident relief.

"Thank you." Stephen let Clorinda and Evie precede him, but only by a half step. Hobbes wouldn't try to keep him out, but he wouldn't put it past the women to slam the door in his face.

Anne had already shed her cloak and was heading for the stairs. He stepped past Clorinda and grasped her elbow. "I said we needed to talk."

She glared at him, but he thought he saw a touch of fear in her eyes as well. That made him even angrier. She couldn't be afraid of him; she must know he'd never hurt a woman, and he'd certainly never hurt her.

"I said you could come in; I didn't say I'd talk to you." Anne shrugged one shoulder and looked away from him. "I'm tired."

"Exactly," Clorinda said, removing her cloak and handing it to Hobbes. "We are all tired." She looked pointedly at Stephen. "Very, very tired. You go on up to bed, Evie. I'm sure we'll be along shortly."

"Very well." Evie looked uncertainly from her sister to her cousin to him. "Thank you for escorting us tonight, sir. Even though things seem a bit . . . unsettled at the moment, I wish to say I truly had a wonderful evening."

He forced his lips to unlock so he could bend them into something approaching a smile. "I'm very glad to hear it, Evie. And I would say you were a complete success. You'll have all the young men of the *ton*—and some of the older ones—at your feet."

A shy smile lit her face. "Oh, do you really think so?" She blushed.

His face loosened more and he grinned. "I really think so."

"And your brother . . . ?" Her blush deepened. "He was very amiable."

He laughed. Oh ho, did the wind blow in that direction? It would be awkward if he couldn't settle matters with Anne—and Nick was still very young—but it might be a good match. "Poor Nick was completely bowled over by your charm and beauty, Lady Evangeline."

"Oh, now you are funning, sir." She looked extremely embarrassed and equally pleased.

"Weren't you on your way to bed, Evie?" Clorinda asked.

"Yes, of course. Good night." Evie curtseyed and then almost skipped up the stairs.

"At least someone's happy," Clorinda said, watching Evie. Anne kept her eyes on the newel post, inspecting it as if it were some strange, new architectural marvel. Clorinda speared him with a dark look. "And now, sir, as I've said, we are all tired. This had better not take long."

Did Clorinda think to chaperone them? She would be very much in the way. "There is no need for you to stay up, madam. Your presence is not required."

"Of course it's required. You are not yet married to Lady Anne, Mr. Parker-Roth."

"I'm betrothed to her."

"And betrothed isn't married, is it?"

Anne made an odd, little sound—a cross between a slightly hysterical giggle and a snort of exasperation. "You may go up to bed, Clorinda. Mr. Parker-Roth is not going to r-rape me."

"Anne!"

Clorinda sounded as shocked as Stephen felt. He wasn't some shy virgin, but to hear that ugly word on Anne's lips, to think of that ugly action as having anything to do with what was between them was sickening.

Anne swiped at her eyes—was she crying? "I'm sorry. I really am tired. It was a more stressful evening than I anticipated."

Clorinda put her arm around Anne's shoulders. "And Mr. Parker-Roth is a beast for even thinking of keeping you up another instant. You can talk to him in the morning. Come—"

Anne shook her head and slipped out from under Clorinda's arm. "No, it's best he and I speak now. I couldn't sleep if I did go upstairs. I'm too"—she waved her hand vaguely—"agitated to rest. You go on ahead."

There was real concern in Clorinda's eyes and voice. "You're certain?"

Anne nodded. "Yes. And don't wait up. I'll be fine, truly."

"Well, all right. I *am* tired . . ." Clorinda gave Stephen one more stern look. "I expect you to behave like a perfect gentleman, Mr. Parker-Roth. I am relying on your honor."

He bowed. "You may do so without the slightest

hesitation, madam. I do sincerely care for Lady Anne's welfare, you know."

She examined him a moment more and then nodded. "Very well. Good night then."

"Good night."

They watched Clorinda make her slow way up the stairs. Once she'd disappeared from sight, Anne turned to Stephen. "Are you going to ring a peal over my head now?"

Stephen looked around. Hobbes had left as soon as he'd locked the door behind them. They were alone, but he did not wish to have this discussion in such an exposed place. Sound carried, especially when spoken in a marble hall with a wide staircase. "Isn't there a place we can be private—other than the study or the odd room with the obscene knickknacks?" Neither option appealed at the moment.

Anne jutted out her chin. "We *are* private."

There was no point in wasting more time arguing. He took one of the candlesticks and Anne's arm and directed her toward the back of the house. "Do I need to open every door, or will you tell me when we arrive at a suitable room for our talk?"

He passed the odd room and the library. They didn't need much space; just a door that closed and walls that would absorb their words.

Anne grumbled and stepped ahead of him. "The green sitting room should do," she said, pulling open a door near the end of the hall.

It was a small room with an assortment of chairs and tables and a large chaise-longue. The fire had been banked; the air was chilly. Anne shivered.

Stephen shut the door behind them and then struggled out of his coat. He draped it over Anne's shoulders and went to throw a log on the fire.

Anne pulled the coat tight around her. It was warm

with the heat of Mr. Parker-Roth's body. She buried her nose in the cloth—he was turned away from her; he wouldn't notice—and breathed deeply. It smelled of him, too.

Oh, God, what was she going to do about Brentwood?

Panic threatened to strangle her. She couldn't think about it now. She was far too upset.

She watched the muscles in Mr. Par—no *Stephen's*—back shift as he poked the fire, bringing it back to life, and she felt something flicker deep inside her.

He was angry with her. He would tell her how she shouldn't have acted the way she had waltzing with Brentwood.

She didn't want to argue. She didn't want his anger. She wanted his strength, his warmth. Him.

He'd awakened something in her, this little flickering need. It had stirred when he'd first kissed her, and it had grown stronger when she'd seen how he'd looked at her before the ball, when he'd teased her in the carriage on the way there, when he'd taken her into the garden and kissed her.

She'd been angry with him; he was angry with her.

She didn't want to be angry any longer. Not now. Now she wanted a different kind of heat, something to make her forget anger and fear. Forget shame. Forget Brentwood.

The fire must finally be burning to his satisfaction; he put the poker down and turned to face her. The lawn of his shirt was so fine, she could see his arms through the fabric.

If only he weren't still wearing his waistcoat.

"Don't look at me that way, Anne." He sounded tense again, but not angry.

"What way?" The fire was working amazingly quickly; she was quite warm now. Hot, even. She slipped

Stephen's jacket off her shoulders and hung it carefully over the back of a chair.

She walked toward him. She felt . . . reckless.

She stopped when she got to within a few feet of him. Closer and she might completely embarrass herself by starting to unbutton his waistcoat. Her fingers itched to do so.

She wanted to feel his hands on her again. She wanted to taste his mouth again. After her waltz with Brentwood, she needed to feel Stephen's touch to feel clean again.

She closed her eyes briefly. She should tell him her secret; she should not lie to him with silence.

She didn't want to tell him, not now. What harm would there be in delaying?

She would tell him . . . later.

"Are you going to give me a thorough tongue-lashing?" she asked.

Oh! A jolt of heat shot from her breasts to the place between her legs. She should not have mentioned tongues.

"I should." Stephen's voice wasn't much more than a strained whisper. He was staring back at her, an air of . . . hunger about him.

She wet her lips and watched his eyes follow her tongue. "Why?"

He blinked. "Why, what?"

She was having a hard time following this conversation as well. Her body was shouting at her to stop talking and do something better with her mouth. "Why do you wish to give me a dressing-down?"

His eyes flicked over her. She *had* said "give me a dressing-down" and not "take my dress down," hadn't she? She was certain she'd said the former; she wished she'd said the latter.

"Yes." His eyes snapped back to her face. "Yes, I want . . . I want to . . ."

He stepped toward her and grabbed her shoulders. He shook her, not hard, but hard enough that one loose hairpin fell, sending a length of hair tumbling down to cover his fingers. He dropped his hold on her as if scalded, whipping his hands behind his back.

"What were you thinking this evening?" His voice was hoarse.

"When this evening?" She could easily reach his waistcoat buttons now. They were calling to her. "In the garden with you?"

She flushed. She should not have said that either; she did not wish to tell him what she'd been thinking—and feeling—then. Though if she did, would he be so kind as to make her think and feel those things again? The door was closed. She was already a fallen woman. At twenty-seven, she would likely not get many more chances for this kind of . . . activity.

Once he knew the truth—once everyone knew the truth—she'd get no more chances at all, unless she wished to take up the usual occupation of fallen women.

"No, damn it." Stephen sounded goaded. "When you were dancing with Brentwood."

Brentwood. Oh. She felt trapped and dirty again.

And what had Stephen been doing while she'd been suffering with Lord Brentwood?

Perhaps anger *was* better than this cold, sick feeling.

"I'm surprised you noticed. I thought all your attention was on your partner—your *mistress*—Lady Noughton."

His brows snapped down. "Did Brentwood tell you Maria was my mistress?"

He'd called the woman by her first name.

Anne bit her lip. It felt like he'd stabbed her with a knife.

Stupid! It was nothing to her what Mr. Parker-Roth

did. She and he were strangers, brought together by scandal and this sham betrothal. They would part ways—to her great delight—by the end of the Season. Sooner, if possible.

If she tried to speak, she'd cry. She nodded, but one ridiculous tear leaked out anyway.

He must think her the most pathetic creature in Christendom.

His hand came up to cradle her jaw; his thumb caught the tear and wiped it away. His voice was now as gentle as his touch.

"She was my mistress, Anne, but she is no longer. We parted ways in February. It took me too long, but I finally saw what a petty, grasping woman she is."

Now both his hands held her face tilted up toward his. He was staring at her mouth. Her lips felt swollen. Her heart—and an organ rather lower down—started to pound. She put her hands on his waistcoat.

"There's been no one else in my bed since." He brushed his lips over her forehead, over her cheek. "And never anyone in my heart."

His mouth touched hers then, just touched it, not pressing, not mashing her lips against her teeth as Brentwood had done during that terrible house party.

She wanted more pressure, but she made herself stay still. If this was her only chance, she would not rush it. Though she was no longer a virgin, she knew nothing about physical love. She wanted to see if there was more to it than the embarrassment and pain Brentwood had given her. What better way to find out than to let the King of Hearts be her teacher?

He lifted his head, his hands sliding up into her hair, plucking her pins free, dropping them to the carpet. She felt her wild red mane tumble down over her shoulders and back.

"Your hair is beautiful." He buried his face in it, then turned to kiss her neck just below her ear.

Her breasts ached; the place between her legs ached. She was so hot she felt she was burning, and her temperature had nothing to do with the fire in the grate. She wanted to press herself against him, but she stayed still. She would not rush blindly ahead and so, in her ignorance, miss something wonderful. And she did think it would be wonderful.

But it would be more wonderful without his annoying waistcoat. She slipped the top button free.

He chuckled by her ear. "Are you undressing me, Lady Anne?"

Her fingers froze for a moment. Was she being too bold? But he'd sounded amused. She swallowed and moved trembling fingers to the next button. "Surely you must be too hot."

He gently sucked on the skin below her ear and her nipples tightened. "You are right, I am a trifle over-heated." He straightened, making it easier for her to reach all his buttons. "Thank you for thinking of it. I will definitely be more comfortable with fewer clothes."

She met his gaze briefly and then dropped her eyes to her fingers' work. His look was too intense; he might read her secret in her face if she wasn't careful. She loosened the last button and pushed aside the waistcoat, running her hands over his shirt. This was better. Not perfect—his bare skin would be perfect—but it was much, much better.

"Are those all the buttons you mean to loosen, Anne?"

"Y-yes." She knew which other buttons he meant; it was hard not to know. Just below his waistcoat, only inches from her fingers, his erection was straining against his fall so it seemed almost a charity to free it, but she was not yet that bold.

"A pity, but I suppose you are wise." He shrugged out of his waistcoat, threw it over a chair, and then grinned at her. "You know, I find I'm still rather warm. Would it offend you if I removed my shirt as well?"

Her mouth went dry, as dry as another part of her was wet. "No," she managed to whisper. "It would n-not offend me at all."

"Splendid." He shed his cravat and then pulled his shirt up and over his head.

Oh! He was beautiful. The firelight flickered over his broad shoulders and muscled arms and lit the hair that dusted his chest and trailed down over his flat stomach to the waist of his breeches.

She'd never seen a man without his shirt. Brentwood had kept his on—and his waistcoat and coat as well—when he'd taken her virginity. They'd been in Baron Gedding's garden, after all, and it had been chilly.

If only he had shed his clothing, the sight of his pale, soft flesh might have shocked some sense into her and she would have fled. But no, she'd fancied herself in love. When he'd taken her into that secluded section of the garden, she'd been thrilled. She'd thought him romantic and brooding—and she'd thought herself daring.

She'd never been daring before—or after until right now. It had been out of character, but she'd been seventeen and stupid—and perhaps a little angry Papa was adding to his family again. She knew she'd be given charge of the baby—or babies as it turned out.

So she'd gone into the shrubbery with Brentwood. As soon as they'd reached an especially leafy spot, he'd backed her up against a wall and thrust his tongue into her mouth, almost gagging her. His hands had been all over her body, pinching her breasts, grabbing her bottom. She'd tried to feel thrilled and passionate and womanly, but it was difficult when she was also trying to breathe. And then suddenly she'd felt cool air on her thighs and, before she could free her mouth to protest, a burning pain as something hard and long was shoved into the most private part of her body. She'd stiffened in shock, but Brentwood hadn't noticed. He'd been too busy grunting and moving against her.

At least it had been over quickly.

"Anne, are you all right?"

"What?" She blinked. Damn, she'd let that cursed memory blind her to what was happening now. Stephen was frowning at her, concern clear in his eyes.

"You look . . . stricken."

He stooped to pick up his shirt. Was he going to put it back on? No. She would not let Brentwood ruin this, too. She pulled it out of his hands. "It's nothing. Just . . . hold me. Please?"

"Of course." He wrapped his arms around her, bringing her up against his bare chest.

It was wonderful. He was warm and solid and strong. She felt safe, not trapped as she'd been with Brentwood.

She could not remember the last time anyone had just held her.

"Better?" he murmured. His breath whispered over her hair, and then his lips brushed the top of her head.

"Yes." She wrapped her arms around his waist and let the past go, at least for now. She wanted to live in the present—this present with her cheek on Stephen's naked chest and his warmth all around her. Mmm. She slid her hands up his broad back.

"Anne."

"Hmm?" Was his skin sweet or salty? She touched him with her tongue, and heard—and felt—him in-hale sharply.

Salty. His skin was faintly salty.

She felt his erection press against her belly and she smiled. She kissed one of his nipples. He caught his breath again—and then he pushed her away.

"No." She tried to get back to his warmth, but his hands on her shoulders kept her from her goal.

"Anne." He shook her just a little and she looked up. His face was guarded; his jaw, clenched. "Anne, what do you want? I will hold you, but if you keep on this way, I'll be tempted to do far more than that."

"Good." She would tell him what she wanted. She ran her hands up his arms, over their rock hard muscles. "Kiss me."

His gaze sharpened; she'd swear she could see little flames in his eyes. His muscles under her fingers tensed. He was so strong . . .

"But gently. Don't crush me. I want to be able to breathe."

He laughed. "Very well. I will try, but if I get carried away and become more enthusiastic than you like, you must tell me." He relaxed his arms, bringing her a little closer. "If your lips are otherwise engaged, you may give me a slight push." He brought her closer still so her bodice almost touched his chest. "Or, if that doesn't work, a strong shove. Will that be acceptable?"

"Yes." She tilted her head up. "Now perhaps you could attend to my request and use your charming lips for something other than discourse."

His lips turned up slightly. "My pleasure, madam." He lowered his mouth so it just touched hers. "Is this what you had in mind?"

"Yes." Mmm, this was what she wanted. This was where they'd been headed before she'd let thoughts of Brentwood intrude.

She would *not* think of that disgusting creature again.

She opened her mouth and let Stephen's tongue in. His hand came up to play with her breast.

"Is this still gentle enough?" he whispered.

"Mmm."

His touch was exquisite, but her bodice was very much in the way. She wished she could shed it as easily as he had shed his shirt.

And then his nimble fingers slipped under the satin, and the neck of her dress loosened. She sucked in her breath as she felt it slide down.

"Would it be all right with you, Anne, if we move to that lovely chaise-longue? I'm finding standing to be rather a challenge."

She was finding standing to be unusually difficult as well. Her knees were refusing to support her weight any longer. "That's an excellent notion."

Stephen scooped her up as if she weighed nothing and deposited her—gently—on the chaise-longue. He stretched out beside her and leaned up on one elbow. "You are so beautiful," he said.

Her breasts were now exposed for anyone to see, and Stephen was obviously looking. She didn't care. She was feeling reckless again, and perhaps a touch wanton.

His fingers plucked her nipples, and she sucked in her breath. It was as if there were a vibrating string between that part of her body and her womb. The opening Brentwood had so rudely entered ten years ago grew wetter. If Stephen were to—

Good God, she couldn't be considering such a thing, could she? It had been so painful and so embarrassing last time.

This time felt nothing like that time.

Stephen gave her a lingering kiss and then slowly—gently—his mouth moved down to her jaw and her throat, her collarbone. Was he going to . . . ? He was. He did. His mouth took his fingers' place on her nipple and sucked. Her hips shot off the chaise-longue.

"Oh!"

He looked up at her, his mouth suspended above her breast. "Aren't I being gentle enough?"

What the hell was he talking about?

"You're growling." He flicked his tongue over her poor nipple. She whimpered—and then grabbed his head to hold him exactly where she wanted him.

He blew a little puff of air over her wet, hard peak, and laughed. "You are a demanding woman, Lady Anne."

"Just—oh." One of his hands had wandered down to the hem of her dress. Now it was sliding slowly up her leg, higher, closer to—

The tip of his finger gently probed her wet folds and touched a tiny, hard spot she'd never known existed. Her hips jerked and then twisted. His finger circled the spot, slipped over it. Each touch wound her tighter and tighter.

Someone was making small, mewling noises and she very much feared it was she. She had never felt—

Oh! She grabbed Stephen's shoulders and stiffened. Almost. There was something almost within her reach. She didn't know what it was, but her body did—and Stephen did. His finger teased her with another gentle touch and another and then—

"Ohh." Wave after wave of pleasure cascaded through her. When the last wave subsided, she lay in Stephen's arms like a rag doll. Every one of her muscles was limp. "Mmm." She kissed his collarbone, the part closest to her lips. "That was lovely. I had no idea."

"Of course you had no idea." He kissed the top of her head. His voice sounded amused, but somewhat strained, too.

She moved closer to him and discovered the obvious

problem. He was not limp at all. His erection, still very large and hard, pressed into her hip.

He moved back so he was no longer touching her.

Now he would want to do what Brentwood had done. She should be distressed, but she was too sated with these new sensations to care.

No, that wasn't true. She wanted him to do it. She wanted to give him pleasure like he had given her. She was almost sure it wouldn't hurt this time. The King of Hearts would know how to make it, if not pleasant, at least not painful. But how could she invite him in?

She reached for the bulge in his breeches.

"No, Anne." His hand moved hers firmly away. "It's late. I should go."

She could persuade him to stay. She reached for him with her other hand, but he deflected her again and stood up, taking a step back.

"You are playing with fire," he said.

She sat up, her breasts exposed, her clothes in complete disarray. "Perhaps I want to get burned."

His eyes focused on her bosom and then jerked up to her face. He ran his hand through his hair and gave a breathless little laugh. "I suppose I'm glad you do, but you will have to wait. I'm not taking your virginity on a chaise-longue in a sitting room with an unlocked door."

"Oh." She felt a hot flush sweep up her body.

He couldn't take her virginity. She didn't have it to give him.

"Don't look so stricken. It won't be long. I think after our recent activities, I should get a special license. I can't wait until the end of the Season to have you in my bed."

The thought of being in Stephen's bed caused her exhausted female organs to perk up. She didn't want to wait till the end of the Season either—she didn't want to wait till the end of the week—or perhaps even the end of this hour.

But she would have to wait forever. She couldn't marry Stephen.

She should tell him now. She *would* tell him if only her traitorous body would stop insisting she could— she *had* to—wed him . . . and if she didn't dread seeing the surprise and then the disgust in his eyes when she told him.

He picked up his shirt and pulled it over his head. "Get dressed, will you? You don't want a servant to see you that way—it would be all over London by tomorrow's dinnertime." He buttoned up his waistcoat and reached for his coat. "We may be betrothed, but I'd rather not entertain society with accounts of our amorous activities."

She just stared at him, so he came over to tug her bodice back into place for her. "I've always tried to be discreet." He grinned. "Kissing you on the square was the one notable exception to that practice."

"Oh." He was so matter-of-fact. Had she imagined his passion? She looked down at his breeches.

She hadn't imagined it. Part of him was still very enthusiastic.

"Stop that," he said.

"Stop what?"

"Looking at me that way." He grabbed her upper arms and hauled her to her feet. "You need to go to bed, Anne—alone—and I need to leave." He pushed her toward the door. "Now."

"Oh, very well." She walked, his hand on the small of her back, urging her out of the room and down the corridor. When they finally reached the front door, she paused. "Do I get a good night kiss?"

"No." Stephen grabbed his hat from the side table and jammed it on his head. "Definitely not." He opened the door and stepped out so quickly she wondered if he was afraid she'd tackle him. Probably. She felt a bit desperate.

"Lock up behind me," he said before he slammed the door closed.

She sighed, turned the key, and headed up the stairs, hoping she'd be able to fall asleep before dawn.

Chapter 13

There was no chance in hell he was going to be able to get to sleep any time soon. Stephen paused outside Crane House to adjust his breeches. The ache in his groin was damned uncomfortable. He was amazed he could walk.

Hell, he deserved a medal for self-control. When he'd seen Anne, half naked, replete with sexual satisfaction, reach to touch him where he most wanted to be touched, it had taken all his willpower to pull back. If he'd stayed in that little room one more moment, he'd have had his breeches off and his cock buried in her sweet body in record time. Not a good way to introduce a woman to physical love.

He started down the pavement. Blast, his damned cock still throbbed and his bollocks felt like rocks. He could not think about Anne on that chaise-longue any longer or his private parts would explode.

He should find out why she had such a strong reaction to Brentwood. After her emotional performance at Damian's ball this evening, every last member of the *ton* must be speculating about her relationship with the marquis. There were probably a dozen theories circulating already. He'd meant to ask her tonight, after he'd finished castigating her for not hiding her feelings better—or at all—during that cursed waltz, but he'd got . . . distracted and hadn't managed to attain either of those goals.

He'd seek out Gedding, that's what he'd do. Chances were the fellow was too far in his cups to have anything of interest to say—not that a sober Gedding would be much more informative—but it was worth a try. He had to do something—sleep was definitely not in the cards for at least an hour or two.

He found Gedding at White's in his usual spot, nursing a brandy bottle.

"Mind if I join you?" Stephen lowered himself into the chair next to the baron. The man blinked at him.

"Parker-Roth." Gedding hiccupped and shrugged. "Want some brandy?"

"Thank you." Damn, Gedding had obviously been imbibing all evening. He was more than likely wasting his time talking to him, but then he had time to waste. He took a sip from the glass Gedding handed him and pondered how to raise the topic of that long ago house party.

"Heard you're betrothed to Crazy Crane's chit."

Stephen almost sprayed brandy over his lap. Perhaps this wouldn't be wasted time after all. "Yes, I am."

Gedding nodded drunkenly. "Glad to hear it."

"Oh? Why?"

The baron shrugged. "Always felt a little bad about the girl. Invited her to a house party as a favor to Crane, you know. She was only seventeen, needed a little polish before her come-out."

Stephen waited, but Gedding fell silent, staring into his brandy glass. Perhaps he needed a slight prod. "And?"

The man startled as if he'd forgotten Stephen was there. "And what?"

Thankfully, White's was sparsely populated tonight; no one was sitting close enough to overhear. "You said you felt bad about Lady Anne. Why?"

Gedding frowned. "No reason, really." He took another swallow of brandy and sighed somewhat drunkenly. "Though I probably should have kept more of an eye on her. I'd told Crane my cousin Olivia would chaperone the girl, so he'd sent her along with only a maid in attendance, but damned if Olivia didn't come down with a dreadful cold at the last minute. She had to stay home, so Crane's daughter spent the house party without a proper duenna. Didn't think it would be a problem, though. The chit seemed the quiet, biddable sort."

Anne—quiet and biddable? Were they talking about the same woman? "*Was* it a problem?"

"Hmm?" Gedding pursed his lips, then shook his head. "No, no I don't think so. Not really."

Gedding didn't sound so certain. Stephen clasped his hands to keep from grabbing the baron by the shoulders and shaking the information out of him. "Was Lord Brentwood there as well?"

Gedding nodded. "Yes. Bit of a dirty dish, that one. I didn't invite him—he came with Heddington—but I couldn't very well turn him away when he showed up on my doorstep. He *is* a marquis."

"Right." Stephen kept his voice neutral. "You couldn't turn him away."

"But I did worry. He was a womanizer even back then, you know, and he started flirting with Lady Anne. Didn't mean anything by it—he never does—but I'm afraid she was a bit taken in. Stands to reason she would be, her being so young and green."

"Yes." It was hard to keep his voice even. Poor Anne.

Supposedly, Brentwood had been something of an Adonis ten years ago. "He didn't do anything besides flirt, did he?"

"I don't think so. You know the way of it. Some meaningful looks, a bunch of silly compliments, a walk or two in the garden, and then once he's caught a woman's interest, he moves on to his next conquest." Gedding sighed. "Lady Anne seemed to take it hard. She left early, saying her stepmother needed her at home, but I never believed that excuse. And then not to see her in society again . . . It's been weighing on my mind a bit."

Gedding met Stephen's gaze. "I'll tell you, sir, I'm glad it looks as if she's found some happiness. I wish you both well."

"Thank you."

Gedding poured himself some more brandy. "You're a good sort. They may call you the King of Hearts, but you ain't like Brentwood. You don't go collecting ladies' love like snuffboxes just because you can." Gedding snorted. "Though I'll wager he has fewer successes these days. Man's got rather stout, hasn't he?"

"Rather."

"But he's still a marquis. Some ladies don't care what a man looks like, if he's got a lofty title." Gedding waved his hand at Stephen. "Oh, not Lady Anne, obviously, but others." He snorted. "I'd like to see Brentwood taken down a peg. The man's too full of himself."

Stephen stood and bowed slightly. "And I'd be delighted to oblige you and the rest of the *ton* by teaching the marquis a little humility."

"Splendid. I look forward to seeing it."

Stephen nodded at a few friends as he made his way through White's, but he didn't take up any of their invitations to join them in a bottle or a game of cards. He wasn't feeling particularly sociable.

What had Brentwood done to Anne? It must have been more than an aborted flirtation. Yes, Anne had been young and impressionable then—and maybe she'd even been quiet and biddable as Gedding had said, though he had a hard time believing that of his fiery fiancée—but she'd never been an idiot. She might have been disappointed when Brentwood lost interest in her, but she'd have learned from the experience and moved on. She wouldn't have hidden herself away for a decade nor would she have such a strong reaction to Brentwood now.

The only thing he could imagine that would provoke such a response was . . .

Bloody hell, if what he suspected was true, he'd castrate the bastard with a blunt knife.

He reached White's front door. Good. He had a lot of thinking to do, thinking·better done alone in the dark. He would just—*damnation.*

The door swung open to admit the Marquis of Knightsdale followed by the Duke of Alvord and the Earl of Westbrooke.

"Parker-Roth, just the man I'm looking for," Knightsdale said. He turned to Alvord and Westbrooke. "You go ahead; I'll join you shortly."

Westbrooke laughed. "Lucky you, Parker-Roth. I suspect you're in for one of Charles's bear-garden jaws." He clapped Stephen on the back. "Don't worry. Charles won't run you through—he left his sword at home."

"Robbie, you are not helping matters." Knightsdale looked at Alvord. "Will you take this idiot away, James?"

Alvord grinned. "With pleasure. Come along, Robbie. Let's start on a bottle while we wait for Charles."

"An excellent idea. Take your time, Charles," Westbrooke said. "No need to hurry on our account."

"Right," Knightsdale said. He turned to Stephen. "If you'll follow me? We should be able to be private in here." He led the way into a small antechamber.

"Is there a problem, Knightsdale?" May as well take the bull by the horns.

Knightsdale closed the door firmly behind him. "With Emma, there is always a problem."

Damn, damn, damn. He was trapped, he knew it, but he wouldn't give up without a fight. "No offense, Knightsdale, but your charming wife's interest in my affairs is not welcome. Nor appropriate. *I'm* not married to her sister."

Knightsdale just looked at him.

Blast it, he knew it was a weak argument—no, in truth it was a perfectly good argument, if one were arguing with a reasonable person. But Emma was not reasonable. She was a damned officious busybody. The mere possibility that his activities might affect her sister in any way was enough in her demented mind for her to meddle. And if Emma was involved, Knightsdale would be involved. He obviously loved his wife completely, even though they'd been married almost five years and had two sons as well as charge of Knightsdale's two nieces.

Knightsdale clasped his hands behind his back. "Emma wishes to know if this is a sham engagement you are involved in."

How the hell had she guessed that? Stephen crossed his arms in front of his chest. "I publicly announced my betrothal at dinner this evening—you and Emma both heard me. I cannot honorably withdraw now, even if I wanted to, which I do not."

Knightsdale nodded slightly, never breaking eye contact. He must have been a damnably intimidating officer when he served on the Peninsula.

"Lady Anne's waltz with Lord Brentwood was quite

a spectacle. Society is buzzing over it, though no one seems to know quite what to make of it." Knightsdale's gaze sharpened, if that were possible.

Stephen shrugged. "Society loves to speculate about everything."

"True. But if I were to speculate, I would say your betrothed has a pronounced dislike for Lord Brentwood."

"Does anyone of good sense like the marquis?"

Knightsdale inclined his head. "No. However, Brentwood doesn't always return the dislike. My guess is the bastard means to cause Lady Anne problems, and any problems Brentwood causes are usually markedly unpleasant."

Stephen could be intimidating, too. "I invite him to try."

Knightsdale relaxed slightly. He was still standing straight as a board, but he didn't look dangerous any longer. "If you need any assistance in dealing with him, I shall be delighted to help."

"Thank you, but I think I can handle the man on my own."

"Still, the offer stands, and I know Westbrooke and Alvord would lend their support as well." Knightsdale grinned suddenly. "You might be interested to know Brentwood is far up River Tick. It's not common knowledge, but the cent-per-centers will soon be camping on his doorstep unless he finds a way to come about."

So Brentwood was in dun territory, was he? That was interesting. Men drowning in debt were usually willing to grasp at anything to keep their head above water, taking all manner of ill-advised risks. Stephen smiled. He would very much enjoy manipulating some of those risks to his advantage. He would begin by buying up the bastard's vowels. "Thank you. That does open up a number of attractive options, doesn't it?"

Knightsdale laughed. "I thought you'd see it that way."

* * *

"What have you been doing, miss?" Clorinda snorted. "Not that I need to ask."

"Eep!" Anne jumped and almost dropped her candle. She did drop her hold on her bodice which drooped guiltily. Clorinda was standing in the doorway to her bedroom, attired in a rather alarming puce dressing gown and frilly white nightcap. "I thought you'd gone to bed."

Clorinda looked her up and down from her pin-less, wild hair to her sadly crumpled skirt. "Obviously."

She could say that things weren't as bad as they looked, but they were almost that bad and she didn't at all wish to debate the matter. "I'm so sorry if I kept you up." She stepped toward her own bedroom door. "I'll be going to bed now. Do sleep well."

Evie poked her head around Clorinda's body. "Anne!" The poor girl's eyes almost popped out of her head. Her expression was a mix of horror and fascination.

Anne flushed an even brighter red, she was sure. "Why aren't you asleep?"

"We were waiting for you"—Evie turned red, too— "and talking about the ball. I was too excited to go to bed right away. And then when you didn't come up . . . I was on the verge of going downstairs a number of times, but Clorinda stopped me."

"I didn't want poor Evie to get too advanced an education," Clorinda said. "Thank God the boys are asleep."

Anne covered her face with her left hand, her right still being occupied with the candle. She was finally unmasked as the jezebel she was, except this time she didn't feel at all like a jezebel. Yes, it was embarrassing to have Clorinda and Evie guess what she'd been doing—though she hadn't been doing *that*, not exactly—but she wasn't truly sorry she'd done it. Worse, she'd like to do it—and more—again. Soon.

"Oh, Anne, what a beautiful ring!" Evie's voice had more than a touch of awe in it. "Did Mr. Parker-Roth give it to you?"

Anne held out her hand. Her gloves had been misplaced somewhere—she'd best check the green sitting room in the morning before the boys were up—so Stephen's ring was very evident.

"He must have, Evie. Where else would she have got it?" Even Clorinda sounded impressed. "Come into my room so we can look at it more closely."

Anne hadn't seen it properly herself; the garden had been too dark and she'd had her gloves on in the ballroom. She sat on Clorinda's love seat and turned her hand this way and that. The ring *was* beautiful—a single ruby in a simple gold setting, exactly what she would have chosen if she'd been the one making the selection. The candlelight made the ruby glow as if there were a fire burning in its heart.

If only she were truly betrothed. Though after what had just transpired downstairs . . .

"Here, have some brandy." Clorinda handed Anne a glass, and then poured more into her own and Evie's.

"You two are going to be tipsy if you aren't careful," Anne said, taking a sip. The brandy burned a path down her throat and started a pleasant, warm glow in her stomach.

Clorinda grunted and reached for Anne's hand to examine the ring. "Exquisite. The man has taste, and obviously spared no expense. Perhaps he does mean to go forward with this marriage." She glanced at Anne's drooping bodice. "You'd best hope so."

Anne flushed and took another sip of brandy.

"Of course Mr. Parker-Roth means to marry Anne,"

Evie said. "How can you think otherwise? I imagine that's what they were doing downstairs all this time. He gave her the ring, and they discussed their wedding."

Clorinda grunted. "That and other things."

Anne smiled and drank more brandy. There was no need to explain exactly when Stephen had presented her with the ring.

Clorinda leaned forward, gesturing with her glass so a drop of brandy splashed onto the carpet. "If you do mean to wait until after the Season to wed," she said, "you'd better wait until then to do other things as well. A few weeks one way or the other make no difference, but a few months . . ." Clorinda raised her eyebrows significantly. "The *ton* may be a great collection of idiots, but they *can* count—at least as high as nine."

Anne's face felt as if it were aflame.

"What do you mean?" Evie looked from Clorinda to Anne and back again. "What has counting got to do with anything?"

"Babies, Evie." Clorinda took another swallow of brandy. She'd obviously had a swallow or two too many to be talking so freely with Evie. Anne should stop her, but she was too embarrassed to speak.

Embarrassed and something else, something hot and yearning. The thought of having Stephen's child, a baby they'd made together . . .

"Babies?" Evie said. "You mean . . ." She looked at Anne. "But Anne would never do that before she was married." She blushed. "Not that I know what *that* is, of course. And Anne mustn't know either. Mama will tell her the night before her wedding."

Anne examined her ring very closely.

Clorinda had definitely had too much brandy. "Evie, my dear, I expect while we were up here waiting, Mr. Parker-Roth was busy giving Anne a very thorough idea of exactly what *that* entails."

"Oh." Evie looked at Anne.

"No." Anne cleared her throat. "No, he wasn't." *Not completely at least.* "But, Evie, Clorinda makes a very good point; young women—debutantes like you— need to be very careful." She certainly did not want Evie following in her disreputable footsteps. "Men can all too easily lead you into trouble and ruin your reputation. Since I'm older and betrothed, I'm allowed a little more leeway."

Clorinda snorted and waggled her eyebrows. Anne ignored her. This conversation had obviously gone as far—further—than it should. She glanced at the clock.

"Heavens, look how late it is!" She stood and shook out her wrinkled skirt. "The boys will be expecting an excursion tomorrow; if we leave them cooped up here any longer, they will get into any manner of mischief."

Evie laughed. "Papa will come home to find all the knickknacks broken."

"We will be lucky it's all the damage they do," Clorinda said. "How can you bear to live with them all the time? They are exhausting."

"They are ten-year-old boys," Anne said. "One becomes used to the constant high spirits."

Evie nodded. "They can be annoying—they often *are* annoying—but I can't imagine life without them. I love them."

"Hmph. Well, I for one hope Mr. Parker-Roth discovers a suitable tutor very soon."

Evie blushed again. "I believe there was some talk that Mr. Parker-Roth might enlist his brother's help." She turned an even deeper shade of red. "And during our waltz, Mr. Nicholas Parker-Roth told me he would be happy to come by to meet the boys; if they got along, he might be able to act as their tutor for a while as he didn't have any definite plans for his time."

Was Evie enamored of Stephen's brother? Anne

frowned—and then mentally shrugged. Surely nothing would come of it. The Kenderly ball had been Evie's first London social event; she would meet and dance with many more men before the Season was over. And Stephen's brother was very young to be thinking of settling down. "I wouldn't be surprised if the two Parker-Roth gentlemen come by tomorrow, then."

"Oh, do you think so?" Evie leapt up from her seat, looking at the clock also. "Oh, dear. You're right, Anne; it's very late. We'd best get to bed immediately." She rushed out the door so quickly she almost knocked over her brandy glass.

"What is it about the Parker-Roth men?" Clorinda shook her head. "The boy seemed pleasant enough, but nothing to set one's heart aflutter."

"That's because your heart is no longer seventeen, Clorinda." Anne put the brandy glasses back on the table by the decanter. "I'm sure Evie will fall in and out of love any number of times before the Season's over."

"Perhaps." Clorinda pinned her with a sharp look. "But neither your heart nor your head is seventeen, miss. Whatever were you thinking tonight?"

Anne flushed. If only she'd hurried out with Evie. Why did Clorinda suddenly feel the need to take her chaperonage duties seriously? Had she finished all the bird books in the library? "I assure you that while things did become a bit passionate, nothing of a serious nature occurred."

Clorinda was regarding her as if she had suddenly sprouted a second head. "What are you talking about?"

"What, ah, happened—or, rather, what *didn't* happen—downstairs."

"Pshaw!" Clorinda poured herself a little more brandy. "That's not what I meant."

"No?" Anne suddenly had a very bad feeling about

this. "What did you mean?" She started to edge toward the door. Clorinda could finish her brandy in solitude.

"That dance with Lord Brentwood! It looked very much as if you two had some kind of history."

"Gaa."

Clorinda frowned. "Excuse me?"

Anne swallowed and tried to get her heart to slow down. "I mean, where would I have met the marquis?"

"That's a very good question." Clorinda raised her eyebrows.

Anne raised her hand and rested it on the doorknob. She would rather fry in hell than tell Clorinda the tale of her initial meeting with Lord Brentwood. Thankfully Clorinda didn't press her.

"Well, what did you and Lord Brentwood talk about?"

It was all a horrible blur. "Er, dressmakers and, ah, my betrothal."

"Lady Dunlee said it looked like a lover's spat."

"It was definitely not that!" "Love" and "Brentwood" did not belong in the same sentence—in the same paragraph. In the same library. "I'm sorry to offend you, since I know Lord Brentwood's mother is your friend, but I cannot like the man."

"*That* was exceedingly evident." Clorinda shrugged. "Frankly, I thought Mr. Parker-Roth was going to discuss the issue with you tonight—he was obviously in a pet when we got home—but"—Clorinda eyed Anne's drooping bodice again—"apparently he was more interested in other topics."

Anne gripped the doorknob rather than pluck at her poor bodice again. Could she leave now? No, Clorinda was shaking her finger at her.

"You don't want to get the gabble-grinders in a frenzy and annoy Mr. Parker-Roth, Anne. You're quite lucky to have snagged him, you know. If he's not quite rich as Croesus, he's very well to grass—splendid head for investments, Dickie told me tonight. He's been quite the catch on the Marriage Mart ever since he made his bows."

"I see." So the man was not only handsome but rich as well. No wonder all the women were glaring at her tonight.

"I confess I thought your betrothal was all a hum at first—the man reeked of spirits when Lady Dunlee dragged you both into the study—but now it does look as if he means to have you." Clorinda gestured at the betrothal ring glowing on Anne's finger. "What I still don't understand is how you formed this tendre."

"Ah."

"And don't fob me off with that tarradiddle Evie told me about you being introduced to him at a house party ten years ago. Really! Only a child could swallow that tale."

"Ah."

"So?" Clorinda looked expectant.

"So?" Anne smiled. How was she going to get out of this room?

"How *did* you become attached?"

"Ahh . . . it's rather complicated." Anne turned the doorknob at last. "Far too complicated to discuss now. I really am exhausted. Thank you for the brandy; I'm afraid I must be off to bed now. Good night."

She opened the door and fled to the safety of her room.

Chapter 14

Stephen whistled as he rapped on the door to Le Temple d'Amour. The morning had been extremely profitable. Knightsdale's information was correct, of course—Lord Brentwood did owe many, many people money. He grinned and patted his pockets, stuffed full of the IOUs he'd just purchased. But now the marquis had just one creditor—him.

Once Anne told him what Brentwood had done to her, he would decide on the most appropriate way to use the man's vowels.

He rapped again, harder. It was early, but Mags would just have to bestir herself. She was one more link in the chain he intended to draw tight around Brentwood's neck.

He finally heard a stream of invectives on the other side of the flimsy door and then it was flung open.

"What the bloody hell do you think—oh." Mags's jaw dropped. "It's you."

"It is indeed." He stepped past her; he didn't want to give her the opportunity to slam the door in his face. She was wearing a faded blue dressing gown and a nightcap that might once have been white but was now a dingy shade of gray. She looked significantly older without all her rouge and powder, but he found he liked her better this way. She seemed more human.

Mags closed the door behind him. "And what are you doing here? All my girls are still asleep—as I was before you started banging on my door." Mags made a sound of disgust. "Not that I think you're here for the girls. Mags's place ain't good enough for you, is it?"

"Mags, you know I don't frequent brothels." Though if he did, this one would be at the bottom of his list. It wasn't that it was rundown; it was that no one—neither Mags nor her girls—cared much about cleanliness. Picking up a few lice would be the least of his worries.

Mags, looking extremely mulish, crossed her arms. She clearly wasn't going to offer him a seat. Just as well. He'd prefer to remain standing. Any manner of vermin might infest the furniture.

"So why are you here, Mr. Too-Good-For-Me Parker-Roth?"

"I wish to speak with you about the Marquis of Brentwood."

Mags spat into a corner. "That piece of dung? I don't know nuttin' about him and I care less." She stuck her nose in the air. "He don't want to dirty his precious little cock—and it *is* little—dipping it into the likes o' me when he's got a fancy lady who'll spread her legs for him. Talk to your whore, Lady Noughton. She's the one he's swiving now."

"Lady Noughton is not my anything." It was revolting to consider he'd ever visited Maria's bed. He'd let his cock do his thinking for him, but now even that organ cringed at the notion of having anything more to do with the widow.

"That's right. Brentwood said he pushed you out of her bed."

"Mags, do I look like I would let Brentwood push me anywhere?"

Mags looked him up and down. "Well, no."

"Of course not. Lady Noughton and I parted company months ago; Brentwood is welcome to her—they are birds of a feather."

"Aye, you can say that again." Mags's lips curled. "They can burn in hell together."

Mags's reaction was only slightly more violent than the men from whom he'd bought Brentwood's vowels. Brentwood was most unpopular, but then bullies usually were. Everyone was eager for him to get his just deserts. "So you wouldn't be unhappy should poor Lord Brentwood encounter a spot of bad luck?"

"Unhappy? I'd stand up and cheer, and that's a fact. All the girls would."

"Then perhaps you and they would like to whisper in your customers' ears that Brentwood's pockets are to let." Brentwood had hidden his penury well; not only would he be furious when the truth got out, he'd find his credit cut off immediately.

"He's really in Queer Street?" Mags looked simultaneously skeptical and hopeful.

"He is. He's been punting on the River Tick for months. I've got his vowels to prove it." He pulled the wad of papers out of his pocket far enough for her to see it.

Her nostrils flared. "The bloody bastard. I'd like to boil his cock in oil. I'd never have let him in the front door if I'd known that. The lying whoreson told me he was going to buy me a new house closer to Mayfair. Make me one of the top madams." She snorted. "I should have known it was all talk. Half the time he didn't pay me for my night's work—and it *was* work. Maybe Lady Noughton don't mind his tiny prick, but if I'm giving a man a free tumble, I want something out of it, if you know what I mean."

She looked pointedly at Stephen's crotch. "And I'm sure you know what I mean. Lady Noughton must be colder than ice if she's happy with Brentwood after having your—"

Stephen yanked out his pocket watch. "Look at the time!" He had no desire to discuss Brentwood's—or his—performance in the bedroom. "Sorry, but I've got to run—promised my fiancée I'd take her young brothers to see some of London."

"So I can't interest you in a quick ride? I'll not charge you for the pleasure." Mags grinned at him, revealing several missing teeth. "It'd be *my* pleasure."

"Thank you, but no."

Mags frowned and looked as if she might take offense. He didn't want to insult his new ally, but he was not at all interested in her generous offer. How could he—of course. He was betrothed now—he would hide behind Lady Anne's lovely skirts.

"My fiancée would not approve."

Mags's frown turned immediately into a shout of laughter. "That's rich—the King of Hearts is to be a hen-pecked husband!"

"You've found me out." He took the opportunity to step outside. "But I hope I may prevail upon you to keep my secret."

"Aye." She dimpled at him as if she were a coy, young miss. "I'm more interested in spreading the word about a certain penniless bastard."

"Splendid. I encourage you to do so at every opportunity."

He grinned and bounded down the steps. Mags's girls entertained all manner of men—peers temporarily under the hatches as well as footmen and tradesmen. The news of Brentwood's distress should spread from all directions and be common knowledge in a day or two.

Stephen was very much looking forward to watching the marquis squirm.

"What are you grinning about, big brother?" Nick was in Stephen's study, sprawled in one of the wing chairs by the fire, a glass of Madeira dangling from his fingers. He did not look happy.

"I've had a profitable morning." Stephen poured himself some Madeira and sank into the other chair. "What's gnawing at you? I thought you'd be chomping at the bit to get to Crane House."

Nick shot him a wry look. "Mama and Da are here."

"What?" Stephen jerked upright, spilling a few drops of Madeira on his breeches. "Damn." He pulled out his handkerchief and mopped at the spot, before looking back at Nick. "They can't be here."

Nick rolled his eyes. "Well they are. They've gone off to the Pulteney."

Stephen's heart was lurching about in his chest in a most distracting manner. He loved his parents, but he loved them more when they were home at the Priory. "You must be mistaken. Mama wouldn't leave baby Jack, and Da wouldn't leave his study."

Nick looked up at the ceiling as if he thought he might discover some intelligence there, as he clearly felt Stephen lacked any. "I may be eight years your junior, dear brother, but I'm not a knock-in-the-cradle. I do recognize our parents. I assure you Mama about hugged me to death. And yes, Da just looked as if he wanted to get back to his sonnets." He cocked a brow at Stephen. "But I'd say they both were somewhat keen on talking to you."

"Bloody hell." Stephen downed his Madeira and

poured some more. "Mama could not have got wind of the betrothal." He took a more judicious swallow and shook his head. "And even if she had, there's no way in Hades she could have made it to London this quickly. The notice was just in the papers this morning." And the thought hadn't been in his head before yesterday, but he wasn't about to tell Nick that.

"I suspect she decided about five minutes after I left home that she didn't care to have me loose in London with only my brother, the King of Hearts, to provide supervision."

Stephen cringed. Damn that nickname. "I'm not your keeper."

"I know that. You know that. I think even Da knows that. Mama, however, is of a different opinion."

Nick was likely correct. Mama *would* expect him to look out for his brother. And he would, of course, but his notion of acceptable behavior for a young man about Town and Mama's were certain to be vastly different. "I could have sworn nothing short of the end of the world could separate Mama from her new grandson."

"Well, yes, but I imagine she convinced herself in short order that my visit to London, a cesspool of sin and vice, qualified as world ending."

Stephen snorted. "But what about the girls? Shouldn't she be home riding herd on Juliana and Lucy?"

"Meg and John aren't so besotted with their baby that they can't see the girls don't run amok—and anyway, the girls can look after themselves. Juliana just turned seventeen, you know. If she hadn't singed her eyelashes off in the explosion after her last experiment, she might be making her come-out this Season."

"Good God!" Little Juliana, here for the London

Season? She *had* looked rather grown-up at Jack's christening. He'd obviously been away from home too long.

"And of course, once Mama got to London and heard you were betrothed—and yes, she definitely has heard, but not from me—wild horses couldn't drag her away from Town, you must know that."

"Zeus." Stephen looked longingly at the Madeira, but he couldn't have any more. He was promised—he and Nick were promised—to Crane House. The twins would be expecting their outing. "When do you think they'll be back?"

"I don't know. They didn't say." Nick sat up and put his glass on the occasional table at his elbow. "But I suggest we leave promptly so we aren't here when they do return."

Evie was driving Anne to distraction. "Will you sit down and stop looking out the window? You're worse than the boys."

Anne was already on edge, thinking about seeing Stephen—Mr. Parker-Roth—again. What must he think of her? She'd behaved like a complete wanton last night. Worse, she was tempted to behave in exactly the same fashion today.

Evie flushed and sat down on the edge of her chair. "Shouldn't they be here by now?"

Anne glanced at the table clock which Evie could see as well as she. "It's just five minutes past the hour."

"They're late."

Anne put aside her sewing. She obviously wasn't going to get any more work done. "When a gentleman says he will call at two o'clock, he doesn't mean *precisely* two—as you well know."

Evie picked an invisible speck of lint off her skirt.

"Well, of course I know that. It's just that your Mr. Parker-Roth struck me as very punctual."

"You've only just met him; I don't see how you can have formed an opinion of his habits."

Evie shrugged. "He just seems very precise and capable. He must be, if he organizes all those expeditions, don't you think?" She raised her gaze to meet Anne's. "But you've known him for years—am I right?"

O what a tangled web we weave, when first we practice to deceive. Sir Walter Scott got that exactly right. "I, ah—"

Footsteps pounded down the stairs out in the hall accompanied by Harry's manic barking and the boys shouting and whooping.

Evie sprang out of her chair and twitched back the curtain. "They're here!"

Anne frowned. Evie was much too delighted by this outing. She grabbed her sister's elbow before the girl could go dashing out to greet their visitors as enthusiastically as the twins. "Evie, you don't want to give Mr. Nicholas Parker-Roth the wrong impression."

Evie flushed. "I don't know what you mean."

"You do. You will make the man think you favor him too much."

Evie turned a deeper red. "I *do* favor him."

Good Lord! "You can't. You've only just met him. And anyway, he's too young. You're too young."

Evie's jaw hardened. She was usually possessed of the sunniest of dispositions, but occasionally something would stir her passions and she would dig her heels in. This appeared to be one of those times.

Anne's gut clenched. Surely Mr. Nicholas Parker-Roth had not stirred *those* passions?

"He is not too young," Evie said, "nor am I. You were just my age when you met his brother, if you'll recall."

Damn! Why the *hell* had she said she'd met Stephen

at Baron Gedding's house party? She just did not have enough experience with lying. "But that's different."

"I don't see how, except you wasted ten years of your life pining for your Mr. Parker-Roth. I do not intend to be so nonsensical."

Anne heard the door open. Stephen and his brother must have entered the hall; Harry was barking as if he were possessed. She still had her hand on Evie's elbow. She shook it to emphasize her point.

"Just be cautious, please? Men are very different from women. You can't assume you know what they are thinking." She'd certainly made some disastrous assumptions about Brentwood's thoughts.

Evie pulled herself free. "I know that. I'm not a child, even though *some* people seem to think I am." She gave Anne a speaking look before she pulled open the door and stepped into the entryway.

Anne closed her eyes briefly, her stomach twisting into a tight knot. She'd been just as certain she knew everything when she was Evie's age. No one could tell her anything—and look where it had got her. She wouldn't let that happen to Evie.

She took a deep breath to calm her nerves. Really, the situations were not all that similar. Yes, Evie was young, but she had a good head on her shoulders, and she didn't have any of the foolish anger Anne had had over the then-impending birth of the twins. And, most importantly, Evie had Anne by her side to keep a sharp eye on Mr. Nicholas Parker-Roth.

Stephen stuck his head into the sitting room, and she jumped. He laughed.

"Are you coming out of there, Anne? We're getting ready to leave. The boys and Harry are quite eager to be off."

"Oh." She could barely get her breath. She was as

silly as Evie; just seeing Stephen made her heart pound. "Where are we going?"

"To the Tower to see the Royal Menagerie. It's a sad little collection of animals these days, but the boys said they don't care. It won't take long, and then we can take Harry for a romp in the park."

"Ah. Yes." Her heart wasn't the only organ pounding. Did he remember their activities of last night as clearly as she did?

"I see you're wearing another one of Celeste's creations." His eyes slid over the gold-toned walking dress as he stepped all the way into the room. He had a hat box in one hand. "Very nice." He grinned. "But I still like the red dress better."

"The red dress would be completely inappropriate for day wear, as you well know." She eyed the box. She was too polite to ask what was in it, but she was sorely tempted.

His grin widened. "I've brought you something." He handed her the box.

A present. She felt foolishly thrilled. "I'm sure you shouldn't have."

"I'm sure I should have. Go ahead, open it."

She untied the strings and lifted off the top. Nestled inside was a bonnet trimmed with gold ribbon and bunches of forget-me-nots. She lifted it out and held it up. "Oh! It's beautiful, and it goes perfectly with this dress."

"It should. I asked Celeste which frock she'd send first."

She'd never had a bonnet so lovely. Much as she might denigrate London hats, she was very taken with this one. However . . . "I can't accept it."

"Of course you can."

"But—"

Stephen held up his hand. "You can. Come, you

must admit I owe you a bonnet after I ground yours into the mud." He took it from her and put it on her head, tying the ribbons under her chin. Then he turned her to look in the mirror. "See? This bonnet sets off your hair instead of hiding it."

Anne stared at her reflection. The bonnet did look very nice. It framed her face and made her look almost elegant. "Thank you."

"You're welcome. Now, we'd best be off—I imagine your brothers are getting impatient. Come along. The day's warm. You won't need a pelisse."

They stepped into the hall, but it was already empty. Anne wasn't surprised to see the boys and Harry gone, but Evie hadn't waited for her, either.

Perhaps that wasn't so surprising. Evie likely didn't want another helping of unwanted advice from her older sister. "How are we going to get there? We can't all cram into one carriage."

Stephen opened the front door and she saw the answer. Two carriages stood in front of Crane House, one with the Earl of Kenderly's coat of arms on its side. A footman stood by Stephen's coach, holding Harry's leash.

"Damian lent me his equipage—looks like everyone's piled in there," Stephen said, pulling the front door closed behind them.

Anne paused and frowned at the earl's carriage. So much for keeping a close eye on Stephen's brother. "I'm not certain—no, actually I am *quite* certain your brother and my sister should not be alone in a coach together."

Stephen laughed. "They aren't. Philip and George will prove to be more than adequate chaperones. If I remember correctly, ten-year-old boys are very observant and would be completely—and loudly—revolted if Nick attempted any kind of lovemaking." He took her arm and led her over to his coach. "And see, they've left Harry to accompany us and ensure *my* animal instincts don't get the better of me."

This last he murmured by her ear as he helped her into the carriage, sending a shiver of . . . something through her. So he *did* remember last night's activities. Her breasts and her, ah, nether region sprang to attention, letting her know in no uncertain terms they would thoroughly enjoy a repeat performance.

Stephen's weren't the only animal instincts threatening to lead her astray.

Harry followed her into the carriage while Stephen said a few words to his coachman. She wrapped her arms around the dog and buried her face in his neck. Perhaps if she held onto Harry, she wouldn't attack Stephen when he got in.

She'd never have guessed she'd ever wish to engage in any activities that involved the lower portion of her person. Not after her distasteful experience with Brentwood. But Brentwood hadn't done any of the things Stephen had. She hadn't known her body could feel such sensations.

She was like a child with a new toy. She wanted to play with it all day.

Stephen finally climbed into the carriage and settled on the bench across from her. Their knees almost touched. Her treacherous body thrummed with delight.

He grinned at her, and then turned to open the carriage window.

She ordered her body to behave itself and her thoughts to focus on something other than Mr. Parker-Roth's broad shoulders and talented hands. This was the perfect time to broach the issue of his brother and Evie.

She let go of Harry and sat up straighter. "Mr. Parker-Roth—"

He laughed. "Stephen, my love. After the intimacies we shared last night, such formality is rather ridiculous, don't you agree? Especially in the privacy of my carriage."

The coach jerked into motion. Harry, the traitor, leapt for the open window and stuck his head out. Stephen, the rogue, leapt for Harry's place beside her.

She slid toward the carriage wall, but the bench was narrow and the scoundrel merely followed her. She could feel his hard thigh pressing along the whole length of hers. "Ah." All thoughts of Evie and Nicholas scattered.

"Don't tell me you've forgotten all the lovely things we did in that sitting room yesterday evening?"

"Ah." Was she such a complete idiot she couldn't manage to formulate a coherent word?

He shook his head. "I'll just have to remind you." His hand brushed the side of her bodice.

"Eep!" It was as though current ran from his fingers to her nipples and the other small bit of flesh lower down that he'd discovered last night.

He frowned. "Is that a yes 'eep' or a no 'eep'?"

Her heart was pounding—and her breasts and nether region were throbbing—so it was very difficult to think. Her mind—and her morals—told her to say a clear, loud, unmistakable "no," but her body screamed "*yes!*"

"You can't. I can't, ah, arrive at the Tower looking all m-mussed. Everyone will know what we've been doing."

"Ah, so that was a yes, but be careful 'eep'."

She gave a breathless little laugh. "You are absurd."

"But correct, hmm?" He reached down and lifted her skirt to her knees. "I blush to say it, but I have had enough experience to know how to manage things without leaving any wrinkles or other evidence for suspicious gossips to detect."

His hand was caressing her left calf, sliding up her leg, rubbing, playing.

"I-I had intended to discuss your brother's interest in my sister," she said. He was stroking her knee now.

He kissed her cheek. "Sounds like a dreadfully dull topic, but I'll try to listen if you wish to talk." His mouth hovered over hers. "Open for me, will you?" he whispered.

He did not mean her mouth.

Where was Harry when she needed him? With his head hanging out in the wind, silly dog. He was a terrible chaperone.

"Please, Anne?" He slipped his fingers between her thighs. His eyes were deep blue pools of temptation.

And she was a terrible, needy woman. She parted her legs.

His large, warm palm slid slowly, tantalizingly, up the inside of her thigh.

"We are in public." Sadly, her body didn't seem to care where they were, but her mind was still fighting.

"We are in my coach."

"Someone could see us."

"No one is looking, and it is not so easy to see inside a coach." He kissed the corner of her mouth. "We will be most discreet."

Discreet! Good God, they were being anything but that. Her knees were exposed, and Stephen's hand was under her skirts. But he was correct—no one was looking. Traffic proceeded placidly along on the roadway, completely oblivious to the scandalous goings on in this vehicle.

"And what would be the penalty if we were discovered? We are already betrothed."

"Um." The small spark of rational thought that still

struggled to make itself heard in her sensation-drugged brain begged to differ with the man's assessment of the situation, but that voice was easy to ignore, especially as her poor body was begging most strenuously for her to allow his hand higher. A certain spot was weeping, it was so frustrated.

His thumb was now drawing circles on her bare skin. She spread her legs a little wider.

His eyes, still looking into hers, got bluer—and hotter—as his palm slid up another inch. His fingers were *so* close. He reached the very top of her thigh—and stopped.

She was panting. Just an inch—less than an inch. She needed him to move just the smallest measure of space toward her center. If he only touched her *there*, she'd explode like she had last night. She tilted her hips, twisting, trying to move him closer. She whimpered.

"Now, Anne?"

Words were far beyond her abilities. She nodded.

He moved, brushing his fingers lightly over the hard little point, once, twice—and then the now familiar waves of intense pleasure radiated through her. She clung to him so she wouldn't be washed away entirely; he covered her mouth with his to muffle the little noises she made until the last wave passed and she collapsed against him.

"Oh." She couldn't move. She should feel embarrassed—Stephen's hand was still covering her under her skirts—but she was far too satiated to feel anything but deeply, oddly content. She lifted her head—it took more effort than it should—and pressed a kiss to his jaw.

"Are you all right?" he asked.

"Mmm." Far more than all right.

She dropped her head back to his chest and listened to the clop of horse hooves, the rattle of carriage wheels, the steady, comforting sound of his breathing. She never wanted to move again.

Finally he cupped her chin, turning her face up to his. "I'm very glad I seem to have stolen away your senses, my love, but you need to try to return to the present now. We are approaching the Tower."

"What?"

He grinned, but she thought his eyes looked a little tense as he slipped his hand out from under her skirts, brushing them back into place. He flinched a bit when he moved as if he were in pain . . .

She looked down at his breeches.

"Oh, you poor man." She reached for him.

He dodged her hand. "Don't."

"Why not? You must be most uncomfortable."

He smiled rather tightly. "It will pass."

"But can't I—" She reached for him again, but he captured her hand in his. "But you're so . . . stiff. Surely I can help if you'll just tell me what to do."

"What you need to do is change the subject. Shall we discuss our siblings in the other coach?"

"What?"

He shifted gingerly on the seat. "You remember Nick and Evie—my brother and your sister? They're in the carriage behind us."

"Oh, yes, well—"

Harry started barking wildly. He looked as if he were going to squirm through the window.

"Harry!" Anne grabbed his leash. "What is it?"

"Damn." Stephen was looking out the other window.

"What? Are we not at the Tower?"

"Oh, we're there all right." He sat back and dropped his head into his hands. "And so are my parents."

Chapter 15

"Your parents!" Anne gaped at him. "As in your mother and father?"

"Yes, of course." He ran an expert eye over her. He'd done a good job of keeping her clothing and hair in order, and the shock of his parents' arrival seemed to be draining away her heightened color.

Something needed to drain the blood from his poor cock or his father, if not his mother as well, would immediately discern what he'd been doing. Damn these tight breeches and cutaway coats. He'd have to hide behind Anne's skirts. "What did you imagine—I sprang from the ground fully formed?"

His tone was sharper than he'd intended, but frustrated desire was making him tetchy.

"Aren't they in the country?"

"Obviously not." He had to get a grip on his emotions. It wasn't Anne's fault Mama and Da had tracked him down. He should have waited at his rooms for them, but who'd have thought they'd follow him to the Tower?

Heh. How appropriate. If only he were here to have his head chopped off.

"What will they think of me?" Anne had clearly moved from shock to panic. That would be all he needed.

"They will love you, Anne. Why wouldn't they?" He'd swear he could see the whites of her eyes, as if she were a horse ready to bolt.

"I'm Crazy Crane's daughter. I haven't been brought out; I've never been to London before; I have no polish. I'm old." Her lovely voice was thin and rising; she was talking too fast to breathe properly. "And I was just doing"—she turned beet red again, damn it—"what I was doing with you."

He forced aside his sexual frustration and tried to speak soothingly. "No one can tell by looking at you what we've been doing." What they could tell by looking at him was a different affair, but fortunately his dimensions were finally shrinking. "Just smile and try not to look guilty."

He should have left off the bit about not looking guilty. She flushed again.

"Truly, you have nothing to worry about." He laughed. "Though you might try not to glare at me."

"I'm not glaring at you!"

He elected not to argue the point. "Anne, my mother will be over the moon I'm engaged. I've just turned thirty, and my older brother and younger sister are both married and have presented her with grandchildren. She was hounding me at my nephew's christening to find a bride; in fact she made it painfully clear she planned to turn her full attention to my marital status as soon as possible. Your appearance has saved her a great deal of trouble, I assure you."

"But the odd circumstances of our betrothal! That *must* cause her dismay."

"Not at all. You know our family specializes in odd circumstances and scandalous marriages. Jane was

enceinte when she wed Motton, and John had compromised Meg many times over. The tittle-tattle was in
all the papers."

She flushed again, but not so violently. "Yes, it was."

"So there you are; the manner of our betrothal was
almost expected."

She didn't look completely convinced, but at least
she had calmed down—as, thankfully, had his cock.
There was no time to say anything else in any event.
The coach was finally swaying to a stop. Harry had his
nose to the door.

"Sit, sir," Stephen said. "I cannot let you out if you
crowd me so."

Harry obligingly backed away. Stephen closed the
window, and then opened the door and let down the
steps.

"Stay," he commanded as Harry tried to bolt.

He climbed out and reached back to help Anne.
Harry scrambled down behind her. Nick, Evie, and the
boys had already got out, and Nick, good man, was oc-
cupying Mama and Da with introductions.

"How did they find you?" Anne whispered as Harry
tried to tug her over to the group.

"I imagine my valet told them where I was going.
They'd stopped by my rooms earlier, but I was out."

Mama must have had one eye on their coach, because she turned almost immediately to smile at them,
her sharp eyes missing nary a detail. Thank God his
male organ had finally resumed its normal proportions. He saw Da put a hand on her arm to keep her
from rushing toward them.

"Here we go then. Don't be nervous," he muttered
to Anne. He was the one who was nervous. He led her
over to his parents, feeling a bit as if he were Daniel
and they were the lions.

"Mama, Da, what a surprise."

Mama's brows dropped and she gave him one of her looks. All right, yes, it was a silly thing to have said, but he was fresh out of witty conversational gambits.

"I don't know why you should be surprised; I'm sure Nicholas told you we were in Town."

"Ah." He couldn't very well deny it with Nick standing right there. "Yes, well, in any event, let me make known to you Lady Anne Marston, the Earl of Crane's daughter." He turned to Anne. "Anne, my parents, Mr. and Mrs. Parker-Roth."

"And who might this be?" Da asked. Harry was sniffing his boots and breeches.

"That's our dog, Harry, sir," Philip said. "He's quite friendly."

"I can see that."

"We are taking him for a romp in the park after we've visited the menagerie."

"The menagerie, eh? I haven't seen the menagerie in years," Da said. "May we join you?"

"Of course, sir," Philip said. He and the others started up the path to the Lion Tower. Mama stayed with Stephen and Anne.

"Are your father and stepmother here in London with you, Lady Anne?" Mama asked.

She must know they weren't; Stephen felt sure she'd ferreted out every detail of Anne's visit to Town the moment she'd learned of their engagement.

"No." Did Anne sound the slightest bit bitter? "My father and Lady Crane are currently in Greece, investigating a new discovery of antiquities. But my cousin, Miss Clorinda Strange, is acting as our chaperone—or, my sister's chaperone. I am far too old to require her services."

"Oh, yes, I can see you are indeed ancient." Mama laughed. "Don't be nonsensical, Lady Anne. You are in the prime of your life."

Anne flushed. "Oh, no. That is, I'm twenty-seven. Quite on the shelf."

Mama raised her brows in a manner that clearly said, "Are you a complete cabbage-head?" "Perhaps you *were* on the shelf, my dear; now I understand you are betrothed to my son."

Anne's flush deepened. Her mouth opened and closed twice, and then a determined look entered her eyes. Damn. She was going to tell Mama the complete story. He couldn't let her do that.

He put his hand over hers where it rested on his arm and squeezed gently. She glared at him, her mouth opening once more. He squeezed harder. Her eyes narrowed, but at least she snapped her lips closed.

He felt Mama scrutinizing them. She must suspect something—with six children she had perfected her ability to sniff out even the slightest whiff of subterfuge— but at least she couldn't know exactly what was amiss.

"Yes, indeed, Mama. Lady Anne has made me the happiest of men."

"This is somewhat sudden, isn't it?" Mama directed her question to Anne, obviously having concluded she would have far more success extracting the truth from her.

"Yes and no." Stephen spoke quickly to forestall Anne's reply. "We met years ago at a house party. I was too young to consider marriage then, but I couldn't banish Anne from my thoughts." Mama's eyes widened. It *was* quite a plumper to swallow, but Mama was a romantic at heart—perhaps she wouldn't choke on it. "When I saw her again, I had to propose." He smiled and delivered his winning thrust. "I grant you, I was a bit impetuous, but I'm definitely old enough to marry, as you were just telling me at Jack's christening." He grinned. "So you see you are at least partly responsible for our betrothal, Mama."

Mama nodded, acknowledging a direct hit, but she was a fighter where her children were concerned. She wouldn't give up easily. "At whose house party did you meet?"

"Baron Gedding's."

Mama's eyebrows rose. "I didn't know you were on intimate terms with the baron."

"One doesn't need to be on intimate terms with one's host to get an invitation."

"I don't remember you ever attending such a gathering."

He raised his own brows. "I hesitate to inform you, Mama, but I've attended many gatherings of which you are not aware."

She frowned and pressed her lips together. To give her her due, she had never tried to keep any of her children in leading strings. She might not be completely happy about it, but she recognized her sons needed their freedom, and though she kept her ears open for any gossip that came her way, she didn't actively seek it out or pry into their personal affairs.

She looked at Anne again. "And were you also taken with my son?"

Anne blushed. "Oh, yes."

Zeus, she sounded sincere; Stephen hadn't thought her that accomplished an actress.

Was she acting? Could she possibly have developed a tendre for him? An odd, warm feeling started in the vicinity of his heart.

He shook himself mentally. He'd started believing their Banbury tale. He'd not actually been at Gedding's gathering; he hadn't met Anne before their encounter in Hyde Park. Of course she had no special feelings for him.

The warmth faded, leaving behind a cold, irritable

feeling. As cork-brained as he admitted it was, he wished Anne truly was in love with him.

Nick walked toward them, almost dragging Harry barking insistently behind him.

"My heavens, what is all the commotion about, Nicholas?" Mama asked.

"Harry took exception to the lions, I'm afraid."

Stephen laughed. "Perhaps he thinks they are merely overgrown versions of Lady Dunlee's cat, Miss Whiskers."

"Lady Dunlee!" Mama grimaced. "Surely you haven't been associating with that woman?"

So Mama hadn't heard all the details of the scandal . . . yet. Unfortunately, she'd get a complete, most likely embellished accounting of his actions at the first society event she attended. Not that the incident could be embellished much and still be fit for female ears. He *had* behaved outrageously, though he didn't regret a moment of that encounter—well, except for the fact that it had caused Anne some distress.

"Unfortunately, Lady Dunlee lives next door to Crane House, Mrs. Parker-Roth," Anne said.

"Oh, you poor dear." Mama made a tsking sound and shook her head. "That woman is a terrible busybody. She was the one who spread the tale of my oldest son's encounter with Meg—his wife now, but not then—in Lord Palmerson's garden." She smiled mischievously. "Though I suppose I really should thank her. If she hadn't gossiped far and wide, John might never have pulled his head out of his plants long enough to notice Meg, and I couldn't ask for a better match for him. She's very interested in botany herself, but she's also a delightful girl—and she's presented us with a wonderful grandson."

"Oh, Lord," Nick said, "don't get Mama talking

about her grandchildren. She'll go on until you scream for mercy—and she only has two so far."

"Nicholas!" Mama tried to sound offended, but she couldn't quite keep a thread of amusement from her voice. "I hope I am not such a bore."

"Of course you aren't, Mama." Nick rolled his eyes.

Harry, having subsided for a moment, decided to redouble his efforts to get back to the lions. He jerked on the leash so vigorously, he almost pulled Nick over.

"If you'll excuse us, Harry and I will retreat to the carriages and save you your hearing." Nick pulled back on the leash. "I think everyone will be following shortly, so if you do want to see any of the animals, you'd best go on now."

"How can they be leaving so soon?" Mama asked. "They just arrived."

Nick shrugged. "I'm afraid the menagerie proved rather disappointing. Come, Harry."

Harry offered a few more protestations, but finally gave up and followed Nick with fairly good grace.

"Disappointing?" Mama looked surprised as they continued up the path. "How can that be? Didn't you find it exciting when you were young, Stephen? I'm sure I did whenever we visited. You don't see a hyena or a jackal every day."

"No, indeed." Anne nodded. "I can't imagine how the twins could fail to be thrilled."

"The menagerie has declined over the years, Mama," Stephen said. "There's only a handful of animals left." He paid their entrance fee, and they went through the gate and down to the animal cages. They got jostled a bit by the crowd, but he was able to keep Mama and Anne from the worst of it.

Da came over as soon as he saw them and took Mama's arm. "It's not the same menagerie we remember, Cecilia. It's much smaller and a bit shabby."

Philip nodded. "It's all a hum, Mrs. Parker-Roth. There's only a panther, a leopard, a tiger, four lions, and a bear."

"And they don't do anything," George said, clearly disgusted. "They just lie there."

"They are in such dreadfully small cages," Evie said. "It's so sad. The animals all look mangy and tired."

"Only one tiger and one panther?" Mama asked. "And no jackal or hyena?"

"That's right," Da said. "Here, come see for yourself."

They stepped over to the nearest cage where they saw a rather moth-eaten looking tiger, sound asleep. Mama, Da, and Evie moved on. Stephen started to follow with Anne.

"Anne," George said in a slightly whiny tone, "me and Philip have seen everything already."

Anne let go of Stephen's arm to turn to the boys. "Philip and *I*, George. And we won't be much longer."

"But can't we go find Harry now, Anne?" Philip asked. "Please?"

"Well . . ."

A pack of boisterous boys pushed between Stephen and Anne. He lost sight of her for a moment. When he saw her again, she was going back up the ramp to the gate with George and Philip.

Damn it, what was she thinking? A pair of ten-year-old boys couldn't provide her adequate protection.

"Da." He pressed through the group of people around the leopard's cage and grabbed his father's arm. "I have to go after Anne. She and the boys have gone to the carriages. Will you take care of Evie for me as well as Mama?"

Da nodded. "Of course."

Stephen didn't wait to discuss the matter further, but pushed his way through the crowd. Bloody hell,

Anne and the boys were already out of sight. Wait, was that Anne's bonnet? If he hurried—

He bumped up against the back of a very large woman. She turned to glare at him. Blast!

"My apologies, madam. I hope you will excuse me. I'm trying to catch up to my companion."

The woman put her massive arms on her hips so she blocked even more of the walkway. "Trying to catch up to your companion, are you? You think that gives you the right to abuse anyone you wish?"

An equally sizeable man, who'd been slightly ahead of the woman, stopped and came back. "Is this fellow annoying you, Madge? I'll be happy to take him outside and deal with him."

The only way this puff-guts could "deal with" Stephen would be to sit on him, but Stephen didn't have time for an argument. "Sir, I was just apologizing to this lady. I very clumsily bumped into her." He turned back to the woman. "Madam, please accept my abject apologies. I was completely at fault. My only excuse is my concern for my fiancée. We became separated and now she is in the crowd alone."

"Well, why didn't you say so at once?" Madge smiled at the large man. "The boy's in love, Bert. I suppose we can't hold that against him, can we?"

Bert laughed. "No, I suppose we can't. I was like that once, too, wasn't I?"

"I believe you were—thirty years ago."

The couple still hadn't got out of his way. He was becoming desperate. Surely Anne wouldn't run into trouble in such a short time? Surely the boys would have the sense to stay by her.

Surely he wouldn't start bellowing if these people didn't move very, very soon.

"If you will excuse me, then? I am most anxious to find my fiancée."

"Of course you are," Madge said. She finally stepped aside. "Hurry on, then. Go find her."

"My heartfelt thanks." He almost ran past them.

"Ah," he heard Madge sigh. "There's nothing like young love, is there, Bert?"

"Oh, I don't know," Bert said roguishly. "Let's go home and see, shall we?"

He put Bert and Madge firmly out of his mind as he threaded his way through the crowd. Why did so many people walk so slowly? He'd swear everyone was purposely getting in his way.

There. Anne was across the yard, standing all alone by the wall. The boys were nowhere in sight, damn it. She was—

Bloody hell! Brentwood had just come up to her. So there was still a hyena in the menagerie. Well, he'd put a stop to that.

He was starting toward them when a hand grabbed his sleeve.

"Stephen," Maria said, "how lovely to see you."

"Lady Anne, what a delightful coincidence."

Brentwood sounded pleasant enough, but Anne heard the threat in his voice. Her eyes narrowed. "What are you doing here?"

His brows shot up. "I had a sudden desire to view the animals. The menagerie *is* open to the public, you know. Did you think I slipped in without paying my admission fee?"

That was the most shocking bouncer she'd ever heard. She no more believed he was here by coincidence than she thought the moon was made of cheese. "You're following me."

His smile was repulsive. He *did* belong at the menagerie, but inside the cages. "Perhaps. I enjoy looking at you and imagining what I'll be doing with you in just a few days." He waggled his brows. "I find anticipation is half the pleasure, don't you?"

"Anticipating having anything to do with you makes me ill." She'd like to tell him she'd die before she'd go to his bed, but she couldn't, not yet. First, she needed to come up with a plan to mitigate the damage his revealing her secret would do to Evie's Season—and be sure Evie knew never to be alone with the man; then she could allow herself the satisfaction of letting him know exactly what she thought of him.

And she had to tell Stephen the truth first as well. Even though telling him in person meant she'd be compelled to watch his expression turn from amiable to disgusted, she owed him that courtesy. She could not let him find out from gossip.

Brentwood's eyes narrowed. "I hope you aren't considering reneging on our bargain, my sweet. I assure you that would be a very bad decision. I will have no compunction about ravaging your reputation—and perhaps your charming sister—completely. Neither of you will be able to hold your head up in society. All doors will be shut firmly in your face; everyone will give you the cut direct. You will be forced to flee London with your tail between your legs."

His lips slid into a lecherous smile. "Much better to let me between those lovely legs." His eyes wandered over her. "But this time I'll have you naked, so I can see all your charms and watch my cock slide into you."

She swallowed bile and clutched her skirts to keep from slapping him—or kneeing him in the groin.

He laughed. "Such spirit! If you look down at my

breeches, you'll see I am most, most eager to enjoy all that fire."

"I will fight you."

"I do hope you will. That will make the encounter all the more exciting. I plan to have you many, many times—on your back, on your knees, maybe even against the wall like I did the first time."

Her face was flaming; her gut was a hard, tight knot. "You are disgusting."

"Indeed I am." He touched her cheek and she flinched away from him. He laughed again. "And I wager you'll enjoy every disgusting moment. You have the hair—and the soul—of a whore, you know."

"I do not." She *would* hit him if she stayed here another moment. "And I will hate every second."

He shrugged. "Very well. It makes no difference to me." He leaned close. "I've often found an unwilling partner is even more . . . stimulating."

Hadn't anyone noted her discomfort? Surely someone would step in to assist her. The twins were long gone, but perhaps the others? She looked hopefully back toward the animal cages—and saw Stephen . . . with Lady Noughton.

"Don't think your fiancé will help you," Brentwood said, following her gaze. "On the contrary, he'll be delighted with your disgrace. Even the highest stickler wouldn't fault him then for ending his betrothal. And once free of you, he can wed Maria."

"He doesn't care for Lady Noughton." She knew Brentwood was lying. He must be. Stephen had told her he was done with his mistress. He wasn't making the slightest effort to hide his annoyance with the widow now. She watched him firmly detach himself from her grasp.

"Did he—the King of Hearts—tell you that? Oh, sweetheart, you are so gullible."

She looked Brentwood in the eye. "And I should believe you, the man who seduced me with talk of love and marriage when I was just a seventeen-year-old girl? The man who lured me into Baron Gedding's garden and took my virginity with all the gentleness of a rutting bull?"

"Is that how you've justified it to yourself?" Brentwood's voice was cold with derision. "You red-headed whore. Don't lie to yourself. You wanted it. You were as bad as a bitch in heat. I was doing you a favor, scratching your itch for you."

She was too angry to speak. Fortunately, Stephen reached them before she could find her voice. A moment later and she might have completely dropped the reins on her temper.

"Lady Anne, are you all right?" Stephen took her hand and rested it on his arm, covering it with his strong, warm fingers. "You look"—his voice hardened and he turned to glare at Brentwood—"distressed."

She took a sustaining breath and let the comfort of his nearness calm her. "Thank you, but I'm fine now."

"Of course you are," Lady Noughton said, pushing past Stephen. "Lady Anne and Lord Brentwood are old friends, aren't you, Lady Anne?"

Lady Noughton should have asked Brentwood if she wanted agreement. "Friends?" Anne said, injecting all the incredulity she could into the word. She shook her head. "Oh, no. Acquaintances, merely—and hardly that."

Brentwood laughed. "Come now, my dear. Acquaintances? We are far more . . . intimate than acquaintances."

Was the miscreant going to reveal her secret now? Anne waited for the cold dread in her stomach to blossom into panic.

Surprisingly, what she felt was a thread of relief.

She was able to keep her voice level and force one

eyebrow to rise. "I'm afraid you've confused me with someone else, Lord Brentwood."

He opened his mouth to call her a liar, and she braced herself, even as she realized she'd spoken the truth. She wasn't that young girl who'd so foolishly gone with Brentwood into Baron Gedding's garden any longer. She'd changed.

Stephen's muscled forearm tensed under her fingers, and his hand squeezed hers slightly. She smiled. It felt so good not to be facing Brentwood alone.

Brentwood paused and then closed his lips. He must have realized he'd lose any hope of getting her to crawl into his bed at the end of the week if he gave up the sword he was holding over her head now. He bowed slightly. "I cannot contradict a lady."

She inclined her head. "Then if you'll excuse me?" She looked up at Stephen. "I think I'd best leave. I imagine the boys are at the carriages already."

"Of course." Stephen nodded at their unwelcome companions. "Brentwood, Lady Noughton, good day."

They walked across the yard and out the gate. Once they were away from the crowds, Stephen looked down at her. "Care to tell me what that was all about?"

"Not now." George was running toward them with Nick, Philip, and Harry not far behind. "Later. The story will require some privacy."

He nodded. "Very well."

"Perhaps when we are in the carriage." Her stomach twisted at the thought, but there was no point in putting off the inevitable.

"Unfortunately, Mama and Da have sent their conveyance back to the Pulteney and will be riding with us."

"Oh." She couldn't deny she was relieved, but the reprieve was only temporary and necessarily brief— Stephen wasn't a slowtop. He must suspect some of the truth.

"Tonight," he said. "I will arrange it."

George reached them then, just as Evie and Mr. and Mrs. Parker-Roth came up from behind, so there was no more opportunity to discuss the issue. She walked next to Stephen, listening with half an ear to everyone's opinion of the menagerie.

She would tell him tonight. Her stomach shivered with nerves, but she would do it. And then all this would be over.

Pride mixed in with her nerves. She had faced down Brentwood and she would tell Stephen the truth. She glanced up at him. He was teasing Philip about something. If only . . .

No, no "ifs." No wishes. Just the truth.

She would tell Stephen tonight, but she dearly wished she had nothing to tell.

Chapter 16

"When do you and Stephen plan to wed?" Mama asked Anne.

They were headed back to Crane House. Harry had been banished to the other carriage with Nick, Evie, and the boys. Mama obviously wanted nothing to distract her from this inquisition.

Stephen looked over at Da, but his father was studiously gazing out the carriage window. He'd been married to Mama too many years not to recognize the futility of trying to stop her when she was determined to venture into sensitive subjects.

Anne looked miserably guilty, not at all like a newly betrothed woman anticipating marriage with the man she loved. "We, ah, haven't given it any thought." She cleared her throat. "Yet."

"You haven't?" Mama shot him a look laden with suspicion. Blast! Why couldn't she be like other society women, interested more in the latest fashions than her children?

"We thought we should wait until Anne's father and stepmother return from Greece to make any plans." He took Anne's hand. "Though I'm all for a special license. No one knows when Lord and Lady Crane will return."

Mama snorted. "That's no surprise. I've always thought the earl and his second wife consider no one but themselves—certainly not their children—when they go haring off after antiquities."

"Mama!" She must be more upset about his betrothal than he'd guessed; she wasn't usually so tactless. "You should not criticize Lord Crane. Have you forgotten his daughter is present?"

Mama flushed. "My apologies, Lady Anne."

"No, you are quite correct." Anne freed her hand from his. "Papa and Georgiana do run off without warning or consideration about how their absence will affect their family." There was definitely an undercurrent of bitterness in Anne's voice.

"And you are the one left in charge?" Mama sounded sympathetic.

Stephen shifted in his seat. He must be on guard; he'd seen Mama work this way before, especially with the girls. She'd appear sympathetic—well, she probably *was* sympathetic—and before you knew it, you'd spilled all your secrets. Anne was in great danger.

"Yes," Anne said. "I don't mind so much when we are home at Crane House, you understand. I know exactly how things should be run there; I've managed the estate forever. But here in London . . ." She bit her lip. "As I said, Papa did engage to have our Cousin Clorinda come stay with us."

Mama snorted again. "Please. I am familiar with Miss Strange. If the thing doesn't have feathers and a beak, it's of no interest to her."

That surprised a choked laugh out of Anne. "It is not quite that bad, but she has not been a great help with Evie's come-out. And since I know next to nothing about London society . . ." She shrugged.

"You poor thing. I cannot imagine how Lady Crane could have gone off like that when her daughter was to make her bows to society. And to leave you with no guidance! Did she and your father stay for a few days at least to help you get situated?"

"They dropped us off on their way to the docks to catch their boat."

"Oh!" Mama pressed her lips together. "I think it would be best if I not say anything on that head, except—"

"Cecilia." The warning was clear in Da's tone.

Mama swallowed. "Yes, well, I do feel for you, my dear. You have been given a very challenging task." She suddenly turned her gaze to Stephen. "I'm afraid I have very strong feelings about the importance of parents raising their own children."

Why the hell was she looking at him in such an accusatory fashion? He didn't have any children.

Yet.

"As you can see from Lady Anne's experience," Mama continued, "it is very hard on children when their parents—or parent—are absent frequently."

"Eh?" He looked to Da for help, but his father was treating him to a similarly serious gaze. He was in deep trouble if Da was taking up arms with Mama.

"I do hope you intend to curtail your trips after your wedding," Mama said.

"I hadn't thought . . . I mean I had thought Anne could go with me."

"In the beginning," Da said, "but not after you have children."

"Yes, I know, but . . ." He glanced at Anne. She was studying her skirt rather intently. He couldn't condone the way Crazy Crane had dumped all his responsibilities on her shoulders . . . and yet, wouldn't that be exactly what he'd be doing if he took off on months-long expeditions?

"You're quite wealthy; you've no need to go traveling. Stay home and tend your own gardens like John," Mama said.

"I don't think John will agree with you, Mama. He benefits too much from my travels."

"There are other men who can supply him with his specimens," Da said.

An uncomfortable silence settled on the coach.

Damn it, there *were* others who could do the job, but he liked the hunt. He liked exploring unknown lands, tracking through jungles, dodging competing plant hunters . . . falling in rivers, sleeping in the mud, being eaten alive by insects . . .

Perhaps he *was* ready to settle down. He could try breeding plants, like John did. Plants and—he looked at Anne—babies.

Anne cleared her throat. "I should say with regard to Evie's come-out, if it hadn't been for your son's help, I don't know what we would have done. He found us an excellent dressmaker, got us invitations to the Earl of Kenderly's ball, and convinced Nicholas to act as Philip and George's tutor."

Da laughed. "I'll wager it was your sister and not Stephen who persuaded Nick."

"Oh, I'm sure Evie never said a word to Nicholas about taking charge of the boys." Anne looked worried.

Now Mama laughed, too. "Lady Anne, Evie didn't need to say a word. Nicholas isn't blind, you know."

"Oh." Anne flushed slightly. "Evie *is* very beautiful—everyone remarks on it."

"And do they also remark on the beauty of her sister?" Da asked, raising an eyebrow.

"Her sister?" Anne frowned. "But I'm her only . . . oh."

She turned bright red and then laughed awkwardly. "No, of course they don't."

"And why not?" Mama lifted her brow as well. "None of my sons is blind, Lady Anne."

"Cecilia is a painter, my dear," Da said, "so I'm afraid you'll have to believe her on this. She has an eye, you know."

Mama nodded. "You're not in the common way, but why would you want to be? Life would be deadly dull if everyone looked alike." She gestured toward Stephen. "Certainly my son has already told you all this—I don't think he's a complete clod pole. Given his ridiculous nickname, one would think he'd be quite adroit at such matters."

It was a sad situation if he had to take pointers from his parents when it came to wooing his betrothed. "Of course I've told Anne she's beautiful," Stephen said, taking her hand again. She was now redder than a ripe apple and wouldn't meet his eye. "Several times. Haven't I, Anne?"

"Er, yes. But please do stop. I appreciate your kindness, but—"

"It's not kindness. It's truth." Stephen pressed her hand, but he wanted to shake her. Clearly she wouldn't believe a word they said.

"Yes, well—Oh, look. There's Crane House." She sounded so relieved he expected her to jump from the carriage before it stopped, but she managed to restrain herself. She smiled somewhat weakly at Mama and Da. "Would you care to come in and see Clorinda?"

Da looked as if he'd be happy to decline, but Mama nodded. "That would be splendid," she said.

They climbed out of the carriage and started for the front door when Stephen saw Damian's coach with Nick, Evie, and the boys approaching. "You go on ahead. I need to have a word with Kenderly's coachman."

Stephen talked to the coachman while Nick helped Evie and the boys alight.

"I assume Mama wished to speak with Miss Strange," Nick said when Stephen turned to him.

"Of course. You know she must ferret out every detail she can when one of us is involved."

Nick laughed. "Then I'm sure my presence is not required in the drawing room. I must begin my duties with the boys."

"Coward."

Nick grinned. "I prefer to view it as a strategic retreat."

The boys and Evie had fled by the time Stephen and Nick entered Crane House. Anne was waiting with Mama and Da. Nick gave Mama a quick kiss and then was allowed to escape—he was not the focus of Mama's interest today.

"Miss Strange is in the blue parlor," Hobbes told them. "Lady Brentwood is with her."

"Oh." Anne turned pale. "Thank you, Hobbes." She led the way down the corridor. "I've brought Mr. and Mrs. Parker-Roth in to see you, Clorinda," she said at the parlor door. "I hope we're not intruding."

"Of course not. Do come in—and ring for more tea." Miss Strange eyed Stephen and Da. "And perhaps some brandy. Do you know Lady Brentwood?"

"Of course we do," Mama said. "How are you?"

Lady Brentwood was smiling, but her eyes looked suspiciously red. "I confess, I've been better, Mrs. Parker-Roth. And look! You have your husband with you. Whatever could have caused you to tear yourself away from your sonnets, sir, and come all the way to London? I thought you detested Town."

"I do," Da said as he and Mama took a place on the settee, "but I was the only one available to escort my wife—and she insisted on making the trip."

"Of course you came because of the betrothal—but how did you learn of it so quickly?" Clorinda gave Anne a very puzzled look. "Did you perhaps know of it before-hand?"

"No." Da looked at Mama who jumped into the slightly awkward pause.

"We were coming up to see how our younger son was doing in Town and were completely surprised by Stephen's news. I assume we'll find his letter alerting us to this happy event when we return home." She sent Stephen a speaking look. "And we had the great plea-sure of meeting Lady Anne at the Royal Menagerie just now. We are, of course, delighted at the match."

The tea and brandy arrived then, thank God. Stephen cradled his brandy glass and listened to the conversation with one ear while he studied Anne. What was her connection to Brentwood?

He would find out tonight. But where could they have the discussion? She'd said the tale required pri-vacy. It was obviously something that was hard for her to talk about, so they'd need a place where they would not be interrupted.

They couldn't go to his rooms—that would be far too scandalous, even for an engaged couple. But her room . . .

"And how is your son, Lady Brentwood?" Mama asked. He saw Anne stiffen.

Lady Brentwood shook her head and dabbed at her eyes with her handkerchief. "I'm afraid he is a great trial."

Mama's brows furrowed. "Oh, dear. I'm sorry. I don't mean to intrude—"

"No, please. I'd like your advice. You've managed to raise three sons—and three daughters as well."

"Raising children is a great challenge." Mama

smiled gently and then sent Stephen a significant look. "As is dealing with them once they become adults."

Stephen took a mouthful of brandy. He should have fled with Nick, but he couldn't very well desert Anne.

Could he desert her later? Could he leave her alone with his children for months on end while he was thousands of miles away?

Damn. He did not like that notion.

Perhaps his initial plans concerning his marriage did need some revision.

Lady Brentwood twisted her handkerchief. "Lord Brentwood—Walter—was always a willful child. If only I could have given him brothers and sisters, perhaps—" Her voice caught. "Well, it was not to be, but I often think if he'd had siblings, he'd be less focused on his own pleasures now."

Mama leaned forward and touched Lady Brentwood's knee. "My dear Lady Brentwood, I've learned looking backward never helps. I'm sure you did the best you could at the time."

"That is exactly what I've been trying to tell her," Clorinda said. "But I suppose since I am a childless spinster, my opinion holds no weight."

Lady Brentwood shook her head. "No, Clorinda, I value your words very much."

Da grunted. "It's true you can't worry over what's past, but if we *were* to lay blame, I'd say the lion's share belongs to your deceased husband, Lady Brentwood. I'm afraid the tales of his debauchery still circulate in the clubs."

Da was right. Brentwood's father had died at least fifteen years ago, yet men continued to talk about the man's sexual exploits. Just last week Stephen had heard an account of some orgy the old lord had hosted.

He'd always been very glad Da lived a boring life. As

Lady Brentwood had said, Da hardly ever left the Priory. Stephen smiled down at his brandy glass. His father might be lost in a creative haze much of the time, but the man could focus quite sharply if necessary—as Stephen had learned to his regret when he'd got in a bit too much mischief as a boy.

How could he leave Anne the burden of raising his sons—and daughters—alone? And how could he miss seeing them grow up?

Perhaps Mama and Da were right; perhaps it was time to give up traveling.

"But what am I to do now?" Lady Brentwood blew her nose. "Walter shows no interest in marriage— I cannot get him to consider any one of the suitable young women I suggest. He is past thirty—it is time for him to produce an heir."

"Indeed it is," Mama said, "but I have discovered that once children are grown, we mothers can no longer control their actions." She sighed. "I have stopped trying to do so."

Unfortunately, Stephen was swallowing a mouthful of brandy when his mother made this pronouncement. He managed—barely—to get the liquid down without coughing it out his mouth or sending it into his nose. Mama given up trying to control his actions? This was news to him. He glanced at his father. Da looked more than a bit surprised as well.

"But how did you persuade your oldest three children to wed? There was no title at stake, and, in any event, your husband is obviously very much alive."

Da laughed. "Thank you, Lady Brentwood, for that astute observation."

Mama laughed, too. "I must tell you, when he gets lost in creating one of his sonnets, I sometimes wonder whether he is still breathing."

"And what about when you are in your studio painting?" Da said.

Oh, God. Stephen saw the expression in his mother's eyes. He feared he knew what was coming.

"You are quite aware that I'm alive, sir. You are usually there with me, are you not?"

Not only was Da with her, he was usually posing naked—and, much as Stephen shuddered to imagine it, one thing generally led to another. He'd learned very early in life not to disturb his parents when they were together in Mama's studio.

He took another swallow of brandy.

"I must confess, Lady Brentwood, that I had nothing to do with my children's matrimonial choices," Mama said, "though it certainly wasn't for lack of trying. Jane was firmly on the shelf in her eighth Season when she settled on Viscount Motton. And John . . . I thought I'd have to convince some young woman to dress up as an exotic flower to catch his attention."

Da snorted. "They both managed to get themselves caught up in a scandal—that's what forced them to the altar."

"Ah, but you know they are both deeply in love, sir," Mama said.

"Oh, yes, but if it weren't for the scandal, I'll wager John, at least, would not have had the wit to marry." Da raised his brandy glass to Stephen. "Congratulations on being the first of our children to propose without the weight of society's displeasure forcing you to bended knee."

An uncomfortable silence seized the room. Stephen studied his brandy as if it were the elixir of life.

"Is there something you've neglected to tell us, Stephen?" Mama asked.

* * *

Anne waved good-bye to Mr. and Mrs. Parker-Roth as Stephen's carriage pulled away. They were both very pleasant even after they'd learned the embarrassing details of their son's betrothal, but still Anne had never been so happy to see two people's backs in all her life.

"Shall we go for a stroll in the park?" Stephen asked, gesturing to the center of the square.

"Yes. That would be lovely." She did not want to go back inside and risk encountering Clorinda and Lady Brentwood again. And they did need to discuss how and where she'd meet him to tell him her secret.

They crossed to the little park. She could tell him now . . . Her stomach clenched, and sweat blossomed on her palms.

Yes, she was a coward; she wanted to put that interview off as long as she could. And the park was not private enough. Anyone could stroll by at the most inopportune moment or be close enough to hear her confession. If Stephen reacted violently—she wasn't concerned he would hurt her, of course, but he might well raise his voice or reveal his anger in his gestures— she didn't want any witnesses. She wanted an enclosed spot where she could be certain he was her only audience.

She swallowed her nerves and looked up at him. "Why didn't you accompany your parents to the Pulteney?"

He grinned as he unlatched the park gate and held it open for her. "I didn't want to subject myself to an inquisition. You may have noticed my mother can be very tenacious."

"But shouldn't you tell them the truth?"

"What do you mean?" Stephen led her over to a bench and dusted it off with his handkerchief.

She sat, looking around while he took the place next to her. She didn't see anyone else, but it paid to be cautious. She leaned toward him and whispered, "You should tell them our betrothal is a sham."

"Anne, my love, our betrothal is not a sham—it is very real. I announced it at Lord Kenderly's dinner and the notice has been published in the papers."

"Shh!" She glanced around again. "Lower your voice. Anyone might hear you."

"I don't care if they do. In fact, I think I'll climb up on this bench right now and shout it out in case anyone is nearby."

Dear God, surely the man wouldn't be so nonsensical?

It looked very much as if he would; he was beginning to get to his feet. She lunged, grabbing his arm. "You can't do that."

"I can. Watch me." He started to peel her fingers off his person.

"No!" She bit her lip and tried to speak quietly. "Please don't, at least not until after I tell you . . . what I have to tell you."

He looked at her. "It won't change anything."

"It *will*."

"It will not." He raised his eyebrow. "What did you do, murder someone?"

"Shh!" She looked over her shoulder. Why would he not be more discreet? "No, I—" She should tell him right now . . . but she couldn't. Tonight in private, she would tell him then. She must. She was dissembling with him far worse than he was with his parents. "I will tell you everything tonight, I swear. Have you hit upon a place for us to meet?"

His blue eyes had turned gray with concern, but he didn't press her further. "I think the best place might be your room."

"My *bed*room?" Her voice squeaked, her heart suddenly beating a wild tattoo in her chest. To have

Stephen in her bedroom . . . the notion was beyond shocking. What if they were discovered?

She took a deep breath to calm her nerves. They would not be discovered—she would be sure to lock the door. And they would be very much alone. No one would disturb them. They would have all the time they needed to discuss their situation.

And there was a bed . . .

She shook her head. Whom was she fooling? Once Stephen heard she was no longer a virgin, he would leave in disgust.

But if he didn't leave . . . Perhaps he would be willing—since he'd then know he couldn't take her virtue as she had none—to finish what he'd started in the green sitting room and again in his carriage.

She would ask him to do it. Once she'd managed to tell him her secret, she'd have nothing to lose. She wanted to know what the act was like in a bed with a kind gentleman. And this time she would be able to give him some relief for his painful stiffness.

"Unless you object, of course." He was watching her carefully. "I couldn't think of a better place that met your requirements for privacy."

"N-no, I don't ob-object." She took another deep breath. "But how is it to be accomplished without anyone knowing?"

"You are promised to the Palmerson ball this evening, aren't you?"

"Yes." A hideous thought struck her. "Will your parents be there?"

"Possibly." Stephen smiled. "But you will not."

"I won't?"

"No, you'll be sick. Pick any illness you care to, as long as it's not dire. Tell your cousin and Evie you have the headache or an unsettled stomach or are merely out of curl. Just make it something you can recover from by morning."

More lies—though this wouldn't truly be a lie. Her stomach was definitely unsettled and her head was pounding. "And what if they decide to stay home to keep me company?"

"Assure them you will do much better alone as all you need is a bit of quiet and a chance to rest or maybe even sleep. Tell them you intend to go directly to bed as soon as they leave."

Go to bed . . . her stomach shivered. "All right."

"Good. Now where is your room?"

"On the north back corner. I'll be sure the curtains are open so you can see the light."

"Splendid. And is there a tree or a sturdy vine nearby?"

"What?" Stephen wasn't intending to pursue his botanical interests now, was he?

He looked slightly exasperated. "So I have something to climb to reach you. I could come up the servants' stairs, but that is more risky. You'd have to make certain the servants' door was unlocked, and I might run into a maid or footman."

"Oh. Yes, there's a tree, and it's in serious need of pruning."

"Good." He frowned. "The boys will be asleep by, say, nine o'clock, won't they?"

She nodded. "They are in the old nursery area on the floor above the rest of us, and they are very sound sleepers."

"Excellent. I will drag Nick along with me when I come to escort your sister and cousin to the ball. Then I'll make some excuse at the appropriate time and leave, delegating the duty of bringing them safely home to Nick." He paused as if waiting for her concurrence.

She nodded again; what else could she do?

"I'm not certain when I'll be able to get away from the ball. I hope it will be no later than ten o'clock, but too much depends on circumstance. I don't want to raise anyone's suspicions."

Good God, if people suspected he was visiting her bedroom— "No, you don't want to cause any more gossip."

"So listen for me. I will throw some pebbles against your window."

"Yes, yes. Of course." She hoped she could hear anything over her thundering heart.

"Splendid." Stephen rose and offered her his hand. She took it; his grip was so strong and confident. He looked completely at ease as he walked her back to Crane House.

"You might wish to begin to act sick now," he said when they approached the front door.

She nodded. That would not be a problem. With the combination of dread and anticipation churning in her stomach, she felt quite, quite ill.

Chapter 17

"Here without your betrothed, Stephen?"

Stephen turned to consider Maria. She'd obviously sought him out—he was standing in a remote section of Palmerson's ballroom, half obscured by potted palms. Everyone else had realized he did not wish to converse this evening and had left him alone. Why did Maria need to see him?

He could think of no pleasant reason.

"Unfortunately, yes. Lady Anne is not feeling quite the thing tonight."

"I'm so sorry." Her expression and tone belied her words.

He frowned. How had it taken him so long to see the pettiness beneath her beauty? He'd always thought himself most astute.

Apparently not when he was letting his cock do his thinking.

"Don't frown." She looked at him from under her lashes. "Come dance with me"—she dropped her voice suggestively—"or walk with me in the garden. I'm sure I can raise your"—she lowered her gaze to his breeches—"spirits."

He wanted to cover his privates like a bashful maiden—or perhaps he only wished to protect himself from attack. "No, thank you. I'm quite content where I am."

Maria tittered. "Oh, you don't have to pretend with me, Stephen."

"Pretend?" What the hell did the woman mean?

She snorted. "That you wish to marry this girl, of course. I know you only proposed because of the scandal." She sighed and shook her head. "You have such a misplaced sense of chivalry."

Anger curled through his gut. "You are mistaken. I am quite eager to wed Lady Anne."

She laughed unpleasantly. "If you think your little red-headed whore will warm your bed, you are far from the mark. Brentwood says she's as cold as ice." She curled her lips into a sneer. "He says having her is like swiving a bloody statue."

He'd thought he was angry before, but he'd been mistaken. The rage now burning through his veins might well cause the nearby palms to combust. He clenched his hands to keep from strangling Maria. "You will not repeat such lies."

"They aren't lies." She raised her eyebrows. "What, did you think your betrothed was a virgin? You poor deluded man—she must be a better actress than I gave her credit for."

Damn it all to hell, Maria wasn't lying. Detecting deception was a crucial skill to have when hunting plants; far too many people were eager to take advantage of foreigners. He'd honed his sensitivity to falsehood to a sharp edge over the years.

Anne was waiting to tell him a secret. Was this it?

Maria shrugged. "I suppose you can hope she's got better at bed games through practice. Brentwood had her years ago. Who knows how many men have slid between her thighs since?"

He hadn't thought to tell Nick he was unwell when he left early, but now it was the perfect excuse, no matter if society might wonder at Anne and him both taking sick. And he didn't need to worry whether his brother was as good at spotting falsehoods as he was. He could not remember ever feeling so nauseous.

Maria leaned closer. "And don't think you can come crawling back to my bed. My offer tonight was given only out of pity. By the time you realize your mistake, I'll be the next Marchioness of Brentwood."

It wasn't well done of him, but he couldn't stop himself. He'd trade unpleasant truth for unpleasant truth.

"Oh? You love the man so much you'll follow him into poverty?"

"What?" Maria didn't mask her alarm fast enough; he heard it in her voice, saw it in her eyes. She forced a laugh. "Oh, I see. You are lying to pay me back for telling you the truth."

"I'm not lying."

"You are." She smiled, though the expression didn't reach her eyes. "Brentwood is a marquis."

"Maria. How long have you been in society? You know a title is not a guarantee of funds—more than one marquis has found himself at point nonplus."

A tiny frown marred the perfection of her brow. "You *must* be lying. If Brentwood was in dun territory, I would have heard it. There's not been the slightest rumor."

"Yet." He shrugged. "That will change."

Her frown turned to a glare. "Why?"

"Because I now hold all his debts." He smiled rather grimly. "I don't know how he's managed to stave off the cent-per-centers so far, but whatever his ploy, it won't work with me." He narrowed his eyes and felt his lips pull into something certain to resemble a snarl. "I'm not feeling especially generous where Brentwood's concerned. Now, if you'll excuse me, I've discovered this gathering is a dead bore."

He didn't have to push his way past Maria—he must have looked intimidating enough that she stepped aside of her own accord. Somehow he located Nick, told him he wasn't in plump currant, and left the ballroom. He hoped he didn't raise too much speculation, but he found he didn't much care if he did.

Could Anne have done what Maria suggested? She'd said she had a secret to tell him, something that would keep her from marrying him.

Bloody hell! He wanted to hit something.

The footman at Palmerson's front door must have thought he was a possible target. He handed Stephen his hat exceedingly promptly and took a step back the moment the exchange had been made. Damn. He slipped the man a larger vail than normal before he ventured into the darkness. He would walk. It wasn't far to Crane House.

"Sir!" Blast. His coachman had seen him. "Are you leaving early? Shall I bring up the carriage?"

"No, Albert. Everyone else is staying. Nick will tell you when he needs you."

"But, sir—"

"I prefer to walk."

Albert looked doubtful.

"I wish to clear my head," he added. *And calm my spleen.*

"But the streets aren't safe, sir. Please let me take you home. I'll be back in plenty of time for the others."

"No, thank you. I am not concerned. I've been in far more dangerous places than London, you know." If only some misguided miscreant *would* accost him. He'd enjoy a good fight right now. "Oh, and I don't know when I'll be home—tell Nick not to worry."

"But—" Albert clearly struggled with his misgivings and then forcibly swallowed them. He tipped his hat. "Very well, sir."

Stephen nodded and set off down the walk. The last thing he wanted was to be cooped up in his coach—or to have Albert know he wasn't going home but to Crane House. Albert was discreet, but not *that* discreet.

He waited for a carriage to pass before he crossed the street.

Anne and Brentwood. Damn. The thought made his stomach turn.

He sidestepped a pair of drunken dandies who were singing some bawdy song—which song it was impossible to tell as they couldn't carry a tune or remember the lyrics between them.

Had Anne been playing him for a fool all this time, laughing behind his back?

He turned a corner and crossed another street.

Of course not. He was letting his imagination run away with him. Yes, there was a kernel of truth in what Maria had said, but only a kernel. He was as good at judging character as he was at recognizing lies.

Anne was no light skirt. She obviously had some history with Brentwood—unpleasant history judging from her reaction to him in Hyde Park, at Damian's ball, and at the menagerie. He'd even suspected Brentwood had raped her. But he would make no assumptions. He must remember who had told him the tittle-tattle. Maria could be as venomous as an adder.

He would wait. Anne would tell him tonight; he just needed to be patient and let her do so. Accusations and harsh words never encouraged confidences.

He saw Crane House up ahead. It had been a good choice to walk. He still wasn't completely calm, but at

least he wasn't as angry as he'd been when he'd left
Palmerson's ball.

Damn it all, he had to admit he was almost happy.
Just the thought of seeing Anne made his heart—and
another organ—lift.

He glanced around. Fortunately, the square was deserted. He'd seen Lady Dunlee at the ball, so he needn't
worry she'd spy him skulking about. He scooped up a
few pebbles and hefted them as he slipped through the
shadows to Anne's window.

Anne paced back and forth in front of the fire. She
was far too nervous to read or even sit still. She
checked her clock—it was only five minutes later than
the last time she'd looked.

Clorinda and Evie had believed her without question when she'd said she was ill—not surprising as she
must have looked like death. The more she'd thought
of encountering Stephen's parents or Brentwood at
the Palmerson ball, the more her stomach had twisted.
Add to that the knowledge she must tell Stephen the
truth tonight, and she was amazed she hadn't embarrassed herself by bringing up the little she had in her
stomach right there in the blue parlor.

Evie had immediately offered to stay home with her,
of course, but Anne had managed to persuade her she
neither wanted nor needed company. She smiled. The
fact that Mr. Nicholas Parker-Roth would be coming
with Stephen to escort them might also have been a
factor in Evie's decision to attend the ball.

Before Evie and Clorinda left, however, they'd insisted on seeing Anne dressed in her nightclothes and
tucked into bed. Anne pushed her loose hair back off
her face. It was beyond scandalous to receive Stephen

this way, but then conversing with him in her bedroom would put her beyond the pale anyway.

She snorted. Why was she worrying? She was already hopelessly ruined; that horse had bolted years ago.

She looked at her clock again. It was almost eleven. Stephen must not be coming. She should try to get some sleep.

She pulled back the covers, climbed into bed, and closed her eyes. Brentwood's ugly face appeared like a nightmare.

Her eyes popped open and she scowled up at the bed canopy. Blast it, Stephen *had* to come tonight. She wouldn't be able to sleep until she told him her damn secret. Brentwood had almost spilled the soup at the menagerie today; he might not control himself the next time he was provoked. If Stephen found out from someone besides herself . . .

Her stomach knotted. She *was* going to be sick. She'd better get the chamber pot out from under the—

Ping!

She froze. Dear God! Was that . . . ?

Ping! Ping!

It was. Pebbles, bouncing off her window. Stephen must be out there.

She was tempted for just a moment to pretend she didn't hear him, but then she thought of Lady Dunlee and shot out of bed.

She jerked the window open—and dodged as a pebble flew past her.

"Sorry," Stephen called.

"Shh!" She leaned out and peered between the tree branches. He was standing in a pool of moonlight. "Come up before someone sees you."

"Don't worry, Lady Dunlee's at the Palmerson ball."

That was a relief, but still, Lady Dunlee was not the only person in London with sharp eyes and a ready tongue. And it was quite possible one of the Crane House servants might see Stephen and, thinking him a thief, attack him. There was more to worry about than mere gossip.

"Just hurry and come up."

He grinned. "Eager to see me, are you?"

Did the man have no sense? "Stop talking and start climbing."

He bowed. "Your wish is my command." He slipped out of his coat, waistcoat, and shoes and then jumped to catch the lowest tree branch. He pulled himself up and reached for the next, moving quickly and confidently.

She leaned farther out to see if anyone was watching. No, thank God, but the ground was a long way down. What if Stephen fell?

She had a sudden vision of him lying broken and bleeding on the grass. "Be careful."

"Don't worry, I've climbed many trees in my life." He wasn't even breathless.

"When you were a child." He was obviously in splendid condition, but he *was* thirty.

"No, recently as well."

"In London?" What kind of a fool did he take her for?

Well, he was the King of Hearts . . . perhaps he had visited other bedrooms this way.

"Of course not in London." He was finally level with the window. "I sometimes take to the trees when I'm hunting plants." He grinned again. The man was amazingly lighthearted. "When I'm pursued by wild animals, angry natives, or competing plant hunters."

She gaped at him. "I had no idea plant hunting could be so dangerous."

He shrugged. "It can be." He grabbed the branch above his head and lifted a brow. "Now did you want me to come in, or were you intending to keep me hanging out here all night?"

What was the matter with him? "Come in, of course. I cannot imagine why you haven't done so already."

"Because you are standing in the window, and I don't want to knock you over. If you'll step aside?"

She jumped back as he swung himself over the windowsill. Then he turned to slide the window shut and draw the curtains. His shirt pulled tight across his shoulders.

Mmm. He had a lovely back. It tapered down to his narrow waist and hips. And his arse—what would it look like naked?

His chest and arms had been wonderful to see—and touch—when he'd taken off his shirt before. What if he shed every stitch of clothing and stood here completely as God made him? She moistened her lips. She was feeling quite . . . hot. She—

She jerked her wayward thoughts back to the subject at hand, which was *not* Mr. Parker-Roth's attractive arse.

She had to tell him her secret. Once she did so, he'd fling open that window and scramble back down the tree as quickly as he could manage.

He'd turned and was regarding her intently. "Is it hot in here? You look very flushed."

"Yes, I—" Damn it, *she* was hot, not the room, as he'd clearly surmised. She cast around for a different subject. "When is your next expedition?"

He crossed his arms and leaned against the wall. "Perhaps in a month or so. Nothing has been firmly decided."

Her stomach dropped. So soon?

No, the sooner the better. Once he knew her shameful secret, he'd want nothing more to do with her. She couldn't abandon Evie; she had to stay in London until the end of the Season or until Papa and

Georgiana returned. It would be easier if she didn't have to encounter Stephen at every social gathering. And if he left without ending their betrothal—at least publicly—she'd be spared much social embarrassment. She would ask him if he'd do that. After all, he had kissed her on the street. If he hadn't done something so outrageous . . .

Well, and she had kissed him.

She would never make that mistake again. If there were ever a next time, she'd know to scream and fight the man off . . . which she would have done this time if it had been any other man than Stephen.

She closed her eyes briefly. She was not blameless, but neither had she been the one to initiate the disaster. Surely Stephen would admit his culpability and be willing to grant her this small request. Then she would tell Evie and warn her to have nothing to do with Brentwood. Not that Evie would want to. If the marquis had been attractive ten years ago, he certainly wasn't any longer.

To give the marquis his due, Anne had gone with him willingly. She had, in a manner of speaking, asked for her ruination. Evie would never be so stupid— especially once Anne related her story.

So all she had to do now was tell Stephen the truth. She frowned at him—and noticed his eyes were examining her nightgown. She looked down.

Good God! She could see her nipples clearly through the worn cloth—

She ran to one of the chairs by the fire and threw herself into its concealing embrace, covering as much of herself as she could with a shawl she'd left draped over its back. She poked her hand out of the fabric to point at the other chair.

"Come sit down. I'm sorry I don't have any brandy to offer you. I didn't think to—"

"Anne," he said, walking toward her, "this isn't a social call."

"N-no." Why wouldn't the man sit down? His current position put her eyes on level with the organ that was making a very interesting bulge in his breeches. She could see its outline distinctly. She opened her eyes wider. Was it growing?

She glanced up. Stephen's eyes were hooded and his lips curved slightly. The man knew exactly what he was doing to her. Well, he was the King of Hearts; what else could she expect? He'd probably perfected every method of seduction there was.

"Sit down!" She spoke sharply, mostly out of desperation. If he didn't move immediately, she might give into temptation and unbutton his breeches. She must be the only fallen woman in the world who'd never seen the instrument of her ruination.

Ugh. Thinking of Brentwood and Stephen at the same time was obscene.

He sat. "You seem somewhat agitated."

Somewhat? That was the understatement of the year. She wished she *had* thought to secrete some brandy in her room. She could use a good swallow at the moment. "Why do you say that?"

He grinned. "There are almost too many reasons to enumerate, but, for one, you're clutching your shawl tightly around you when your face is almost as red as your hair."

Her face promptly grew two shades redder.

"I grant you it does seem very warm in here." He touched his cravat. "Would you mind very much if I got comfortable?"

"N-no. Of course not." Anne's eyes were glued to his fingers. "P-please, take off—I mean, do what you like. As you say, this isn't a social call. We should be comfortable."

She watched his hands as he slowly unwound his cravat.

It wasn't good of him to tease her, but he couldn't resist. Her eyes held such innocent passion.

He should forget Maria's nasty words. Anne's expression didn't lie. No matter what her past, she wasn't a light skirt. She didn't welcome men indiscriminately to her bed. And if she had known a man before him . . . Did he really care?

His cock was telling him emphatically he did not.

Being in Anne's bedroom with her temptingly rumpled sheets nearby made his desire almost unbearable. She was in her nightclothes, for God's sake—her worn, thin, translucent nightgown. When she'd stood there in front of him, he'd seen the curve of her breasts, the outline of her nipples and delicate waist, and, most maddening of all, the shadow of her nether curls.

He could get her to come willingly to bed with no effort. The way she'd stared at his crotch and now studied his bare throat almost pleaded with him to do so. He would be doing them both a favor.

But he would not seduce her. This wasn't one of the many widows he'd taken to bed in the past. This was Anne, the woman he intended to marry and to build a family with.

Seduction had its place, but this first time, she needed to choose freely.

And then there was her secret. She must tell him that before they went to bed. There should be only truth between them from now on.

"Anne, you said in the park this afternoon there was something you needed to tell me that required privacy. What is it?"

She turned as white as a sheet. Was she going to faint? He moved to kneel by her chair and grasp her hands—they were ice cold.

"Anne."

She bit her lip, shook her head. She would not look at him.

"Tell me, Anne. I've come here so you can do so. There is no point in putting it off."

"I know," she whispered. "I . . . oh." She sniffed and pulled her hands free, swiping at a tear. "You will hate me once I tell you. You will be disgusted by me."

"No, I won't."

"Yes, you will. You must."

"Anne, you can't know how I will react until you tell me what you have to say." He captured her hands again and shook them a little. "And I can't help you unless I know what the problem is."

"You can't help me—no one can."

"Anne, nothing is that bad."

"This is."

He raised an eyebrow. "So is Lady Noughton correct? You've lifted your skirts for too many gentlemen to count?"

"What?" The shock of Stephen's words almost took her breath away. "No! It was only once, and I didn't lift my skirts at all—Brentwood did that."

Stephen frowned, but he didn't recoil in horror. He didn't even let go of her hands; his warm grip was a comforting anchor.

"Ah." His voice was hard, even if his grip was not. "Brentwood raped you."

She almost wished she could claim it *was* rape. "No. I . . . I wanted . . . Well, I didn't want . . . I didn't know . . . I thought he only meant to kiss me."

She looked down at their clasped hands. Stephen's were so much larger and stronger than hers.

Would she have gone into the garden with Brentwood if she'd known what he intended to do? She'd thought she'd loved him—just as she thought she loved Stephen.

Was she on the verge of making the same mistake?

No. She tightened her grip on Stephen's fingers. She was older now. Wiser. She didn't expect marriage or anything else. She just needed to know for her own sake if the . . . deed would be better with a kinder man. Doing the thing with Stephen would either wipe away an unpleasant memory, like drinking chocolate after taking medicine, or would show her it hadn't been Brentwood so much as the action itself that was embarrassing and uncomfortable.

Oh, she should not lie to herself. It was more than that. She *did* love Stephen. This feeling was far stronger than the weak emotion she'd entertained for Brentwood.

But first she had to give him the truth.

"When Lord Brentwood took me out to Baron Gedding's garden, I did want to go." She should give herself some credit, not that it forgave her stupidity. She met Stephen's eyes. He looked very angry—no more than she deserved. "I truly thought he only meant to kiss me again—and it wasn't that I'd liked his kisses"— she'd never felt the need for Brentwood that she did for Stephen—"but he'd liked kissing me." She looked down. She'd been so naïve. "Even though Georgiana had warned me not to be alone with a man, I thought she only meant I risked being kissed. I didn't know anything else could occur."

"Anne." Stephen cupped her cheek. His voice and touch were gentle, even though his expression wasn't. "You don't have to say any more."

"But I do." She had to say it all. Maybe if she confessed every horrible detail, she'd finally feel at peace. "He took me to the back of the garden where no one could see us. I was a little nervous—we were quite alone—but I didn't say anything. It was exciting, too. I thought he wanted privacy to profess his love. I even thought he meant to propose." She cringed. She had been so stupid.

"Anne."

She pulled back from Stephen's touch, and he let her go. She forced herself to look him in the eye once more. "Brentwood didn't want to tell me he loved me. He wanted to . . ." God, she almost gagged at the memory. "He backed me up to the garden wall, lifted my skirts, and—"

She *was* a coward. She couldn't meet Stephen's gaze while she said it. She dropped her eyes to his shirt. "At least he did it quickly. I imagine it hurt less that way." She raised her eyes to his chin. "I went home the next day and was very glad to discover a week later I wasn't increasing."

"Anne." He tilted her face up so she had to look at him again. She couldn't hide.

Amazingly, he didn't look disgusted. He looked regretful and sad.

He was going to tell her how sorry he was, but she was correct. He couldn't marry her. She steeled herself to accept it calmly. She would try very hard not to cry.

"Anne, you *were* raped. You are not to blame for what happened."

What? Had he not understood her words? She jerked back, but this time he wouldn't let her go. "Didn't you hear me?" she said. "I wanted to go with him."

"Of course you did. You were young, at your first house party. Brentwood was older and experienced. You wanted to go, but you didn't want what happened."

"No, I didn't, but that doesn't excuse the fact I chose to walk alone with a man in a secluded location. I should never have done so; I knew it was wrong. And the moment he lifted my skirts, I should have screamed and struggled." She sniffed; tears were threatening to fall again. Helplessness and, yes, a bit of self-pity flooded her. "But it all happened so quickly. I didn't understand what he was doing until I felt . . . something"—she blushed furiously—"there. And then almost immediately I felt a burning pain when he . . . did what he did."

"Oh, Anne." Stephen pulled her gently toward him, so her cheek lay on his chest. She didn't have the energy or determination to resist.

"I didn't even slap him," she said in a small voice.

"You were too shocked to do so."

"And afterward, he smiled and said, 'Thank you, that was very pleasant.' But it *wasn't* pleasant—not for me. It was horrible."

She squeezed her eyes shut, but that didn't help. The ugly scenes—and feelings—were burned into her memory.

"He escorted me back to the drawing room. I tried to talk to the other guests, but I couldn't pay attention to anything they said. And then I-I felt something wet dripping down my leg. I ran up to my room to discover blood and Brentwood's seed on my thighs."

She took a deep, shuddery breath and inhaled Stephen's warm, clean scent. His hands held her securely and stroked her hair. She heard his heart beat calmly, steadily under her ear.

She exhaled and felt some of her tension leave with her breath. "And you want to know the funniest thing? I still don't know exactly what he did to me."

She felt Stephen's lips brush the top of her head.

"Let me show you," he said.

Chapter 18

Stephen wanted to castrate Brentwood. To take an innocent girl's virginity was bad enough, but to do so in such a callous manner was despicable. The man had given no thought to Anne. He obviously hadn't cared whether she understood his intentions, and he'd certainly not tried to make the experience pleasurable for her.

Anne leaned back to look at him. She was blushing again. "*Would* you show me? I'd decided to ask you to, so you saved me the struggle to get the words out." She dropped her gaze back to his chest. "I imagine you can do a better job of it than Brentwood did."

Bloody hell. He'd cut off Brentwood's testicles slowly with a very blunt knife. "Anne."

She glanced up briefly, but almost immediately went back to studying his shirt.

"Anne, look at me." He put the edge of his hand under her chin. She resisted at first, but then, with a small sigh, let him raise her face to his. He caught her gaze and held it.

"What Brentwood did to you was indeed rape, no matter that you willingly went with him. You did not invite him to take those liberties, and even if you had, he should not have accepted unless he intended to wed you."

She started to open her mouth, but he would not let her blame herself again. He put his fingers on her lips to stop her.

"What we shall do in your bed will have nothing in common with that. We are betrothed. This is not some furtive coupling."

God, that was true. An odd warmth spread through him. Anne would be his wife; they would have a life and a family together.

He'd spent his adult years guarding against by-blows, but now, here, with Anne, he needn't worry—he could even hope—that he'd give her a child.

She jerked out of his hold and stood, turning away from him. "No."

"Yes. I will get a special license tomorrow and—"

"No. You don't have to marry me." Dear God, she wanted what he offered so much—but what was he offering? Pity? He *must* be disgusted with her—she was disgusted with herself.

She didn't want his pity; she wanted his love.

Oh, blast it, why must she be so greedy? She could have a life with him, children, all the things she'd thought she'd never have—but she wanted more. Not duty, not even lust—but love. If she had his love, she might even be able to bear his leaving her again and again to go off on his expeditions.

"Of course I have to marry you," he said.

She kept her back to him. If she faced him, she might give into her weakness and take what he offered. "You do not. I know our betrothal is at heart only a way to escape scandal—or at least defer the worst of it—until Evie has her Season. Now you know I have no reputation to protect. Once the Season is over, we can go our separate ways. It makes no difference if society thinks me a jilt of the worst sort."

"Perhaps our betrothal is only a ruse to you." He sounded almost angry. "It was never so to me. You must know the moment I told Lady Dunlee we were betrothed I was bound by my word. Gentlemen cannot break an engagement."

"Oh!" She was panting now, but not with desire. Anger—this was what she needed. Now she turned to face him. "That's right—it's all about your bloody honor. You don't want to wed me; you only want to keep your word."

His brows lowered. "I didn't say that."

"You told Clorinda as much." How could he look so bewildered and . . . hurt. "Don't deny it. You and Clorinda were standing in the entry hall to Crane House before Lord Kenderly's ball as I came down the stairs. Your words carried. I heard each one quite clearly."

"I don't know what you're talking about."

He had almost seduced her. He was far more skilled than Brentwood; he'd used compassion and understanding—gentle words and touches—but the result was much the same. Worse perhaps. Her heart felt as pierced as her body had been in Gedding's garden.

No, she wasn't being fair. Stephen hadn't seduced her as much as she'd seduced herself. She'd let herself be blinded by what she wanted, rather than forcing herself to look clearly at what was before her. Had she learned nothing in ten years?

She swallowed the annoying lump in her throat. "Oh, yes, you do. Clorinda promised you she or Papa would get me to cry off, but you needn't worry. I shall do so of my own volition as soon as the Season is over."

He was scowling at her. "I don't want you to cry off, and I'm certain I never told your cousin I didn't want to marry you." He snorted. "I would never have such a confidential conversation with that woman."

"So how do you explain what I heard?"

"I don't know—I don't remember what I said."

Well at least he was being honest. "It doesn't matter. I know what you meant."

"How can you possibly know what I meant? You aren't a mind reader." His gaze was unpleasantly direct. "I'll have my exact words, if you please."

She lifted her chin. She didn't remember his exact words, but that made no difference. "You said what you just said here. You are bound by your word, no matter how unpleasant the consequences."

"I *am* bound by my word." He looked at her as if she were completely daft. "Of course I am. Any gentleman is. But I'm very sure I said nothing about 'unpleasant consequences.' I certainly didn't say any such nonsense just now." He raised his brows suggestively. "In point of fact, I was anticipating some very pleasant consequences before we got into this silly brangle."

She flushed. "It's *not* silly. It's—"

He reached out and captured her upper arms; the weight and warmth of his fingers shot directly to her treacherous breasts and the place between her thighs.

"Anne, the night before Kenderly's ball, I arrived at Crane House far too early, I was that anxious to see you. Unfortunately, your cousin was downstairs early, too. I was forced to endure far too much time with her. I ended up so angry—she was not speaking of you in a way I could like—I hesitated to say much of anything to her for fear I'd lose all gentlemanly restraint and tell her exactly what I thought of her."

He held her eyes with his. "I was willing to marry you then, but I didn't know you as well as I do now. Now I'm very, very eager to make you my wife."

"But if it weren't for the scandal—"

"I was very much the author of that scandal."

"You were drunk."

"I've been drunk before." He smiled a little. "Too often recently, until Harry tumbled me into that mud puddle. Even in my cups, I've never kissed a woman—gently bred or baseborn—on the street."

Anne studied his face. She'd swear he was not prevaricating. Could he possibly care for her? "But what if Brentwood tells everyone I'm not a—"

Stephen stopped her lips again. "He won't. I hold his vowels. I can ruin him at will. He'll dance to my tune."

Her damn heart leapt with hope. Stupid organ. She wasn't as naïve now as she'd been at seventeen.

"I still don't understand." She ran her hand through her hair, giving him a delightful view of her fire lit breast.

"What don't you understand?" His cock swelled in immediate appreciation and reminded him what they'd been on the verge of doing before they'd been diverted by this argument.

He wanted to pull off her thin nightgown. He wanted to see every exquisite inch of her without anything—even that worn cloth—obscuring his view; he wanted to run his hands over her smooth, soft skin; to feel the weight of her breast in his hand; to smell and to taste her from the red hair on her head to—

"Stephen!"

"Yes?" Damn. He jerked his gaze from her chest. "Did you say something? I'm afraid I wasn't attending."

She frowned. "You shouldn't ask a question if you aren't going to listen to the answer."

"Very true." He forced himself to look only at her face . . . and her lips and—

No. Concentrate on her words. He was not out of the woods yet. She obviously was in no mood for anything but conversation at the moment. "I promise to pay strict attention now."

She gave him a long look. "Very well. What I said was I don't understand why you would wish to marry me. The King of Hearts can have any woman he wants—I assure you, I've not forgotten all the glares directed my way in Lord Kenderly's ballroom. So why do you want a red-headed spinster with no social graces to speak of"—she blushed—"and no virtue."

"Anne—"

She looked away. "I'm not a virgin."

"Neither am I." He put his hands on her shoulders. "Of what consequence is a small scrap of flesh really?"

She was angry again. "It is everything."

"No. You've made it everything because you've had the great misfortune of having it stolen from you. I wish I could change that for you, but I can't. It happened—ten years ago. Let it go."

"I can't let it go. I'm not what I appear, don't you see? I'm not a virtuous maiden. I'm a lie."

"*That* is the lie. You are one of the most virtuous women I know."

"Don't be ridiculous. I—"

"No, don't you be ridiculous. You *are* virtuous." He'd like to shake her, but that wouldn't help. She needed to accept the truth herself. "You love and take care of your sister and brothers; you forgive your father his absence; and—perhaps most amazing—you put up with your cousin."

Anne's laugh was watery. "Clorinda means well."

"If you say so." He could tell she wasn't convinced. "Anne, what happened at Gedding's house party shaped who you are today. It made you stronger in some ways and weaker in others. Who knows who you'd be if things had happened differently? Maybe you'd be a matron with several children hanging on your skirts—or maybe you'd have wedded a drunkard who beat you."

Anne was staring at him as if he'd given her a whole new way of looking at things. Good.

"It makes no difference who you might have been. You are who you are. You need to put Brentwood's despicable actions in the past where they belong." He did shake her now, just a little. "You are giving the man far too much power over your life by dwelling on his perfidy."

"Oh." She bit her lip, and her eyes glistened with tears. "Perhaps you are right."

"Of course I am right." He pulled her toward him and was happy to see that she came to him willingly and laid her head on his chest. He cradled her against him, listening to the fire hiss and pop. He would love to take her to bed, but she'd likely had enough emotion for one evening. "I should go and let you get your rest."

"No." She looked up at him. "Stay."

"I'm not certain that's a good idea."

"I am," she said, but her smile wavered.

"Anne, we can wait. We have years before us."

"No, I want to begin now." Her voice sounded more determined. "It wasn't just a scrap of flesh Brentwood took from me, it was my dreams of love and marriage and children." She rested her hands on his chest. "I want you to show me now how it should be."

He closed his eyes briefly. If he'd thought his poor cock was going to explode a moment ago, he was sure of it now. But he must go gently. Anne's body might not be strictly virginal, but her heart was.

He held her eyes with his. "All right, but first, know that anything I do—or you do—we do together—*with* each other, not *to* each other. If you ever want me to stop, you need only say so."

Anne searched his face and then nodded. "Very well. How shall we begin?"

"I think you first need to admit that you are beautiful."

"What?" She stepped back. "Don't be silly."

"I'm not being silly. Married love is more than the spiritual communion bad poets celebrate; it's physical communion as well. There are many women I'd be happy to have a conversation with that I'd never wish to take to bed." He reached for her again. "And there are women I've taken to bed that I do not care to converse with. You are the only woman with whom I wish to do both."

"No."

"Anne, it will become very annoying if you keep contradicting me. You must bow to my greater experience in this matter, if you please. And my experience tells me that it's important you see yourself as desirable in order to believe I sincerely desire you. Therefore, we will begin by removing your nightgown."

"But then I'll be naked!" She sounded horrified.

"Well, yes."

"That's indecent."

Stephen smiled. "It would be if you were to walk into Almack's dressed—or, rather, not dressed—that way. The patronesses are very particular about attire, you know. I have to wear silly knee breeches every time I subject myself to the place."

"I know that." Dear God! Just the thought of stepping into that exclusive club without any clothing made her heart pound.

"But here in the privacy of your room, who can object? You shed your clothes to bathe, do you not?"

"Well, yes." She flushed. "Briefly."

"Do you never look at yourself in the mirror?"

"Of course I do. See?" She stepped over to the cheval

glass. Stephen followed, standing close behind her. He was so much bigger than she.

"I meant do you never look at yourself naked in the mirror?"

"Good heavens, of course not!" She paused, a titillating thought making her blush more. "Do you?"

He laughed. "Only if I happen to glance at it as I walk by."

"As you walk by? Do you mean you walk naked around your rooms?"

He grinned. "Generally just in my bedchamber." He lowered his head to whisper by her ear. "I hesitate to shock you more, but I sleep naked."

"You"—she tried to clear her throat—"do?" Instead of feeling shock, she felt a jolt of shocking need.

"I do, though I need plenty of blankets to keep away the chill on a cold night." He kissed her temple. "I'm sure in the future you will help me keep warm. Now, let's get rid of this nightgown so I may begin a proper seduction."

"But . . ." She stared at herself in the mirror. She would die of embarrassment . . . wouldn't she?

"Please, Anne?"

Why not? There was no point in being bashful now. She would let Stephen be her guide. As he said, he was far more experienced than she in such matters. "Very well."

She'd hardly got the words out before her poor, threadbare nightgown went flying off into a corner.

"Eep!" She saw a shocking expanse of white flesh and squeezed her eyes tightly shut.

"There—that is much better." Stephen wrapped his arms around her waist and pulled her back against him; the lawn of his shirt was soft on her skin, but his breeches were rough.

She felt a pronounced ridge rise against her backside.

"Anne." His voice was husky now and, if it weren't such a ridiculous notion, she'd say there was a touch of awe in it. "Open your eyes."

Open her eyes? That would be far too embarrassing. "I can't."

"You certainly can. You must. I cannot continue seducing you if you do not."

"Oh, for goodness sakes." She cracked one eye open. Oh, dear. Her breasts and her thighs were on complete display. She couldn't bear to—

Oh. One of Stephen's hands was sliding over her skin to her breast. She opened her other eye to watch it. It was . . . odd to feel his touch and see his fingers, so dark against her flesh.

"I've lain awake hours thinking of you, Anne, imagining how you would look naked, but for once my imagination wasn't up to the task."

His words, dark and drugging, whispered in her ear, stirring tendrils of hair.

"Your skin is like silk. And see how your breast fits perfectly into my palm?"

She did see. She saw—and felt—how the tip of one of his slightly calloused fingers was circling her poor nipple causing it to harden into a tight, aching point.

She sagged against him—her knees no longer cared to support her weight—and felt the ridge pressing against the cleft in her bottom grow even larger.

"See how beautiful you are," he said, "flushed with desire?"

Her face—no, her entire body—was flushed. She should be mortified, but apparently there was no room for mortification in her soul at the moment.

She looked up at his face reflected in the glass—his eyes were half closed, intent and focused on her body;

his lips tilted up into a lazy smile. He looked as if he truly wanted her.

She definitely wanted him—and at the moment she especially wanted him to stop teasing her nipple and touch it.

He must have read her mind. He not only touched the sensitive point, he rolled it between his finger and thumb.

"Oh!" Exquisite sensation shot through her, right to the damp, empty place between her legs. She parted her thighs, thus looking even more wanton. But she needed to feel the room's cool air on that heated flesh.

No, she needed to feel Stephen's fingers . . .

She watched his other hand—the one not fondling her breast—splay itself across her belly. If only it would move a little lower. There was one specific spot in amongst her curls that was crying for his touch.

She waited. Perhaps he would read her mind again.

He didn't. His hand stayed where it was as if grafted to her skin. The heat and weight of it felt wonderful, but she felt certain it would feel much, much more wonderful an inch or two lower.

Well, if the mountain would not come to Mahomet, Mahomet must go to the mountain. She tried to flex her hips to bring her ache closer to his fingers, but he was holding her so tightly, she couldn't move. In fact, her motion must have encouraged him in a way she'd not intended—he pressed her more firmly against his erection.

"Is that a growl I hear, Anne?" Humor laced his voice; the annoying man knew exactly what he was about. "Am I doing something to displease you?"

"Yes—I mean no."

"Yes and no? I don't understand. Perhaps if you tell me instead of merely growling at me?"

She growled. "It's not what you're doing—it's what you're *not* doing. I want you to move your hand."

"What, this hand?" He lifted his fingers from her breast.

"No. Of course not." Her teeth were gritted now. "The other one."

"Ah, *this* one." He stroked her belly. At last he was moving in the right direction.

"Yes."

His lips nuzzled a spot just under her ear. "And where would you like me to move it?"

"You know."

"Anne, I am no more a mind reader than you are. Tell me."

He knew; she knew he knew, but she had no patience to discuss the matter. "Lower. Move it lower."

"An excellent suggestion. Like this?" He slid his fingers through her curls, but skimmed over the spot that most needed him.

"Not quite." Desperation exploded in her. "I need you to *touch* me."

He acted confused, but she saw the devilry and heat in his eyes. "But I *am* touching you."

She was no longer in the mood for teasing—one did not dangle a loaf of bread in front of a starving man. She grabbed his hand and tried to push it where she wanted it to go, but he was far too strong. She couldn't move him at all.

"Impatient?" He kissed the skin below her ear again and circled her nipple with the tip of his finger.

"Yes." If he enjoyed torturing her, she would try torturing him. She pushed her bottom more tightly against his erection and wiggled a bit. She heard him inhale sharply. "*Touch* me!"

"So demanding." She was savagely delighted to hear a thread of need in his voice. "Let me see . . . is this the spot?" He brought his finger down until . . .

"Ahh." Her body shivered. "Yes." This was nothing at all like her encounter with Brentwood. Stephen had loosened his hold on her a little, so she tilted her hips and spread her legs wider, offering him a bold invitation. She no longer cared what she looked like.

He accepted it. His finger slipped over and around her.

"You're so wet for me, Anne." His voice was husky; he sounded very pleased.

"Ah." She twisted. It felt so good. It felt—

He stopped, his hand cupping her. "I think it's time we went to bed, don't you?"

Bed sounded like a very good idea, but . . . "You won't stop doing this, will you?"

"Only for the time it takes us to move from here to there. And then I will do this and other, even more delightful things—things much easier to do on a comfortable mattress."

"And you'll be naked, too?"

He kissed her jaw by her ear; she heard him panting slightly. "Yes. In fact, I do believe it's past time I shed my clothing."

He let her go. She turned, trying to ignore the insistent throbbing between her legs, and attacked the buttons on his fall as he pulled his shirt over his head.

"Ohh." As soon as she undid the last button, his long, thick male organ fell into her hands. Her eyes widened. Now she understood why it had hurt so much when Brentwood had done what he'd done in Baron Gedding's garden.

Stephen *was* a mind reader. "It will be different this time, Anne." He stroked his hand over her hair. "Your maidenhead is gone, and you are ready for me—the wetness that helped my finger slide over you will help my cock slide into you."

"Oh." It was true she hadn't felt this damp throbbing when she'd been with Brentwood.

"Yes. And I will stop at any point if you wish me to." Stephen had a rather strained expression on his face. "Just please decide sooner rather than later."

"I won't ask you to stop." How could she have given Brentwood even a moment's thought? This would be *nothing* like that time. Brentwood was selfish and cruel; Stephen was generous and kind . . . and she loved him.

And lusted after him, too. She stroked his male organ. How odd it looked, nothing like anything females had. It was hard, but soft as well. She ran her finger from its base to its tip and saw it jump as if it were a separate living creature. She found a drop of wetness and spread it over the velvety skin.

"Anne," Stephen said.

She heard the pain in his voice and dropped her prize immediately. "I'm sorry. Does it hurt when I touch you there?"

He gave a strangled kind of laugh. "Not at all—quite the contrary." She saw him swallow. "But if I don't sit— or better yet, lie—down soon, I shall collapse."

"Oh, dear." His expression did look strained, but the rest of him looked wonderful. His chest and shoulders were so broad; his stomach, flat, the narrow trail of hair leading down to—she'd swear his male organ swelled even larger as she inspected it. Were his breeches too constricting? Perhaps he would feel better if she removed them. "Then we must get you to bed immediately."

"Ah, yes, an excellent— What are you *doing*?"

She'd dropped to her knees to pull his breeches down to his ankles. His poor swollen organ was bobbing around by her face, so instinctively she'd given it a quick, soft kiss. "I'm sorry. I won't—"

"No, don't apologize." He pulled her up as he kicked off his breeches. "You may do that with my blessing— my fervent blessing—but you must wait until we're lying down." He scooped her into his arms and strode toward the bed.

Chapter 19

He was going to die if he couldn't bury himself in Anne immediately.

No. He slowed his pace. He couldn't jump on her like a rutting animal. She wasn't ready for that, and he certainly didn't want to do anything that would recall Brentwood's rough handling.

He laid Anne gently on the mattress and climbed in next to her, propping himself up on an elbow so he could see her beautiful body—and her face. He wanted to watch for even the slightest shadow of alarm.

She turned her head on the pillow, frowning at the lit candles. "Shouldn't you snuff them?"

"No." He cupped her breast and watched her blush. "I want to see you."

She grinned. "And I definitely want to see you." She ran her hand over his chest and then pushed slightly. Did she want him on his back? She pushed a little harder. Apparently.

He flopped down on the pillow. He would let her have the lead if she wished, though it was hard to imagine where her inexperience would take them. "What are you doing?"

She pushed herself up to her knees. "You said I could continue what I'd been doing once we were lying down."

"Huh?" He was having trouble thinking. The sight of her glorious red hair tumbling over her shoulders and breasts was extremely distracting. Add to that her slightly parted knees that allowed him to see the hair between her thighs and a hint of her entrance where he would finally be in just a short while, and he was doing well to remember his name. "I, ah, thought you wanted me to continue doing what *I* was doing."

"In a little while. I've discovered I want a turn now." She directed her attention to . . .

Zeus! He closed his eyes and took a deep breath. Anne was kissing his cock. Her lips moved lightly, maddeningly, all over it. If only she would . . .

She did. She touched him with her tongue, tentatively at first as though she were taking the slightest taste of him, and then more boldly. Much more boldly. She put her mouth—

"Anne!"

"What?" She frowned and bit her lower lip. "Don't you like this? I thought you did. You were making little noises and moving about."

He'd swear he actually blushed. "Of course I like it, but I'm afraid I can't take any more." He combed his fingers through her hair. "You've brought me to the brink, Anne. I want to be deep inside you when I finally lose control."

"Oh." Anne blushed, too.

"Come." He tugged gently on her hair. "If you don't object, I think we must leave the long, slow lovemaking for another night."

"I don't see what the hurry is," she said, but she allowed him to guide her down onto the bed.

The moment her back hit the mattress, he came

over her, his lips latching onto one of her nipples. If he hadn't been on top of her, she was sure she would have shot right up to the ceiling.

Perhaps she did understand the need for haste.

His mouth moved to her other breast while his fingers played with the one he'd just left. Her hips twisted. She understood it very well. She was feeling rather desperate herself. She spread her legs wider to give him the hint he should move in that direction.

He was a very intelligent man. He proceeded promptly to exactly the location she needed him to be. Soon he would do what Brentwood had done, but this time it wouldn't hurt; it would be wonderful. It would—

Her head shot up. He couldn't be . . . He was between her legs and he was . . .

"*What* are you doing?!"

He raised his head. "Kissing you."

"*There?*"

"Don't you like it?" He dipped his head and flicked his tongue over the tiny, throbbing point hidden in her curls. "I'm just kissing you the way you kissed me a few moments ago."

"Ohh." She moaned as his tongue slid slowly over the point again. He was drawing her tighter and tighter, as he had in the green sitting room. Very, very shortly she would shatter, but this time she wanted him with her. She reached for him. "Stephen, I need you."

"In a moment—"

"No. Now." She couldn't wait. "I want you now."

"Yes, madam." Stephen rose up over her. He paused and looked into her eyes. "You are certain? This is your last chance to tell me no."

She had no breath left to waste on words. She grabbed his hips and pulled him toward her.

"I will take that as a yes," he said, and then he was sliding into her.

She shivered. This was nothing like the time with Brentwood. There was no pain; there was only pleasure. She was in a warm bed, naked, with the man she loved, his body heavy on hers, his hard length deep inside her, and his heat all around her. It was heaven . . . well, a very carnal heaven.

He slid almost out and then back again slowly. In and out. The tension kept growing until she couldn't stand it any longer. She gasped and gripped him so tightly she might leave bruises on his back and hips. She was close . . . so close.

"Ahh." She was there. The tension peaked and shattered. Pleasure washed through her and in the midst of it all, she felt the warmth of Stephen's seed spurt deep into her womb.

Had he given her a child? She hoped so.

He relaxed onto her. He was sweaty and heavy—and he was still inside her. She wrapped her arms around him. She never wanted to let him go.

"Are you all right?" He was looking concerned again.

"I am wonderful."

He laughed. "And I am too heavy for you." He lifted himself off, leaving her very cold and empty.

She stretched up her arms. "Don't go."

"I—"

Someone knocked on the door, and they both jumped.

"Who can that be?" Stephen whispered.

"I don't kn—"

"Anne, the door is locked." It was Evie's voice. "Are you all right?"

"Tell her you'll be right there," Stephen murmured, "or she'll set the household to searching for you." He moved soundlessly out of the bed and across the floor.

"I'll be right there, Evie." Anne's nightgown came sailing through the air to her. She glimpsed Stephen's white arse like a moon low in the corner, before she scrambled into her clothes. He had his breeches on by the time she emerged from the voluminous white fabric and was pulling his shirt over his head. She'd never seen anyone get dressed so quickly.

"Anne!"

"I'm coming."

Stephen stopped her as she hurried toward the door. "Sleep well, love." He kissed her quickly. "I can't wait until we'll sleep together."

"Yes, I—"

Evie rattled the doorknob. "Anne."

"Go." He gave her another quick kiss and headed for the window.

By the time she reached the door, Stephen had disappeared.

Stephen stretched, linked his hands behind his head, and grinned up at the bed canopy. His heart literally felt as if it would burst from his chest, he was so happy. Well, and that wasn't the only organ swollen with joy. He glanced down to where his cock was making an obvious tent in the bedclothes. His valet, MacInnes, would be rather startled if he happened to come in and see this display.

He sighed. If only Anne were here, he could address the issue very satisfactorily.

His damned eager cock leapt at the thought.

Last night had been so different from his previous encounters he might as well have been a virgin himself. He'd engaged in sexual congress many times with many women, but the act had always been merely a pleasant physical release. One woman was as good as another, assuming she was relatively clean, free of lice, and unlikely to be carrying the pox. And while he'd always striven to help his partner find release—he *was* a gentleman—the effort had sprung more from pride in his performance than from any true concern for the woman.

All that had been different last night with Anne. Oh, his animal instincts had been very much involved, of course, but so had his heart. He was making love to *Anne*, not merely enjoying a quick tumble between the sheets with some willing female. Every touch, every kiss had been for Anne, with Anne. He'd have been happy to forgo his pleasure if that were necessary to give her hers.

He snorted. Well, not *happy*, but he would have done so without a second thought.

And he'd never wanted any of the other women here in his own bed. He'd not even wanted to sleep with them; it had made Maria cross as crabs that he always left her room shortly after he left her body. But Anne . . . He wanted her here with him. If she were . . . He grinned again. She'd still be naked from their lovemaking the night before. He'd just roll over and . . .

His cock was going to poke a hole in the bedclothes if he didn't get up. He'd splash some cold water over himself and confine his appendage with breeches and a

sturdy fall before going out to procure a special license.
He wanted Anne as his wife as quickly as possible—and
in his bed immediately thereafter.

He was just heading to the washbasin when MacInnes
opened the door. The blasted valet saw his cock—it was
rather hard to miss as it was roughly the size of a carriage axle and stuck straight out from his body—and
raised one of his damn Scotch eyebrows. "Had some
pleasant dreams this morning, then?"

Stephen wished he'd already washed so he'd have a
wet towel to throw at his impertinent valet. "I am going
out; you may help me dress."

"Aye, ye'll need some help getting that into your—"

"MacInnes!"

MacInnes laughed. "Testy, are you? Well, I'm afraid
you've got more annoyances in store for you. You've
got a visitor."

"Oh?" Stephen could tell by the glee in MacInnes's
eyes there was something odd about this caller. "Who
is it?"

"A female calling herself Mags."

"Damn." Mags would only come here if she had
urgent news of Brentwood. He grabbed the first pair of
breeches that came to hand.

MacInnes handed him a shirt. "At least this woman
has solved the problem of getting your fall buttoned."

Stephen glared at the man and then pulled the shirt
over his head. "Where have you put her?"

"In the kitchen."

"Give her some tea, will you, and tell her I'll be
down immediately." Stephen pulled a pair of socks out
of his clothes-press.

"The female doesna look like she drinks tea."

"Then get her some brandy—just don't let her go

until I've spoken to her." Where the hell had he put his shoes?

"I'll tie her to her chair if I need to." MacInnes stopped at the door. "If you're looking for your footwear, I see one shoe under the desk." He grinned. "Were ye drunk on brandy or Lady Anne's kisses last night?"

Stephen feared he was blushing. He grunted noncommittally and bent to peer under the bed. "Just go deal with Mags." Ah, there was the other shoe, but he'd have to crawl almost halfway under the bed to fetch it. He didn't care to entertain MacInnes with *that* spectacle. He glanced back at his valet—the man was still standing by the door. "Well, go on."

"Aye, I will, but first . . . Well, I just wanted to say we're all—even your parents—happy about Lady Anne, ye ken."

Stephen was definitely blushing now. How the hell did his valet know his parents' thoughts on the matter? Not that it was surprising, really. No one stood on ceremony at the Priory; everyone knew everyone else's business.

"Yes, well . . ." He cleared his throat. "I plan to get a special license today as soon as I hear what Mags has to say."

MacInnes grinned. "Splendid. I will go deal with her immediately."

"You could have dealt with her more immediately if you hadn't stayed to tease me," Stephen muttered after MacInnes left. He scrambled under the bed, rescued his shoe, and followed his valet.

When he arrived in the kitchen, Mags had a glass of brandy in her hand, and MacInnes was watching her as if she might steal the silverware—which she probably would if given the chance.

"Thank you, MacInnes. That will be all."

MacInnes folded his arms, assuming his threatening mad Scot look. "I'm happy to stay."

"That will not be necessary." Did the man think he couldn't handle Mags? He must know better—MacInnes had seen him win battles with much more intimidating opponents.

MacInnes hesitated long enough Stephen feared he'd have to bodily eject him, but fortunately it didn't come to that. "Verra well. I'll be just outside if ye need me."

"And don't have your ear to the keyhole," Stephen murmured as MacInnes walked past. MacInnes gave him an innocent look, which confirmed he'd be eavesdropping. Oh, well. Mags couldn't have anything of a confidential nature to disclose.

Mags took a long swallow of brandy and sighed. "That man's got a fine arse. You know I've always liked Scots."

"I didn't know that, Mags," Stephen said, hoping MacInnes *was* listening.

Mags nodded. "Aye. I swear they've the biggest cocks—don't you think so?"

Good God. "I have not made a study of male genitals."

Mags laughed. "No, I guess you haven't—but I have." She looked at the kitchen door. "Think he knows about the Temple?"

"I have no idea."

"Tell him, will you?" Mags winked. "I'll give him special service."

"Ah. Yes. I'll be sure he knows." He'd wager MacInnes would not be interested. In their travels together, he'd found the man as fastidious about such matters as he was. "Now tell me why you're here."

Mags gazed longingly after MacInnes a moment

more before she apparently shook herself out of her lecherous woolgathering. "Oh, right. I came about Brentwood, of course. He showed up last night, drunk. Said Lady Noughton had found out he was all rolled up and had shown him the door."

Damn. He should have realized Maria would confront Brentwood immediately.

Mags took another swallow of brandy. "I told him I knew it, too. We had it out—quite a brangle—and I showed him *my* door." She grinned. "Had him tossed out on his arse—I much enjoyed seeing Lord High-and-Mighty in the gutter." She downed the rest of the brandy. "But you'd best be careful. He's mad as a buck, and he knows you're behind his troubles. I'd say he's looking for revenge."

Bloody hell, he had to warn Anne. "And you waited until now to tell me?"

Mags shrugged. "Had another customer. I *am* a business woman, you know."

He wanted to shake her for delaying even a moment. Instead, he swallowed his bile and slipped a sovereign into her open palm. "My thanks. Now if you'll excuse me? I have urgent business to attend to."

"But how am I to get home?"

He put more money into her hand. "Take a hackney," he said, and then jerked open the door. Sure enough, his valet almost tumbled into the room. "Perhaps MacInnes here can help you."

It looked like rain.

Anne sat by her window, gazing out over the back garden, nibbling on the toast a maid had brought up with a cup of chocolate. She hadn't wanted to go down to breakfast and risk encountering Clorinda, Evie, or the boys. She didn't want to be with people yet. She wanted to savor this moment in private.

For the first time in ten years her heart felt light. She'd told Stephen her shameful secret, and he'd accepted it. She giggled. If she *had* been a virgin, she definitely wasn't one now.

She saw Harry appear, sniffing at the base of the tree Stephen had climbed last night. Oh, dear. Had someone let him out by himself? That was not a good plan—the dog was quite capable of escaping from— No, there were Philip and George. Good.

She took a sip of chocolate, cradling the cup in her hands. Now, in the morning, it was hard to believe last night had not been a dream. But it had indeed happened—the ache in a particular part of her body confirmed it. Stephen had actually been here in this room, in that bed—in *her*.

The place he'd been most intimately throbbed at the memory, and she shivered with pleasure. She wanted to do it all over again as soon as possible.

To think the same body parts had been involved in her encounter with Brentwood, yet the experiences had been as different as night and day.

The boys were throwing something at each other, and Harry was barking furiously at them. Lady Dunlee would not be happy about the noise. She should go out and stop them. She would, in a moment.

Could she have conceived Stephen's child?

She'd prayed so hard ten years ago that she wasn't enceinte. She hadn't been able to sleep, she'd been so full of dread, and during the day she'd burst into tears with no provocation. It had been such a relief when her courses had started. But now . . .

She laid her hand over her belly. She hoped Stephen's seed had taken root.

She frowned. There was still the problem of Stephen's

travel. He would be gone so much. Yes, he'd said she could come with him . . . until they had children.

She put aside her chocolate and toast.

She could not put her children through what Papa and Georgiana had put Evie and the boys through—being raised by their older half sister and servants. Well, and she'd missed Papa, too, when she was younger.

But if she stayed home . . . how would she bear the months and months Stephen was gone? She'd pine for him and worry about him.

She looked out the window again. The boys and Harry were no longer in the back garden. Where had they gone? The clouds looked quite threatening. She'd best go see; there was no telling what mischief they could get into. There would be hell to pay if Harry was disturbing Lady Dunlee's precious Miss Whiskers again.

She got up and shook her skirts out. In any event, a breath of fresh air would be most welcome; she'd always loved the windy, slightly wild air before a storm.

She had the bad luck of running into Clorinda in the corridor.

"How are you this morning, Anne?"

Clorinda looked genuinely concerned. Why? Oh, right—her excuse to stay home last night. "I'm very much improved with sleep, thank you, Cousin. It was a passing upset."

Clorinda's face lit with comprehension; Anne's face, she was certain, lit with embarrassment. Blast, had Clorinda guessed her secret? No, she couldn't have; she looked amused, not angry.

"So you had troubles of a female nature, did you? Why didn't you just say so? We all have—or in my case, had—that time of the month."

"Er . . ." Her "troubles" had definitely been of a

female nature—last night's events would never have occurred if she weren't female—but her courses for this month had come a week or two earlier.

"I'm sorry I doubted you when you said you were unwell," Clorinda was saying. She matched her step to Anne's as they walked down the stairs. "I don't know why I did. I should have realized you wouldn't wish to miss seeing your betrothed."

Anne ducked her head so Clorinda couldn't see her eyes and her heighted color when the thought popped into her head, completely unbidden—she *had* seen Stephen, all of him.

They reached the foot of the stairs and Clorinda stopped to pat Anne's arm. "As Evie may have told you—she said she was going to stop by your room last night—Mr. Parker-Roth was clearly disappointed when he learned you would not be attending the gathering with us."

"I think Evie did say as much." Anne couldn't say for certain what Evie had said—she'd been too overwhelmed by what Stephen had so recently done with her to pay a scrap of attention to Evie's bibble-babble.

"Oh, yes. He was most out of sorts and left the ball early—and angrily—after speaking to that Lady Noughton. He told his brother he wasn't feeling well, but the gossip is he left so abruptly because he finally broke with the widow."

"Oh?"

Was it true Stephen had just now given Lady Noughton her congé? He'd said they'd parted ways in February.

Had he lied? And if he'd lied once . . .

Last night had seemed too good to be true because it was.

Anne tasted bitterness. She was such an idiot, thinking the King of Hearts could be in love with her.

Apparently her judgment had not improved at all in ten years.

"Are you certain you're feeling quite the thing, Anne? You look rather pale all of a sudden," Clorinda said.

"No, I'm fine." Anne did not want to get into a discussion on the subject. "I'll be better after I take some air. I was just on my way outside to see where the boys are."

"An excellent idea. A little gentle exercise used to help me when I was in your situation, but do keep an eye on the clouds. And don't be out too long or get excessively windblown. I wager your betrothed will be over shortly to check on your health."

Anne nodded. Stephen probably *would* come by; it would be in keeping with his role of attentive fiancé. She put on her new bonnet—it didn't give her any of the pleasure it had yesterday.

"Perhaps Evie should go with you. I believe she's still in her room. Shall I—"

"No, thank you." Anne did not care to have company at the moment. The twins didn't count. They were boys—they would most likely not say ten words to her. As long as she wasn't dying loudly, they'd never notice anything was amiss.

"Enjoy your walk then." Clorinda headed toward the breakfast room. "But don't be long; you don't want to be away when Mr. Parker-Roth arrives."

Actually she *did* wish to be away when that occurred—in Inverness, perhaps, or Boston—but she merely nodded.

She sighed with relief the moment the front door was securely shut behind her, and turned her face up to the sky. The wind felt good, even if the damp added to the chill of her heart.

She'd recovered from Brentwood; she'd recover from Mr. Parker-Roth as well.

Ha. This wound was far, far deeper.

She bit her lip. She could not be crying on her doorstep; Lady Dunlee might see. She clasped her hands tightly together as if she could grasp her runaway emotions.

She should not jump to conclusions. The gossips were often wrong, though it was true Stephen had spoken with Lady Noughton last night. He'd told her he had. She'd forgotten in all the . . . excitement of the evening.

What had he said? That Lady Noughton had told him Anne had lifted her skirts for countless men?

Oh, she would like to strangle the woman—and perhaps Stephen as well.

Now where were the boys? Ah, there they were. She heard Harry's bark and Philip and George's shouts. They were indeed in the park across the square.

She stepped to the edge of the walkway and then saw a black carriage turn the corner. Would it wait for her to cross? No, she'd swear it was picking up speed. Reckless driver! One would think he'd exercise a little restraint in residential neighborhoods, but likely he was some half drunk young buck. She would wait for the vehicle to pass before attempting to reach the park.

Oddly, the carriage slowed just in front of her. Did the fellow need directions? He would quickly discover she was not at all knowledgeable concerning London streets.

A nasty-looking man with his hat pulled low and a muffler pulled up over his face was on the box and another jumped out of the coach body.

"May I help you, sir?" She did not at all care for the look of the fellows.

"Aye." The man grabbed her, knocking off her bonnet. "Ye can help me by coming along quiet like."

She drew in her breath to scream, but his hand, smelling of sweat and dirt, slapped over her mouth. He was strong. He held her so tightly, no matter how much she struggled, she couldn't free herself.

"Got 'er," he shouted to the man on the box. "I'll— Ow!" She'd managed to get her teeth into his palm. "The bloody whore bit me. Brentwood'll have to pay me extra iffen she's drawn blood."

"Brentwood don't have to do nuttin'," the coachman shouted back. "Hurry up! We don't want to be found out."

Anne heard the boys yell and Harry bark. Out of the corner of her eye, she thought she saw them running toward her. If she could just delay a few more seconds . . . but the man was too strong.

"Right," he said and threw her over his shoulder, climbing into the carriage and slamming the door on her hope of rescue.

Chapter 20

Stephen leapt from the hackney as it pulled up to Crane House. Before he could pay the jarvey, the front door flew open and Clorinda tottered out, her handkerchief clutched in one hand, Anne's crumpled bonnet in the other.

"Oh, Mr. Parker-Roth, I am so glad to see you."

Ice filled his veins. Had Brentwood been here before him? "Where is Lady Anne?"

"Gone!" Clorinda shuddered. "With only her poor bonnet left behind. Oh, if only I'd come out with her, perhaps I could have done something." She hid her face in her handkerchief.

"Stay here," he told the jarvey. "I may have need of your services immediately." Assuming he could get any coherent information out of anyone, that is. Obviously Clorinda would be no help. Perhaps Evie or Hobbes had seen something useful.

Hobbes was hovering just inside the door as he'd been the day the twins had gone missing, Charles the footman, by his side. "Thank God you're here, sir," he said.

Clorinda, still sobbing, tugged on Stephen's sleeve. "You will rescue Anne, won't you?"

"Yes." He would die trying, if necessary, but the sooner he left, the better. Time was not in their favor. He turned back to the butler. "When did this happen, Hobbes?"

"Only about five minutes ago, sir. We were just about to send Charles here to alert you."

Stephen looked at the footman. "Did *you* see anything?"

"No, sir, but I believe the boys may have."

"I'll speak to them, then. Where are they?"

"In the blue parlor," Clorinda managed to say between her tears, "trying to comfort Evie."

"Very well. Hobbes, send word to my rooms telling my brother and my valet they should come to Crane House at once. And have them bring my horse."

"Yes, sir. I'll send Charles."

"Excellent. Take the hackney." Stephen strode down the hall, Clorinda in his wake. He heard Evie sobbing even before he got to the door. When he stepped over the threshold, he saw the twins, sitting close to their sister and looking very pale and anxious.

"Mr. Parker-Roth!" George saw him first and dashed over, followed closely by Philip.

Clorinda took their place on the sofa, wrapping her arm around Evie's shoulders. Evie glanced up—she managed to look beautiful even with a red nose and swollen eyes—and smiled at him as if he were Michael the Archangel arrived to vanquish Lucifer.

"They've snatched Anne, sir," Philip said. He was clearly trying hard to be brave as would befit a proper Viscount Rutledge, but his face was white as death and his eyes glistened with suppressed tears.

George nodded. "Philip and I had taken Harry out to the park in the square. We saw Anne come out of the house and step toward the road—and then a black carriage flew round the corner and stopped in front of her."

"We couldn't see who they were, sir," Philip said, "but there were at least two of them."

"One man had his hat pulled low and his muffler pulled up to his nose," George said. "The other fellow must have been riding inside the coach."

Philip nodded. "There wasn't a crest on the door, at least not on the side we could see, but the man in the coach—the one who actually grabbed Anne—howled how Brentwood needed to pay him more."

George grinned and said with definite pride, "Anne bit him, sir. She's pluck to the backbone, isn't she?"

"She most certainly is." The ice in his veins dropped about twenty degrees. Anne was now in a carriage with an angry man, likely from one of London's worst stews. He could only hope the rogue was enough afraid of Brentwood that he wouldn't harm her. There was clearly no time to waste. "Did you see which way they went?"

"Down Upper Brook Street." Philip shook his head, looking thoroughly disgusted with himself. "We gave chase, but the coach was too fast. We lost it at Park Street."

"We wouldn't have lost it if you hadn't kept me from dashing across in front of that curricle."

"The curricle would have hit you; you couldn't help Anne if you were run over." Philip glared at George, and then looked up at Stephen. "That was the right thing to do, wasn't it, sir?" The boy looked completely miserable.

"Of course it was." Stephen put a hand on each boy's shoulder. "You both did exactly as you should have. George, it was valiant of you to want to keep after the coach, but you would have lost it in any event. A carriage moves much faster than your legs can."

George sighed and nodded, but brightened quickly. "We did see it turn right on Park Lane."

"Splendid. I'll—"

"What's going on?" Nick burst into the room. "The footman said something about Lady Anne being abducted." He caught sight of Evie. "Zeus, Evie, don't cry. We'll find your sister." He sat down next to her and likely would have snatched her out of Clorinda's arms if he hadn't had an audience.

"Brentwood has taken Anne, Nick. I want you to stay here and lend the ladies your support." He knew better than to mention the twins, but they also needed a sensible fellow like Nick around.

Nick frowned. "Don't you need help?"

"I believe I'll do better on my own, but I'll be sure to send word if I can use your assistance. I'll tell MacInnes when he gets here to check all Brentwood's holdings to see if he's gone to ground at any of them. I somehow doubt it, but we need to be sure."

Nick nodded. "MacInnes was right behind me. He should—"

Hobbes appeared at the door. "Your valet and horse are here, sir."

"Splendid. Then I'm off to have a very thorough chat with Lady Noughton."

"God-speed," Clorinda said. "We'll be waiting to hear you've found Anne safe and can bring her home."

Stephen nodded and left, hoping he'd be able to do exactly that, but with the head start the miscreants had—

No, he would not entertain such thoughts. He *would* be successful—he had to be.

Anne's heart raced. She tried to throw open the window and scream for help, but it was nailed shut. Damn. What could she—

The vehicle careened around a corner; she grabbed

a hand strap to keep from being thrown from her seat.
If she were lucky, they would crash and, if her neck
wasn't broken, she could escape.

"Ye may as well sit still; yer not goin' anywheres."

Her abductor glowered at her from the other side of
the coach. He'd removed his muffler and hat; it was
not an improvement. A scar ran through his right eyebrow, and his nose resembled a cauliflower. He must
be a former pugilist.

He held up the hand she'd bitten. "Yer lucky ye
didn't draw blood, ye know." He crossed his arms.
"That and Brentwood said he wants ye in good order."

She nodded—there really wasn't anything to say to
that—and stared at the window. She couldn't actually
see out it, since the curtains were nailed down, too, but
it was better than staring at her captor. She busied herself praying for a broken axle or a herd of cows to
block the road.

Unfortunately, nothing occurred to detain or delay
them. The coachman appeared to be skilled with the
ribbons. They avoided capsizing and had now settled
into a fast, steady pace—too fast for her to try leaping
from the carriage.

She tightened her grip on the hand strap. "Where
are we going?"

"To Brentwood, o' course."

"To Lord Brentwood's estate?" She relaxed slightly.
Brentwood's estate was not so far from Crane House.
She could—

"No."

Her heart sank. "Then where?"

"Ye'll find out when ye get there."

She forced herself to breathe slowly and deeply. She
couldn't panic—she had to come up with a plan.

Eww. The carriage smelled of old vomit, sweat, and
dirt. The squabs were so flattened they might as well

not have been there and the springs—they hit a bump, and she felt the jolt from her seat to her head.

It would be nice to know where she was going, but it wasn't essential. "Away" was the only direction that mattered once she arrived at wherever Brentwood was. Surely she could find some soul to take pity on her and offer her sanctuary until Stephen could come fetch her. And he would come—his honor, if nothing else, would demand it.

She regarded her companion again. Could she convince him to assist her? "Neither my father nor my fiancé will be happy you've abducted me. If you take me back now, I promise no one will be the wiser."

The man spat into a corner. "Brentwood will."

She swallowed and tried not to show her revulsion. "My father will deal with him."

"Yer father ain't in England."

Too true. "But my fiancé is."

The villain finally looked uncomfortable. He shifted on his seat. "Brentwood said Parker-Roth would be happy to get his freedom back." He looked her over. "Stands to reason. Why would the King of Hearts want to marry a scraggy female like ye?"

Why indeed? She pushed her own doubts aside. "Perhaps he wishes to marry an earl's daughter."

The man snorted. "Crazy Crane's get? I don't think so."

"My father is very wealthy."

"Parker-Roth is richer."

The man was impossible. "Mr. Parker-Roth despises Lord Brentwood. He would not like it if the marquis stole an old boot from him, but to steal his betrothed . . ." She shook her head. "He'll be furious."

Did she see sweat on the villain's brow? It was too dim in the carriage to be certain.

He fidgeted. "Brentwood says—"

"Lord Brentwood knows nothing. He is not in Mr. Parker-Roth's confidence." Was she swaying him? She would dangle money before him. That should work. "And I assure you, my fiancé will be most appreciative. He'll pay you as much or more than Lord Brentwood has offered you if you return me now, unhurt."

"Ye think so?" The man was definitely wavering.

"I am certain." Surely, no matter what Stephen's true feelings, he would help her in this?

"Well . . ." The man scratched his head. Anne bit her lip to keep from shouting at him. "I gotta ask Gus."

Gus must be the coachman. "Pray do so at once."

He reached to give the signal to stop, but the coach was already slowing. "Looks like we're here." The man shrugged. "A bird in the hand is worth two in the bush. His lordship will pay us now, and we'll be done with this."

"But you can't give me to Lord Brentwood." Anne grabbed the man's arm. "My father or my betrothed will pay you double what he's offering, I swear it."

"And Brentwood will shoot us now if we don't give ye to him." He picked her hand off his arm and went to open the door, but it was already opening.

Anne clutched the carriage strap. It was a futile effort; her abductor easily pried her fingers loose and then shoved her out the door. She tripped and fell—straight into Brentwood's arms.

"Ah, my dear Lady Anne, how lovely to see you again."

"Her ladyship is not at home, Mr. Parker-Roth." Maria's butler looked slightly alarmed to see Stephen on the doorstep.

Stephen shoved past him into Maria's entry hall. It was decorated in the Egyptian style; he hadn't realized just how much he hated it. He grimaced at a chair that had two sphinxes supporting its arms. "Now Wentwood, we both know Maria never leaves her bed this early in the day."

"But sir . . ." Wentwood wrung his hands, obviously recognizing Stephen would not be nay-said. "My lady is not at home to visitors."

"I'm not precisely a visitor. I have urgent business with her; I cannot wait." Stephen started up the stairs. "I expect I'll find her still abed, won't I?"

"Mr. Parker-Roth, sir, please . . ."

"Don't worry, Wentwood. I can find my way." He'd no time to argue with the butler; every second wasted increased Anne's danger.

He pushed Maria's bedroom door open without knocking. As he'd expected, she had a companion. The man—boy, really; one of Nick's friends—saw him and dove under the covers.

"Why, Stephen." Maria sat up, treating him to a view of her naked breasts. "Have you come to make this a threesome?"

"Not at all." He addressed the lump under the covers. "Don't worry, Puddington. I won't tell your mother where I found you."

"My thanks," the lump replied in a wavery voice.

Maria cupped her breasts invitingly. "Since you're here, the least you can do is join us." She smiled in what she must imagine to be a sultry fashion. "You can give young Thomas a tutorial. I'm sure he'd like to observe the King of Hearts at work." She patted the lump beside her. "Wouldn't you, Thomas?"

The lump shook; poor Thomas was likely terrified by the notion. "No, thank you, madam."

The "madam" obviously hit a nerve. Maria scowled and looked on the verge of kicking Tom out of bed.

"Maria." Stephen had no time for this. The clock was ticking. "I am in a great hurry."

"Then be about your business. I certainly did not invite you here."

He couldn't very well strangle her, though he was sorely tempted. "I will leave as soon as you answer a question or two. Thomas, you are not to repeat any of this."

"I would never, sir."

Maria scowled at the lump and then at Stephen. "Why should I help you?"

"Because I alerted you to the fact Brentwood hasn't a feather to fly with. And because I know a variety of secrets you wouldn't want society to learn."

"That's blackmail."

"You can call it that if you wish, just know I'm not leaving until I get my answers."

For a moment, Maria looked as if she was considering defying him, but then she shrugged. "Very well, ask your questions, but I don't promise I'll answer them."

She would answer if he had to shake the answers out of her. "Did you have a little chat with Brentwood after I left you at the ball last night?"

"Of course I did." She patted the lump. "I brought Thomas home to help me forget that unpleasant tête-à-tête." She sighed. "Unfortunately, he is like most young men. Splendid to look at, all eagerness, but in and done far too quickly. Perhaps I should take him on as a pupil. Would you like that, Thomas?"

Thomas mumbled something. Stephen couldn't distinguish the words, but the boy's tone did not indicate enthusiasm. It would be damn amusing, if he wasn't in such a hurry.

"Did you tell Brentwood I hold his vowels?"

Maria yawned. "I believe I may have."

He hadn't thought Mags had lied, but he'd had to

confirm her story. He couldn't afford to be wrong. At least now he was quite confident, especially given what the twins had overheard, that Brentwood was behind Anne's disappearance.

"Where would Brentwood take someone he'd abducted from London?"

Maria smiled maliciously. "Oh, my, did evil Lord Brentwood steal your betrothed, Stephen? How sad."

He reminded himself he did not strangle women. "Where did he take her, Maria?"

"I'm sure I don't know."

He did *not* strangle women, but perhaps just this once . . .

He forced his anger under control. "Don't you want Brentwood to get his just deserts, Maria? I would think you'd be eager to see him taken to task after the way he deceived you."

"True," Maria said, "but I'd also like to see Lady Anne suffer for stealing you from me."

What was this? "Maria, you and I parted company in February. Ours was a pleasant, but temporary affair."

Maria shrugged and finally reached for something to cover her nakedness. "You may have thought it temporary; I did not."

Was she serious? "Think about it, Maria. If we wed, I would want you to have children and to give up London most of the year to live with me in the country. You would not like that."

"No, but I know I could persuade you to stay in Town."

"No, you couldn't."

"But—" Maria was staring at him as though he'd suddenly turned into an exotic beast.

"And I would expect fidelity, Maria." He gestured to the lump. "You like variety. You'd be loathe to give that up."

"Well . . ." She patted the lump again. Poor Puddington must be getting very warm under the blankets.

"Lady Anne has done you a favor."

She shrugged a shoulder. "Perhaps."

"So will you tell me where Brentwood has taken her?"

She sighed, looking suddenly older. "I really don't know." She stroked the lump while she pondered the possibilities. "He wouldn't take her to his town house, of course—Lady Brentwood is in residence. I suppose he could go to one of his estates, but I don't think he would. Most are too far from London, and the servants would not approve of such behavior. From what I've gathered, they are still very loyal to Lady Brentwood and don't much approve of her son."

That made sense. "So where else might he have taken her?" He wanted to shout, but he restrained his impatience. At least Maria was seriously considering the question.

The lump mumbled something. Maria lifted a corner of the blanket. "What is it, Thomas?"

He mumbled something again.

"Ah, very good, dear. I think you are likely correct." Maria dropped the blanket back into place and smiled at Stephen. "Thomas suggests you might try Baron Sambleton's house in Richmond."

"Sambleton? I thought he was forced to go abroad after Lord Dashling's daughter was discovered with him at an orgy in that house."

"Yes, and he's still abroad," Maria said. "But he left Brentwood a key to the place, so he could host smaller gatherings from time to time or use it for his own private enjoyment."

"Splendid." Stephen knew exactly where to find that house. Last year he'd gone with Baron Tynweith to see if Sambleton's parties were as bad as they were rumored to be. They were, and he and Tynweith had left quickly. Funny how straight-laced Tynweith had become now that he was a husband and father. "I will be on my way then and let you and young Puddington get back to what you were doing when I so rudely interrupted."

"Thank you," Maria said. "And I do wish you luck, Stephen."

"And thank you for not telling Mama," the lump said.

Stephen closed the bedroom door and ran down the stairs. He paused for a moment to dash off a note to Damian, asking him to meet him at Sambleton's house. Damian would be an excellent ally if Brentwood proved difficult.

"Send someone running to deliver this to Lord Kenderly, if you please, Wentwood," he told Maria's butler as he strode out of the house. He threw a coin to the stable boy holding his horse and leapt into the saddle.

He could make it to Sambleton's in less than half an hour going cross country. The carriage had a good start on him, but, if he pushed his horse, he should arrive only shortly after it. At least he hoped so.

Anne's well-being might depend on it.

"Milord, ye promised us our coin when we delivered the gentry mort." The unpleasant man who'd shared the coach with Anne spoke with bravado, but Anne thought she heard a thread of fear in his voice. Clearly, he would not defend her against Brentwood.

"Very well. Hold her while I get my purse."

Brentwood shoved her into the man's grasp. Anne screamed as loudly as she could.

"Feel free to muffle her," Brentwood said.

"She bites."

"Does she now?" Brentwood looked her over, making her flesh crawl. She screamed again. "Well, she'll soon tire of making a racket. It's not as if anyone but us can hear her." He pulled out his purse and extracted a few coins. "Here you go."

The man holding her pushed her back into Brentwood's grasp and counted the money.

"Is it all there, Ned?" the coachman shouted down from his perch on the box.

"Aye." Ned tied the coins in a dirty handkerchief and leapt up to join his companion. As soon as his arse touched the seat, the coach thundered away down the drive.

"And now, Lady Anne," Brentwood said, smiling in a most revolting manner, "time for a little fun, hmm?"

He had his hands wrapped firmly around her upper arms, but if she was going to escape, she'd best make her attempt now before he managed to drag her into the house. She jerked her knee up, but he'd anticipated that move. He blocked her with his thigh.

"Tsk, tsk, my love. That's not very polite, is it?" He chuckled, and the hair on the back of her neck stood on end. "You were much more eager for me in Gedding's garden, but no matter. I like a bit of a struggle before I have my prize."

"You are disgusting."

"Perhaps. Do come inside now." He jerked her toward the front door. "I may as well tell you there are no servants to look to for help. It is just you and me, my dear."

Anne dragged her feet, trying to slow her forward progress. "I thought you were giving me to the end of the week. That was our bargain."

"Regretfully, I don't have until the end of the week.

I leave England on tonight's tide, right after I have my wicked way with you."

Her damn heart leapt into her throat. She couldn't afford to panic, least of all now. They were almost to the door. Brentwood might be ten years older than he'd been at Baron Gedding's and have let himself go to fat, but he was still stronger than she. She could not stop him.

"You may have a terrible reputation, but I've never heard you abducted your bedmates."

He shrugged. "There's always a first time."

"You won't be able to show your face in society ever again."

"I won't be in England to care, my dear."

She tried one last time to jerk herself free. "Mr. Parker-Roth will save me."

"Oh, I doubt that. This isn't my house; I can't see how he could guess I've brought you here."

He swung open the door and hauled her into the entryway. "I'd intended to hold you for ransom," he said, almost conversationally. "Parker-Roth has all my blasted vowels, you know. But upon further reflection, I concluded he and his powerful friends and relatives would make my life hell as long as I remained in England. So if I had to say farewell to my native shores, I might as well soil them quite thoroughly first." He grinned horridly. "And I shall oh so thoroughly enjoy getting my revenge on your bloody betrothed."

He slammed the door closed behind them, locking it and slipping the key into his waistcoat pocket. "I do wish I could stay to watch him struggle with what I'm leaving him, though. He's so damned honorable, I wager he won't put you aside, but he'll have to wait to have you to see if my seed has taken hold." He chuckled. "Or, even better, if he's sown in your field since last I saw you—you *were* absent from Palmerson's do last night and he left early—he'll spend his life wondering if his firstborn is his . . . or mine." He laughed. "Oh, I do hope it's a boy."

"You can't do . . . that to me." Anne wasn't above lying. "I have my courses."

"Do you?" He shrugged. "That's not a problem—I'm not especially fastidious."

Anne looked away from him and finally noticed her surroundings. Dear heavens! There were manacles hanging from the walls and a basket of what looked like whips where an umbrella stand should be. "What is this place?"

"Have you heard of Lord Sambleton?"

"No."

"No, I suppose you haven't. I'd forgotten you were such a country mouse. This is his house—he used to give wonderful parties here."

Anne could not imagine a wonderful party that included manacles and whips.

"His house is quite delightful. Would you like a tour?"

"No, thank you."

Brentwood laughed. "That was a rhetorical question, my sweet. Come along." He pulled her into a large room that looked somewhat like the harem room at Crane House, except the walls were covered with mirrors instead of paint or paper—and the obscene statuary was larger and more abundant. She stumbled over the edge of a carpet and reached out to steady herself, grabbing hold of a long, smooth—

"Eep!"

"Like that, do you?"

Anne shook her head. She stared at the enormous penis and the statue of Pan to which it was attached.

"I gave that to Sambleton. Got it from Griffin after Lord Wolfson died. Griffin had scores of them, and with Wolfson gone—" He shrugged. "Not that it makes a difference to you. I had it affixed to this pedestal so it wouldn't tip over—the huge cock makes it a bit unstable."

Anne thought an organ that size would make anyone unstable.

"The ladies are especially fond of it. The cock twists off"—Brentwood dropped his hold on her to remove Pan's member—"and makes a splendid dildo."

She'd never heard the term, but she could guess its meaning as Brentwood flourished the phallus under her nose.

"It is too bad Sambleton had to flee to the Continent. His gatherings were so . . . stimulating. They were almost as good as Griffin's—would have been better, but Sambleton wouldn't allow animals in the house."

Anne hoped she wasn't following Brentwood's meaning. She began to edge as stealthily as she could toward the door.

"All these couches were covered with naked men and women in all possible combinations and positions. It was a rare sight to behold."

"I'm sure." Anne took another step closer to escape. The front door was locked, but there must be another exit.

"We will have to imagine it while we—or at least while I do my poor best to recreate the proper licentious atmosphere." He grinned. "I will begin by divesting you of that lovely outfit."

"No!"

Brentwood's grin turned darker. "Will I have to chase you and strip you? That could be fun."

He would have to if she couldn't come up with a better plan. "No, I mean why do I have to go first? I think it would be much more exciting if you shed your clothing before me." She swallowed and tried to sound enthusiastic. "I can't wait to see you naked."

Brentwood's eyebrows rose. "Really?"

"Really." Anne swallowed again and hoped she wouldn't choke on the lie. "I'm sure your . . . appendage must be so much more impressive than Pan's."

He looked at the disembodied penis in his hand. "Well . . ."

"It certainly felt more impressive in Baron Gedding's garden."

"Thought about our tryst often, have you?"

"Daily." Unfortunately, that was not a lie.

"You gave me the very distinct impression—flat out said it, I believe—that you weren't interested in repeating the experience."

Anne shrugged. She would lie until her tongue shriveled up and her nose grew as long as Pan's member if it would save her from Brentwood. "I was betrothed to Mr. Parker-Roth—what else could I say?"

"Hmm."

"I'm not an idiot; I realize you have me trapped. I may as well enjoy the encounter."

"Well . . ."

"And as you say, this room is quite inspiring."

"True." Brentwood grinned. "I believe women are more randy than men by nature, you know. You are not the first one to be overtaken by lust here. Quite amusing, really, how the most meek and proper miss becomes a lusty, panting fornicator with the right stimulus. And you do have the hair—and perhaps the soul—of a whore." He gave her a speculative look. "Hot for me, are you?"

"Oh, yes." *May God—and Stephen—forgive her.* "I am

desperate to see you naked. You kept all your clothes on last time."

"So I did. I trust you will give me some good bed play if I humor you?"

Anne nodded. The bile rising in her throat precluded speech.

"Very well, I will grant you this boon." He began to unbutton his coat. "I think Parker-Roth must have had you last night. Did he teach you some amusing tricks? I will want you to show me them all."

"Of course."

Brentwood removed his coat and waistcoat. She was tempted to bolt when he had his shirt up over his head, but she made herself stand where she was and try to look expectant.

His chest was nothing like Stephen's. It was pasty white with thick black hair that covered it like a rug and appeared to continue on over his back. If he had any muscles, they were well hidden. His belly, not his erection, strained against his breeches.

He opened his fall and his pitiful male organ flopped out, dwarfed by his stomach. How could that little thing have hurt so much?

She tensed. In a moment . . .

He got his breeches down to his knees—and realized he'd forgotten to take off his boots.

She took off running.

"Hey, you—ack!"

There was a delightfully solid thud behind her— Brentwood must have hit the floor—and then a stream of curses.

She checked the front door quickly, just in case a miracle had occurred, but sadly, it was indeed locked.

"I'll get you, you bitch."

She glanced behind her—Brentwood was rolling

around on the floor, trying to get his clothing to rights. She picked up her skirts and ran again.

She tried every window she came to—they were all shut tight. Lord Sambleton's staff was to be commended; they had closed the house up exceedingly well when the man took off for the Continent.

Perhaps she would have more luck in the kitchen. There must be a door there.

"Tally-ho!" The cry rang through the hall. Brentwood must have untangled himself from his clothing.

She fled to the back of the house. Yes, here was the kitchen with . . . a securely locked door. Damnation. Where was the key? Could it be hidden in one of these drawers? She pulled them out randomly. Knives, forks, spoons, ladles—no keys.

Was that the crack of a whip she heard?

She shot out of the kitchen and through the breakfast room. It looked like the library lay ahead. Perhaps she'd find French windows to a terrace there.

Behind her she heard a slap, slap, slap against the kitchen floor. Was that the sound of bare feet? Surely the man had pulled his clothing on, not off?

She darted into the library. Yes, there were French windows. She tugged on them, but they refused to budge even an inch.

"I've got you now!"

She looked over her shoulder. Brentwood, stark naked, was running toward her, snapping a long coach whip. She slammed the library door. She needed a weapon of some kind. What?

A heavy book would have to do. It was all she had at hand. She grabbed the largest one she could reach as Brentwood burst in. She swung it below his huge belly at his puny private parts. Desperation gave her strength. He howled with pain and doubled over, dropping the whip and stumbling toward the French windows.

She followed and swung the book at his head. It was too heavy for her to lift high enough to hit him squarely on the crown, so she smacked him on the ear. He lost his balance and crashed into the windows.

Glass shattered, wood splintered, and then Brentwood lay naked on the floor, still as death.

Chapter 21

Anne held the book ready to bash the bounder if he moved. He didn't. In fact, he looked most unwell. All the color had drained from his face.

Frankly, he closely resembled a corpse.

Dear God, had she killed him?

She dropped the book and backed away, horrified. She'd never killed anything in her life. Not that she'd had a choice in this instance nor did she wish Brentwood alive, but to be the one who had . . .

She slapped her hands over her eyes so as not to see the body and started to shake uncontrollably.

"Anne."

Someone touched her; she screamed. She would run; she'd find a place to hide; she'd—

"Anne, it's me, Stephen."

Stephen? She swallowed, fighting down her panic. Could it really be Stephen? She forced herself to look.

It *was* Stephen.

She threw herself into his arms and burst into tears.

"Did he hurt you, Anne?" Stephen tried to rein in his panic. He'd ridden as fast as his horse would carry him, his fear for Anne's safety constantly urging him to go faster. When he'd arrived and found the door locked and the house apparently deserted, he'd tasted bitter despair. He'd had no idea where to look next, and even if he'd had a plan, he knew he'd arrive too late to save Anne. Thank God he'd decided to search the house's perimeter. He'd just been turning the corner when he'd heard the glass shatter. "Are you all right?"

"Y-yes, I'm f-fine."

She didn't sound at all fine. She was stiff and trembling.

"Is . . . is he d-dead?" she asked, keeping her face buried in his chest.

"It looks so." He didn't want to let go of her, but he should ascertain whether the bloody bastard still breathed. "I'll check—wait, here's Kenderly . . . and Knightsdale as well."

He'd been hoping Damian would arrive soon, but how the devil had Knightsdale got word? Surely Emma couldn't divine his location by studying her tea leaves or something?

"Hallo, Stephen." Damian, followed by Knightsdale, stepped through the French window Stephen had forced open. "Hope you don't mind I brought Knightsdale along. Actually, he brought himself. He was with me when I got your note and insisted on coming." He looked down at Brentwood and gave a long, low whistle. "Here's a bit of a mess."

Knightsdale stooped to examine the body, using his handkerchief to lift the head. "Definitely dead. Piece of glass cut right through the jugular."

"Indeed," Damian said. "Look at all that blood."

Anne moaned and pressed her face farther into Stephen's waistcoat.

Knightsdale laid the head back down and frowned

up at Anne's back. "I'm sorry to cause you pain, Lady Anne, but could you tell us what happened here?"

"No one blames you, of course," Damian said. "You were clearly defending yourself from Brentwood's advances, but we need to know a few details, such as how Brentwood found himself hurtling through the window. Did he trip or"—Damian cleared his throat—"did you, er, assist his progress in some way?"

While Damian was talking, Knightsdale pulled a Holland cover off one of the chairs and draped it over Brentwood's body, leaving only his large, ugly feet exposed.

"Tell us, Anne." Stephen massaged the back of her neck. She was so tense. "And then I'll take you away."

Knightsdale nodded. "Yes. Kenderly and I will stay and handle all the odds and ends."

Stephen felt Anne take a deep breath; then she straightened and turned to face Damian and Knightsdale, averting her eyes from Brentwood's draped corpse. He kept his arm around her waist, hugging her to his side.

"Lord Brentwood was ch-chasing me. When I got to this room, I was t-trapped. I grabbed a book and when h-he came in, I h-hit him—twice—as hard as I could. He f-fell."

"And the book?" Damian asked.

Anne pointed. "It's on the f-floor there."

Damian picked up the tome. "It's certainly heavy enough to do the job." He glanced inside and his eyebrows shot up. "Very interesting." He turned the book sideways and examined one of the pages intently. "The illustrations are extremely educational"—he slammed the book closed—"and obscene."

Stephen didn't care if the book were Satan's diary, he just wanted to get Anne away from there. "Are you done with Anne now?" She was trembling again.

"Yes," Knightsdale said. He got up and took one of

Anne's hands in his. "I will tell you what I told many soldiers who were under my command, Lady Anne. Don't let Brentwood's death bedevil you. It wasn't your intention to kill him, but to save yourself."

"I-I know," she said quietly. "Th-thank you."

Stephen ushered Anne out the French window, being careful to give Brentwood's body a wide berth. The sky was still threatening rain.

"Damian, Knightsdale," he called back.

Damian glanced up from the corpse. "Yes? What is it?"

"I'll have to take Anne up on my horse, so we'll be traveling slowly. If it starts to rain, we'll seek shelter. Could you send word to Crane House to let them know we're all right in case we're delayed?"

"Of course—don't worry about that."

Knightsdale looked up at the sky. "You'd best be off if you want to have any chance of beating the rain."

Stephen led Anne around to the front of the house. She looked straight ahead and didn't speak. She was so tense, he feared even one word would shatter her. He lifted her onto his horse and then swung up behind her, encircling her with his arm.

They rode slowly, Anne sitting stiff as a rod before him. She was obviously not ready to talk about what had happened, but he would encourage her to do so soon. The first time he'd killed anyone—another plant hunter who'd spent too long alone in the jungle and had greeted him with a knife—he'd been haunted by nightmares for weeks. They still occasionally returned—the remembered feel of sliding a blade through human flesh, blood spraying—

The wound crusted over; it never healed completely.

A fat raindrop plopped onto his glove. Fortunately, there was a small inn just up ahead. The storm restrained itself long enough for him to help Anne dismount and give his horse to a stable boy, but as soon they stepped in the inn's front door, the heavens opened.

"We were lucky," he said. Anne only nodded. The sooner he got her private, the better.

"Have you a room for me and my wife?" he asked the innkeeper, a fubsy fellow, almost as fat as he was tall, with a genial expression. "It's started storming; I don't believe the rain will let up any time soon."

"Right ye are, sir," the innkeeper said. "I can feel it in my bones—it'll be raining cats and dogs all night." He picked up his keys. "Happen I do have a room, but only one, if that'll do. I've had a rash of business just in the last hour—lots of travelers decided to put up for the night when they saw how threatening the sky be."

"One room will be perfectly adequate." Better, even. Anne shouldn't be alone with her thoughts.

"This way, then." The innkeeper led them up the steep, narrow stairs to a small but clean room. "Here ye be."

"Thank you—and please send up a light repast with a pot of tea as soon as possible"—Stephen looked at Anne—"and a bottle of brandy immediately."

"Very good, sir." The man bowed, making his corset creak rather alarmingly, and closed the door behind him.

"I do hope he makes it safely down the stairs," Stephen said, watching Anne closely. "I was afraid he'd suffer an apoplexy on the way up. You'd think a man who must climb those stairs many times a day wouldn't be so fat, but perhaps his size in an endorsement of the quality of the establishment's food. I hope so. I missed nuncheon, so I'm famished. Aren't you?"

Anne blinked at him. "What?"

At least she'd said something. "The boys told me you bit the fellow who abducted you."

"Yes."

"Did he hurt you?"

"No."

Thank God for that. "The twins were very alert; if it hadn't been for them, I wouldn't have been certain to go after Brentwood. They heard the man who took you mention his name."

"Oh." Anne was hugging herself and staring at the floor.

Someone scratched at the door, and then a servant entered with the brandy and two glasses. "A cold collation and tea will be up in just a moment, sir."

"Splendid." Stephen poured Anne a glass of brandy as the servant left. "Drink a little of this, Anne."

She shook her head.

"It will help."

She shook her head again. It broke his heart. Where was his passionate, prickly love?

"Then come sit with me before the fire." He led her to the settee and drew her down beside him, holding her close. He offered her the brandy again. "Take one sip at least."

"No, I don't—"

"Trust me."

She stared at Stephen and then sighed and took the glass, obediently putting it to her lips. The brandy burned a fiery trail over her tongue down her throat to her stomach where it bloomed into sudden warmth.

"Better?" Stephen asked, taking the glass and putting it on the table by his elbow.

"A little."

She rested her head on his shoulder and watched the orange and yellow flames play in the fireplace while his hand slid comfortingly up and down her arm. She heard the servants come in again, deposit the food and tea, and leave.

He had said he was hungry; she should let him go. "You wanted to eat."

"Later."

He gave her another sip of brandy. He was so large, so solid. Slowly, slowly, she relaxed against him. The heat of the fire and the warmth of the brandy and Stephen's body cracked the ice encasing her heart. Painful feeling leaked out.

She covered her face with her hands. She was shaking again and crying.

Oh, God. She'd been so afraid in the carriage. And when Brentwood had grabbed her . . .

"Anne, Anne." Stephen turned her so her body was tangled up with his, both his arms around her now. "Let it go." She felt his lips brush her forehead. "It's over."

The tears kept coming. She cried because of the horrible events of the last few hours, but she cried also for the young girl who'd lived so long with shame and broken dreams.

Finally, after Stephen's shirtfront was thoroughly soaked, the tears ran dry. She wiped her face on her sleeve and rested her cheek on his chest. She listened to the comforting beat of his heart. His hand stroked her hair.

She felt safe, warm and safe at last.

Brentwood was gone. She could put him firmly in her past. She was free.

And what would she do with her freedom? Where would she go—where would she *choose* to go—now?

The answer was obvious.

"Take me to bed, Stephen."

He frowned slightly. "To sleep?"

It felt odd after crying so much, but she smiled. "Eventually."

That made him smile a little, too, but didn't chase away his frown. "Are you certain? You've had a very upsetting time of it. Perhaps it would be better if we just sit here quietly."

She loved the warmth of his arms around her, but she wanted more. She wanted him around, above, and in her. She was still partly frozen. She needed his love, hot and real, to thaw her completely.

"I'm certain."

He kissed her then gently, cradling her head in his hands, stroking her cheeks with his thumbs.

"Very well. We'll do it slowly this time, shall we?" he said. "There's no hurry. Hear the rain beating on the windows? We shall have to stay the night."

"Mmm. That sounds wonderful."

"Relax, then, and let me love you."

He pulled her forward, resting her against his chest while he worked on the tiny buttons at the back of her dress. In short order, he had her bared to the waist. Her nipples tightened in the room's cool air—and Stephen's intent interest. The heat of his gaze—and the fire's heat—flickered over her skin. Longing throbbed in her heart and in the place still hidden beneath her skirts.

His hands smoothed the sides of her breasts, cupping them, lifting them . . .

"To bed, Stephen. Please?"

"Patience, love. Remember we are doing this slowly." He touched one of her nipples and sensation shot directly to that hidden place, increasing its ache. "I shall not be hurried."

He leaned her back and settled her so she rested comfortably, half sitting, half reclining against the settee's arm. Then he bent his head and kissed her breasts, first one and then the other, teasing her, coming close but never quite touching her nipples. She wove her hand through his hair. She would not force him where she wanted him to go. She would relax as he had told her to. He would take care of her.

He did. His tongue flicked out and she moaned. She was empty—all of her was empty—and she needed him to fill her.

"Stephen, I can't wait any longer."

He stood then and pulled her up, freeing her from the rest of her clothes. He carried her to the bed.

She stretched out on the mattress, completely naked and feeling pleasantly wanton, and watched him slowly remove his waistcoat. How different he was from Brentwood in all things. "You are so beautiful."

He laughed, pulling his breeches off so she could see just how beautiful he was. "You are mistaken, my love; it is you who are beautiful."

She wouldn't argue with him; she was too happy. She couldn't believe she would have the pleasure of him every day . . . every night . . . Well, whenever he was in England.

She pushed that thought away. "Are we really to wed?"

He grinned. "I think it best, and the sooner the better. I'm planning to make another attempt to get you with child—in case my first try was unsuccessful, that is."

She spread her legs a little. She was very hot. "Brentwood wanted to r-rape me, so if I did increase, I'd never know for certain the father of my baby."

Stephen climbed into bed and gathered her close. "Don't think about him, Anne. He'll never trouble you again."

"I killed him." She was growing cold once more, even in Stephen's arms.

"As Knightsdale said, you did not mean to; you were defending yourself." He put a hand on her breast and the warmth came back. "And you saved me the trouble of doing it myself. If he hadn't died by your hand, I would have dispatched him to hell with pleasure as soon as I arrived."

He kissed her lips and then kissed her belly. She spread her legs more and arched to encourage him. Her emotions were still tentative, but her body was not. It knew exactly what it needed.

Stephen knew what she needed, too. His tongue touched lightly, teasingly, the sensitive nub hidden in her curls until she was frantic with desire.

"Stephen." The sensation she longed for was so close. "Now."

He did as she wished and moved over her.

She closed her eyes, waiting for the exquisite feeling of him sliding deep inside her.

Nothing happened. She flexed her hips to remind him what he was about.

"Anne."

This was hardly the time for a chat.

"Anne, look at me."

She opened her eyes. Stephen's face was so serious.

"Anne, I've never said this to any woman—I love you. I want to marry you not because of any scandal, but because you hold my heart."

"Ah." Her chest hurt, she loved him so. "And you hold mine."

He came into her then, slowly and deliberately. She felt every lovely inch of him. In, out, in—and that was enough. She came apart—and felt his warm seed pulse into her as she did.

When he was done, she held him tightly, feeling a little desperate. "I wish you never had to leave me."

He leaned up on his elbows, keeping them joined. "I'll never leave you, Anne."

"But you will." She tried to smile. "Aren't you off on another expedition very shortly?"

"No. I've decided to take my mother's advice for once and stay home to manage my estate." He grinned. "To plant"—he flexed his hips and she felt him stir inside her—"and tend my own garden. To help you raise our children."

"Oh, I am so glad." She kissed him, running her hands down his back to his hips. She was crying again but with happiness. She tried to laugh. "And will you give up your crown as well? Cease being the King of Hearts?" She cupped his jaw and looked up at him. "Will it be enough to be king of only one heart—mine?"

"Yes," he said and turned his head to kiss her palm. "For you are queen of mine."

Dear Readers,

The Naked King concludes—at least for now!—my *Naked* series. I've had a wonderful time exploring this *Naked* world, and I hope you have, too.

While all the books stand alone, I've had fun discovering new characters and weaving former characters into whatever my current story is. For those of you who are interested, here's the chronology of when the stories "happen." The year in parentheses is the year the book was published.

> 1816—Roughly concurrently: *The Naked Duke* (2005), *The Naked Baron* (2009), "The Naked Laird" in *Lords of Desire* (2009)
> 1816—A few months later: *The Naked Marquis* (2006)
> 1819—Roughly concurrently: *The Naked Earl* (2007), *The Naked Viscount* (2010)
> 1820—*The Naked Gentleman* (2008)
> 1821—February: "The Naked Prince" in *An Invitation to Sin* (2011)
> 1821—April: *The Naked King* (2011)

Thanks so much for "reading *Naked*"! Please visit me in cyberspace at www.SallyMacKenzie.net or on my Sally MacKenzie Facebook page or Twitter @Sally_MacKenzie.

Sally

GREAT BOOKS,
GREAT SAVINGS!

When You Visit Our Website:
www.kensingtonbooks.com
You Can Save Money Off The Retail Price
Of Any Book You Purchase!

- **All Your Favorite Kensington Authors**
- **New Releases & Timeless Classics**
- **Overnight Shipping Available**
- **eBooks Available For Many Titles**
- **All Major Credit Cards Accepted**

Visit Us Today To Start Saving!
www.kensingtonbooks.com

All Orders Are Subject To Availability.
Shipping and Handling Charges Apply.
Offers and Prices Subject To Change Without Notice.